'A complex and often heart-and-gut-wrenching novel. This book intelligently explores the need to confront and acknowledge evil before it can be exorcised ... Armstrong's supremely confronting basic material is crucial to our understanding of ourselves as "warped timber" humanity.'
Adelaide Advertiser

'A bold adventure of a novel ... Here is a consummate writer at the top of her form ... The dialogue is often witty, and the narrative whips along. Admirable, too, is the sheer amount of information she manages to convey without being heavy-handed ... A fine fictional debut from a writer who's already made her mark.' Sara Dowse, *Canberra Times*

'Diane Armstrong has taken [a] little-known historical footnote and fashioned it into a popular fiction that explores how easily tribal bloodlust can affect the most ordinary of citizens. For a book that focuses on murder and religious persecution, *Winter Journey* is, not surprisingly, a sober story about the need to acknowledge national culpability for past misdeeds. However, it also captures shards of light amid the gloom, with incredible tales of valour and self-sacrifice on record to balance the most heinous details ... Armstrong treats distressing subject matter in the novel with unflinching assurance.' *The Age*

'Profoundly moving, compelling and superbly written'
Australian Women's Weekly

'Diane Armstrong has done it again with an absorbing page-turner from the opening sentence. An intriguing yarn that would make an excellent movie.'
The Australian Jewish News

P9-DGZ-959

'Truth is stranger and often a lot more deadly than fiction and Armstrong has found a suitably horrific story to bear testament.' *Sunday Times*, Perth

'The twists will keep you reading late into the night, while the subject matter raises issues about culpability. The novel is testament to the strength of human nature.' *Daily Telegraph*

'A harrowing heart-wrenching drama. A novel that works on many levels and many layers, *Winter Journey* resonates with humanity, compassion and wisdom and is not only a book you won't be able to put down, but one that will stay with you long after you finish its final page.' *High Life*

'Diane Armstrong is a master of the elaborate plot which fits together like a beautiful puzzle and her command of characters and their complex motivation is assured. The redemptive power of forgiveness and the possibility of changing attitudes, especially of the young, make this a powerful novel which is impossible to put down.'
Australian Jewish Historical Society Journal

'A story of love, loss and hope, where the human spirit at its best is inspiring; at its worst defies all understanding ... Armstrong's descriptions of characters and events are profoundly moving and evoke strong emotions. A deeply moving and inspiring novel.' *Good Reading*

'This is a good story, well told ... a cleverly crafted mystery tale with a serious, almost polemical purpose. Armstrong's skill in weaving an elaborate fabric out of her characters and subject matter stands her in good stead ... Telling and effective.'
Andrew Riemer, *Sydney Morning Herald*

Winter Journey

Also by Diane Armstrong

Mosaic: A Chronicle of Five Generations

The Voyage of Their Life:
The Story of the SS Derna *and its Passengers*

Nocturne

Winter Journey

a novel

DIANE ARMSTRONG

HARPER PERENNIAL

'Someone Diggin in the Ground' extract from *The Essential Rumi*
by Coleman Barks © Coleman Barks

HarperPerennial
An imprint of HarperCollins*Publishers*

First published in 2005
This edition published in 2006
by HarperCollins*Publishers* Australia Pty Limited
ABN 36 009 913 517
harpercollins.com.au

Copyright © Diane Armstrong 2005

The right of Diane Armstrong to be identified as the author of this work has been asserted
by her under the *Copyright Amendment (Moral Rights) Act 2000* (Cth).

HarperCollins*Publishers*
Level 13, 201 Elizabeth Street, Sydney NSW 2000, Australia
Unit D, 63 Apollo Drive, Rosedale, Auckland 0632, New Zealand
A 53, Sector 57, Noida, UP, India
1 London Bridge Street, London SE1 9GF, United Kingdom
2 Bloor Street East, 20th floor, Toronto, Ontario M4W 1A8, Canada
195 Broadway NY, NY 10007, United States of America

National Library of Australia Cataloguing-in-Publication data:

Armstrong, Diane, 1939– .
 Winter journey.
 ISBN 0 7322 7695 0.
 ISBN 9 7807 3227 6959
 I. Title.
A823.4

PS material prepared by Annabel Blay
Cover design by Katie Mitchell
Cover image by photolibrary.com
Author photo by Keith Arnold, Red Rocket Design
Internal design by Katy Wright, HarperCollins Design Studio
Typeset in 10.5/14.5 Hoefler Text by HarperCollins Design Studio
Printed and bound in Australia by Griffin Press on 50gsm Bulky News

To Michael,
For all the journeys we've taken together

Prologue

The madness began around the time of the summer solstice, as soon as the Bolshevik trucks roared away behind clouds of dust. At first everyone went crazy with joy. Barefoot children chased the departing trucks, poking out their tongues, yelling, and mimicking Cossack dances until they flopped down in the dirt. After the suspicion and fear of the past two years, the arrests and accusations and deportations, everyone was smiling once more. Even grumpy old Antos, who had sworn never to play his harmonica again, struck up a mazurka and hopped around on his wooden leg. It seemed to Piotr Marczewski as though a sorcerer's spell had been lifted and his dead village had come to life.

And then the other madness started. Piotr first noticed it on market day. He was riding in his high-sided wooden horse cart when he passed his neighbour Janina.

'Thank the Lord those godless Bolsheviks have gone at last, and my Stach and all the others will come home again. Now we'll have a reckoning!' She shook her fist. 'We'll make them pay for what we went through. *Pan Bóg dał nam się doczekać!*' The Lord has answered our prayers.

Stach's wife had always been a meek woman and Piotr was taken aback by the venom in her voice.

Perched beside her father on the wooden seat, Kasia brushed away the summer flies that buzzed around his battered felt hat. The mare had an easy trot and all Piotr had to do was emit a low whistle from time to time to encourage her to keep up the pace and avoid the ruts in the road. As the cart swayed alongside fields of corn and rye, they passed old women in thick stockings and gumboots, leading cows to pasture. '*Szczęść Boże*,' he greeted them with the traditional blessing, and as usual they responded, '*Daj Boże*.'

Piotr gazed at the fields that rolled all the way to the horizon, and then far beyond, all the way to Stary Most. That was all a man needed: a field planted with corn, beets and potatoes, sunshine and rain to help them grow, strength to harvest his crops, and children to pass it on to. Of course there was one other thing that made life complete, but he tried not to dwell on that. The Lord must have had a reason for taking Anielcia, although he couldn't figure out what that could have been when he and the children needed her so much down here. Still, it wasn't for him to question God's will.

When they reached the shrine at the crossroads, he pulled on the reins so that Kasia could jump down as usual and pick daisies and cornflowers. He liked watching the deft way her small strong hands twisted the stems together to weave the garland she placed beneath Christ's bleeding feet.

'When we've sold our chickens, we'll buy some bread from Berish,' Piotr said. Kasia nodded happily. She pulled at her wispy plaits to make them meet on top of her head, but no matter how she stretched them, they barely reached the tips of her ears and she needed a very long ribbon to join them. Every week the baker would survey her with a solemn expression and declare that the ribbon was getting shorter. Then, while she giggled, he would put his hands behind his back and she would have to guess which hand held the raisin bun. Before they returned home her father sometimes bought her a new ribbon.

Carts clattered over the cobblestones of the marketplace as peasant women wrapped in grey and brown shawls arrived with their baskets. They laid out cottage cheese in muslin bags, eggs collected that morning and still smeared with chicken droppings, pickled cucumbers in wooden barrels and pats of glistening butter. Housewives picked over the goods with critical eyes, searching for defects to lower the price. Bantering and bargaining were part of market day. The Catholics came to market to sell their produce, and then bought saucepans, shirts and leather goods from the Jews. Later the men would gather at Szmuel's tavern for a glass of vodka. It had been like that in the village as long as anyone could remember.

As soon as their chickens were sold, Kasia pulled her father towards the bakery. Most of the shops around the square were owned by Jewish cobblers, tailors, grocers and haberdashers, who stitched, mended and sold their goods in the front and lived out the back. The warm, yeasty smell of freshly-baked *challahs* wafting from the bakery made them both breathe so deeply that their toes curled. As usual on Fridays, the shelf behind the counter was stacked with the braided loaves glazed with egg and sprinkled with poppy seeds that most of the villagers, not only the Jews, queued to buy. Berish was a big man with a ruddy complexion and a genial disposition, but today he looked as white as the dough he kneaded. Silent and preoccupied, he hardly noticed Kasia and for once he didn't tease her about her hair.

Piotr counted out a few *groszy* for the bread and was about to leave when Berish let out a long sigh. 'They say the Germans will be here soon,' he said. Piotr waited. He had known the Jewish baker and his family all his life, and had occasionally borrowed money from him to tide him over till the next harvest. 'Those *Endecja* thugs can't wait for the Nazis to get here. Their hands are itching to beat us up,' Berish went on.

Piotr didn't know what to say. The nationalist party accused the Jews of having collaborated with the Bolsheviks. They were threatening to take revenge, but threats were one thing, actions another. He started to say this in his slow way when the baker held up his large hand. 'I can feel the hate in the air,' he said. 'I know the signs. It's not the first time. But it's not me I'm worried about, it's my family.'

Piotr remembered Berish's daughter, Malka, a tall girl with unruly reddish hair and a mischievous smile who used to serve in the bakery before she married and moved to Stary Most. Berish was looking at him with such unnerving intensity that he shuffled his heavy boots on the wooden floorboards.

'Our rabbi says that life is like market day and when we meet our maker we all have to answer whether we traded honestly,' the baker said.

Piotr scratched his head. He wasn't sure what Berish was getting at. 'You people worry too much,' he mumbled. Putting the loaf under his arm, he stepped outside. He quickened his pace past the crowd that was gathering around the *Endecja* banner and headed straight for his cart. Casting a regretful look in the direction of the haberdasher's store,

4

Kasia followed him. There was no point pleading when he had that look on his face.

As the cart rumbled over the loose planks of the bridge, Piotr noticed three lads hiding in the reeds, spying on the village girls. Just as he had done the first time he'd seen Anielcia wading into the creek, her skirt rucked up above her knees. How his throat had contracted at the forbidden flash of her round white buttocks. She had gone into peals of laughter when she turned and saw him staring open-mouthed, and splashed him from head to toe so he had a hard time explaining to his mother why his clothes were wet.

He was still smiling at the memory when he looked up and pulled so hard on the reins that the horse and cart jolted to a sudden stop. A row of shiny cars and motorcycles, modern ones that had never been seen in these parts, were choking the road to the village. Edging closer, Piotr saw German soldiers in helmets and leather gloves. Everything about them was crisp, polished and perfect, from their high glossy boots to the jackets that seemed moulded onto their bodies. The scent of eau de cologne wafted from them, like brides.

They had stopped in front of the triumphal arch that was decorated with flowers, ribbons and banners. Hanging from it was a photograph of Hitler, surrounded by signs thanking the Germans for liberating Poland from the communists and the Jews. Piotr watched as several village girls ran in front of the vehicles and handed the Germans bunches of asters and cornflowers and chunks of bread, and wondered who had organised this welcome. When one of the officers bowed to acknowledge the gifts, the death's head insignia on his cap gleamed in the sunlight.

A crowd of villagers had gathered, some of them waving flags and smiling. Even Father Olszewski was there, leaning against the white wall of his church, his shrewd eyes taking everything in.

'You'd think they were greeting heroes,' Piotr muttered to himself. Less than two years ago, this army had made mincemeat of Polish soldiers, poor boys who had tried to defend their country with weapons dating from Kościuszko's time. Horses and lances didn't stand a chance against machine guns and tanks. It didn't seem right to be welcoming them now, even if they had declared war on the Russians. Piotr had left school at twelve and expressing ideas didn't come easily to him, but some things were as clear as the priest's black cassock billowing in the light breeze.

In the days that followed, the group that congregated under the *Endecja* poster grew larger and their voices became louder and more menacing. 'Jews are traitors. They suck Polish blood.' The tendons in Władek Bułka's thick neck swelled with every word. The most vehement men were those who, like Piotr's neighbour Stach, had recently been released from Soviet jails. They accused the Jews of conniving with the Bolsheviks to persecute their Catholic neighbours. One man yelled that the Jews exploited decent Poles and turned them into drunkards. Another shouted that they had killed Christ. Voices grew angrier. It was time to get even.

Piotr heard that in neighbouring villages Jews had been beaten up, synagogues had been vandalised and Jewish shops and homes smashed and looted. Although he didn't know whether to believe the rumours, he didn't trust Władek Bułka, the leader of the local nationalist party. In the 1930s,

Bułka had organised a militia armed with clubs to stand guard outside Jewish shops to make sure that no Catholics entered. Most of the villagers kept away but Agata, who was about to get married, ignored them and went into the Jewish haberdasher's to buy a length of satin for her wedding dress. Two of Bułka's supporters burst inside, dragged her into a lane behind the square, knocked her to the ground and kicked her until she lost consciousness. Piotr remembered how bitterly she had wept because the doctor told her that she would never have children.

Piotr was riding to the mill with his grain one sultry afternoon, mulling over the past, when the sky darkened and zigzags of lightning speared the horizon. The clatter of his big wooden wheels along the stony road sent a flock of ravens flying across the cornfield, but the branches of the poplars and birches were still and the birds were silent. The mill wheel turned over the foaming stream as usual, but inside the millhouse Yankel Rabinowicz was pacing up and down, stroking his black beard.

'These are hard times,' he said, hoisting the bulging sacks into the cart. 'You're my first customer today. The fascists have become much bolder since the Germans got here. Why have they all turned against us? We suffered just as much as they did under the accursed Bolsheviks. They sent my uncle and nephew to Siberia and I don't know whether they're alive or dead.'

It was too confusing for an ordinary man to figure out, Piotr thought, tugging the reins to head for home. Soon the horse was trotting faster as they approached the bridge. He had stood near this spot as a boy when a villager's horses had bolted. The harder the man pulled on the reins and lashed them with his whip, the more maddened the horses became, snorting and rushing down the hill, tossing their heads, foam flying, hooves raising clods of earth as the cart swerved from side to side. Piotr had been glued to the spot, his eyes wide with alarm but also with excitement, because he knew that this could only end one way and no one had the power to stop it. Faster and faster the horses galloped until they reached the narrow bridge. The cart overturned and crashed into the water, dragging the horses with it. Piotr remembered the wild eyes of the struggling animals and then the ever-widening ripples. Everyone rushed down to the stream, but the driver was pinned beneath one of the horses and drowned before they could lift the animal off him. The horses were injured and had to be shot.

Piotr had just swung the cart into Kościuszko Street when four youths swaggered along the dirt road towards him, swearing and brandishing sticks. 'We'll show the motherfuckers!' one of them yelled. It was Stach's son Bogdan, a sullen lad who reminded Piotr of a dog that's been chained too long. As his cart drew level with the youths, the reek of moonshine hung in the air.

'With all that *bimber* inside you, you'd better not go near any lighted matches!' Piotr called out.

Stepping in front of the cart, Bogdan hissed, 'You son of a bitch, watch yourself or we'll come and fix you after we've finished with them!' Peering inside the cart, he shouted, 'So you've been getting flour from Yankel the Yid?'

As he raised his stick to stab the sacks, something glinted in the light and Piotr saw that the tip was studded with pieces of razor blade. Piotr swung his whip towards Bogdan's shoulder but one of the youth's drunken cronies pushed him out of the way in time.

'*Ej*, Bogdan, who gives a shit about the old fart. Get a move on. We've got better things to do!' And they lurched along the road, yelling and cursing.

Bogdan was a lout, Piotr thought, and his father wasn't much better. In fact the only decent person in that family was the girl, but he hadn't seen her around for a long time.

Thunder growled in the distance and large drops of rain pattered onto the splayed plane leaves as he drove into the farm. He and Anielcia had cleared the land to plant apple trees, beets and potatoes, sometimes disturbing the badgers that had burrowed deep in the earth. In May, when the purple lilac filled the air with its wistful perfume, Anielcia used to walk ahead of him, scattering potato seedlings from her apron while the blade of his plough sliced through the soil.

Piotr grunted with the effort of pulling off his rubber boots, dropped them on the doorstep and went inside the dimly lit farmhouse. As always, he glanced at the wedding photograph beside the plates on the sideboard and Anielcia's kind strong face looked back at him. Usually her presence comforted him, but today's events left him feeling uneasy. 'Something is brewing,' he told the photograph.

Kasia threw more wood into the stove and soon steam rose from the blackened pot and the floury sweet aroma of boiled potatoes filled the cottage. Although she was only twelve, since her mother's death she had taken over the running of the household. She had Anielcia's brains and Piotr was sorry he'd had to take her out of school, but someone had to look after the little ones while he was ploughing fields or felling trees. He comforted himself that women's wisdom didn't come from books.

After placing an earthenware bowl of potatoes on the table, Kasia filled the jug with buttermilk and called the children for dinner. They all bowed their heads, crossed themselves and murmured a hasty prayer to thank Lord Jesus for their food. They were looking hungrily at the potatoes, waiting for their father to start, when they heard a crash in the distance, like walls of glass shattering. A moment later, they heard screams that made the skin prickle on their backs. Their forks, poised to spear the potatoes, froze in mid-air. Marysia, the youngest, began to whimper. Eight-year-old Tereska was the first to speak.

'*Tata*, what was that?' she whispered.

Piotr didn't answer. Accustomed to her father's taciturn nature, Tereska didn't ask again.

After the meal, although it was still twilight, he closed the wooden shutters and sent the children to the bed they all shared in the corner of the room, below the picture of the Blessed Virgin with the infant Jesus. 'Don't forget to say your *paciorek*,' he said.

But Satan had been let loose and he sensed it would take more than prayers to rein him in.

At dawn, when Piotr left the house, Kasia handed him two chunks of bread with a slab of lard tied up in a gingham cloth. This time he went straight to his neighbour's house. Stach was in the yard, his sandy hair falling across his bony face as he sharpened his axe.

Dispensing with niceties, Piotr said, 'It's Bogdan I've come about.'

Stach gave a knowing wink. 'There was some excitement in town last night — he's sleeping it off.' He put down the axe and rubbed his hands. 'The miller won't be grinding flour for a long time.'

Piotr could feel the colour draining from his face while Stach spat a gob of phlegm into the dirt. '*Cholera psia krew*,' he swore. 'They thought they could lord it over us with their friends the Bolsheviks. Well, now we'll show them who's boss. We'll soon flush the blood-suckers out.'

Piotr cleared his throat. 'Your son is a drunken lout. Cursing, frightening my horse with a stick, threatening to spill my flour.'

Stach shrugged. 'Just lads having a bit of fun,' he said. 'Don't you remember when you were young?'

'You'd better warn him that if he ever threatens me again I'll let him have it.'

Stach's smile vanished. He picked up his axe and stood so close that Piotr could smell the nicotine on his breath. 'You watch yourself or you'll be the one that gets it,' he hissed. 'Things are going to be different in this town from now on. The Bolshevik lovers will swing from the trees.'

In a calmer voice he added, 'Bułka is holding a meeting at the *Rada* tomorrow morning and wants all the men to come. He's the *burmistrz* now.'

Piotr couldn't conceal his shock. Bułka, their mayor?

'What's the meeting about?' he asked.

Stach became unusually voluble. 'Remember the day Commandant Wurtzburg arrived in town? Well, he asked Bułka what the council intended to do about the Jews. He said this situation couldn't go on.'

'What situation's that?'

'They said we've got too many Yids here. Anyway, Bułka told him we'd deal with the Jews ourselves.' Stach moved closer to Piotr, his eyes gleaming. 'Listen to this.

Wurtzburg told Bułka he'd better leave a few Jewish tradesmen, but Bułka said there was no need. "We've got our own Christian tradesmen." That's what he told them!'

Stach, a carpenter who envied his Jewish rivals, was so delighted with this that he repeated it in a ringing voice. 'Bułka wants everyone to come tomorrow so he can tell us what we're supposed to do. He's thought of everything, even organised a militia to make sure none of them get away. They've already started sorting them out in Stary Most.'

Piotr felt a strange sensation in the pit of his stomach, which seemed to be folding in on itself, and as soon as he could get away from his neighbour he headed for the woods. The pine forest breathed out a cool resinous scent and his chest glistened with sweat as he swung the axe in a steady rhythm. Nothing existed but the regular movement of his arms, the clean sound of the axe striking the wood, and the chips that flew off the moist trunk. Trees were living things. Their breath smelled sweet, sap coursed from the trunk to every bough and they talked to each other in soughing whispers. Some days, when he stretched out on the soft pine needles and closed his eyes, he thought he could understand what they were saying. You knew where you were with trees; there was no evil concealed in their roots. He had tried to say this to Anielcia once, embarrassed by his awkward way of putting things. But he knew she had understood.

He smelled smoke. Putting down the axe, he wiped his face and neck and followed the sunflecked track out of the forest to see what was burning. The horizon to the east was a dull red and black smoke was billowing above it. Stary Most was on fire and the smoke was blowing in their direction.

That evening, by the flickering light of the kerosene lamp, Piotr was pencilling his expenses into one of Kasia's old exercise books, taking great care with each letter. Suddenly the dog chained in the yard gave a warning growl. A moment later he heard frantic knocking on the door. Putting down his pencil stub, he peered through the window and saw two figures huddled together. As he opened the door, the woman crumpled like a rag doll and sank to the ground. Piotr caught his breath. It was Malka, the baker's daughter.

The couple stared at him with an expression that reminded him of a picture he had seen of Judgment Day where wild-eyed sinners with gaping mouths were being speared, garrotted, burnt and torn apart. Malka's blistered lips moved but no sound came out. Struggling to help his wife up, the man whispered, '*Woda. Woda.* For God's sake, give her some water.'

Piotr stared at the young couple in front of him. With a sharp gesture he motioned them inside and quickly closed the door, hoping his neighbours hadn't seen them. He poured a glass of water from the enamel jug but the woman's hands were shaking so violently that most of it spilled before she could raise it to her lips.

Yossel was watching his wife anxiously. In breathless bursts, he said, 'Help us, please help us. We've walked all the way from Stary Most. Had to hide in the cornfield so they wouldn't find us. It's hell on earth there. *Gehenna.* They want to kill us all. They bashed old men with iron bars, grabbed children from their mothers' arms. They chased my sister and when they caught her ...' He exploded with loud sobs. 'Help us, please. We have nowhere to go.

We're not lepers or criminals, but no one would even give us a glass of water. They said if we didn't go away, they'd call the police. One woman wanted to let us in, but her husband slammed the door in our faces and threatened to set the dog on us.'

Malka gulped the water down and spoke for the first time. 'You're Piotr Marczewski, aren't you? My father told me to come to you if we ever needed help.'

Piotr's hands were clammy and he could feel his feet sweating inside his socks.

Holy Mother of God, what was he going to do with them? They were people just like himself, even if they didn't pray to the Virgin Mary. But they were also strangers. Apart from buying bread or clothes from them, and occasionally borrowing a few zlotys from Berish, he didn't really know them. He felt sorry for them, but it wasn't his fault. He hadn't arranged the world into Jews and Catholics or Bolsheviks and Nazis.

Father Olszewski said that the Jews had been condemned to wander the world because they had crucified Our Lord, but Anielcia had said that the Jews in their village weren't the ones who had done that, and she knew about these things. Stach said they had it coming because they were communists, but the Bolsheviks had said the Jews were capitalists and exploiters of the workers. Could they be communists and capitalists at the same time? If they were communists, how come so many of them had been deported to Siberia? And if they were capitalists, then how come most of them were as poor as everyone else?

All this thinking made his head ache, but Malka and Yossel were still sitting there, not taking their eyes from his face. He had to do something.

'All we need is a bit of hay in the corner of your barn,' Yossel pleaded.

Piotr looked down, struggling to find a comfortable place between his conscience and his fear. Did he dare to go against Bułka, Stach and the others? He glanced up at the photograph. Anielcia, what should I do?

A shadow fell on the wooden floor and he turned to see Kasia standing there. What if someone asked her if she'd seen any Jews? He'd heard rumours that a couple in a nearby village who had hidden a Jewish family had been strung up from the tree in their own yard, beside their two sons. He couldn't endanger his girls. Anielcia had been told that the last pregnancy would kill her, but she had placed a higher value on the baby's life than on her own. As she lay dying after giving birth to Marysia, she had entrusted the children to his care. That settled it. He didn't have the right to risk their lives.

Kasia was tugging at his sleeve. 'They could stay under the barn.'

Twenty years before, when war had broken out with Russia and the front had come close to their village, Piotr had helped his father hollow out the bunker under the barn. They heard the shelling and saw drunken Russian soldiers, caps askew, staggering around looking for vodka, watches and women. He'd been a small boy at the time and had heard the women whispering about girls left bleeding in ditches after the soldiers had finished with them. His father had built the bunker to protect his mother and sisters but, thank the Lord, it had never been used.

Piotr surveyed the couple before him. Malka was plumper than he remembered her, and the bunker was quite small, but he reckoned they'd be able to manage down there. He could let them out at night. Anielcia wouldn't want them to die.

'God will reward you,' they kept saying, grasping his hand. He pulled it away in embarrassment.

'It's just for a few days until you sort out what to do.' He spoke more gruffly than he intended.

Every morning, after her father had left for the fields, Kasia gave her sisters their breakfast of bread and milk, and walked into the barn with the bucket in which she usually carried swill for the pigs. Looking around to make sure no one was loitering near the house, she removed the hay that covered the trapdoor and looked into the dark musty hole where the fugitives spent their long hours. It was already three days since they had arrived and she wished she could let them out into the fresh air, but she knew the danger to them all if they were seen. Quickly she handed them a bowl of potatoes and a jug of water, took out their waste in the bucket and replaced the trapdoor, leaving them in the dark again after that blinding stab of light.

Heavy-hearted, she walked back across the yard where Marysia and Tereska were chasing the chickens. Putting down the bucket, she drew a hopscotch in the dirt with a stick and showed them how to play. 'If you step on the line, you'll go to hell,' she said. Her sisters were jumping around and giggling when she heard rustling in the lilac bushes behind them. A twig cracked. Throwing down the pebble, she went to see what the noise was but found only a few chickens scratching around.

Next morning, as Piotr sharpened his scythe in the yard, the front gate creaked and he looked up to see his neighbour walking towards him. Stach seemed to be sniffing the air. 'They're all over the village,' he said.

Piotr continued sharpening to keep his hands busy. 'Who is?'

'Some of the Yids got away from Stary Most and we're looking for them. If we find any of them around here ...' Instead of finishing his sentence, Stach made a slicing movement across his throat.

Piotr tried to sound casual. 'Why come to me?'

Stach shrugged. 'Just thought I'd mention it.' He gave a wolfish grin. 'Wouldn't want any of my neighbours strung up from their apple trees!'

As soon as he left, Piotr went to the barn, his lips moving as he rehearsed what he would say. The Lord wanted us to help each other but He didn't expect us to die for others. Making sure no one was watching, he pushed aside the hay, lifted the trapdoor and leant down.

'It's Malka!' Yossel gasped. 'She's in labour!'

Shocked, Piotr peered into the bunker. When his eyes grew accustomed to the darkness, he saw Malka sitting with her head in her hands, her bulging stomach clearly visible. 'Mary, Mother of God, have mercy on us,' Piotr murmured. What a time to bring a child into the world. His next thought made him break into a cold sweat.

'Well, now, a baby,' he said. 'You never told me there was going to be a baby.' He swallowed and wiped the perspiration off his forehead. 'It's not just about me. I have three children to think of,' he stammered. 'Babies cry a lot ... everyone will hear it ... you know what's going on out there. If someone hears a baby crying, we've all had it. You, me and my children ... *Panie Yossel*, I'm sure you understand ... you know what I'm trying to say ...' His throat closed up.

Yossel stared at him with wild eyes. 'But she can't have it down here, there's not enough room.'

Piotr could only shake his head. That was life for you. You took a path and followed it, not knowing where it would lead, until suddenly there was no turning back.

Down in the bunker, Malka was rocking and moaning as spasms seized her body.

Piotr's mind was made up. He closed the barn door and hasped it from inside. 'Give me your hand,' he told Malka.

With Yossel pushing from below, and Piotr pulling from above, they managed to hoist Malka up. Her face was ashen and contorted with pain. She held her belly and bit her lip, trying not to cry out. The contractions were coming faster now. Piotr smoothed out the hay that he had piled over the entrance to the bunker so that she could lie down. Looking away, he handed her a piece of wood.

'Bite on this when the pains come so you don't make a sound,' he said.

Malka gripped Yossel's hand and the tendons in her neck stood out like ropes as she heaved and grunted to push the baby out, while he wiped her moist forehead, hoping she wouldn't see the despair in his face.

Suddenly Malka's body arched and a low howl came through her clenched teeth as the slippery little body slid out, smeared with blood. It was a boy. Tears flowed down Malka's face as Yossel cut the cord and placed the baby on her belly.

Above her, the two men looked at each other for a long moment without speaking and both knew the terrible meaning of that glance.

As the baby's first cry filled the barn, Yossel placed his hand over the tiny mouth. Tears streamed down his face as he invoked curses on the heads of the persecutors of the innocent for ever and ever. The cry died away and the tiny body grew limp.

Without saying a word, Piotr handed Yossel a small wooden box and walked slowly into the farmhouse, avoiding Anielcia's accusing gaze.

One

The smoke was thick and black and above it orange flames clawed at the roof. Shards of burning wood fell to the ground and fiery embers sparked all around her. She coughed so violently that it seemed her chest would rip open. Above the rising panic, she heard a woman whispering, 'Run. Quick. While there's still time.' But there was no way out and she was so tightly jammed against the others that she couldn't move, not even to brush away the scorching cinders. The fire crackled, so close that she felt its suffocating breath on her face, but when she opened her mouth to scream there was barbed wire in her throat and no sound came out. Suddenly, shrill music blared outside. At last! Someone had come to rescue her. At the thought of deliverance she almost wept, but the music only grew more strident, conjuring images of a witches' sabbath as it mocked her hopes. The flames were leaping all around her now, her lungs were about to explode. She was going to burn to death and the rest of her life would become a heap of ashes. 'Oh no,' she gasped, 'I can't die here, please don't let me die, not like this.' The sickening smell of singed flesh filled her nostrils and the flames licked at her hair. 'Oh no, please, no ...'

Halina Shore snapped awake, arms flailing, tears streaming down her face, shocked that the moaning was coming from her own mouth. She was in her bedroom, her silk nightdress drenched with perspiration. She walked unsteadily to the window and looked out into the darkness of the Paddington street. Through the iron arabesques of the balcony she saw the disappearing tail lights of a car speeding towards the city. She glanced at the clock on her bedside table. 4.10 a.m.

Something soft swished against her bare legs and she looked down into the reproachful gooseberry eyes of her cat, Puccini. Her violent movement had startled him out of his comfortable sleep on the pillow beside her. She picked him up and stroked his mottled black and pumpkin fur until her heartbeat slowed and her breathing became more even.

Pushing the thick hair back from her face, she padded downstairs to the kitchen. Puccini ran to his bowl, sniffed it, then turned away with a disdainful look. 'Yes, I know,' she murmured. 'But the vet said milk was bad for cats.' Everything was constantly being turned upside down. Milk used to be good for humans as well as for cats, but now it seemed it was harmful for both.

What the hell, she thought, and poured him the fat-reduced milk she always drank. While he lapped it gratefully, she poured herself a generous slug of Metaxa cognac, tapped a cigarette out of the pack of Marlboro Lights she kept in the bottom drawer for emergencies, and struck a match with trembling fingers. The first mouthful of cognac stung her throat. The second spread warmly through her veins. Closing her eyes, she drew back on the cigarette and exhaled a column of smoke towards the ceiling. One day soon she would quit, but not just yet. As the kitchen filled with the comforting aroma of nicotine, she tried to shake off the numbing effect of the nightmare.

Scanning the CDs she kept in alphabetical order on the shelf, Halina reached for Schubert's *Winterreise*. She sank back in the deep leather armchair, closed her eyes and sipped the brandy while Dietrich Fischer-Diskau's mellow baritone filled the room with songs of a journey of love, loss and loneliness acted out in a snowy landscape. Lyrical and tender, these songs usually soothed her nerves but this time in the pianist's accompaniment she heard the wayfarer's suffering. She thought of Schubert, dead at the age of thirty-one with so much music still inside him, and tears welled in her eyes, but whether they were for the composer or for the person in her dream, she couldn't tell.

Puccini licked his paws, wiped his milky whiskers and jumped into her lap, but slid off when she rose and stood by the window. The music had stopped and she felt calmer now. Night was retreating and gauzy wisps of apricot and peach floated over the Sydney skyline. The silence was broken by the blare of a clarinet next door. Halina slammed the window shut, shaking with indignation. The new neighbour was a jazz musician, clearly unable to tell night from day.

She scrawled him a note: *I'm sure one day you'll be famous and I'll be paying big bucks to hear you play and lining up for your autograph, but until then please have some consideration and confine your practising to daytime hours.* She ran outside and slipped it under the door of the adjoining terrace.

Back in her own bedroom, still shaken by the dream, Halina searched for some logical explanation. It was not surprising that on this unusually hot October night she had dreamt she was on fire, and that the piercing notes of the clarinet had crossed the boundary of reality and entered the realm of dreams. Everything could be explained: all we had to do was observe and unravel the clues. That was why she had chosen her profession. She enjoyed seeing the expression on people's faces when she told them she was an odontologist. When she was in a kinder mood, she would say 'forensic dentist'. Most people gave her a strange look when she explained that she spent her days examining the teeth of the dead. In the shocked pause that usually followed while they struggled for something to say, she guessed what their response would be. She was rarely mistaken. Some nodded politely and said, 'That's an unusual job for a woman.' Sometimes, as their eyes slid from her stylish haircut to the designer clothes and Italian shoes, they asked what had prompted her to choose such a gruesome profession. 'My mother always wanted me to be a dentist so I'd get to wear a white coat and work in hygienic surroundings,' Halina would reply demurely. That usually ended the conversation.

Outside, a tomcat was yowling and spitting at the indifferent object of his lust. An ambulance siren shrilled as it sped towards St Vincent's Hospital and she wondered whether the patient would arrive in time. These days patients were referred to as 'clients', an expression she found irritating. Her clients were never rushed to hospitals: they were smashed to smithereens, dredged up from rivers, incinerated in fires or decomposed in shallow graves.

When the flesh was gone, only the teeth were left to identify the body. Like the remains that a dog had dug up in remote bushland in the Blue Mountains the previous week: naked, decomposed, without face or fingerprints. All they could tell so far was that it was a young female and, judging by the rate of decomposition and the condition of the surrounding soil, it seemed she had lain there for at least five years.

Halina's thoughts shifted to the forthcoming trial in which she would testify for the prosecution. Having examined the bite marks on little Tiffany Carson's body, she had no doubt that the police had charged the right man with the murder, but she would need to be focused and clear-headed when she gave evidence. She knew that Clive Bussell would be watching and hoping she'd slip up. He wasn't the only one in her department who thought she had sharp elbows, but she shrugged off their envy. It wasn't possible to be promoted without arousing resentment. Ever since she had been elected president of the International Association of Odontologists, the smiles of many of her colleagues, including those she had considered good friends, had become cooler and their comments more guarded. The change was subtle but unmistakeable, like the sour tang lurking inside a ripe plum.

Stepping under the shower, Halina glanced into the mirror as usual to check that no loose skin slackened the contour of her jawline or concealed the cleft in her chin. Her eyes slid from her short hair crisply cut into the nape of her neck to her long slim body. Not having children probably helped her look younger than most of her friends whose boobs had succumbed to child-bearing and gravity. Boobs. Her mother had shuddered in disgust whenever she said that word. '*Tfui!* So vulgar,' she'd say in her heavy Polish accent. 'You go to good school, Halina, don't talk like *analfabeci*.'

There was no point explaining that using slang expressions didn't mean you were illiterate. Halina sighed as she often did whenever she thought about her mother's comments. 'Vy you buy old house?' Zosia had grumbled when Halina had brought her to see her new Paddington terrace. Wrinkling her nose, she had sniffed at the door of every room like a retriever. '*Wilgoć.* Damp,' she said. 'You get sick. Air not good.'

When they had arrived in Sydney in the late 1940s, Paddington was a rundown working-class suburb generally regarded as a slum, and her mother had continued to think of it that way even though half a century later you had to be a millionaire to buy one of those terraces. Her mother had no sense of history. Looking back on those early days, when they had rented a room in a Newtown boarding house permeated with the strong smell of lamb chops, dripping and mashed potatoes, Halina marvelled that a woman who had barely finished primary school, had devoted herself to providing her daughter with the best possible education. How she had managed to scrape together enough money from scrubbing floors and washing dishes in restaurants to send her to a private school was a miracle, but one that Halina had accepted without question at the time.

Instead of evoking gratitude, Zosia's sacrifice had caused her embarrassment. Surrounded by girls who rode horses on country properties during the holidays and wore the latest fashions, Halina was ashamed of her frugal lifestyle, darned socks and mended sweaters. Every speech day when Halina received prizes, her mother always arrived wearing the same old faded dress and squashed felt hat stuck on her greying hair, smelling strongly of perspiration because she had rushed across town to get there. Halina squirmed whenever Zosia spoke loudly and ungrammatically in her choppy Polish accent. She could see that her mother lacked the finesse of the other women, who wore tailored suits, white gloves and had lace handkerchiefs perfumed with Helena Rubinstein's Apple Blossom. She also noted that their pleasant smiles and Anglo politeness gave no sign that Zosia was not one of them.

Shampooing an auburn rinse into her hair in the never-ending battle to conceal the grey, Halina thought with regret about her mother, a closed person who spoke little and avoided confrontation. She would give a brief opinion whether it was solicited or not, but if it met with an argument, as often happened in conversation with her daughter, she tightened her lips, shrugged and changed the subject. Now that it was too late, Halina wished she had found a way of breaking down that wall and reaching the woman on the other side. She didn't even know what had prompted Zosia to leave her native land. Whenever she had asked about their life in Poland, her mother had shrugged and said, 'Past is past. Nussing to talk about.'

Halina dried herself energetically to erase the sound of her mother's voice that filled her head. She needed some coffee to clear her thoughts. A few minutes later, the Gaggia espresso machine, a recent extravagance, spat and spurted as it frothed the milk for the cappuccino that had become an essential part of her morning ritual.

'That machine sounds like a jet about to take off,' Rhys had said with his deep rolling laugh the first time she had made coffee for him. He had stolen up behind her and, with a rough movement, pulled her against him. 'Leave that and come to bed,' he'd murmured. 'You make my balls ache with lust.'

Rhys's turn of phrase, so quaintly vulgar, never failed to excite her. No man she had ever known had desired her with such urgency. She had left the machine spluttering. By the time they came downstairs again, it had burnt out and the kitchen was filled with an acrid smell.

That was months ago, and the coffee still had a bitter taste even though she'd had the machine fixed. And Rhys hadn't phoned for two weeks and three days.

Halina looked at her watch. Too late to go back to bed, too early to meet her friends for breakfast and too hot to jog in the park. She heard a thump in the front yard and the sound of a car speeding away as the thick rolls of the weekend newspaper struck the tiles of her verandah.

She scooped them up and peeled off the clingy plastic wrapping on her way inside, rolled it into a ball and threw it to Puccini. He backed towards the wall, climbed up several centimetres with his hind legs, then launched himself towards the ball with the spring of an athlete about to attempt a long jump. His paws skittered on the polished floor and, instead of catching the ball, he pushed it under the settee. Repeated attempts to extricate it failed and he looked at her expectantly. As Halina reached down to dislodge the ball, she saw why it was caught.

Two

Did she have a right to go through her mother's papers? Perhaps the life Zosia had always kept private should be left in the scuffed cardboard box, unopened. Suspended between integrity and curiosity, Halina felt like a thief sneaking into an empty house. Parents' lives were always a mystery to children, a mystery that deepened with age, but now that Zosia was no longer here to protect her secrets, she hesitated to raise the veil.

How could two adults be part of each other's lives for over fifty years, yet understand so little about each other? Sitting cross-legged in the pool of sunlight on the polished floorboards of her lounge room, Halina thought about her mother's last days in the nursing home. An invisible screwdriver turned in her chest, tightening her ribcage so that she had to sigh deeply every few moments to suck enough air into her lungs. It was painful to remember the over-perfumed deodorant intended to mask the pervasive odour of urine, and the residents in their solitary rooms looking up eagerly at every footstep. Every Sunday afternoon it had been a guilty relief to say goodbye to her mother, slumped in the wheelchair, silent and withdrawn, and to walk out into the light and feel the sun on her face again.

Zosia had never demanded anything of Halina other than that she should study hard. 'You want to be cleaner, like me?' she used to taunt whenever Halina pleaded to go out with her friends. After a day spent scrubbing and vacuuming other people's homes and travelling across the city by bus and train, Zosia ironed Halina's school blouse and uniform, darned her lisle stockings with tiny stitches, and cooked their *bigos* stew or rolled out pastry for the *pierogi* she stuffed with mashed potatoes or mushrooms. She never asked Halina to help. 'Go and study,' she would order, waving her large reddened hands towards the textbooks.

Halina looked again at the box on the floor in front of her. It was covered with faded paper patterned in a paisley design and secured with string. She recognised it from her primary school days, when she had filled it with the required lengths of cesarine and headcloth. With the sewing teacher's help she had fashioned the material into shapeless aprons and skirts, and embroidered the edges in clumsy cross-stitch. It had lain under the sofa for several weeks, since she had brought it from the nursing home along with her mother's other belongings. She had intended to go through everything then, but the task had proved too distressing and she had pushed the box under the settee and forgotten it until now.

The string was knotted so tightly that when she tried to undo it, her nail broke and she had to cut it with a knife.

As she raised the lid, her heart beat with anticipation. Perhaps she would finally find out something about her father. She knew that his name was Józef, and that he had died fighting for Poland when she was a toddler, but her mother had refused to talk about him. Through sadness, Halina assumed. She had never even seen his photograph.

'Photographs?' her mother had said scathingly whenever she mentioned the subject. 'I had to leave everything when Warsaw was bombed. I carried you on my back. And you ask about photographs!' Pressed for details, her mother had become so upset that Halina always dropped the subject. She resented being rebuffed but had always believed that one day she would catch her mother off-guard and persuade her to talk about the past. That moment never came.

During her last visit to Wentworth House, she had wheeled her mother onto the terrace but neither the luscious perfume of the mock orange nor the warmth of the sun had brought a smile to her face. After Halina had asked about the nurses, the food and the other residents, and Zosia had replied with shrugs and monosyllables, there was little left to say. She would have liked to talk about her work, but the nursing home was hardly the place to describe the triumphs of identifying corpses by examining their dental remains. As for Rhys, Halina had never told her mother about him. Zosia would have been appalled by an affair with a married man and, even at her age, Halina wasn't prepared to expose herself to her mother's disapproval.

Usually she broke the awkward silence with gossip about her friends, problems with the taxation department, or some minor irritation caused by the council's incompetence. On that last day, however, she had good news. Her mother would be proud that she had been elected president of the International Association of Odontologists.

As she told her about the appointment, she had noticed the milky fog lift from her mother's eyes. The colour of her irises had deepened to some indefinable colour beyond the earthly spectrum, and her expression was unnerving, as though she was trying to drink her daughter in. Impaled on that impenetrable gaze, Halina felt naked, all her selfishness exposed. A moment later, her mother's eyes were dull and unfocused once more.

The following morning, the phone had rung before she was awake. As usual her thoughts had leapt to Rhys, and then lurched from disappointment to anger with herself.

'You'd better come over right away,' the matron had said. 'She's failing.'

It was Halina's first bereavement. The end of a life was a disappointingly small moment that hung on the final exhalation of a breath. Although she had studied anatomy and examined bodies on mortuary slabs, Halina struggled to comprehend that her mother's light had been extinguished for ever. She sat beside the bed, watching as her mother's face stiffened like a wooden mask, and smoothed the grey strands away from her jowly cheeks, wondering what had gone through her mind in those final moments. But her mother had died as she had lived, in silence.

Although she was accustomed to dealing with the deaths of strangers, Halina felt unequal to the task of mourning for her mother. It seemed to her that she should feel something more significant than a numb sense of unreality.

The burial rites had posed a problem. Although she was born and raised a Catholic, Zosia had not been a churchgoer and, from the few conversations they had had on the subject, Halina knew she had little time for God or his earthly representatives. 'Does God hide in churches when there is so much suffering in the world?' she would say. 'If God exists, he doesn't need priests or churches.'

Halina had arranged for a cremation, but changed her mind at the last moment when she thought of the teeth that would be left after incineration. Instead, she had her mother buried in the Catholic section of Rookwood cemetery, where worms consumed the dead of all religions without prejudice. At the funeral, she had spoken briefly about the simple woman who had brought her small daughter to a foreign country, worked hard all her life, and lived by old-fashioned values.

The box contained very little. An entire life reduced to a slim manila folder. At least her mother had left a daughter behind. Who would look through her own belongings and remember her after she was dead, Halina thought.

Puccini was brushing against her, and as she stroked his mottled fur she recalled her mother's exasperation when she took in the starving creature she had found miaowing piteously in her yard. 'A woman needs a child, not a cat. Cats don't cry for you when you're dead.'

When Halina had married at the age of twenty-three, she had assumed they would have children, but it hadn't taken long to realise that she had made a bad choice. Gary had felt threatened by her ambitious nature and had resisted everything she aspired to. To stay married to him she would have had to work part-time in a suburban practice, filling and scaling teeth all day, so that his status and income would surpass hers. She had left him after four years of compromises that satisfied neither of them and arguments that grew increasingly rancorous. In the years that followed, Halina discovered that she despised weak, insecure men who needed her too much, and resented strong ones who didn't need her enough.

Lying on top of the papers in the folder was her mother's document of naturalisation, signed by Harold Holt, who later disappeared mysteriously while swimming at Portsea.

She wondered how his relatives had coped with the fact that his body had never been found. Lack of closure was endless torture for families. The next document referred to their change of name. Halina had almost forgotten that as soon as they had become Australian citizens, her mother had changed their name by deed poll. Mortified every time she had to spell out the long consonant-heavy Polish name that usually provoked stares and giggles from her classmates, she had been relieved when Szczecińska became Shore. But when the teacher said she would call her Helen, she had jumped to her feet and retorted with a flaming face, 'My name is not Helen, it is Halina!' There was a shocked intake of breath around the classroom but Halina hadn't cared. She must have been angry even then.

Each document took her back in time. A sheet of paper dated December 1947 was covered in copybook copperplate. It was her report from the convent school in Warsaw, the year before they had left Poland. She remembered the day she had been forced to kneel on dried lentils as a punishment for talking in class. The lentils had dug into her knees but it was the humiliation rather than the pain that had made her stand up and face the teacher. 'You shouldn't hurt children,' she had shouted. When Sister Czesława struck her legs with a ruler for insolence, Zosia had hurried to the convent the following day, so angry that she could hardly speak. 'You all pretend to be saints but you're sadists,' she told the astonished nun, and took Halina out of the school.

As she opened the double page of the report, a cardboard cutout of a heart fell out. Clumsily embroidered in large stitches were the words *Na dzień matek życzenia od Haliny.* Mother's Day wishes from Halina. Her mother was not a sentimental woman and Halina was surprised that she'd kept this all her life. Her eyes skimmed over the report card. *Bright but inattentive. Halina is an intelligent child but needs to gain control over her temper and her tongue.*

At the bottom of the box lay a black and white photograph with serrated edges. Her heart thumped in anticipation but the photo had been taken in Australia, shortly after they arrived. Zosia had been stout and grey for so long that Halina had forgotten how she had looked when she was young. Studying the photograph, she saw a buxom young woman with an open face and sturdy arms and legs. And there was Halina, standing beside her mother but not touching her. Already nearly as tall as Zosia at the age of nine, she had her hair braided in that old-fashioned Polish way, each plait doubled under and tied with a bow, with a bigger bow on top of her head. And there were those prominent central incisors, the left crossed over the right, clearly visible in the photograph even though she was smiling so carefully to conceal the defect.

Beside her stood a couple with a small boy in baggy trousers and a sleeveless vest, grimacing into the camera. The woman had a protective arm around her husband, a thick-set man with a brooding expression. Halina had no idea who they were.

She returned the papers to the folder and replaced the lid on the box with a twinge of regret. No secrets there.

Three

The beachside café was already crowded when Halina arrived. Waitresses squeezed past the wobbly tables on the pavement, balancing plates of scrambled eggs, roasted tomatoes and berry pancakes high above the diners' heads. A schnauzer tied to a lamp post strained at the leash and barked hysterically, drowning out the twenty-somethings complaining about their love lives and the forty-somethings complaining about their lack of it.

On a ledge of sandstone below the café strip, a young brunette sprawled on a towel, her bare breasts frying in the sun. Like Sydney, Halina thought, self-indulgent and carefree. Looking round for her friends, she saw Claire waving to attract her attention. A moment later they spotted Toula weaving in between the tables, a worried look on her pale face.

'Sorry I'm late,' she said. 'I had to pick up some feta and olives for my mother.'

Toula's life revolved around people who took advantage of her. Her critical husband, her angry daughter and her demanding mother. 'You're a perfect example of the saying that no good deed ever goes unpunished,' Halina said.

'Why doesn't your brother help take care of your mother?' She spoke more sharply than she had intended.

'He's moved to Newcastle.'

'How convenient.'

Toula sighed. 'It doesn't make any difference. He's always too busy, wherever he is.'

Claire was nodding. 'No matter how many brothers or sisters you have, it's always just one that does all the caring.'

The three women met here on the last Saturday of every month for breakfast to catch up with the unscripted soap operas of their lives. They were close confidantes, affectionate rivals and stern critics who used each other as yardsticks to measure their own progress and validate their triumphs.

Claire was studying Halina. 'You look wrecked,' she said. 'Another night of passion?' Claire considered sex a waste of energy better invested in more worthwhile endeavours.

'I had a bizarre dream last night,' Halina replied.

Claire and Toula didn't take their eyes off her while she described it, her voice trembling as she relived the nightmare.

'God that's horrible. What do you think it means?' Claire asked.

Halina already regretted mentioning it. 'It was just a dream.'

'You said you were terrified and trapped,' Claire pointed out. 'Do you feel trapped?'

'I do now!' Halina laughed. 'Claire, it was a dream, not a psychiatric case study. And it wasn't about me. The brain is a computer, and dreams are the by-products of nightly testing of its software.'

'Always the scientist,' Claire said. 'Don't you know that there are more things in heaven and earth ...'

Toula leant forward. 'I went to see a clairvoyant last week. She was amazing. She told me I was worried about my sick mother, and needed more self-confidence.'

Claire snorted. 'You didn't need to pay fifty bucks to find that out, did you?'

Toula wasn't discouraged. 'She also said I should be ready for a big change in my life.'

Halina burst out laughing. 'This is unbelievable. An intelligent woman like you, ready to believe charlatans who tell you that the month you were born can affect your personality and your destiny!' She knew she was wasting her time. Most people preferred to believe in the stars than to trust logic and scientific proof.

Claire was surveying her with an ironic smile.

'What?' Halina asked. 'What's on your mind?'

'I always know what you're thinking, but I hardly ever know what you feel.'

'Are you saying I live in my head?'

Toula was looking from one to the other, anxious to lighten the conversation, when a woman walked past, her face stretched into masklike stiffness over a newly resculpted nose and pouting lips. Claire stopped spooning her pancake into her mouth and nudged Halina. 'That's the second cosmetic surgery she's had. She'll end up looking like Michael Jackson. I think it's sad not to be comfortable with your own face at this stage of life.' Claire was a big woman who wore loose tops, baggy pants and no make-up. 'My face is as furrowed as a Dubbo paddock in a drought, but I've worked hard to earn my wrinkles and grey hairs and I'm not giving them up!'

Halina made no comment as she sipped her latte. She knew she would never give up her regular visits to the hairdresser, the beautician or the gym. Eternal vigilance was the price you paid for having a lover considerably younger than yourself.

'If I thought that keeping my husband interested depended on the colour of my hair or the shape of my bum, I'd leave him right now. Right now,' Claire was saying.

Soon after graduating Claire had married her first boyfriend, who still doted on her, while Halina's life was a graveyard of relationships that had suffered an early death.

Claire was watching her. 'At least you've had the sense to leave those front teeth alone.'

Halina ran her tongue over the overlapping tooth. As soon as she started earning money, she had made an appointment with an orthodontist. He had extracted two molars and inserted what felt like a suit of armour in her mouth, which had lacerated her tongue and the inside of her cheeks for eighteen months. She could hardly wait for the day when the braces would be removed and she would see a row of perfectly straight teeth in the mirror. But her joy had been short-lived. Within two years, her teeth had moved back and the left incisor overlapped the right as before. The prospect of going through the agonising process once more, with no guarantee of success, had discouraged her, particularly as her husband had found the irregularity appealing. 'It looks cute,' he had said. Conscious of her height, Halina had never expected anyone to find her cute.

'I probably should have them straightened again,' she said now. 'These days techniques are less invasive and more successful than they used to be.'

Claire shook her head so vigorously that her short iron-grey hair flew up. 'No way, Halina. Surely you don't want a Hollywood smile. That tooth gives your face character. Otherwise it would be too perfect.'

Halina burst out laughing. 'That's the weirdest compliment I've ever had. It's good to know that an overlapping tooth saves me from looking too perfect!'

But Claire's mind was no longer on Halina's dental irregularities. 'So, how *are* you feeling?' she asked.

Halina frowned. 'Now that you've made me feel vain and superficial for tinting my hair, but saved by having a crooked tooth, you mean?'

'God, you're a pain. I mean how are you feeling in general? That was a pretty traumatic dream.'

Under Claire's intent gaze Halina felt like an insect on a glass slide. This relentless delving into emotions was tiresome. 'Read my lips,' she said. 'I'm fine.' She looked intently at her fruit platter and took a long time deciding whether to spear a strawberry or a chunk of melon.

After a pause, Claire said, 'You haven't really grieved yet, you know. Losing your mother means losing part of yourself. I think you're still in denial.'

Halina picked at her broken fingernail. 'I hate that pretentious jargon. It reduces every emotion to a formula.'

Despite their differences, Halina admired Claire's assurance just as she admired her passion for social and political issues. Instead of establishing a private law practice, Claire had chosen to work for human rights groups and was always caught up in the plight of raped women in Rwanda, child soldiers in Sierra Leone or girls sold into prostitution in Cambodia. Issues that titillated and horrified readers of weekend magazines were her daily concern. Halina, on the other hand, found it easier to deal with dead bodies than living people. As for political causes, she could always see both sides. She thought that made her open-minded but Claire said that ambivalence indicated a reluctance to commit.

Halina turned to Toula. 'You're very quiet this morning.'

Toula sighed. 'It's Katy. After going through all those interviews and getting the job she applied for, she's decided not to take it after all. She says she doesn't want to work in a corporate firm and never wanted to do law anyway. Now she's going to India to meditate with some guru. Says it'll help her find herself.' Her dark eyes looked more tragic than usual.

'She's given up a job with a good salary and good prospects to pursue a dream.' Claire whistled softly under her breath. 'That takes guts.'

Toula shook her head. 'She's angry with me as usual. Apparently it's my fault she did law. Says I've never taken her needs into account, that I've always tried to push her into a mould. But all I ever wanted was for her to be happy.'

'It has nothing to do with you. She's just dumping her shit on you.' Claire shrugged. 'Tell her to fuck off and come back when she's grown up. And you should stop being your family's slave and put yourself first for once. When you cark it, they'll put on your grave, "Here lies Toula who lived everyone's life except her own."'

'That's easy for you to say,' Toula shot back. Suddenly she giggled. 'You know what? I really wish Katy would find herself. Whoever she finds is bound to be easier to get on with than she is!'

Whenever Toula talked about her daughter, Halina was relieved that she had no children. At the age of thirty-two Katy caused her mother more angst than she had done as a teenager. Halina couldn't understand why parents put up with such ungrateful children, or why bright young people spent years trying to find themselves. Who was Katy expecting to find on her journey of self-discovery? Who did she think had been living in her skin all these years?

Toula was sighing. 'I don't know how long she'll be away. First she's stopping off for a holiday in Bali, to chill out, as she calls it. I wish she'd meet someone and settle down. My mother drives me crazy. When is Katy going to get married? What will people say? That's all she thinks about.'

While Toula moaned about her family, Halina's gaze wandered to the cliffs. Their sharp edges might have been hewn off by a giant's axe. Beneath the overhangs that curled above the sea, the sandstone had been whorled into creamy caverns and red-streaked crevices where yellow gazanias had taken root. Waves crashed into smooth flat-topped boulders below, spilling over them like miniature waterfalls, and cormorants flew onto the rocks and spread out their wings to dry. The honeyed scent of alyssum wafted down from the hills above the beach. Why aren't we delirious with joy at the beauty all around us, Halina wondered.

The topless sunbather rolled up her towel, wrapped a sarong around her tanned body and strolled languidly along the beach, trailing her beach bag along the pale sand. On the edge of the sandstone platform, a child crouched down to pick bait out of a red plastic bucket and handed it to the fisherman beside him, who fixed it onto his hook. A moment later, the sun glanced off the reel and the rod flickered as the fisherman cast out. The child leant over the edge of the rock, peering at something in the water. The tide was coming in and the waves foamed as they crashed into the rocks and exploded high in the air like shattered crystal.

Toula was talking about her work at the Maritime Museum and the migration exhibition she had recently curated. Her question brought Halina's attention back to the table.

'What ship did you come out on, Halina?'

'No idea. My mother never talked about the voyage.'

'That's not unusual,' Claire said. 'In those days people didn't talk about the past. They kept a stiff upper lip and just got on with it.'

'You might be able to find out the name of the ship from the Maritime Museum,' Toula suggested.

Halina looked down at the rock ledge again. The fisherman was bending over his red bucket but she could no longer see the child. She craned forward, looking from side to side several times, as tense as a cheetah stalking its prey. Following her gaze, Claire and Toula saw the churning water and spotted the small head bobbing among the waves in the same instant as Halina. Toula's hand flew to her mouth; Claire's eyes widened. Pushing her chair back so suddenly that it crashed onto the pavement, Halina kicked off her sandals, sprang up and started running. Her long legs moved so quickly that her feet left shallow imprints in the sand and it seemed as though she was moving faster than the seagulls she had panicked into flight. A young mother sitting under a tangerine umbrella with her chubby toddler opened her mouth to complain at the sand being kicked up in their direction.

'Get help!' Halina screamed and kept running, over the rocks now, not daring to take her eyes off the child being swept further away.

Before she knew what she was doing, she was in the water, she was swimming. Her shorts ballooned, weighing her down. Too late to take them off now. Her nose filled with the sharp salty taste of the sea and her arms and legs felt heavy. She put all her strength into her stroke but the water felt like liquid lead. Buffeted by the current, she made little progress. Suddenly she was back in the Himalayas, trudging along an almost perpendicular slope that poked into the pitiless sky, her feet encased in cement boots. 'It's not hard, it's just up,' the sherpa had said. She repeated the mantra now, over and over. *It's not hard, it's just up. Keep going. It can't be far now.*

Hidden in the hollows of the waves, the small head disappeared from view and bounced up a moment later. He was about five years old and there was panic in his eyes.

'Hold on, I'm coming!' Halina shouted, but the shriek of the gulls and the splashing of the waves blew the words away. A giant wave slammed into her and she went under, saltwater flooding her nose and mouth. Time and movement stopped, the universe was still and silent. She was floundering in slow motion, going under.

In the dark stillness, she became aware of her mother's presence. 'Come on, Halina, you can do it,' Zosia was saying. Just as she had said when Halina was a small girl too scared to cross the road by herself. Paralysed with fear, she had stood on the kerb, crying. 'Come on, Halina, the light is green now, you can do it,' her mother had called from the other side, stretching out her hand as if to guide her. Fighting the current but feeling calmer now, Halina saw that green light all around her, and she looked straight into her mother's face as Zosia held out her hand to pull Halina up through the solid wall of water.

She came to the surface, spluttering, and grabbed hold of the drowning child. A piece of seaweed straggled over his face. One arm hooked around his sparrow-thin shoulders, Halina managed to tow him towards the beach. Someone ran into the breaking rollers, took him from her and carried him ashore. Halina staggered onto the shell-encrusted sand, not aware of the cuts on her feet, and flopped down, her heart drumming against her throat.

Someone turned the boy on his side and applied pressure on his back to force out the water he had swallowed. Someone else was punching numbers into a mobile phone and repeating the word ambulance in a panic-stricken voice. In the background, an agitated voice was saying over and over, 'Jesus God, I only turned me back for a second and he was gone. Only a second. Jesus.'

'It's a bloody miracle more of them don't get swept away fishing on the rocks,' a man was muttering. 'Then they fucking sue the council. He's a lucky devil. If that woman hadn't jumped in, the kid would've been a goner.'

A flash went off in Halina's face. Someone was asking her name. Her breath came in gulps and her limbs weighed a thousand tonnes. Summoning her remaining strength she shook her head, mumbled 'No,' and closed her eyes.

When she opened them again, she was looking into the white faces of Claire and Toula. They were kneeling beside her on the wet sand, their eyes full of concern as they rubbed her cold hands. Was she all right? Did she want some water? Should they call an ambulance?

To all their questions, she shook her head. 'Don't fuss,' she said. 'I'm fine. Just tired. I'll be okay in a few minutes.'

As soon as they got her home, she gratefully sipped the cognac that Claire poured her.

'What on earth made you do that?' Toula asked, gripping Halina's hand. 'You're not even a good swimmer! You could have drowned!'

Claire pushed a strand of hair away from Halina's eyes. 'That was unbelievable! We were just sitting there watching, but you plunged in and saved him. What made you do it?'

Halina sat up and tried to smile. 'I got bored with the conversation. Maybe I didn't want to have to identify another water-logged corpse.' Then she shrugged. 'I have no idea why I did it.'

'That was the most heroic thing I've ever seen,' Toula said.

'You're being melodramatic. I didn't think about the danger or anything. I just moved. It's as if it wasn't really me.'

Halina was irritated by their repetitive chatter and admiring comments. There was only so much you could say about the incident, and they had said it all several times. She felt a desperate need to be alone and sighed with relief when she heard the front door close behind them.

Stretched out on the sofa with Puccini lying across her stomach, she stroked his fur absently and replayed the incident at the beach. The unthinking impulse to jump into the water, the terror of being swirled beneath the surface by the undertow, the icy dread at realising she wouldn't be able to rescue the child. She shivered as she recalled the panic of being sucked down, of knowing that her strength was gone, that she would soon be defeated by the power of the waves. She was a pebble, slammed by the tide towards the bottom of the sea. But by some miracle her arms had kept thrashing through the water. A voice outside herself had urged her on. Had she been hallucinating in her exhausted state?

Halina sat up and shook her head in disbelief. How could a vision have such power? But she knew without a doubt that it had been the sound of her mother's voice and the touch of her hand that had spurred her on to keep struggling through the current and lifted her to safety through the churning waves.

Four

Rhys was looking into her face as though trying to see behind her eyes. 'Some people will do anything to get into the newspapers.'

'Well, I had to find some way of getting your attention.' She smiled to dilute the sting.

As usual, he refused to engage. 'I told our photographer if he took another hopeless shot like that I'd push the fucking camera up his arse.' He gave a throaty laugh, clearly pleased with himself.

Halina looked at the page-three article with the blurred photograph of her turning away from the camera. It was captioned: *Mystery heroine dashes into dangerous surf to rescue child.* 'Talk about sensationalism. Thank God I didn't give them my name.'

He was still studying her face. Moving closer, he traced the outline of her mouth with his index finger. 'You did a very brave thing yesterday. Even if it was to get my attention.'

Rhys always avoided the subtext, and she was too proud to say that she wished he called more often, so they frequently sparred like this without achieving anything.

She waved her hand dismissively. He took it in both of his, turned it over and pressed his warm lips against her palm. Her fingers tingled. She already knew how this would end.

'I'm taking you to bed,' he murmured, holding her so tightly against him that she could hardly breathe. 'It's not every day I get the chance to fuck a heroine.'

Effortlessly, he lifted her up and carried her towards the stairs.

'I must have built up all these muscles from typing,' he said and they both laughed. At the bottom of the staircase he stopped.

'I can't wait till we get upstairs,' he said hoarsely.

He threw off his shoes, unzipped his trousers and, with a rough movement, pulled off her silk underpants. 'Let me look at you,' he whispered, kneeling between her legs. He breathed in deeply and closed his eyes as though inhaling some expensive perfume. Unlike her former lovers, who enjoyed sex in a scrubbed and sanitised way, Rhys was excited by all its flavours, smells and juices.

'You're rosy inside and out,' he murmured, gazing at her with the enchantment of a scientist who has discovered a new species. 'Such a tender juicy pink.' She was still laughing when he thrust his thick hot tongue inside her, setting off flickers of electrical shocks that made her moan with pleasure. 'You taste like the sea,' he said. As they rocked together, her blood turned pirouettes in her veins. 'You feel like the ocean,' she whispered.

They lay in each other's arms, damp with sweat. Halina smiled in post-coital languor, stroking the familiar coarse texture of his back.

'I'll make coffee,' she said.

But Rhys was already pulling on his trousers. 'I don't have time. I have to get back for the afternoon news conference.'

It was always like this.

They had met eight years before at a forensic conference in Hong Kong. The first speaker had been Dieter Neumann, an international expert on microbiology. Pausing occasionally to push up the glasses that kept slipping down his nose, Dr Neumann outlined the uses of DNA testing in odontology in his German accent.

Halina yawned. She was familiar with his research and humourless delivery. As she looked around, she became aware that a man was staring at her from the back of the function room. Drawn to his bold gaze, she glanced in his direction several times. She seemed to be entering into some kind of mental duel which could only be won by refusing to look back, but his insistent scrutiny threw down a challenge she was unable to resist.

Dieter Neumann was coming to the end of his speech, and his concluding remarks returned Halina's attention to the conference.

'What makes mitochondrial DNA a unique and invaluable tool in identifying bodies, ladies and gentlemen, is its mode of inheritance. Because unlike nuclear DNA, half of which is passed down from each parent, mtDNA is inherited only from the mother, with no paternal input. So mtDNA tells us the history of women, and can through matrilineal descent for generations be traced. Theoretically, all the way from Eve. So all we need is a living descendant on the mother's side, *ja*? And even decades after death, mtDNA can usually in the bones be found. But the best source of all is the pulp of a tooth. This testing is not in so many labs performed, but believe me, it will in our lifetime take place.'

As Dr Neumann bowed stiffly in response to the applause, Halina's heartbeat quickened. What a breakthrough, to be able to identify a body by comparing its mtDNA to that of a descendant, especially as tooth enamel was the toughest part of the body and most likely to remain intact after the flesh had decomposed. With the advancement of molecular biology techniques, perhaps this type of testing would become available within a few years. The danger was that technological developments were fast outstripping people's ability to think, and she made a mental note to warn her students that technology would never replace human powers of observation and deduction.

It was time for her to present her own paper and she moved towards the rostrum while the chairman was introducing her. 'We are very fortunate to have Dr Halina Shore, president of the Australian Association of Odontologists, to talk about odontology in mass disasters.'

'With the proliferation of air travel, odontology is bound to play an increasingly important role in identifying victims of mass disasters,' Halina began. 'Now that the airline industry has been deregulated, and companies are increasingly cutting down on maintenance and training hours, pilots are pressured to fly with what the industry euphemistically calls "unserviceabilities". Let's not kid ourselves: that's doublespeak for risky business. When planes carrying several hundred people crash, the bodies disintegrate. In conditions like that, there's little left to identify the dead apart from their teeth.'

The man at the back of the room was still there, not taking his eyes off her.

'When you remember that one hundred deaths means ten thousand cross-matches,' she continued, 'it's obvious that we need to organise planning procedures and train teams of forensic dentists all over the world.'

She recounted the shambles she had witnessed after a recent plane crash in Thailand, where thousands of body parts were strewn over a huge area in 100-degree heat with no cold storage for the remains and no experts on the ground. It still made her shudder to recall the cameramen photographing faces that had slammed into a mountainside at over 600 knots, then handing the images around for distraught relatives to identify.

'Now that cities are becoming more densely populated, and office blocks, apartment buildings, hotel towers, shopping malls and underground trains contain hundreds, and sometimes thousands, of people, the potential for mass disaster is growing. If we don't organise planning procedures now and train more odontologists, one day we will regret it.'

As soon as she stepped off the podium, she was surrounded by colleagues sharing experiences and asking questions. Above the buzz of conversation she heard someone shout, 'Halina! You look marvellous! Come and have a vodka with us like a good Polish girl!' It was Marek Janowski, the Polish odontologist she had met in Paris several years before. Marek had an inexhaustible fund of jokes and an anecdote for every occasion. After an evening spent with him the world always seemed a more cheerful place, but noticing the young brunette clinging to his arm, Halina made an excuse. She glanced around for the man who had been watching her but he had gone.

In the dimly lit bar on the top floor of the Orient Pearl Hotel, she was sipping a Metaxa when suddenly everything blurred and the voices of the other patrons reverberated in her ears. She doubled up as though a knife had plunged into her stomach. Running towards the toilet, hand over her mouth, she banged into a table and knocked something over but kept going.

She flung open the door of the cubicle, knelt down and vomited in painful spasms. As she groaned, she became aware that someone was standing behind her, rubbing the back of her neck. She supposed it was one of the women from the conference. Wiping the threads of vomit from her mouth, she staggered towards the wash basin and splashed her face with water. When she opened her eyes, she was looking into the face of the man who had been watching her in the conference room.

'I don't make a habit of going into women's toilets, but the way you threw that glass over me and kept running I thought you might be in trouble,' he said, handing her a wad of paper towels. His voice was as dark and mellow as the brandy she had been drinking.

Mortified at being seen in this condition, Halina thanked him hurriedly. She tried to hold her aching head high as she walked out ahead of him, but her legs buckled. Reluctantly she took his proffered arm and leant against him on their way back to the bar.

'We had a buffet for dinner,' she said in a hoarse voice she hardly recognised. 'It must have been something I ate.'

He steered her to a table, sat her down and held out his large hand. 'Rhys Evans. Southeast Asia correspondent for the *National Observer*.' He looked into her face. 'You need water and I need a whisky.'

He turned, clicked his fingers twice, then looked around with a gaze that implied that he knew everything about everyone in the room and what he didn't know he would soon find out. 'The service is appalling tonight, Carlton,' he said to the Chinese barman in a loud voice so everyone could hear. A moment later, the waitress came running with their drinks.

While Rhys tipped the Jack Daniel's straight down his throat, his lips not touching the rim of the glass, Halina sipped a Perrier. Below them shadowy sampans were moored in the bay and floating restaurants lacquered scarlet with gilded dragons trailed long ribbons of light in the water.

'What were you doing at the conference?' she asked.

'I came to hear you speak.'

She raised her eyebrows.

'No, really,' he protested. 'I saw that a Sydney forensic expert was listed among the speakers, and thought I might get a story to send back. I was fascinated by what you said.' He dropped his voice until it strummed invisible strings deep in her body. 'Tell me, how did you get into this profession?'

Halina was about to give her usual sardonic reply but something in his searching gaze changed her mind. 'Everyone was shocked when I chose this dark corner of dentistry, but violent death has always fascinated me,' she said quietly.

He listened attentively while she spoke. It was refreshing to talk to a man who was neither over-awed nor threatened by her. The nauseous feeling was passing and she began to relax.

'Sometimes I think the most important decisions in life are made for reasons we don't understand,' she mused.

'I always wanted to be a doctor, but when I found out that women dentists were treated more equally than women doctors, I changed my mind. Besides, if you were a "lady doctor" back then, you ended up doing general practice part-time or becoming a dermatologist and spending your life treating pimples and rashes.'

He was looking into her eyes with such admiration that she broke off and sipped her Perrier, amused but flattered.

'A dollar for your thoughts,' she said lightly.

'I'm thinking what an extraordinarily attractive and interesting woman you are.'

If anyone else had said it, it would have sounded corny, but his Richard Burton voice infused the words with sincerity.

'And you. Why did you become a journalist?' Halina asked.

He tipped another neat whisky down his throat. 'I grew up in a narrow grey house in a narrow grey town, surrounded by grey-minded people.' As he described his childhood in a dour household in south Wales, she could almost smell the coal dust and see the discontented tight-lipped mother who told him he'd never amount to anything. Rhys had run away from home at thirteen, packed fish on the trawlers, driven forklifts on the wharves and repaired sleepers on the railways, until he got a job as a cabin boy on a ship that brought English migrants to Australia. He shrugged. 'I was lucky. I got to know how the world works while other lads were fidgeting in classrooms learning useless facts. Not bad training for a reporter.'

The crowd in the bar was thinning out. Halina looked at her watch. 'This conversation is getting way too serious, and I need some air.'

'Shall we drive to The Peak?' His voice, low and tender, made even simple words sound seductive.

As the road wound towards the summit, they left the glass towers and cement office blocks behind. It was quiet and a light breeze cooled the air. Hong Kong's dramatic harbour was spread out beneath them.

But Rhys wasn't looking at the view. 'I love the way the tip of your nose moves when you talk. May I kiss it?'

Halina burst out laughing. This was original. But instead of the light peck she had expected, he placed his mouth over her nose, enclosing it in a hot sensual kiss that she found disturbing. Deep inside she felt the fluttering of a moth's wings in a room long unopened. She pulled away and her voice was cold. 'I think you've made a false assumption.'

His mouth was still smiling but there was a sardonic look in his eyes. 'I assumed you'd let me kiss your nose and you did. So what's the problem?'

The blood rushed to her face. The evening had been a disaster. First she had made a fool of herself by spilling a drink over him and vomiting, and now he was mocking her. A taxi pulled up nearby and, without saying a word, she got in, slammed the door and looked straight ahead as it drove away. Thank God she was flying home the following day and would never have to see the arrogant bastard again.

Several months later, when Hong Kong had become a distant memory, the phone rang.

'I'm back in the Sydney office,' the deep rich voice was saying. 'I would very much like to see you. Will you have dinner with me?'

She was shaking her head but she heard herself saying yes.

'He's nine years younger than me, and he's married,' she had blurted out to Claire over breakfast a few weeks later. 'He and his wife have drifted apart and lead separate lives. When the boys are old enough he's going to leave.'

'Oh, please!' Her friend's voice was heavy with sarcasm. 'Aren't they all! Wake up, Halina, he's a cliché-ridden scumbag.'

'You're being unfair. People can't help falling out of love.'

'But they can help falling out of commitment,' Claire said tartly. 'Anyway, you're wasting your time. Men never leave their wives. Never. Write that on a big piece of paper and paste it above the toilet, because the other woman always has a shit life. Christ, you don't need to settle for this. You have everything.'

'That's right,' Halina nodded. 'I do have everything. A man I'm crazy about who appreciates me and doesn't interfere with my work. I don't need to get married.'

Eight years had passed since then and she still felt the same way. She re-read the article in the *National Observer* about the beach rescue. Thank God no one would recognise her from that photograph. Picking up the clothes Rhys's impatient hands had torn off her and flung onto the floor during their lovemaking that afternoon, she smiled. More sensual and responsive now than she had been in her twenties, Halina had never expected to feel such rapture at this stage of her life. Claire was right in some respects: Rhys was selfish and unreliable. He was also inaccessible much of the time, but this was a small price to pay. She had the best of all worlds: independence, rewarding work, and an exciting lover. She felt like the princess in the fairytale, finally awakened after sleeping for a hundred years.

Five

As soon as shafts of morning sunlight slanted through the blinds, Halina jumped out of bed, pulled on her shorts and jogging shoes and ran to the park. Heavy rain during the night had washed the grime from the streets and light poured from the sky with startling clarity. Dew still glistened on the blades of grass as she ran around the perimeter, pacing herself to maintain an easy stride. Something fell out of a pine tree and struck her head. She looked up and laughed. High in the branches, a flock of black yellow-tailed parrots were chomping on the pine cones, their curved ivory beaks tearing into the fruit and spitting out the woody outer parts.

The sultry sound of a clarinet drew her towards the duck pond. Sitting cross-legged on the grass with his back to her, was her neighbour, Andrew, his long ponytail hanging below a battered pork pie hat. She recognised the Gershwin melody he was playing, and hummed it as she jogged past.

Running in Centennial Park in the mornings usually cleared her mind but this time she couldn't switch off. She ran through the evidence she would soon give in court. There was no doubt in her mind that Kevin Donnelly, the man charged with the murder of little Tiffany Carson, was guilty, but the only conclusive proof was the bite-mark evidence she had collated. Unfortunately there was always a possibility that his defence lawyer might produce someone to disprove or shake the jury's confidence in her testimony. It enraged her that lawyers so often used their skills to ensure the acquittal of people like this, who were released and continued preying on defenceless children. *We don't need more clever people. We need more good people.* Halina stopped running. Her mother used to say that. It was astonishing how often she heard her mother's words in her head these days. The woman who had been such an indistinct figure during her lifetime had become more sharply defined since her death.

Half an hour later, Halina was running towards her car, ignition key in hand, when she saw that someone had double-parked, blocking her exit. That was the trouble with inner-city living. No garages, too many cars, and morons with driving licences. She honked the horn several times, and was thinking of calling the police, when she saw her neighbour hurrying towards her, his clarinet in one hand and keys jingling in the other.

'I'm going,' Andrew grinned. 'Don't bother writing me another letter.'

He had the eager expression of people who are constantly excited by life, and his feet in their worn-down sneakers seemed to skip along the pavement. His relentless cheerfulness irritated her.

'You'll have to come to one of my gigs so you can see that all my practising has paid off,' he said.

'I'm busy that night,' she retorted.

'And the night after that?'

Her foot was already on the accelerator. 'I'll have to check my diary,' she called out.

The sound of his laughter followed her across Sydney as she sped along the western highway leading towards the dental hospital. She entered the main building, a dispiriting box-like structure that had not blown out the public works budget but had won no accolades for the architect either, and quickened her step along the corridor that led to her office. As she passed Clive Bussell's half-open door, she caught a whiff of the pipe tobacco that clung to the tweed jacket with the scuffed leather patches on the elbows, a style he must have adopted in Oxford back in the 1960s. Inclining his large head in a stiff motion without smiling, he looked away. Of all the negative emotions, envy was the hardest to conceal. He had hardly spoken to her since she had been appointed president, and now that she had been granted a part-time assistant, he had lodged a complaint. His lectures had been cut through lack of funds and he demanded to know how the board had found money to pay Luong's salary.

Luong was already in the office, going through a pile of journals searching for references on bite-mark evidence. She read with her chin resting on her chest, her face so close to the print that Halina could only see the hair that stood up on top of her head like a hedgehog. The neon tube flickered as it cast its harsh light over the books and magazines that were stacked on the floor because the shelves were overflowing. She had wondered how her new assistant would fit into an office hardly bigger than a broom closet, but Luong was so tiny and unassuming that she didn't seem to take up any space at all.

As soon as Halina came into the office, Luong closed the journal she had been reading, placed it carefully on top of those on the floor so that the edges corresponded and handed her the relevant articles she had found.

'What time did you get here?' Halina asked.

'I think maybe eight o'clock,' her assistant said. Her voice was like a wisp of chiffon brushing against a bare arm.

Halina flung her bag down. 'Luong, it's wonderful that you're so keen but you know I can only pay you for four hours.'

Luong shook her head. 'I do not ask more money,' she said.

For the next few hours, Halina read through the articles Luong had marked for her attention, poring over the incidence of hypocalcination, and calculating the statistical probabilities to support her testimony.

She finished reading and looked at her watch. If she hurried, she'd have time to detour to Darling Harbour before heading home. The migration exhibition that Toula had mentioned had stirred her curiosity about the past. Even if she didn't know the name of their ship, it would be interesting to see other ships and their passengers from that era.

Rushing past the restaurants, ponds and museums that now filled what used to be a run-down industrial part of the harbour, Halina came to the restored sailing ships in front of the Maritime Museum. The exhibition consisted of photographs of post-war migrant ships and a database for accessing the passengers' names. Halina walked slowly past photographs of shabbily dressed Europeans hanging over the rails, sizzling with impatience to see their new land. We must have felt like that, she thought as she looked at the boat people of 1948. A group of migrants pressed against the rails of the SS *Artemis* made her stop. She was looking at a little girl with an eager face, crooked front teeth and a big bow in her unruly hair. Halina caught her breath as she recognised herself.

Her eyes lingered over their names on the computer screen: Zofia and Halina Szczecińska. Sponsored by Jack and Bella Enfield, Carlton, Melbourne.

Who were these people and why had they sponsored them? Of their brief stay in Melbourne she had only a faint recollection. A small cottage with an outdoor toilet where she was terrified to sit on the seat in case of poisonous spiders; a classroom where she couldn't understand what anyone was saying; an elderly teacher with hair like cotton wool balls stuck on a bright pink scalp, who sat with her at playtime and taught her to speak English.

Halina felt a sudden urge to find out more about the past. If only she had tried harder to pierce her mother's intransigence. Perhaps the Enfields were still listed in the telephone directory.

The fourth number she tried belonged to a man with a tired voice and the wary manner of someone on the run from the taxation department.

'Who are you?' he demanded. 'Who gave you this number?'

It took a long time to allay his suspicions.

'Jack and Bella were my parents,' he said, 'but they're both dead now, so I can't help you.' She sensed that the receiver was on its way down.

'Can you just tell me whether they ever mentioned a woman and a little girl they sponsored from Poland in 1948?'

There was a pause. To encourage him she added, 'That was my mother and me.'

'You stayed with us for a few weeks,' he said at last. 'You wore a ridiculous bow that flopped over your forehead like rabbit's ears. You were younger than me and couldn't speak English, but you ran faster than I did.'

'I don't suppose you liked that,' she chuckled.

'No. I told you never to sit on the toilet seat or the spiders would bite your bum and kill you!' He was laughing now.

'Do you know why your parents sponsored us?'

'They never discussed things like that with me. All I know is that our mothers had a big fight.'

As soon as he said it, it came back to her. She had been sitting at the kitchen table, colouring in with her treasured Staedtler pencils, when she heard shouting in the next room. A door slammed. She sat very still, too worried to move. Some time later, her mother emerged from their room. She was wearing her thick grey coat with the large lapels, the brown felt hat jammed on her head, and she was dragging their suitcase which was fastened with rope.

'Get your doll, Halina, we're going,' was all she said.

In her haste, she had left her coloured pencils behind, and cried most of the way to Sydney.

'Enfield isn't a Polish name. I suppose, like us, your parents changed their name when they got here,' she said.

'By the time my father met my mother in Melbourne, he'd already changed his name. I never knew what his real name was,' Richard Enfield said. 'I think the argument was about a letter,' he continued. 'For some reason your mother flounced out and I don't think she ever contacted my parents again. They didn't even know where she went.'

That figured. Zosia was slow to anger and slow to forgive. 'I don't believe in second chances,' she used to tell Halina. 'If someone lets you down once, they'll do it again.'

Now that he had relaxed, Richard became quite garrulous. 'My mother was a hoarder. She couldn't bear to throw anything away. After she died, I found her drawers stuffed with bits of string, used wine corks and stubs of old candles. And her cupboard was stacked from floor to ceiling with tins of salmon, sardines, packets of Continental chicken noodle soup, and rice. You'd think she was preparing for the siege of Leningrad. It's probably because they were so poor in their Polish *shtetl*. She was always scared there wouldn't be enough. When she was a little girl she had to stay in bed in winter under layers of newspaper to keep warm because they couldn't afford fuel. She couldn't go outside because she didn't have shoes.'

'*Shtetl*.' Halina repeated. 'What's that?'

'Oh, sorry,' he said. 'It's Yiddish for a small village.'

It hadn't occurred to her that the Enfields were Jewish. But knowing how little religion had mattered to Zosia, it didn't surprise Halina that she had Jewish friends.

'Mother kept every letter she ever received,' Richard was saying. 'She kept all the birthday cards too, tied in bundles with string. You can't imagine how much stuff she left. Too much. I've been putting off going through her things until I get over my operation.'

Halina's question, asked from politeness rather than concern, elicited an avalanche of aches, pains, operations, complications and complaints about medical ignorance and negligence going back over the past thirty years. His entire life was punctuated with a succession of doctors who had misdiagnosed his illnesses, prescribed medication that produced worse symptoms, operated on him for the wrong reasons, and had enriched themselves, their colleagues and the pharmaceutical industry at his expense.

Desperate to find some way of cutting through the complaints, she said, 'What about your father?'

There was a brief silence. 'I never got to know him. He never talked about his life.'

She recalled the brooding face in the photograph.

'When I was small he terrified me. He often screamed at night and woke me up. Mother would bring a cup of hot milk to calm me down. But no one ever alluded to it in the morning. It was like a guilty secret that we all knew but pretended it didn't exist.'

Richard let out a long sigh. 'I'm exhausted, I have to go and rest now. But if I ever come across that letter, I'll get in touch.'

Six

Turning off Parramatta Road, away from the streaming traffic, Halina swung into a quiet suburban side street and parked outside the liver-coloured building that housed the Department of Forensic Medicine. As she pushed open the door, she wondered whether passers-by realised that this was the city morgue. She flashed her ID at the clerk sitting at his computer behind the glass window, glanced at the clock and sat down to wait for June Blake, who could be the mother of the young woman whose remains had been found in the Blue Mountains.

On the white-painted brick wall facing her hung a print of a country girl with pink cheeks running through a field of scarlet poppies, the ribbons of her bonnet trailing behind her. No doubt the decorator had intended to create the impression of an ordinary waiting room, but neither the dead who were brought here nor the living who came to identify them had eyes for pretty pictures. This was hell's vestibule and offered little solace for the living, whether they recognised the face under the plastic cover or not. Halina had seen it so often: in the paralysing second before the attendant slid the gurney out of its cold tomb, the visitors clenched their fists and held their breath. Some even closed their eyes, not wanting to have their worst fears confirmed. At this moment, even the staunchest atheists weakened as they prayed that the corpse beneath the sheets would not be their loved one. But even if their prayers were answered, and they sank gratefully against the wall, their relief was soon replaced by the dread of knowing that they would have to continue living suspended between hope and despair until the next corpse was dug out of its shallow grave.

Halina looked up when the door swung open. Although they had only spoken over the phone, she knew at first glance that the woman in the violet pantsuit was June Blake. All the juices in this woman had dried up, leaving a brittle shell.

'It's five years and three months since Cathy went missing,' she said. As she took the photograph out of her handbag, her eyes lingered on it before she handed it to Halina.

'Don't worry, we'll take good care of it and let you have it back,' Halina said.

The girl had bleached locks and wore a strapless candy-floss pink dress that seemed about to slide off her full breasts. She took a closer look at the teeth. Part of her left central incisor was missing. Thank God she had smiled at the photographer.

'Cathy was that happy to be her sister's bridesmaid. And to think that only a few weeks later ...' Mrs Blake's bony shoulders slumped and she dabbed her eyes with a crumpled tissue. 'You know, love, it probably sounds weird to you, but after all this time I never go past the bank where she used to work without looking inside and holding me breath, just in case she's still in there. And Bill's a total write-off. He just sits and stares into space of a night. He doesn't talk, but I can tell what's going on in his head. Wouldn't he like to get his hands on that police sergeant. We kept telling him she wouldn't just stay out without letting us know. She wasn't like that. If only they'd started looking for her the day we reported her missing, they might of found her.'

Halina nodded. That was the sad fate of so many families of the disappeared: no peace or finality, only endless rage, recriminations and regrets. Swamped with thousands of reports of missing teenagers every year, the police took the cynical view that they'd probably got drunk or stoned and spent the night with their mates, or else they'd run away and didn't want to be found. By the time they started investigating, several days had passed and by then, if they'd been abducted, it was usually too late. A national database of missing persons would at least make it easier to trace those who had moved or been taken interstate, but in spite of Halina's efforts, each state persisted in regarding itself as a mini-nation instead of pooling information.

In the hope of concealing their victims' identity, killers sometimes cut off fingertips, dissolved their flesh in acid or set them on fire, but they couldn't destroy their teeth or dental records. They dumped the body in remote bushland, hoping it would never be found, but sooner or later an inquisitive dog or an adventurous hiker came across the remains. By then there was usually no face left, especially if the body had been left on its stomach.

Judging by the pelvic bones found in the Blue Mountains, the forensic anthropologist had assessed that the corpse belonged to a woman aged between eighteen and twenty-five, who had never borne children. From the condition of the body and the surrounding soil, it appeared that she had been lying in the shallow grave for five or six years. Only the teeth remained intact. Halina had noticed that the third molar roots hadn't completely formed, which meant that the dead woman was around twenty. The police register showed that nine women in that age group had been reported missing in Sydney during that period. Only dental records would prove her identity.

June Blake was watching her with the supplicating expression of a job applicant too timid to ask whether the interview had been successful.

'We're not sure yet whether it is Cathy,' Halina said as gently as she could. 'The photograph will be a great help.' June Blake's eyes welled with a hundred questions that she was unable to articulate.

'I'll get in touch as soon as we know anything,' Halina said as she accompanied her to the door. She watched the woman walk slowly away with her head bowed. Two images came into Halina's mind: the happy girl in the pink dress, and the faceless skull with its empty eye sockets. There couldn't be a pain as agonising as not knowing whether your child was dead or alive. Murderers didn't just kill their victims; they killed entire families. She couldn't bring Cathy Blake back, but by identifying her she could set her parents free to grieve, to say a final goodbye and get on with what was left of their lives.

The sound of young voices made her look up. Her students had arrived for their first visit to the morgue.

Halina ushered them into the lift and pressed the button for the lower ground floor. 'Grab a pair of rubber boots,' she said as they crowded into a narrow anteroom lined with wellingtons. In the change rooms, the students picked through piles of faded blue cotton gowns and trousers and tied them clumsily with the long tape.

'Make sure you step right into the trough,' Halina said as they pushed open the plastic doors that led to the dissection room and sloshed through the disinfectant bath. She sensed rather than heard their intake of breath as they attempted to correlate this sterile place with their preconceptions of it.

'I find the mortuary strangely peaceful,' Halina told them. 'I don't feel that souls are being disturbed here.' They looked at her with expressions ranging from doubt to disbelief. She didn't expect them to understand.

'This is where fiction and reality collide. It's probably not what you expected,' she warned.

A stout man with a big belly and a cap stuck on top of his large head like a flag on a mountain peak looked up from the stainless steel slab and grinned. 'Ah, new recruits!' he exclaimed in a booming voice that bounced off the metal surfaces.

The pathologist was standing over the naked body of an elderly woman, studying her through large plastic goggles. Her skin resembled candle wax and her head was thrown backwards, the long stringy grey hair almost touching the floor. She had been slit open from the thorax to the abdomen. Plunging his gloved hands through a thick layer of fat, the pathologist removed the burgundy liver and slapped it onto the dissecting table, much as a butcher throws a lump of meat onto the scales. He proceeded to slice thin sections to make slides for histology examination. A visceral smell of human flesh and organs permeated the dissection room, the dark odour of something that had never been open to the air before.

The pathologist stopped slicing and gave the group a long stare. 'What we do here is perform surgery on dead bodies, but if anyone feels they're going to pass out, step back,' he said. 'I don't want anyone falling on top of the corpse. She's already feeling pretty cut up about things.'

A female student giggled nervously, but the males, as usual, appeared defiantly unmoved. Admitting that they were sickened by what they had seen seemed a sign of weakness. 'It doesn't look like a real person,' one of them shrugged. 'More like a figure from Madame Tussaud's.'

A young lab assistant poked her head around the door. 'You coming to the Christmas dinner, Dr Gould?' she asked.

'Christmas? That's two months away!' he protested. 'All right, I'll come as long as you promise there's no kidneys or liver on the menu!'

Halina turned to her group. 'I warned you about the black humour in this place. It's a way of coping with the gruesome reality.'

On her first visit, she had been appalled by the flippancy of the pathologists and their technical assistants who told bawdy jokes and made callous remarks while they sawed through bones and craniums with no more emotion than if they were slicing oranges. Later, she had been even more shocked by the speed with which she herself had become accustomed to seeing the mutilated bodies lying on the tables. She had learnt to excise the mandible and peel back the soft tissue up to the base of the eyes like a glove, to enable her to examine the top jaw. It wasn't pleasant but she did it without becoming emotionally involved. It was surprising how fast she had erected a barrier between herself and these empty shells which no longer bore any resemblance to the living. They were cocoons, abandoned after the butterfly had flown.

One by one the students stepped into a small circular recess. The door slid shut behind them and they stood uneasily in total darkness until the door on the other side opened, leading into another part of the mortuary. A moment later, a man wheeled in a trolley covered with a beige plastic bag. 'It took me a while to find the right serial number, but this is the one we want.' He stopped and looked around. 'I see we have an audience today. All hope abandon ye who enter here!'

Halina turned to her students. 'Meet my poetic buddy, André Legrand.'

André unzipped the body bag and removed several brown paper bags labelled 'field item' while Halina took out a skull with the cranium sliced off.

'The pathologists saw open the top of the skull and remove the brain,' she explained. 'It's too mushy to slice when it's fresh and needs to be kept in formalin for a time. After we've taken X-rays, they pop the top of the skull back, pull the tissue down, stitch up the incisions and you can hardly tell it's been opened up. If the brain has to be kept for examination, the relatives come and collect it later.'

While this was sinking in, André whipped out his Polaroid to take close-up shots of a tooth that had been filled. Halina held up an X-ray against André's magnified shot of the mandible and told the students to come closer.

'See how the root of that tooth fits perfectly? Every root is different, they have lumps and bumps that are peculiar to each individual. Only the right one will fit flush into the socket.'

'The tooth, the whole tooth and nothing but the tooth,' a student quipped to the girl beside him.

'So does that mean you've identified the body?' asked a guy with a red beard.

'Not yet,' Halina said. 'But it's a start. Ideally we need thirty points of concordance to make a positive identification. There are still some discrepancies.' They craned forward to see where she was pointing. 'Her dentist recorded filling one surface of the lower left first molar, but I can see signs of two separate restorations here.' She turned to André. 'You know what probably happened? He probably patched a pre-existing filling without noting it down, but we can't assume that. We'll have to check it out.'

An overpowering smell, sweetish and foetid, made the group sniff, wrinkle their noses and look around. 'Stinks like a fox that's been dead for a month,' one of the students said.

'That's a pretty good description,' Halina said, pointing to what resembled a clothes dryer. 'That's a Ward's boiler, where we boil up badly decomposed bodies to dissolve all the flesh.'

'That's what Shakespeare must have had in mind when he wrote "Oh that this too solid flesh would melt".' The wit looked pleased with himself while the others groaned and rolled their eyes.

'If we scraped the flesh away, we could damage the bone,' Halina continued. 'So we boil it slowly over a long period to remove all the soft tissue and get to the skeletal remains. You can't see the injuries caused by knife wounds until the bone is clearly exposed and you can check for stab marks. It takes a day or two. Defleshing isn't pleasant but it can tell us how someone died.'

'It sounds like something out of a Hannibal Lecter movie,' one of the female students said, her eyes bright with excitement.

In the change room, to lighten the atmosphere, Halina told them about the first known case where odontology identified a corpse. 'Emperor Tiberius's wife, Agrippina, took out a contract on his lover, a woman with a black incisor, so the resident gladiator, who doubled as a hitman, lopped off the woman's head and brought it to the Empress on a platter. When she saw it, she told him he'd killed the wrong woman, but in reply the gladiator raised the top lip. The blackened incisor proved who she was.'

This story never failed to amuse students with its *Pulp Fiction* scenario of Roman hitmen, extramarital affairs, revenge and macabre murder. Halina wondered whether Rhys's wife would consider taking out a contract on her if she ever found out about their affair. One could never tell what passions simmered behind those controlled North Shore voices and bobbed blonde hair.

Seven

Speeding along the M5 in her yellow BMW, Halina hummed 'One Fine Day' along with Maria Callas as she overtook furniture trucks, landscape gardeners' vans and grey-haired women gripping their steering wheels. The convertible was an extravagance she had never regretted, especially at the end of a long summer's day when the sky was still blue and a breeze ruffled her hair. Driving was a meditation that usually blotted out troubling thoughts but this time they continued to intrude. The trial of Tiffany Carson's killer was about to begin and it looked as though only her evidence would be strong enough to convict Kevin Donnelly.

She turned the volume up on the CD player just as the aria was finishing, and wondered whether Maria Callas had been thinking of her own tragic love story as she sang those heart-wrenching notes. The tenors always sang stirring songs about revenge and war, while the sopranos lamented over unrequited love. She was running through her favourite arias to check this theory when she saw a police officer in the middle of the road, diverting traffic.

An Ampol tanker had overturned, spilling petrol across the road in an iridescent pool. As Halina drove closer to the spill, the thick fumes made her gag and her stomach heaved, pumping a sour liquid into her mouth. She'd never reacted like this to the smell of petrol before. Her hands slid on the steering wheel as she broke into a cold sweat, and the more she tried to breathe deeply, the faster her heart raced. She felt an overpowering urge to get out of the car but she was in a long line of traffic creeping bumper to bumper. The panic threatened to overwhelm her and she struggled with the compulsion to jump out. Surely it would be better to hold up the traffic than collapse or cause an accident.

Deathly white and beaded with perspiration, she leant out of the car, propping her head with her clammy hand, and spoke to the young policeman diverting the traffic. 'Officer, I just have to get out of here,' she began.

He bent down, one hand on his hip. As his eyes roamed over the car, taking in the leather seats and GPS display, he smirked. 'You and me and everyone else, lady,' he said, and with an impatient gesture motioned her to move on.

Unable to hold it in any longer, Halina leant out of the window and vomited over his shiny black shoes.

Her head was splitting by the time she swung into her street. As usual there was nowhere to park and she drove around the block several times cursing her decision to move to Paddington. A crazy voice in her head was saying: *If I don't find a spot soon I'm going to leave this fucking car in the middle of the road!*

Puccini was already rubbing against her legs and miaowing as soon as she slammed the front door behind her, but she rushed past him, kicking off her shoes and unbuttoning the silk shirt that clung and stank of sweat.

She stood motionless under the shower with eyes closed, letting the water stream over her body for a long time, but even after she had splashed herself with cologne, the petrol smell persisted. She could even taste it.

Wrapping the lotus-patterned silk kimono she'd bought in Kyoto around her, she went downstairs and shuffled through her letters. Tucked between the bills, the self-congratulatory notices from real estate agents, invitations to subscribe to cable television and offers of lifelong prizes from Reader's Digest, she noticed a slim handwritten envelope. She tore it open.

After our conversation I finally got around to going through Mother's things and came across this letter. Maybe that's what caused the argument, Richard Enfield wrote.

Ignoring Puccini's frantic efforts to attract her attention, Halina sank into her wicker-backed armchair and examined the pale blue aerogramme postmarked New York and embossed with the head of George Washington.

The writer was Polish, and obviously not used to typing, judging by the uneven letters and all the o's filled in. *I'm writing to you in the hope that you can help me,* Halina read slowly, translating one word at a time. *For the past four years I have been searching for my niece Mireleh Lieberman through the Red Cross, and someone mentioned your name to me. If you have any information about her, I would be very grateful if you could contact me.* The date was March 1949. It was signed Esther Kennedy (née Kleinman).

Halina read the letter several times with a growing sense of disappointment. Whoever Esther Kennedy and her strangely named niece were, this letter couldn't possibly have any connection with her mother or the dispute that had severed the friendship between the two families.

Puccini's calculating eyes followed every movement as she took a can of cat food from the cupboard and opened it. While he crouched in front of his bowl, cocked his striped head to one side and took dainty bites, she poured herself a Metaxa to settle her stomach and wondered whether Esther Kennedy had ever found her niece.

The phone shrilled and she jumped up. It won't be Rhys, she warned herself. It was Richard Enfield, but this time his dry, thin voice sounded more animated than before.

'Did you get my letter?' he asked, but didn't wait for her reply. 'I was looking through my mother's books this afternoon. She must have been reading *Crime and Punishment* when she died because she left a bookmark on page 358. Mother was a voracious reader. If she liked a book, she nagged me until I read it too.'

He tailed off and Halina sensed the void left in his life by the woman who had hoarded bits of string, stockpiled food and discussed books with him. She wondered what it would have been like to have a mother with a taste for literature.

'And you know what the bookmark was?' he was saying. 'Another letter from that woman in New York!' Undeterred by Halina's lack of interest, he continued, 'This one is much more recent. She wrote it only ten years ago. Listen to this.'

She heard paper rustling. As he read the letter, it was clear that the intervening years had not been kind to Mrs Kennedy whose agitation leapt from every sentence. A dead son, a paralysed husband and a thousand disappointed hopes had refuelled her desperation to find her niece.

'She must have moved,' Richard was saying. 'The forwarding address is Walnut Lodge in the Catskills.'

Halina chuckled. 'That sounds like a hospice for sick cats!'

He wasn't amused. 'It was a popular mountain resort for New Yorkers of a certain age and background,' he explained. She had to thank him several times for getting in touch before he understood that the conversation was over.

She curled up on the settee with her notes on bite-mark evidence but felt too agitated to concentrate. Her thoughts wandered back to the disturbing episode in the car. The smell of petrol had always nauseated her, but she had never reacted in such an irrational way before. She had been on the point of jumping out of the car and abandoning it on the highway. Get a grip, she told herself. You're losing it.

Her hand hovered above the Marlboro Lights, contemplating the illusion of nicotine-induced relaxation, but the thought of inhaling smoke evoked another wave of nausea. She tossed the packet into the rubbish bin, slammed the drawer shut and went out onto the wrought-iron balcony for some air. Across the road, a row of modern townhouses had sprung up, like boxes glued together, lacking the charm of the secretive old terraces shaded by jacarandas, frangipanis and golden robinias.

Voices floated up from the street. High heels clicked on the pavement and a woman laughed raucously at something her companion said. Under the lamplight, a couple embraced, devouring each other's lips. Three men with shaven heads and tight leather trousers walked towards the pub as they argued about a film. 'I've never seen such crap,' one of them was insisting. 'A successful woman obsessed with a no-hoper like a lovesick schoolgirl. Give me a break!'

Halina wanted to tell someone about the episode in the car, but Toula would have just got home exhausted after making dinner for her mother and Claire was in Melbourne at a seminar on child trafficking. And Rhys? He could be in Indonesia interviewing the foreign minister, in a Chechyan mountain hideout interviewing a rebel leader, or in Sydney having dinner with his wife. She never knew where he was or when she would hear from him, but unpredictability added to the excitement of their relationship. Nothing equalled the elation she felt on hearing his voice after a long absence.

It would have been comforting to have someone there to talk over her strange reaction to the petrol spill, but if she had wanted a predictable life of suburban routine she would have stayed married to her first husband, she thought as she sank into her leather armchair. As she had discovered much earlier in life, living with someone was no guarantee of closeness or sexual intimacy. Couples could spend all day every day together without understanding each other's needs or dreams. 'I don't need a man to make my life complete,' she told Puccini as she switched on the radio to fill the empty spaces in her home.

Eight

In the computer room, Halina studied the screen as the special-effects generator superimposed the photograph of the missing girl over that of the skull found in the shallow grave and the two images coalesced into one. As the images faded in and out, Cathy Blake's happy smile was peeled away layer by layer until it became indistinguishable from the gaping mouth of the skull.

'Look!' She turned to Luong, unable to keep the excitement out of her voice. 'See how the surfaces and roots of every tooth match perfectly?'

The flesh had melted away and the vibrant young woman had become her own skeleton. Halina always found this transposition eerie, a grim sleight of hand that death performed on life. She shivered, as though a tomb had suddenly been opened and cold air had chilled her lungs.

Luong was staring at the image, mesmerised. 'Is same girl?'

Halina nodded and closed her eyes to conceal the unseemly triumph that she always felt whenever hypothesis and fact merged like this. Now that she was able to positively identify Cathy Blake, the anguish her parents suffered would be exchanged for a different kind of pain.

Many years before, when Halina was still in high school, their diabetic neighbour had developed gangrene in his toes. His face became rigid with pain and sometimes she heard him scream and beg for an axe to chop off his feet. After the amputation, he sat in a wheelchair and often groaned with the pain he felt in his phantom toes. It seemed to Halina that he had simply exchanged one kind of agony for another, but her mother disagreed. 'Before, pain tore his flesh like pincers, but this pain he can live with.'

She could still see Zosia as she looked that day, pushing back the strands of hair that escaped from the knot that she twisted hastily at the base of her neck, wiping her large hands on the big apron tied around her thick waist. Her mother had sounded irritable, but now Halina wondered whether perhaps she'd mistaken anger for sadness. Zosia's feelings had always been inaccessible to her.

Luong's eyes, like shiny black almonds, were still fixed on the screen, her legs in their fishnet stockings and laced-up boots with platform heels tucked under the chair. Halina supposed she was making some kind of fashion statement. Perhaps Luong was rebelling against the traditional Vietnamese style of dress, but her delicate features and dainty figure would have been better suited to long smooth hair cascading onto a slinky white tunic.

'I wish we had this technology in Cambodia after Pol Pot,' Luong said softly.

Halina swivelled her chair around in surprise. So Luong wasn't Vietnamese.

'What do you mean?' she asked.

'When I was nine, the Khmer Rouge killed my parents.'

Luong rarely spoke about that time. Every day she made a conscious effort not to think about the events she now described to Halina. She was seven when her childhood ended. That was the day when she and her entire family were forced out of their home in Phnom Penh by soldiers armed with guns. They became part of a river of bewildered people being pushed out of the city, carrying children, sick parents and their belongings, which grew heavier hour by hour. They walked for days until they reached a primitive camp that was their new home. The world became a cruel, harsh place where sadistic guards had the power of life and death over them all. People fell ill and died, but no one cared. There was no medicine and hardly any rice.

The hunger cramps made her curl up into a little ball on the hard ground and sob every night, dreaming of a full bowl of hot rice. Old people shrank until they resembled dried-up leaves and her little brother changed from a chubby four-year-old to a skeleton with a swollen belly and an old man's head. When he died, her father hardly had the strength to dig the tiny grave.

Halina listened without moving.

'One day soldiers come to camp and say, "Teachers, come with us to next village, no teachers there for children,"' Luong continued. 'My parents believe them. They go in truck with soldiers. I never see them again.'

'And you were only nine!' Halina exclaimed. 'The same age I was when I came to Australia. How did you survive?'

'My older brother say we have to run, quick, before Khmer Rouge find us, because we are children of teachers, so they kill us too.' She looked down at her small hands, remembering the terrifying nights spent in dark bamboo forests, listening to its sounds and dangerous silences that made her clutch her brother's hand and tremble. Her voice was almost inaudible. 'Sometimes we so hungry, we eat insects and leaves.'

Halina shook her head. She had worked with this woman for six months without having any idea of what she had gone through.

'When it safe to come back to Phnom Penh, our uncle find us. He only one left in my family. Same for other people,' she said softly. 'The Khmer Rouge kill one third of the population.'

'But weren't the Khmer Rouge Cambodian too?' Halina was ashamed of her ignorance about an event that had been so extensively reported.

Luong nodded. 'Yes, they Cambodian like us. But they torture and kill because Pol Pot tell them educated people bad. They even kill people with glasses. They think when people read too much, they make trouble.'

This mindless communal violence shocked Halina. Every day she dealt with dead bodies, but they were killed by psychopaths and criminals for some personal motive, either greed, jealousy or malice. It was impossible to comprehend that guards, some of them only teenagers, had savagely murdered over a million of their own people. Even in the case of the ethnic cleansing in Kosovo, the violence in Bosnia and the genocide in Rwanda, there was a long history of tribal hatred that erupted after simmering for decades. But as far as she knew, Cambodia had not been divided into rival ethnic or religious groups. The Khmer Rouge had tortured and butchered their own people simply because their leader had ordered them to do it.

'Before they get guns, they same as other people,' Luong said. 'And now they ordinary people again. They live in Cambodia today, no problem.'

Halina recalled reading about an amnesty granted to the Khmer Rouge by Hun Sen, and the pressure exerted by the United Nations to charge them with war crimes. 'It's outrageous that they're allowed to live in comfort instead of having to answer for what they did. Doesn't that make you angry?'

Luong looked thoughtful. 'Life in Cambodia quiet now. If soldiers are charged, maybe they make more trouble. I want justice but my country needs peace more.'

Halina wondered whether peace was possible without justice but the quiet dignity of Luong's words left nothing more to be said.

She had almost forgotten why they were discussing the Khmer Rouge. 'What did you mean about technology?' she asked.

'There is place outside Phnom Penh called Choeung Ek. Sometimes called Killing Fields. Many bodies there in mass graves. There is memorial with nine hundred skulls they find in graves. But we do not know who they are, so relatives cannot burn incense and pray for souls. Maybe my parents killed there too. We don't have DNA technology to help us find family, and now it too late.'

Halina nodded. As Dieter Neumann had predicted in Hong Kong eight years before, mtDNA, which was passed down from mothers to their children, was increasingly being used to identify bodies where a living relative on the female side could be found. Luong may have been able to identify her mother through her mtDNA which could be extracted from teeth long after death. That was how the remains of Tsar Nicholas had been identified after he had been killed in 1917 and his skull smashed to pieces. As for the Tsarina Alexandra, she had been identified when a sample of mtDNA taken from her descendant, the Duke of Edinburgh, was found to match hers.

But Luong would never know whether her parents had been killed at Cheoung Ek.

Back at her desk, Halina picked up a letter with a Polish postmark, addressed to *Szanowna Pani Doktor Halina Shore*: Honoured Madam Doctor. Empires, tsardoms, communes and republics had come and gone, but the Poles had not abandoned their old-world custom of attaching every possible title and degree to the surname. Probably a notice about yet another conference. Halina placed it in her in-tray, unopened. She would look at it later. Before attending any more conferences, she needed some time off. When Rhys had mentioned going to New Zealand at the end of the year to write a series of articles about the political and economic situation of the country he facetiously referred to as Australia's other offshore state, she had suggested joining him and combining research with a driving holiday.

Claire had been sceptical. 'He's never taken you on a holiday so don't get your hopes up,' she said.

Staring out of her office window, Halina mulled over Claire's words and sighed. She needed this to happen, needed it with an intensity that surprised her. Like a schoolgirl fantasising about a longed-for tryst, she visualised them sipping sauvignon blanc in front of a log fire in some secluded cabin, sleeping in each other's arms all night and waking together in the morning. But she knew that the trip meant more to her than the yearning to share a passionate holiday. It had become an indication of Rhys's commitment, a measure of his depth of feeling for her, a validation of their relationship.

Uncomfortable with that line of thought, she checked her watch and sprang up. It was time to go to court. As she hurried along the corridor, she almost collided with Clive Bussell, who lifted his hand in a half-hearted gesture. He slid his lashless red-rimmed eyes over her. 'Elegant in black as usual, Halina!'

Clive had a way of catching her off-balance, making flattering comments in a mocking tone and loading simple statements with sinister subtexts, as though in possession of some secretly damning information.

'Must run,' he said. 'Some of us don't have the luxury of assistants.' Before he had time to throw another barb, she walked on.

Halina was reading through her notes outside the courtroom when the court officer, a stout woman in lace-up shoes, called her name and ushered her inside. As the opaque glass door swung open, twenty-four curious eyes in the jury box turned in her direction, sizing her up. Eight women and four men. Knowing that forensic evidence would form an important part of the case against the accused, had the defence loaded the jury along gender lines, hoping that women would become confused by the testimony and distracted by the obfuscations?

Halina's high heels clicked loudly on the wooden floor as she walked to the witness stand. As she took the Bible in her right hand, the sleeve of her tailored black jacket fell back, showing the cream cuff of her silk shirt.

'Do you swear to tell the truth, the whole truth and nothing but the truth?'

While the court officer administered the oath, the judge stared at her with eyes that had sunk into his pale face like raisins in an undercooked bun. Justice Adrian Woodbridge was a political anachronism who enjoyed the lifestyle of a committed capitalist while spouting socialist ideals. In recent years he had acquired a compassionate image among prisoner support groups, sociologists and left-wing journalists for displaying more sympathy for the perpetrator than the victim, a propensity Halina had discovered several years before when giving evidence at a rape trial.

Spruced up for his day in court, his hair washed and brushed back, a navy wind-cheater over a white shirt and tie that his lawyer had no doubt produced for the occasion, Kevin Donnelly sat in the dock, casting occasional glances at the jury. Although juries tended to return a guilty verdict whenever prosecutors tendered DNA evidence, Halina knew that forensic evidence could also be used to create uncertainty. For every forensic dentist ready to testify that a set of bite marks had been made by a particular individual's teeth, the defence could always find a 'liar for hire' who would cast enough doubt to shake the jury's faith in the evidence presented.

The prisoner's bold stare interrupted Halina's reverie. The jury was also watching him, probably wondering whether an ordinary, inoffensive-looking bloke like Kevin Donnelly, who could have been their next-door neighbour or a mate on the footy team, could possibly have committed the horrible crime he was charged with. Criminals didn't have horns or labels branded on their foreheads, and their ordinariness often created a wave of empathy. But Halina knew more than the jury would ever be told, because past crimes were inadmissible and Kevin's past history would have condemned him in their minds faster than her evidence ever would. As he flashed his barrister a triumphant grin, she caught sight of the teeth whose imprint she had identified on the baby's thighs.

Two-year-old Tiffany Carson had disappeared from her front yard where her mother had left her playing with a doll. An intensive search for the toddler proved fruitless, and the distraught woman appeared on television, pleading for anyone who knew anything to come forward. Halina remembered the tired blue circles under her eyes and the way she tore at her nails, trying to keep back the tears. 'Tiffs wouldn't have wandered away,' she insisted. 'She couldn't even reach the latch on the gate.'

A few days later, an anonymous tip-off led police to a vacant lot behind a mattress factory. They broke the padlock on the cyclone mesh fence and walked towards the large garbage bin in the corner. They unfastened the clamped lid and looked down at the tiny limp body with a gaping wound between her legs, a broken neck and a terrified look in her wide-open eyes.

Halina had been called into the dissection room the following day, and for once the pathologist made no macabre comments as he examined the little body and explained his findings.

'There's something here I want you to see,' he'd said, indicating that she should stand on the other side of the metal slab.

Halina bent down, and nodded. The marks were well-defined. 'Those bite marks could help identify her killer,' she said.

While police were interviewing the single mother and the neighbours, Halina was examining the bite marks.

Eventually the police narrowed the search down to three men who had worked at the Carson home in recent weeks. Two had alibis that checked out, but when they interviewed Kevin Donnelly's flatmate, he recalled that Kevin had come in very late that night, and for once he had put all his clothes in the washing machine before having a beer. He also recalled that his mate had been more animated than usual and said he'd been with his girlfriend. That was the first time the flatmate had heard that Kevin was in a relationship. But when the police asked Kevin about his girlfriend, he said he couldn't name her because she was married.

Halina had urged the detective in charge of the investigation to make an impression of the suspect's teeth as soon as possible, recalling a case where the suspect had his teeth extracted to destroy the evidence. When you bit a person, you left your unique calling card, with all the necessary information just waiting to be decoded.

By then she already knew that Kevin had a history of pathological behaviour that started with torturing animals and progressed to molesting small children in parks. But none of this would emerge in court, to ensure that his past history did not prejudice a fair trial.

'Dr Shore, could you please tell the court which characteristics in the accused's teeth correspond with the bite marks found on Tiffany Carson's body?'

Barbara Lindstrom, the crown prosecutor, looked lined and pale. In all the years they had worked together, Halina had always admired the tenacious nature and sharp mind that had earned her the nickname 'The Terrier', but today there was no sign of that energy. In fact, she sounded weary. For the past few months Halina had heard rumours that Barbara was ill and would soon retire and, looking at her now, she realised that this could be true.

'His teeth have sharp-edged pits like small craters on the tips of the upper and lower right canines,' Halina said. 'The upper pit is larger than the lower and matches exactly the bite marks found on the child.'

Barbara Lindstrom held up a photograph of the bite marks. 'Your Honour,' she addressed the judge, 'I'd like to show this to the jury.'

Adrian Woodbridge nodded.

'Could anyone else's teeth have produced this particular pattern of marks?'

The prosecutor's tone was so flat that Halina wondered whether she would last until the day's proceedings ended. She hoped the jury wouldn't interpret her lack of energy as lack of conviction.

Halina shook her head. 'He has a rare condition called hypocalcination that makes his teeth as unique as fingerprints.'

The defence counsel stood up and from the smug smile on his closely shaved face, she could see that she was going to have trouble. She and Steven Bonelli had crossed swords before, and although she admired his intellect, she sometimes questioned his ethics.

'Dr Shore, you've shared your opinion with us that these teeth are unique. So would you be kind enough to let us know how many teeth you have actually examined?'

Some of the younger women on the jury were sitting forward and Halina sensed their excited solemnity at being part of a court case like those they had hitherto only watched on television or read about in crime novels.

'Do you mean altogether in my twenty-five years' experience as a forensic dentist, or just in connection with this investigation?' she asked.

Bonelli reddened as a titter rippled around the room. Touché, she thought.

'Please spare us the details of your brilliant career, Dr Shore, and just answer the question,' he said crossly, but she had made her point.

'I've examined one thousand canines in connection with this investigation,' she said. 'The teeth of the accused are the only ones that match the bite marks.'

The barrister modulated his voice to a low pitch of incredulity. 'Do you expect us to believe that the accused has the only set of teeth in the world that match these?'

She shook her head. 'Not at all. Just that they're only ones among the suspects in this murder case whose impressions we have taken.'

Bonelli turned towards the jury with a smile that demanded their complicity. 'Would you care to explain what is unique about these characteristics?'

Halina paused and pretended to look in her handbag for a tissue to play for time. What was he driving at?

'Hypocalcination causes pits to form in the teeth,' she said. 'It's not only rare, but it varies with each individual, so even if we were to find others with this disorder, the pits would occur in different teeth and they would vary in shape and number. The teeth of the accused have two pitted canines. Out of the thousand canines that I examined in connection with this case, only two had similar pits as the accused, but even then their teeth had only one pit each, while his had several. Extrapolating from this, even if we could find twenty people in the general population with pitted canines and hypocalcination, they would have a different number of pits. None of them would have left exactly the same mark as these. And I'd be very surprised if any of them were in the vicinity of Tiffany Carson's home on the day she was killed.' The last sentence slipped out before she had time to control her tongue.

Steven Bonelli glared. 'Your reflections on the whereabouts of victims of hypocalcination is outside the scope of this trial. In future, please confine yourself to answering the question.' He turned to the judge. 'Your Honour, I request that the witness's last statement be struck from the record.'

Adrian Woodbridge nodded. 'Sustained.' Turning to the jury, he said, 'You will disregard that statement.'

Bonelli continued to probe and from his questions about hypocalcination and canine defects, Halina could see that he had read extensively on the subject. Glancing at the jury from time to time, she noticed several women yawning. One woman was examining Halina's Hermès scarf, while a rotund gentleman with bloodhound jowls was staring into space with glazed eyes, probably daydreaming about dinner. Halina supposed that their heads must be aching by now from a surfeit of information.

Steven Bonelli thanked her and said he had no more questions. 'I would now like to call the next witness,' he said. The courtroom door opened and Halina stared in dismay. The man being ushered in by the sheriff's officer was Clive Bussell. Of all the forensic dentists in Australia, she wondered why the defence counsel had chosen one of the least competent.

'I would not even assume that these marks were made by human teeth,' Clive said with a complacent smile.

A few moments later he was claiming that even if they were human bite marks, in his experience, pitting did not make them unique. 'Hypocalcination is not so rare,' he said.

Halina gripped the bench with white knuckles as Clive made the most of his fifteen minutes of fame. The jury members were sitting forward, watching him intently. Perhaps it was his tweed jacket with the suede patches and corduroy trousers that gave him an aura of academic credibility as he steadily undermined her evidence, quoting from unsubstantiated research papers written by obscure academics. Kevin Donnelly was sitting forward too, delighted with an expert whose views offered the possibility of acquittal.

In her summing up, the crown prosecutor reiterated the evidence against the accused and summarised all the points of concordance between his unusual tooth defects and the bite marks. 'Even if others could be found with similar defects, which Dr Shore has assured us is most improbable, the owners of those rare defects didn't live in the vicinity of the murdered child's home, didn't return with suspiciously stained clothes from a secret mission that night, and didn't lie about a non-existent relationship.'

As she listened, Halina had a sinking feeling. In the courtroom, style had to match substance and Barbara's delivery lacked flair and passion. Even more worrying was the fact that when two medical experts disagreed on a vital piece of evidence, it was difficult for the jury to decide who was correct. The preponderance of women didn't mean that they would be more likely to believe her. Women often had more confidence in men, especially where technical and scientific matters were concerned.

Finally Steven Bonelli rose to sum up the case for the defence. With a disarming smile, he approached the jury, his energy and confidence in sharp contrast with the prosecutor's weary tone.

'Ladies and gentlemen of the jury, you've heard a great deal of contradictory evidence given by two eminent forensic dentists. They've told us in detail about hypocalcination, pitting, canine defects, video superimpositions and so on. I don't know about you,' he flashed them a confidential smile displaying his capped front teeth — too regular and unnaturally white, Halina noted, 'but I got really confused. It's so difficult for those of us who are not forensic experts to follow these technical arguments. After all, who can decide when dentists disagree?'

His voice became stronger and more portentous as he wagged a warning finger in their direction. 'We all know of cases where innocent people have been convicted on the basis of erroneous forensic evidence. So if you did become confused by their testimony, if you have the slightest question in your mind whether these indistinct marks were really caused by human teeth, if you have the slightest doubt whether only the defendant could have made them, as my learned colleague for the prosecution tried so desperately to prove, then you cannot in all conscience find him guilty of this shocking crime.'

After Bonelli had sat down beside his client, Adrian Woodbridge summed up both cases, then turned to instruct the jury. 'If you have any doubt about the evidence that has been presented before you,' he said, 'if you are not convinced beyond a reasonable doubt that the defendant is guilty, then you are obliged to acquit him.'

The following day, Barbara Lindstrom called Halina. There was pain in her voice as she recounted the final act of the trial. 'The jury found him not guilty. He's a free man.' Barbara sighed. 'That's the criminal justice system for you. But I'm free too. I'm retiring, and I won't be sorry to be out of it.'

Halina couldn't bring herself to speak.

Nine

Staring out of her office window, Halina brooded over the verdict. It wasn't the first time her evidence had been invalidated, but this travesty of justice depressed her more than usual. She couldn't stop thinking about Tiffany Carson's distraught mother. How could she live with the gnawing ache of knowing that her child's killer had been set free?

Forcing herself to concentrate on her work, Halina was about to open the letter from Poland when someone knocked on the door.

The young woman who entered had the sharp features and alert look of a startled mouse. 'I'm Jane Martin from the *National Observer*,' she said, holding out her hand.

At the mention of Rhys's paper, Halina relaxed. He must have suggested a feature about forensic dentistry. Science and medical writers were always looking for material to fill their columns.

Jane rifled in her backpack and placed a tape recorder on the desk. 'I hope you don't mind if I use this? I don't trust my memory! I promise I won't take up too much of your time. I know what it's like trying to fit everything in. The last thing you want is a reporter hassling you!' Her eyes roamed all over the room as she spoke.

'What would you like to know?'

As Jane switched on the tape recorder, Halina noticed the nicotine stains on her index and middle fingers. Now that she had quit herself, she was aware that young women were smoking more than ever.

'So what got you interested in forensic dentistry?' Jane asked.

Halina chuckled. 'Are you writing about forensic dentistry or about me?' It was typical of Rhys to say nothing and surprise her.

'Well, both really,' Jane said. 'After all, you're the one who got it going in Australia. You formulated the dental procedures for mass disasters, and you're the president of the International Association. People read a lot about forensic pathologists and anthropologists but you forensic dentists have kept a very low profile!'

The girl had clearly done her homework.

Halina was describing the methods forensic dentists used, when Luong brought in two mugs of English Breakfast tea and a plate of shortbread biscuits.

'Oh, bikkies, great!' Jane said, crunching into one. She sat forward and dropped her voice. 'You do such fascinating work, Dr Shore. I know you've been involved in lots of famous cases. Can you tell me about your work on the Backpacker murders?'

Halina smiled at Jane's ingenuous manner. 'I identified one of the girls. She had a protruding lower jaw which made identification easier. Luckily her dentist in the UK had kept her records so I was able to do a video superimposition and compare her X-rays with the skull.'

She stopped talking while Jane loaded her second tape into the machine.

'At the moment, dentists are only obliged to keep dental records for seven years, but if you can say in your article how important it is for them to keep records indefinitely, you'll be doing an important service for the whole community,' Halina said. 'That could be a good angle for your story.'

Jane nodded enthusiastically and jotted something down in her notebook.

She had a ghoulish fascination with Halina's work at the morgue, especially the process that separated the flesh from the bones. 'Is there a special name for that?' she asked, her eyes resting for a moment on Halina's framed degrees hanging on the wall. 'And what do you do with all the bits that are left over after you've boiled it up?' She sounded like a schoolgirl, fascinated and repelled at the same time.

'It gets emptied out,' Halina said, deliberately vague.

'But where? Not into the sewerage?'

Halina nodded. 'At the moment, yes.'

Jane's eyes widened. 'What if they had HIV?'

Halina hesitated. It wasn't a subject she wanted to pursue. After the recent scandal about the body parts taken from cadavers and kept in jars in the morgue, the last thing they needed was more adverse publicity for their work. But it was too late to back-pedal. 'We need special holding tanks for HIV-contaminated blood and to prevent the possible spread of Hep C, but at the moment no one is willing to pay for it. The Police Department shifts the responsibility onto the Health Department and vice versa. I'm sure you know how impossible it is to get money out of government departments.'

She steered the conversation back to the important issues. 'It would be good if you mentioned the lack of a national database. At the moment the states are functioning like seven independent nations jealously guarding information that they should be pooling together.'

'Can I quote you on that?' Jane asked.

'You certainly can.' She couldn't resist adding, 'That should keep your editor happy.'

Jane rolled her eyes. 'That would be a miracle. The best I can hope for is not be ridiculed or insulted.'

Halina suppressed a smile. Rhys had won two Walkley awards for investigative journalism, but he would never win any prizes for personal relations. She felt a perverse sense of satisfaction knowing that she was engaged in an intimate relationship with a man who intimidated so many people.

There was a knock on the door and Jane looked up. 'Oh, here's the photographer to do a shot of you, if that's okay,' she said. While he was looking around checking angles, Jane pointed. 'Over there in front of the bookcase would be good, Brett.' Turning back to Halina, she said: 'So people can see what a forensic dentist looks like!'

After they left, Halina returned to her correspondence. The letter from Poland did contain an invitation but not to a conference. The letterhead bore the unfamiliar initials IPN, *Institucja Pamięci Narodowej*, which was translated below as the Institute of National Remembrance. She ran her eye down the page, reading the stiff, unidiomatic English written by someone who had probably looked up words in a dictionary. A suspected mass grave from 1941 was about to be exhumed, and she was invited to join the forensic team that IPN was putting together. They would be profoundly honoured if she would do them the grace to accept, and respectfully requested her reply as soon as possible.

It was an unusual request. Some years before, two of Halina's colleagues had taken part in exhuming mass graves as part of Australia's war crimes investigation, but those graves had been located in the Ukraine. An elderly German called Helmuth Gruber, who had been living in Adelaide since 1947, had been accused of being the leader of an *Einsatzgruppen* death squad which had machine-gunned about five thousand Jewish men, women and children in a Ukrainian forest. She could still see Bill Mitchell's taut white face as he described his first view of the skeletons beneath the top layer of soil. 'Providing the evidence to show that Gruber gave the order for this massacre was the most important thing I have ever done, probably the most important thing I will ever do,' he had said.

When she saw him again a few months later, he had been choked with fury because the Australian government had closed the investigation. They cited the lapse of time and lack of funds as the reason, but he put it down to faint-heartedness and lack of will. 'Now Gruber will never have to answer for his crimes. He gets to live out his life in comfort while those he murdered lie in their grave without justice,' he had told her. Bill had written impassioned letters to the attorney-general's department, the prime minister and the press but to no avail. He suffered a heart attack and died before the year ended, angry and disillusioned.

Perplexed, Halina reread the letter. There were forensic scientists in Poland, but it seemed that the government wanted to widen the scope of the exhumation outside national borders, and being the Polish-born president of the International Association of Odontologists had made her an ideal choice. She knew from experience that working in foreign countries was a professional and emotional minefield.

She had worked in sweltering heat at the sites of plane crashes in underdeveloped countries and had experienced the logistical problems of working in places with an excess of national pride and a shortage of trained personnel and modern technology. You knew you had been invited because of your expertise, but couldn't always tell whose sensitivities you were offending, or whose political agenda you were supporting or undermining.

Still, this was a prestigious appointment, and the prospect of returning to Poland for the first time since childhood stirred feelings she was unable to define. A frisson of excitement combined with curiosity and anxiety. Perhaps it was part of the urge to reconnect with the past that had surfaced since her mother's death. Halina replaced the letter in the tray. She would reply to the invitation as soon as she had spoken to Rhys.

At home that evening, with Puccini purring in her lap like a wheezy engine, Halina began planning their itinerary. It was a warm Sydney night and the scent of jasmine and woodsmoke wafted in through the windows, squeezing her heart with yearning. She told herself she should not call, but longing overcame her pride. She would tell him about the interview. And find out whether he had set a date for their New Zealand trip.

Hearing his voice mail, she hung up without leaving a message, fighting off a sense of anger and desolation. It was childish to feel annoyed just because he wasn't in his office. Or because he was drinking with his cronies or having dinner with his wife and sons while she was alone with her cat.

❋

'Halina, Dr Stanton call you before,' Luong said the next morning. 'Can you please go and see him?'

As the slow lift creaked downstairs, Halina wondered what the dean of the dental faculty wanted to discuss. She and John Stanton had been friends since their undergraduate days, and she always enjoyed his dry sense of humour. He was standing by the window, watching the students crossing the cement yard, and it struck her that he had aged noticeably in the past year. In dragging long strands of thinning hair across his shiny head, he only accentuated its baldness, and his stomach pushed out his trousers so that from the side he resembled Humpty Dumpty. So different from the gangly, freckled student who had made her laugh while he helped her with prosthetic dentistry, a subject for which she had no aptitude at all. The only sound in the room was the ticking of the grandfather clock in the corner as its pendulum swung from side to side.

'Ah, Halina,' John said. He sat down heavily in his high-backed chair, motioning for her to sit too. He didn't kiss her on the cheek as he usually did, but shuffled some papers and cleared his throat a few times, not looking at her. A newspaper lay open on his desk.

'Was there something you wanted to talk about, John?' she prompted.

He cleared his throat again and took off his glasses, swinging them from side to side so that the arms clicked against each other.

'Have you seen today's *Observer*?' His voice was cool.

She shook her head. Without waiting for her to speak, he thrust it before her. 'You'd better have a look at this.'

The first thing she saw was a photograph of herself in front of the skull on her bookcase. The angle of the shot magnified the skull which looked menacing. The headline read: 'New Morgue Scandal,' and the sensational story that followed mentioned a 'soup' of body parts flushed into Sydney sewerage, placing the population at risk of contracting HIV Aids or Hepatitis C. The writer concluded with the indignant observation that this was another shocking revelation about the grisly goings-on in the morgue where forensic scientists acted with little regard for public health or human dignity.

Halina's mouth went dry. Not a word about why she had become a forensic dentist, how invaluable forensic dentistry was in identifying bodies, or the need for a national database.

Her hands shook as she pushed the newspaper away. Jane Martin had tricked her. No, it was her own fault. She had dropped her guard because it was Rhys's paper, and had trusted a clever little snake disguised as an ingenuous mouse.

But Jane Martin was only the messenger.

Her mother's words came back to her. Decent people always underestimate the baseness of others.

John Stanton was surveying her with an expression that reflected reproach, disappointment and disapproval in equal proportions.

'It's a great pity you felt the need to discuss the boiler, Halina. After the muck the papers raked up last time about the stolen body parts at the morgue, the last thing we need is another media beat-up about forensic medicine.' He sighed heavily. 'All we can do is go into damage control and hope the fuss dies down. I'll write a letter to the editor, although they probably won't publish it.'

She was at the door when he added in a voice as dry as the Sahara, 'Oh, and Halina, if there are any more requests for interviews, I'd like you to run them by me first.'

In her office, Halina paced around the room. Her heart pounded so violently that she felt the blood would explode in her veins. She gripped the windowsill to steady herself. 'You bastard!' she said over and over. 'You ruthless bastard!' She wanted to hurl a brick through his office window, slap his smug face, hurt and humiliate him. she wanted to yell *How could you do this to me? Why did you betray me like this?*

Her whole body trembled with rage as she picked up the receiver to tell him what she thought of him, but she replaced it. Rhys was brutally insensitive and the only thing that mattered to him was the paper. She was too hurt and didn't trust herself to speak. Besides, it wouldn't change anything. And she didn't want to listen to his excuses.

She sank into her chair and her fury turned inwards. Why had she put up with his selfish, arrogant behaviour for so long? She cringed to think of the power she had given him. Her friends had warned her but she'd refused to listen. While deluding herself that she was in control, she had allowed him to transform her from an independent, assertive woman into a spineless cliché, the other woman waiting for the phone to ring. Her mother used to say that if you ran with wolves, you'd better not trip. Well, she had tripped and been torn to pieces.

Her ribs were crushing her lungs so hard that she could hardly breathe. 'Never again,' she kept repeating to herself. 'Never again.'

It was clear to her now that Rhys didn't love her and probably never had. Like a naïve schoolgirl she had mistaken lust for love. She buried her head in her hands and wept for the years she had wasted and for the illusion she had mistaken for reality. Stretching ahead of her was a void she didn't think she could bear, but even if she died of loneliness, she would never give him a chance to humiliate her again ... or the satisfaction of knowing how deeply he had hurt her.

Night fell, office doors closed, and the sound of voices and footsteps in the corridor died away. Halina continued to sit at her desk. She was watching the movie of her life while the projector jammed at every disastrous choice she had ever made. I've taken the wrong turning at every crossroad and misjudged everything and everyone along the way, she thought. Halina blew her nose, wiped her eyes and began shuffling papers around on her desk with arms that felt heavy in their sockets. Picking up the letter from Poland, she scanned its contents, hardly aware of what she was reading. She ached with sadness. For the first time in her life she felt vulnerable and alone.

Ten

As the Boeing 747 flew into the clouds, away from Sydney's rim of parchment-coloured sand, Halina felt her body easing in her seat. The prospect of a week in New York on the way to Poland raised her spirits. It wouldn't be the holiday she had looked forward to, and she would be spending it alone, but at least she was leaving Sydney behind.

'You might even meet someone, now that you've got that scumbag out of your life,' Claire had said.

Halina sighed. Claire did not understand the lacerating grief she suffered. It would have been easier to endure if Rhys had died, because she could have mourned, wept and eventually recovered, but this was the endless grieving for a missing person. For the past few weeks she had stumbled around like a sleepwalker. Everything seemed blurred and out of focus, as though seen through a smudged window. She jumped whenever the phone rang, trembling in case it was him, and shaking when it wasn't. Walking along the street, she would imagine she glimpsed the familiar curve of his cheek or heard the treacherous velvet of his voice, and her heart would pound so hard that she had to lean against a wall until the moment passed.

She tried to switch off the mental recording of their last conversation that played incessantly on some subliminal channel in her mind.

'I don't think you understand,' he had said when she finally took his call. 'It wasn't personal. I'm running a newspaper not a public relations company. I have to report on things that the public needs to know.'

Her voice was hoarse with the effort of keeping it steady. 'I've been understanding for too long. Nothing matters to you except your work. You're a ruthless, insensitive bastard.'

There was a long pause. Finally he said, 'I'm very sorry that you're so upset, Halina.'

Choked with fury she had banged the receiver down.

She knew Rhys wouldn't be replaying their conversation. When she hadn't returned his calls, he stopped calling. If he were to draw a circle and divide it into segments to represent various aspects of his life, she would be a mere sliver. 'You're the rainbow in my life,' he had told her once, and her eyes had grown moist at his lyrical tribute. How well he had chosen his metaphor. Rainbows were illusions of light, fleeting and insubstantial. She was the deluded dreamer while he was too much of a realist to hold on to rainbows or lament their passing.

Churned up again, Halina flicked through the glossy pages of the in-flight magazine. In between articles on Grand Prix racing and an inspirational story about the CEO of a multinational company who had started life as its messenger boy, she came to an interview with an American pop psychologist discussing her latest book, *Letting Go*. Skimming through the verbiage, Halina paused at an anecdote about two Buddhist monks who came across a young girl crying by the riverbank, too frightened to cross. Although they had taken an oath of celibacy and had forsworn all contact with women, they carried her to the other side, set her down and continued on their way. Later that day, one of the monks said, 'We shouldn't have done that, we broke our vow.' To which his companion replied, 'I put her down several hours ago but you're still carrying her!'

The art of life is knowing when to let go, Halina reflected as she sipped the French champagne the flight attendant had placed on the starched white cloth. Starting affairs was easy but ending them was hard. It was time she left Rhys on the riverbank.

The romantic comedies and contrived thrillers being shown during the flight didn't hold her interest, and after trying each one in turn she selected the classical music channel. The first item was the love scene from *La Bohème*. Listening to Puccini's music, her mind strayed to her cat, left in the care of her neighbour. She had come home late one evening to find Andrew sitting on the pavement outside her gate, talking earnestly to Puccini while tickling his chin. Usually reserved with strangers, the cat was looking up at him with an unblinking, adoring gaze.

'Looks like you're having an intimate tête-à-tête,' Halina had laughed.

Deadpan, he replied, 'I thought of writing him a letter but decided to be neighbourly and talk to him instead. I think he appreciated that.'

Halina pulled a face. 'Don't you ever let up?'

But she had invited him in for a drink, and surprised herself by agreeing to go to his next gig. On a warm spring night, with a light breeze blowing off the harbour, Halina had sat on the concourse of the Opera House while ferries and hydrofoils plied under the bridge. Sipping a glass of cold sauvignon blanc, she listened to the Gershwin melodies that flowed like liquid honey out of Andrew's clarinet, and felt a rush of love for the city.

During a break, Andrew had joined her and as he talked about some of his musical mishaps, she was disarmed by the guileless light-heartedness that had previously irritated her. By the end of the evening, she realised she hadn't laughed so much for a long time.

'Your cat seems to have a good ear for music,' Andrew had said. 'Would you like me to look after him while you're away?'

She didn't hesitate.

'Don't tell me you feed him those sawdust pellets and water,' he had protested when she brought the cat over with a few bags of catfood and a list of instructions. 'Is it okay if I give him fish and a bowl of milk every now and then?'

Halina had nodded. Puccini would think he was in moggy heaven, she thought now. He probably wouldn't want to come home.

The dinner service had begun and she selected a Beaune beaujolais to wash down the tournedos rossini, grateful that the Polish Institute of National Remembrance had sent her a business-class ticket. She glanced around at her fellow passengers. Behind her a noisy group shouted and clinked glasses. To her right, a woman laughed uproariously at every inane remark her companion made. Thank God she had an empty seat beside her and wouldn't be obliged to make polite conversation during the long flight.

Taking a mental inventory of the forensic equipment she was lugging around the world, Halina stifled a smile as she recalled checking her luggage in at the airport. As she hauled her bulging suitcase onto the scales, the check-in officer had noted the excess weight.

'You obviously don't believe in travelling light,' she said.

Trying to keep a straight face, Halina replied, 'I never travel without my skeleton.'

The officer looked startled, not certain whether to laugh or call the supervisor until Halina presented her credentials.

But Halina hadn't been joking. Inside the trunk that she always brought on these assignments was a military-style rifle box containing a half-skeleton and a full skull and vertebral column. Packed alongside was her portable dental X-ray and developing tank which were indispensable for field work. She was surprised that the airport security machine hadn't picked up the metal detector, which would show up as a suspicious stick with a pad on the end, useful for detecting bridges and crowns in mass graves. Among the other tools of trade she ticked off in her mind were Vernier callipers that measured the size of teeth, a Polaroid camera for dialling up various magnifications, two pairs of overalls, rubber boots and heavy mortuary gloves. Suddenly she stiffened. Had she remembered to pack her field bible, William M Bass's *Human Osteology*? Then she relaxed as she recalled sliding it into the outside compartment of the suitcase.

Another six hours to go before New York. Halina pulled the video out of the console. A forensic pathologist was investigating the murder of a small girl and it was clear in the first few minutes that he would find the killer. She switched it off. Didn't Hollywood scriptwriters ever come into contact with real life? Ever since Kevin Donnelly's trial, she hadn't been able to get Clive's perfidy or the distraught mother out of her mind. She sighed. Another issue she needed to let go.

The road from JFK airport to Manhattan was gridlocked. Huddled in their cars, drivers gesticulated, swore and honked their horns. The jackhammers of road-repair crews droned incessantly. Hunched over the wheel of the cab, the Ethiopian driver, an embroidered cap on his matted hair, alternately implored Allah for patience and consigned the other drivers to the fires of hell. Two hours later Halina stumbled into the foyer of her hotel, an oasis of calm and elegance in a frenetic city. But as soon as the porter opened the door to her room, she was enveloped in a fug of stuffy air. The window didn't open and no matter how much she fiddled with the air-conditioning knobs, the temperature didn't change. The bed occupied almost the entire room, leaving no space for her suitcase, but when she asked for another room, the reception clerk told her that the hotel was fully booked and wished her a pleasant stay.

Determined to spend as little time in the hotel as possible, she spent all day exploring Manhattan. Dutifully she did the rounds of museums and galleries, and lined up at HalfTix at Times Square, shivering in a long queue to see an over-hyped musical. Another night, while listening to a clarinettist at a jazz club, she thought of Andrew whose banter would have enlivened the evening. After several visits to Saks Fifth Avenue and Donna Karan, where she bought a black cashmere coat, even the shopping began to pall. This rich diet of self-indulgence was giving her indigestion and all these activities seemed pointless. On one occasion she felt lonely enough to consider calling Rhys, just to hear his voice and feel connected again, but she gritted her teeth and called Claire instead, like an alcoholic on the brink of back-sliding.

At an exhibition of her favourite photographer, Sebastiao Salgado, Halina wandered from room to room, looking at images of refugees around the world, portraits of dull-eyed children and gaunt-faced parents gazing into the hopeless future. An Eritrean mother with breasts like empty leather pouches was cradling her dying child. The skin on her face was stretched tightly over the bones, and the cracks on her lips stood out so clearly that, without realising it, Halina moistened hers.

Walking along the avenues of Manhattan, past palatial apartment blocks and boutiques displaying coats, shoes and handbags, any one of which would cost more than the people in Salgado's images would see in a lifetime, Halina was haunted by the image of the Eritrean mother's hopeless love for her child. A woman in a shapeless grey coat with big lapels and a felt hat pushed down on her straight grey hair passed her on the street. Halina recalled her mother wearing an old-fashioned coat like that. Whenever the lining frayed with wear, she would mend it, her tiny stitches criss-crossed into a perfect patch. Zosia had rarely bought anything for herself, but whenever she managed to save a few pounds, she would buy something for Halina. Although she never paid compliments, Halina could tell from the way her mother nodded that she approved of the way her daughter looked. In a painful moment of clarity, Halina realised that she had never appreciated her mother's devotion, had never acknowledged it, not even as an adult. Whether through selfishness or arrogance, she had accepted everything as her due. She had regarded herself as superior to her uneducated, foreign mother.

Musing over lost opportunities and questions never asked, she entered St Patrick's Cathedral. The lofty gothic-style vaulting with its stained-glass windows and the smoky fragrance of wax candles evoked a rush of nostalgia for her childhood. She remembered the chapel in the convent school in Warsaw that had smelled of incense and rose petals. Lighting a candle for her mother, she whispered, 'Wherever you are, I hope you're at rest.'

Outside again, she shivered and looked at her watch. A chilly November fog had darkened the city although it was only five o'clock. Too late for galleries but too early for dinner. The man roasting chestnuts on the corner of the Rockefeller Plaza stamped his feet and warmed his red hands over the glowing embers. 'Chestnuts, lady?' he called. Sitting on a bench in front of the fountain, she split open the charred shells and bit into the sweet floury flesh, watching New Yorkers hurry past.

Inside a Barnes & Noble bookstore, she was breathing in the smell of newly printed books when a memoir about life in the Catskills caught her eye. It brought to mind the puzzling letter from the woman called Esther Kennedy who lived in a retirement home in the Catskills. With her mother still guiltily in her mind, Halina felt an urge to follow it up. Perhaps this woman might provide some link, however tenuous, with a vanished past.

She bought the book and headed back to the hotel, buoyed by the prospect of taking action instead of merely filling in time.

Eleven

If you had to live in a retirement home, this area was probably as good as it got, Halina thought. The cobalt lake was surrounded by dense forests of fir and spruce, and above them granite peaks poked into the sky. A greater contrast with the congestion and chaos of the city she had left only two hours before would be difficult to imagine.

When she stopped to ask directions, the voluble postmaster in his engineer's cap, plaid shirt and heavy-duty overalls reeled off a long list of outdoor activities available in Sullivan County, but she doubted whether Esther Kennedy or the other inmates of Walnut Lodge took advantage of the trout-fishing, horse-riding or mountain-climbing that the area offered.

Burying her chin inside the collar of her new coat against the chilly air that blew from the mountain, she pushed open the gate of Walnut Lodge. According to the shingle, the mock Tudor mansion with hanging turrets, gables and dormer windows protruding from its black and white timbered façade was built back in 1885, but the Disney-style decorations had been added much later. The memoir she had bought explained that the Catskills were a long-established holiday area, renowned more for exuberance than elegance. Kitsch would have been more accurate. The inner courtyard was surrounded by yew hedges trimmed into animal shapes. In the centre a fountain spouted water in time to Mozart's *Rondo alla Turca*, relayed from an invisible player.

'Come on into the cathouse!' the matron called out from her office. Halina thought she had misheard until she walked inside. Shelves along three sides of the room were crammed with cats. Big shiny porcelain cats with whiskers and tails that moved, cuddly furry cats, gaunt wooden cats, sleek marble cats, and papier-mâché cats with long necks and sardonic expressions.

'You could call this room a cat-astrophe!' Darlene Jackson was laughing so much that her little round body wobbled. When they shook hands, Halina saw that each of her plump fingers wore a ring.

'I'm a cat person too,' Halina said with a pang of nostalgia.

'Cawfee?' Darlene asked. While Halina pretended to sip the watery brown liquid that seemed to pass for coffee in the United States, the matron was sizing her up. 'Australia!' she exclaimed. 'The place with the kangaroos, right? When you called yesterday I thought you said Austria! My goodness you have come a long way. Just to see Mrs Kennedy, was it?' Without waiting for a reply she went on, 'As I told you, Mrs Kennedy has occasional lucid periods but unfortunately they are becoming rare. She's been with us for, oh, it must be about fifteen years now, maybe more.' Wiping the corners of her mouth carefully with her thumb and forefinger to avoid smudging her lipstick, she lowered her voice. 'Of course she never recovered from the death of her son. That was so tragic.'

Halina only had to raise her eyebrows for the matron to continue.

'It was during the Vietnam War. He took it so badly. Went on those demonstration marches, camped outside the White House with big placards, and I do believe he even talked of killing the president. Then one day he didn't come home. They found his body near a building site. He climbed up the scaffolding and threw himself from the top storey with a note around his neck that said "Stop the war". I always say that if you have enough courage to die, you have enough courage to live, but I guess some people don't see it that way.'

Darlene hesitated for a moment. 'I don't normally discuss the residents but you've come such a long way to see her.' Her conscience appeased, she continued. 'When Esther and her husband arrived in the U S of A, they didn't have a cent, but Mr Kennedy was a real smart man. He invented the first sugar substitute that didn't taste like saccharin, and she's still living off that. They had a grand apartment in that Dakota building where John Lennon and Yoko Ono used to live, right across from Central Park. But all that money didn't do them much good. First their son committed suicide, and then the husband dropped dead from a heart attack. It's just too sad. Poor thing. It's probably easier for her not to remember anything. You can't wonder, can you?'

'At least the money ensured that she would spend her last years in comfort in this beautiful area,' Halina observed.

Matron nodded. 'Walnut Lodge is the crème de la crème as they say. We offer our residents whatever they want. Spas, massage, manicure, aromatherapy, physiotherapy, you name it. Years ago, this was the top vacation area. Maybe you even heard of Grossinger's in Austria. Excuse me, I mean Australia. In our heyday, every stand-up comedian you ever heard of cut his teeth in guesthouses here. Even Woody Allen. If they couldn't cut the mustard here, forget it. But of course these days retirees buy condos in Florida and we're seeing more hikers and climbers coming into the area. The opposite end of the spectrum! But that's life, isn't it? Nothing stays the same.'

'Can she hold a conversation?' Halina was impatient to return to Esther Kennedy.

Matron pursed her mouth and wiped the corners again. 'Not really. Most of the time she lives in a world of her own, and just stares into space. When she does speak, she repeats herself a lot, like a record that's stuck in a groove.' Her pudgy hands dug into the sides of her rose-pink velvet armchair as she hauled herself to her small feet. 'Come, I'll take you to her room.'

As she followed Darlene Jackson through Walnut Lodge, Halina decided that the interior designer must have gained his ideas about décor from casinos, bordellos and Indian restaurants. Beneath twinkling chandeliers, an emerald carpet criss-crossed with orange zigzags vied with crimson wallpaper embossed with gold arabesques. Following her gaze, Darlene said, 'We do like to make the place look bright. If your environment is cheerful, you feel cheerful, that's what I always say.'

In the lounge room, a chubby man of indeterminate age whose smooth pink cheeks did not look as though they had ever required a razor was thumping a medley from *The Merry Widow* on the pianola, to the obvious enjoyment of the residents. Three white-haired women sang along in raucous quavering falsetto while others tapped their feet or swayed to the well-loved tunes. A man with large elf-like ears and a tuft of grey hair in the centre of his ridged scalp seemed to be sleeping, his head drooped on his chest. Suddenly he raised his gaunt face, held up a trembling arm and shouted, 'Quick march! Left, right, left, right!' No one paid any attention to him but when Halina and the matron passed, the women looked around and started whispering.

'They're all wondering who you are and who you've come to see. The gossip factory will be humming today!' the matron chuckled.

The door of each room was decorated with a floral tile with the resident's name painted in ornate lettering. As there was no reply to Matron's soft knock on Esther Kennedy's door, she opened it gently and looked inside.

'I got a visitor for you, honey. Would you like to see her? She's come all the way from Australia to see you!'

A small erect figure was sitting in a wheelchair beside a window that framed the picture-postcard scene, but the large staring eyes seemed to be gazing at an interior landscape. With her thick white hair pinned into a French roll and an intense expression on her thin face, as though she were trying to pierce the darkness of her own thoughts, Esther Kennedy had a regal presence. A stately palace with all the occupants gone and the lights extinguished. Halina turned questioningly to Matron, who shook her head and indicated that they should wait.

'Here's your visitor, honey,' she said, louder than before. Esther Kennedy turned her head slowly and her eyes darted from Halina to the matron while she made agitated movements with clawlike hands.

'My name is Halina.' She was about to say Shore, but said Szczecińska instead. Perhaps that name would mean something to the old lady. Esther nodded impatiently, but a moment later she asked in a querulous tone, 'Who are you?'

'Do you remember a couple called Enfield? Bella and Jack Enfield? They lived in Melbourne.'

The old woman stared at Halina, opened her mouth and fluttered her hands but made no sound. When Halina repeated the names, her hands waved around more violently.

'Who?' Esther shrieked suddenly. 'Who are you?'

'She's too agitated now. She can't communicate when she's in this state. I think we should leave her,' matron suggested. 'I'm so sorry your visit has been disappointing but I warned you about her condition.'

Halina sighed. Inside that white head was the answer to the mystery of those two letters, but the code had become scrambled and the key was lost.

Back in her cat-infested office, Matron was shaking her head. 'It's sad to see a fine intelligent human being disintegrate like that. When she first came here, she read and played bridge. Boy, did she make trouble! She was pretty feisty, said what she thought, but not in a nasty way. Complained that no one could play bridge properly. She didn't like the food, said it was too bland. "It's just like America," she used to say. "There's a lot of it, but none of it is interesting." Thank goodness we had a special writing teacher who got her to write stories or she would have complained all day long!'

While Halina mused about old age and its chilling possibilities, Matron pressed the intercom with her plump finger. 'Betsy, bring us more cawfee, please. And some chocolate cookies!' she added, obviously not in a hurry to return to her duties.

She leant towards Halina in a confidential manner. 'You know, honey, that teacher still comes every week. We have good people in our community who visit our residents and provide activities for them.'

In the common room, the pianist was still pounding the keys with an enthusiastic rendition of *Oklahoma,* and the women were still singing along.

'Our visitors aren't spring chickens any more, but I guess it does them good to do something useful,' Matron pointed out. 'We all need that, don't we?'

Halina looked thoughtful. 'I wonder if the writing teacher remembers any of Mrs Kennedy's stories?'

'Well, it sure was a long time ago, but you never know. If you can come back tomorrow, Celia Graham will be here and you'll be able to ask her yourself. I can recommend a darling bed and breakfast place nearby. If you'll allow me to make the reservation, they'll take good care of you.'

As thin and chirrupy as a grasshopper, Celia Graham had quick brown eyes and fine white hair through which her bright pink scalp showed. 'I surely do remember Esther's stories,' she said with a smile.

A faintly chemical odour emanated from her, and Halina wondered whether it was caused by a medical condition or the medication she took to combat it.

'Writing life stories is very therapeutic, you know. I've been taking groups for over thirty years and it certainly helps people get things off their chest. Why, there was a man I tutored once who never spoke about the past, and didn't want to write about it either, but after a time he started writing odd incidents, and before I knew it, he had written his whole life story. It opened him up. He became a different person.'

Halina wondered whether her own mother might have opened up under Celia's tutelage. She doubted it. 'Did writing change Esther Kennedy?' she asked.

Celia hesitated. 'I like to think it helped her, but after a time she lost interest in writing and everything else. What a memory she had for details though. You could feel the knobbly trunks of the birch trees and taste the herring soup when she described her life in the labour camp in Siberia. Her stories were so good that I included them in the book I compiled at the end of the year. I still do that, every year. It gives them an incentive and we all need that, don't we?'

Like Matron Jackson, the writing teacher also seemed willing to talk all day. It must be something in the air here, Halina decided. They should bottle it and send it to New York and Sydney.

'Did you keep any of those old books?' she asked.

Celia Graham's face lit up and her smile stretched from one side of her narrow face to the other. 'I sure did! I couldn't bear to part with such wonderful stories. You know, I always thought one day I'd write a novel based on the lives of some of the residents — they've all led such interesting lives. Not plagiarising their stories or exploiting them, of course,' she added, reddening to the tips of her ears. 'But I never did get round to writing that book and I guess I never will. Why do we allow unimportant things to distract us from what we truly want? Anyways, the stories just lie there gathering dust, no earthly use to anyone. Like me.' In the long sigh that followed, Halina sensed the regrets of a life that was drawing to a close without achieving the rosy dreams of youth.

Making an effort to smile, Celia said, 'If you like, I could bring them over this afternoon.'

❄

Her long legs stretched out in front of the crackling fire at the Mountain View B & B, Halina immersed herself in Esther Kennedy's wartime experiences. As she turned the pages, she became acquainted with the younger version of the woman who had sunk so deeply inside herself that she had become an empty shell. The young Esther had been a sensual, spirited woman who retained her warmth and sense of humour in circumstances that left little scope for optimism. Halina had read survival stories of Jews who had been interned in ghettoes and concentration camps during the war, but this was the first account she had ever come across of a Polish prisoner's life in a Siberian labour camp.

Esther's first story described the journey to Siberia.

At first, there were only questions. Questions with no answers. Where were they taking us? And why? Why did they deport us? Why did they bolt the doors from outside? How could I let my poor parents know where we were? But the guards stared past us with their expressionless Slav faces as if we didn't exist. Luckily I had a bag of candy because the only food they gave us for three days was salt herring. When the brakes squealed and the train shuddered, we thought good, now we have arrived, but it wasn't so. The guards ran up and down the platform shouting 'Kipiatok! Kipiatok!' The first time I heard that word, I thought it was the name of a place, but it meant boiled water. They let us get down but pointed rifles at us as if we were criminals and I could see that they wouldn't hesitate to shoot. They called us Bourgoi! Being bourgeois was a crime. They said we were the exploiters

of the working classes. I wanted to tell them that they
made a big mistake, because I never exploited anyone, and
my husband was a socialist like them. But it was useless.
Their faces were as hard as their hearts.

The worst thing for me on that journey, worse
than hunger and cold, worse than exhaustion and
claustrophobia, was the lack of privacy. Most of us had
diarrhoea but we all had to use the same bucket in the
carriage. In full view of everyone. Did I ever think
when I was at home that toilet paper could be more
precious than gold? High up there was one tiny window
covered with an iron grille and we took turns to look
outside. The scenery was strange to our eyes. Miles of
nothing. No towns, no villages, no houses even. Where
were we? Thank God I had my dear husband with me
and somehow we cheered each other up. 'No towns means
no shops. Just think of all the money we'll save,' he said.
He always teased me for being extravagant. We didn't
dare break down. We had to be strong for each other and
for ourselves. Anyway the war couldn't last for ever. My
darling put his arm around me and we promised each
other that no matter what happened, we would stay
together and come back home together.

Halina blew her nose. Esther's grit and the immediacy of
her narrative touched her. She felt she was on the train
with that young couple and could hear the relentless wheels
rolling towards an unknown destination.

The next story was called 'Arriving at Archangel'.

Slowly, slowly, the train came to the end of the line. All
around us were dark forests with trees that poked into

the sky. Nothing but forests. I never knew that a place could be so desolate, cold and empty. To me a place with no villages or houses was a dead place but that was at the beginning. Later I found out that emptiness was what was inside your heart, because the forests whirred with life.

'You have come to Archangel,' a Russian guard told us.

'This isn't my idea of heaven,' my husband whispered.

'This must be the workers' paradise they promised us,' I whispered back. 'Can't you see the pearly gates?' I pointed at the icicles that hung from the branches.

Meanwhile the Russian was droning in a staccato voice, 'You are here to help Comrade Stalin build a paradise for workers.'

Misko nudged me but we stopped smiling when we heard the guard's next words.

'Forget Poland. You will never see it again. This your home from now on. You will chop trees and build houses and we will give you food. In Soviet Union people who do not work do not eat. We do not feed parasites.'

Misko squeezed my hand but I was shaking so much I could hardly stand up. How were we supposed to chop trees and build houses? My mother had spoilt me so much that I had never even swept a floor, while Misko was a chemistry teacher, he'd never done any manual work. That night they gave us a bowl of salty herring soup and showed us where we would sleep. I thought about my mother, my sister and her family, and my grandparents, and cried myself to sleep in a barrack where the wind blew straight down from the Arctic Circle and its breath was studded with icy razors.

Riveted by Esther's account of life in exile Halina couldn't budge from her chair, even when she was asked to join the hostess and her family for pecan pie. Esther and Misko suffered blistered hands, frostbitten toes and constant hunger, but somehow they adjusted to their harsh conditions and, to her amazement, came to love the beauty of their surroundings.

In summer, the sun warmed my back and birds sang while we picked blueberries and mushrooms in the woods. In winter the frost encrusted my eyelashes when I walked for miles in my felt boots along silent paths until I reached the clearing where I had to chop the branches. As we chopped more trees, the forest receded and we had further and further to walk. One day I looked up at the plump cushions of snow resting in the forks of the branches. The tops of the trees were so tall that they must have brushed God's feet. Suddenly I felt so elated that my toes tingled in my felt boots and I flung my arms around a tree trunk and put my face up to the sky. I know that this is hard to believe, but in that Communist labour camp at the end of the earth, where I counted myself lucky if I got enough herring soup and black bread to fill my stomach, and didn't know whether I would ever go back home or see my family again, I felt more alive than I have ever felt before or since. I don't know whether it was the crisp pure air that went to my head, or the ethereal beauty of the snow, but I felt insane with joy.

Halina re-read the last sentence several times. Insane with joy. She had experienced a similar ecstasy during a trek in the Himalayas. She was walking through a rhododendron forest, among towering trees covered all over with cerise, scarlet and crimson flowers, on a path thickly strewn with fallen blossoms that formed a soft flowered carpet beneath her feet. Overcome with emotion, she had flung herself down on the bed of petals, gazing up at the bright blue sky and surrendering to the moment. Time stopped and she could feel the heartbeat of the universe pulsating through her veins. Just like Esther, exulting in the wintry beauty of the Siberian woods.

The couple had been at the camp for about eight months when Esther's workload was reduced.

I couldn't believe it. I was pregnant! A new life was about to begin at the end of the earth. Instead of chopping branches, they told me to peel potatoes, but there were sacks of them and they were frozen solid. The skin on my fingers split and bled and I cried as I peeled.

My baby was born in the winter. It makes my heart ache to write about this even now, after all these years. One of the women in our barrack had been a midwife in Warsaw. She draped a sheet around our bed and told me when to push. We called him Gabriel, because he was a little angel come to comfort us in our exile. He looked like a skinned rabbit and couldn't suck properly. My breasts became engorged, the nipples cracked and became infected. The Russian women told me to cover them with cabbage leaves but nothing helped. Trying to suckle him was torture but I knew there was no other way to keep him alive. At times I wished I was dead so I wouldn't have to suffer this torment any more. It's very painful to write this, but there were moments when I wished he had never been born. And God, who grants

our wishes in ways we least expect, listened to my sinful
thoughts because that day my milk dried up. Gabriel
screamed day and night. He was hungry. But when
Misko asked the commandant for some milk, or at least
some sugar to dissolve in water for him, he yelled that
although this was a workers' paradise, there was no milk
or honey for bourgeois parasites and their offspring.

Gabriel's crying grew weaker and weaker, and his
flesh dissolved before my eyes. Then he stopped crying.
Misko dug a hole in the hard icy ground and we buried
him there. It breaks my heart to this day when I think of
my baby lying all alone under that pitiless Siberian sky.

Halina let out a long sigh. How much sorrow and loss
could one human being suffer and go on living? But
Esther and Misko's sufferings had continued even after
the Polish prisoners were released in 1941. Halina's
science-oriented education had neglected history, and
from Esther's memoir she discovered that in 1939 Poland
had been sliced up like a melon between Germany and
Russia. But in 1941, when Germany broke their pact and
invaded the Soviet Union, Russia ended up on the same
side as the Allies so they released the Polish prisoners.
But although Esther and her husband were free to leave
Siberia, they couldn't return to Poland because war
was still raging. For the next three years they roamed
around Central Asia with hundreds of thousands of other
homeless, starving refugees, trying to survive in the
markets of Samarkand and Tashkent.

I always thought that these were such exotic places
but never have I seen such poverty, misery and

degradation. People robbed and cheated each other just
to survive for one more day. One day I saw a man steal
a stale piece of bread from a starving child who was too
weak to run after him. Misko and I were hungry all
the time but we kept telling each other that if we could
just get through one more day, this would soon end and
we would be able to go home again.

Darkness had fallen, and someone came in to stoke the fire, but Halina kept turning the pages, impatient to see what happened next. In 1946, Esther and her husband returned to their home town, anxious to find the family they hadn't seen for six years. With averted eyes, the townspeople told them there was no one left. The Nazis had arrived in 1941 and had killed all the Jews.

If I live for a thousand years, I'll never find the words
to describe what I felt when I heard that. Through those
terrible years, first in Siberia and then in Central Asia,
the only thing that kept me going was the knowledge that
when this was over, I'd see my dear parents and feel my
mother's arms around me again. It took a long time to
sink in that there were no parents, no grandparents, no
sister and no little Mireleh. It took even longer to grasp
that I was the only one left. Not only of my family, but of
the entire Jewish population in the Łomza region.

Esther and her husband moved to Warsaw. She described a proud city reduced to rubble, where people trudged along the icy streets searching for something to eat. When a horse was shot dead, people emerged from cellars, attics and bunkers with knives and fell on the carcass like savages, hacking away lumps of flesh. They ran as fast as they could, blood dripping on the ground, before someone could tear the prize from their hands.

Two years later, while walking along Marszalkowska Street, Esther was overjoyed when she ran into a farmer whose cheese and butter her parents used to buy. He'd heard that a handful of Jews had survived, including a child, but he didn't know any details. Esther's last entry ended with these words:

Deep in my heart, I felt that my little niece Mireleh was still alive. I wrote to the Red Cross and to every organisation I could think of to try and trace her. I placed ads in Jewish newspapers all over the world, hoping to find someone who might be able to tell me something about my family or my niece.

One day a woman wrote to say that at the end of the war she had met a man in a DP camp in Germany, who came from my village. He was about to migrate to Australia. Melbourne, she said. Overjoyed, I wrote to him, and waited on tenterhooks for a reply that never came. Misko desperately wanted us to have another child but for years I refused in case my niece was still alive, because I wanted to care for her. Even after my beloved Seymour was born, I never stopped looking for her. Whenever I passed a girl her age in Brooklyn, I would stare, hoping to see a family resemblance. Misko said I was obsessed, and perhaps he was right. After my dear son died and my husband had a heart attack, I wrote to Melbourne again, but it was no use. I've lost every single person I ever loved. I know now that Mireleh and I are not destined to meet again in this world.

Twelve

'Welcome to LOT Airlines Flight 344 to Warsaw,' the flight attendant enunciated in crisp Polish-accented English. Her fair hair was brushed back from her finely moulded face which, together with her accent, reminded Halina of someone she knew.

The trip to Poland was a professional assignment, but now that she was almost there she regretted having no personal connections with the land where she was born. It would have been comforting to be met by an aunt or cousin who would embrace her, reminisce about her childhood and talk about the family. But she had no contacts. Her mother's mouth had stretched into a forbidding straight line whenever Halina had asked about their life in Poland and, unlike other Polish girls she knew in Sydney, she had not been raised on a diet of nostalgia and Polish heroism. She had never read Henryk Sieńkiewicz's sagas about valiant Crusaders or marauding Swedes, and couldn't recite Mickiewicz's epic poem *Pan Tadeusz*. She had heard about people returning from Poland with stories about new-found relatives and old houses that shimmered with childhood memories, but there was no door in Warsaw on which she could knock to relive the warmth of past connections.

'We hope you will enjoy your flight.' Having concluded her spiel, the flight attendant proceeded to translate it into Polish, and Halina was relieved to find that she understood most of the words.

As the attendant walked down the aisle with a friendly smile, distributing orange juice and mineral water, the resemblance flashed into Halina's mind. It was Meryl Streep in the role of the haunted Polish woman who had been forced to decide which of her children should live, in the movie *Sophie's Choice*. In Polish her name would have been Zosia. Halina wondered what her mother would have thought of this trip to Poland, and whether it would have induced her to tell stories from the past, or at least to give her some names or addresses. She doubted it.

The flight was full. Walking through the economy class cabin to stretch her legs, Halina noticed several nuns with solid silver crucifixes resting on their chocolate-brown habits, and priests in black cassocks. Some were surprisingly young and were chatting animatedly and laughing like any young people on an excursion.

The elderly woman in the next seat started talking as soon as Halina sat down. Her husband had died recently and she was returning to visit the village where she had spent most of her life. Tears welled in the wrinkled corners of her eyes and she mopped them with a large striped handkerchief.

'I going to village to take some of the ... how do you say — *ziemia*.'

'Soil.' Halina was surprised by how swiftly she translated the word.

The woman nodded. 'Our sacred Polish soil. I bringing for grave so he rest in peace.'

This fervent patriotism intrigued Halina. The woman had abandoned her thick stockings, shawl and gumboots, but her spirit had never left her homeland, and her heart was still in the potato and beet fields, beating to the rhythm of the seasons and the horse carts that rumbled to town on market day.

A long queue snaked across Warsaw's arrival hall and Halina waited while the immigration officer, in a cap that fell over his eyes, scrutinised her documents with intense concentration.

'How long do you stay?'

Halina was still formulating a reply in Polish when he stamped her passport and waved her through. She hadn't reached the exit when a stout man with a Lech Walesa moustache and a tan leather jacket loomed in front of her. 'You want taxi?'

She hesitated but he had already picked up her suitcase. 'Come,' he said in a voice not accustomed to contradiction. 'Many drivers in Warsaw not honest. Mafia people. They say taxi but they not.'

For all she knew, he was one of them, but she decided to trust him. It was a cold day with a biting wind that clawed at her face, and under its bruised sky Warsaw looked sad and grey. The old Mercedes had patches of rust on the doors and a manual gearbox that made a grating sound every time the driver changed gear. The buildings that lined the road were all the same height and gave the impression of being one continuous block cut off at regular lengths to allow traffic to pass through. It seemed to Halina that the people on the streets, walking hunched against the cold or stamping their feet as they waited in bus shelters, were as colourless as the buildings. She had hoped to feel a spark of affection, or at least recognition, on returning to the city she had left as a child but it looked foreign and strange.

'So how is life in Poland?' she asked.

'*Proszę pani*,' the taxi driver said, and shrugged. 'Life in Poland is not always bad. Sometimes it is terrible!'

'I thought that now that the communists had gone, things would be much better,' she said.

He gave a loud snort. 'Communists go? Is good if go. But they doesn't go. The jobs change names but people in offices is the same. New government but same faces, *cholera psia krew!*'

His face was red with indignation so she tried another tack. 'But things will be better when Poland joins the European Union, won't they?'

He braked so suddenly that the car swerved. 'Good for who? Is good for me? No. Is good for farmers? No. Is bad for them. Poland will be market for France. For Germany. And who buy from us?'

Pointing to the stepped cement structure that dominated the skyline, the driver sneered, 'A present to people of Warsaw from our beloved Comrade Stalin.'

He continued to expound on Poland's problems, past, present and future, until he pulled up with a lurch under the portico of the Kościuszko Hotel.

'Will you take American dollars?' Halina asked.

'Of course,' he replied with a sardonic smile. 'American dollars we take, Euros we take, Deutschmarks and pounds we take, but Polish zloty we don't like to take.' He shoved the money in his pocket, jumped back into the car and took off so fast that the screech of his tyres echoed around the foyer.

As the car sped into the countryside, Halina saw girls slouching on both sides of the road like wilted sunflowers, turning their heads in the direction of each car as it approached. They pouted and struck sexy poses in their stilt-heeled boots and short skirts. Although the temperature hadn't reached double figures, their skimpy tops exposed white breasts down to their puckered nipples. Halina looked questioningly at her driver.

'Blondes are Ukrainians, brunettes are Bulgarians,' he explained, and shrugged. 'No work over there.'

'So they come to Poland to find a better life,' Halina commented. The women looked young but their faces were hard and defiant. She knew from Claire that the roads of the western world were lined with girls like these, duped by promises of an easy life. 'How much can they make like that?'

'Five dollars. Not for sex but for ...' He struggled for the right word.

'For a blow job?'

He nodded. She shot him a quick look and, as if reading her thoughts, he added, 'The other drivers, they tell me.'

He had been waiting for her in the hotel lobby that morning, the collar of his brown car coat turned up against the cold. '*Pani Halina?*' he asked, coming towards her, hand outstretched. 'I am driver, Jurek is my name. IPN tell me I take you to Nowa Kalwaria.'

'Nowa Kalwaria,' she repeated slowly. New Calvary. A strange name for a town.

Jurek had a round face and the earnest manner of those who leave nothing to chance. As she slid into the back seat of the Mercedes, he handed her a bottle of water for the journey, pulled a map of Poland from the pocket of his car coat and spread it out to show her the route.

'Yesterday I'm checking map to plan how we must go.'

While his finger traced the route towards the north-east, she looked at all the towns, townships, villages and hamlets marked on the map. There were thousands of them, like ants swarming over a honeypot. Every centimetre of this country seemed to be part of some town or village. Accustomed to the vast spaces of Australia, she was astonished at the density of Poland's population. Individuals felt threatened unless they had a certain amount of space around them. What tensions did such close proximity generate?

'Wisła River,' Jurek announced as they crossed the bridge. The torpid flow of the Vistula at this point gave no indication that it bisected the country from north to south. 'Over there is Praga.' He pointed to the other side. 'My father fight in Warsaw Uprising in 1944. He show me, across the river the Russians sit and wait. Here Germans destroy our army, push our people to the countryside and make our city into ruins, but Bolsheviks they do nothing, they drink vodka, smoke their *machorka* and wait. Like spiders.'

Halina frowned, trying to make sense of his version of events. Esther Kennedy had written that at the beginning of the war Russia had sided with Germany, but later the Russians had fought with the Allies.

'So why didn't the Russians help the Poles against the Germans? Weren't they on the same side by then?'

'Russians fight for Russians. Always. They already win war, but they doesn't want Polish resistance. They want when they enter to be boss. No opposition. So they allow Germans to destroy Warsaw.'

He sounded angrier with the Russians for not entering sooner than with the Germans who had wrecked the whole country and terrorised the people for six years. But neither his English nor her Polish was adequate for a political discussion about such a sensitive subject, so she accepted the caramel he offered and looked out of the window.

There was little to catch her eye as they drove out of the city. Above hoardings advertising Nippon Auto, Ikea and McDonald's, the cross on a church spire gleamed in the weak morning sun. On the wall of a grey apartment block where a poster advertised a soccer game, someone had scrawled a large Star of David.

Jurek followed her glance. 'Is not anti-semitic,' he said with a smile. 'Is about soccer competition.'

She shook her head. 'I don't understand. What does a soccer match have to do with religion?'

'The club that is not your club is Jewish.'

'Sorry, I don't get it.'

He tried again. 'My club is Polonia. So we say other club is Jews. All clubs that fight us are Jews. We say so.'

'Do you mean you always call your opponents Jews?'

He nodded. 'Is nothing against Jews. Many peoples doesn't know Jews. Just talk like this.'

Outside the city limits, the Mercedes gathered speed and swallowed up long stretches of road. Stands of trees flashed past. Although it was November and the leaves had dropped off most trees, some still blazed with autumn foliage that took her breath away. Several times she asked Jurek to pull over so that she could photograph the amber and crimson leaves of the maple trees and the sun-drenched birches that shimmered like golden cloaks.

She breathed in the overripe smell of autumn and its underlying odour of decay, and as she kicked up a flurry of leaves an image flashed across her mind. She was running along a carpet of fallen leaves just like these, stopping every few seconds to pick up newly opened chestnuts, her small fingers sliding delightedly over their smooth glossy surface. That must have been in a Warsaw park shortly before they left for Australia. She stood quite still, closed her eyes and sniffed the air, as if the fragrance of dying leaves could evoke memories that eluded her. For the first time since arriving in Poland she felt the nostalgic tug of the past.

Jurek pointed at a flock of small jays overhead. '*Kawki*,' he said as they flew across the fields and became specks in the distance. The click of Halina's camera shutter was the only sound that disturbed the rural silence. She continued gazing at the trees while Jurek stood a small distance away, smoking as he watched her with an indulgent smile.

'*Pani Doktor*, you were born in Poland, yes?' He addressed her in the formal style, through the third person.

'You can call me Halina. In Australia we call each other by our first names. It's friendlier,' she said. 'I was born in Warsaw.'

'But you doesn't speak Polish at home.' It was a statement rather than a question.

She shook her head and turned back to the trees. Her mother's feelings towards her native land were too complicated for a chat with a stranger by the roadside.

He was studying her with his ingenuous gaze. 'What is your work in Nowa Kalwaria?' he asked.

She replaced the lens cap and walked towards him. 'I'll be part of a forensic team, exhuming a mass grave. My job is to examine the teeth we find, to see how many people died there and whether they were adults or children.'

'For who you do this?'

'For the IPN,' she said. 'Your Institute of National Remembrance.'

Jurek looked dubious. 'But for who is good this work?'

It took her a few moments to unravel his syntax. 'Do you mean who will benefit by it?'

'Who will benefit by it,' he repeated, concentrating on each word as if trying to imprint the phrase on his mind.

'Everyone benefits when the truth comes out,' she said.

'Even the dead people?'

'Especially the dead people.'

He studied her for a time before speaking. 'You are lucky person. You are important.'

Her initial reaction was to deflect the compliment and the envy it implied. 'I just do my job,' she said.

Jurek shook his head. 'You go to new country, Australia, and now you do this work in Poland. I stay in Poland and am driver for important people.'

She didn't know what to say and walked slowly towards the car.

He opened the back door for her, but she slid into the seat beside him. Jurek consulted his map, counted out crossroads aloud, and turned off in a north-easterly direction, along a country road where one village succeeded another so fast that Halina barely had time to say the name to herself before it reappeared with a diagonal red stripe across it.

Stands of poplars guarded the entrance and exit to hamlets so small that she wondered how they had managed to exist through the centuries. Probably they had once been estates with fields and forests belonging to the *szlachta*, but what the noble families hadn't squandered, gambled away, pawned or mortgaged, had been confiscated by the communists. Some of the palaces and manor houses had been turned into government offices and all that remained for the descendants of the princes and counts were their hyphenated names and memories of an aristocratic past.

The further they travelled, the further they went back in time. Black and white cows grazed by the roadside near wooden slab huts that hadn't changed in centuries. Untidy nests, vacated by the storks, protruded from the corners of thatched roofs. Halina swivelled her head for another look. When she was small, her mother used to say that a stork had brought her, and she had imagined a bird carrying a swaddled baby in its beak and depositing it inside a house, but this was the first time she had ever seen a stork's nest.

Few cars travelled along this road and occasionally they overtook wooden horse carts with peasant couples riding in front, the man in worn trousers holding the reins and whistling softly to his horse, and the plump babushka beside him, her head covered with a scarf. The fields they passed were bare now. The corn and wheat had long been harvested and the yellow canola too, although here and there bales of hay lay rolled up, waiting to be collected.

Jurek pointed to raised mounds in the fields. '*Kopce,*' he said, surprised she wasn't familiar with the word. An outdoor potato cellar, he explained, to protect the potatoes from the frost and stop them rotting.

A farmer and his wife, bent over the black soil and pulling out beets, looked up when they heard the car and waved. '*Szczęść Boże,*' the woman called out — the traditional blessing. She wore rubber boots, a man's woollen jacket whose sleeves hung over her hands, and thick woollen stockings under her long skirt.

Along a stretch of road that skirted dark pine forests, old village women draped in shawls stood in a row, waving to them.

'Ukrainians or Bulgarians?' Halina joked.

Laughing, Jurek shook his head. 'These ladies all Polish. They sell mushrooms. Look.' He slowed down and she saw punnets of mushrooms with creamy tops stacked on the grassy verge.

Not long after they had arrived in Sydney, her mother had found out that wild mushrooms grew in the woods around Oberon. At Easter time, after the autumn rains, she would take the train west and return with a sack full of mushrooms that never appeared in the shops. Some had wide parasol caps that were salmon pink in colour, and when she cut them they leaked juice the colour of fresh blood. Others were soft and slippery to touch. Wild mushrooms could poison you or cause hallucinations, but Zosia seemed to know which ones were safe to pick and preserve in jars. She marinated them in vinegar, oil and garlic and added bay leaves, but said their flavour didn't compare to Polish mushrooms. Were Polish mushrooms really so good?

'Mmm,' Jurek murmured. '*Prawdziwki* are the best. I buy for my wife.'

He jumped out of the car and she watched him select several punnets with the care of a connoisseur. There was a heated discussion about the price, but he was beaming when he returned to the car. 'For you,' he said, handing her a punnet overflowing with mushrooms. She buried her face in them and breathed in their earthy woodland smell.

Jurek gave her an approving smile. 'If you will come here in summer, we shall buy blueberries and *poziomki* from the woods.'

The memory of wild strawberries flashed across her mind, and her mouth filled with the bittersweet flavour of the small berries that were more scented than roses.

At many crossroads they passed roadside shrines wreathed with garlands of fresh flowers. Inside one recess, the Virgin Mary cradled her infant; in another, Christ hung from a large cross, his thorn-crowned head drooping to the right and a crimson gash in his side.

'The villagers bring flowers to ask *Matka Boska* for something, or to thank her for answering their prayers,' Jurek explained.

Once again he stopped to check his map, confused by the directions. 'One, two three...' He counted the crossroads. 'Ah, now we turn right.'

The narrow dirt road that led to Nowa Kalwaria was muddy and rutted and as the car lurched from one pothole to another, Jurek muttered, '*Cholera psia krew!*' Turning to her with a mischievous look he asked, 'Do you know what means that?'

She nodded. 'In English we say bloody hell. And if we're very angry we say fucking hell.'

He repeated this to memorise it. 'Facking hell.' She tried to correct his pronunciation but gave up, laughing.

As he swung the steering wheel to avoid a deep pothole, the car skidded. He looked agonised as the spotless bodywork was spattered with thick mud. Halina was about to commiserate when suddenly she blanched and shouted, 'Jurek! Stop! Look!'

He pulled up so fast that she bumped her head.

She pointed at something on the road. 'There!' Her voice was trembling. 'A red puddle!'

He looked around. 'Red? Where?'

She was still staring and her voice was low and urgent. 'There! Oh, can't you see it? Just in front of us. Bright red. It looks like blood.'

Jurek was shaking his head. 'Is water.'

Halina turned to face him, her face ashen. 'It's blood,' she whispered. 'I know it is.'

But when she looked at the road again, all she saw was a pool of muddy water.

Thirteen

Inside the presbytery, Father Krzysztof Kowalczyk sucked a lump of sugar as he sipped the scalding black tea that his housekeeper had made for him and absent-mindedly chewed a doughnut filled with rose-petal jam. In front of him lay the bishop's latest dispatch but his attention continually strayed to the window. If he had been blessed with artistic talents, and enough time to indulge them, he would have liked to paint the way the shafts of sunlight slanted between the branches of the maple trees and filigreed the lawn with light and shade. The pattern altered with the drifting of the clouds and the leaves that pirouetted to the ground like miniature ballerinas, and he wondered how artists ever managed to capture a moment in time when the landscape changed while you watched.

The Almighty had created a world of infinite variation and awesome splendour, and even the simple daisies that grew wild in the fields were miracles of perfection, but the more enthralled he became by nature, the less time he had to gaze at its wonders. Perhaps he was growing senile but sometimes he wondered whether the good Lord was disappointed that people spent so little time marvelling at the world He had created for them. He shook his white head and, with a sigh, turned back to his correspondence. His bishop too was a creature of God, and as such merited respect, even if Father Krzysztof privately regarded him as one of the Almighty's less successful creations.

From the bishop's letter it appeared that a group of experts was about to descend on the village. 'Interlopers' was the way Bishop Lewicki described them in his typically brusque fashion. He could hardly have sounded more antagonistic had they been terrorists. According to him, they were coming at the instigation of an organisation of professional busybodies who had taken it upon themselves to poke about and disturb the living and the dead. This was totally unacceptable, the bishop wrote. The dead should be allowed to rest in peace, even if they did belong to the Mosaic faith.

He instructed his parish priest to answer no questions about this regrettable affair, and give no assistance 'whatsoever' to these 'blow-ins' from Warsaw. The word whatsoever was printed in large capitals. Father Krzysztof chuckled. Subtlety was not the bishop's strong point. He concluded the letter by impugning Warsaw's motives in stirring up a hornet's nest in his diocese and blamed 'Polaphobic foreign elements' for causing trouble in Poland.

There was a soft tap at the door. '*Proszę księdza*,' the housekeeper excused herself.

'Ah, *gosposia*!' He smiled as she padded in to remove the plates.

'Reverend Father didn't eat all the doughnuts!' she chided.

He patted his stomach. 'I'm getting too fat,' he said. 'A priest should set an example in moderation, not advertise gluttony!' He couldn't tell her that a message from the bishop always took his appetite away.

A flock of crows flew past the window and their raucous screeching made him look up from the letter. He too was puzzled by the impending investigation. After all, everyone knew what had happened here during the war. The plaque made it painfully clear. In June 1941, the Nazis had locked the Jews in a barn and set it on fire. The priest had grown up in this place, and as a child he had occasionally overheard the adults whispering about the incident. His mother had said that the smell of burnt flesh hung over the town for years afterwards, but when he asked her what human flesh smelled like, she hadn't answered.

He recalled an incident that had taken place in the woods when he was very young. He had been playing with the village boys as usual when Wojtek, the mayor's son, opened a sack he had brought. Four mewling kittens wriggled inside, a tangle of fluff. Taking out a box of matches, Wojtek had said, 'Let's play Jews!' and suddenly there was an air of breathless excitement, of something forbidden about to happen. Wojtek struck a match and grabbed one of the shivering creatures, but it lashed out with a yowl and clawed his hand, and when he dropped the sack the others escaped.

It was a moment that Father Krzysztof scourged himself with whenever he caught himself judging others. He had shared that guilty moment of heart-thumping anticipation with the other boys, and, like them, had trembled on the brink of blood-lust. Only chance had prevented him from being involved in a cruel and despicable act. Even now, after so many years, his skin prickled at the memory of that shameful corner of his soul that had been impervious to the whispers of conscience.

And now he was back in the village where he had grown up. He had left it as a young boy bound for the seminary and had returned after all this time to become its parish priest. For as long as he could remember, he had known he would become a priest, but why that vocation had manifested itself at a young age, he couldn't say. As a small boy, the rituals of Catholicism had enthralled him. The smell of the incense that curled up from the censers the altar boys carried, and the drama of the Mass when the priest raised the chalice and the wafer and offered the body and blood of Christ. Most of all, he had been awed by the hypnotic solemnity of the language. Although he hadn't understood it, the sonorous Latin words excited him. They were a secret code whose mastery might ensure passage into a mysterious world.

'Ever since you were small, I could see that Our Lord smiled on you. Thank God you recognised your calling,' his mother had said, weeping with joy when he announced his decision. 'I used to pray to the Holy Virgin that you would have the vocation, and she has answered my prayers.' Perhaps he had intuited his parents' unspoken wish.

'Krzysio is with the Jesuits,' they told everyone with enormous pride, because the Jesuits were the clever priests and only accepted the brightest boys into their order.

His vocation kept him away from home for many years. No sooner had he settled down and grown close to the people of one parish than he was moved to another. Sometimes he wondered if the bishops deliberately transferred priests so that they would not form close attachments to their flock, especially to the women who, if the truth were told, seemed to find priests, especially young ones, sinfully attractive.

A priest needed strong resolve to turn his back on pretty young women who confessed their fantasies in lascivious detail in the privacy of the confessional, or called at the presbytery to discuss their marital problems with downcast eyes. Some of them clung to their confessor's hand too long and kissed it more passionately than religious fervour demanded.

He knew that many of his colleagues betrayed their vows by sleeping with their housekeepers, widows or spinsters only too happy to fulfil the physical needs of the spiritual pastor of the community. At first he had been shocked by the prevalence of these liaisons, but with advancing years he had decided it was probably the least harmful course of action for all concerned. Although he had never succumbed to sexual temptation himself, and made a habit of employing old women with no physical charms, like his present *gosposia*, he doubted whether Our Lord would condemn a good man who had found solace with another lonely soul. Human failings seemed relatively minor in the scheme of things, when one considered the crime and suffering all over the world.

'*Gosposiu!*' he called. She must have been very close by because she poked her head around the door straightaway. 'What do they say in the village about these scientific experts who are about to descend on us?' he asked.

From the look on her face, she knew plenty and he invited her to sit down on one of the dark high-backed mahogany chairs carved in the German style that he had inherited from his predecessor, a dour priest from Gdansk. His housekeeper knew everything about everybody and, being comparatively new in town, he was not averse to pumping her for information, although he often sensed that she knew far more than she revealed. In the short time he had been here, he had already heard enough about the parishioners' private lives to write several sensational novels. Everyone had guilty secrets, and it seemed that the smaller the place, the bigger the secrets. But although they confessed their sins, when it came to expressing their opinions about political or ethnic matters, he knew that they held back, uncertain where he stood.

'Everyone's up in arms about it,' she said, folding her arms over her ample stomach. 'They reckon it's all because of the Jews.'

He nodded to encourage her to continue. 'And why is that?'

'Because they're always trying to blacken our name. That's what the butcher said when I stopped by for your pork chop for lunch,' she lisped, her tongue catching in the gap in her top teeth.

'And what do the others say?'

'The grocer's daughter in Chicago sent him the latest Polish newspapers which said that American Jews are always causing trouble for us Poles.'

'In what way?'

She hesitated. 'I couldn't say, Reverend Father. That's what I heard.'

He smiled at her indulgently and she flushed. Father Krzysztof had a way of looking at you as if he could read your mind. Everyone knew that the Jesuits were the brainy ones. That's what she had confided to the haberdasher's wife that morning, giving the impression that some of that acuity had rubbed off on her.

Her employer hadn't finished the conversation. 'Did anyone suggest why American Jews would want to start this investigation in our town?'

She sat forward and dropped her voice. 'They're saying it's a conspiracy to make out that it wasn't the Germans who killed those Jews during the war, but the Poles.'

'And what do you think?'

She looked down at her hands. '*Proszę księdza*, I'm not an educated woman, but I know this much. In the old times, when Jews lived among us, everyone lived in peace. Jews had their holidays, we had ours. They had their shops, we had ours. We knew each other. But when things got bad, people blamed the Jews. And now there aren't any of them left, but they're still getting blamed for everything.' She looked as though she were about to say something else but rose heavily to her feet. 'I'd better go and crumb those pork chops or there won't be any dinner.'

Father Krzysztof had experienced several emotions when he received the order to return to Nowa Kalwaria, but joy was not one of them. A transfer from a large town to a remote village could hardly be construed as a tribute to one's intellectual achievements or a reward for a lifetime's devoted service. Nowa Kalwaria was as much a backwater now as it had always been, and he felt deflated to be posted there at the end of his career.

God had His reasons, and there was always a lesson to be learnt from being humbled, but in the deepest recess of his heart he was disappointed. Nearing sixty, he had expected to be allowed to end his ecclesiastical duties in the parish where he had nestled in like a mouse behind a warm stove for the past fifteen years. Nowy Targ was a peaceful mountain town with a river flowing through it. He had spent many happy hours fishing there, like Our Lord had done in Galilee, casting out his rod and pulling out fat carp that his *gosposia* baked in many delicious ways. He had established the best choir in the diocese, rebuilt the church and enjoyed his game of bridge every Tuesday evening, never dreaming that he would have to uproot himself and become the parish priest of a place that had recently become synonymous with Holocaust crimes. 'I feel like going to Nowa Kalwaria about as much as a naked man feels like walking through a field of nettles,' he had confided to his young vicar. On reflection, it had been an apt comparison.

He had decided to throw himself on the bishop's mercy. Perhaps if Bishop Jagoda was made aware of his age, of his attachment to Nowy Targ and the tricky situation in Nowa Kalwaria, surely he would realise that an energetic young priest would be far more suitable. He wrote a letter requesting an audience and, to emphasise his connection with his parish, signed it Krzysztof Kowalczyk, parish priest of Nowy Targ.

Bishop Jagoda, a man with the elegant bearing and knowing expression of the Borgia popes, had summoned him to his imposing residence. With an urbane smile he greeted the priest with the words, 'We are delighted to welcome the parish priest of Nowa Kalwaria!' Father Krzysztof's well-rehearsed pleas fell on deaf ears. Cutting him short, the bishop said, 'That parish needs someone with the wisdom of Solomon and the understanding of a saint. Since neither are available, we have selected you.'

Father Krzysztof wondered now whether part of the reason for the transfer had been the hope that he would counteract the notorious bishop of the local diocese, whose pronouncements on political and religious issues had made him a rallying point for the ultra-nationalists. Although some admired Bishop Lewicki as a fearless patriot who was unafraid to speak his mind on contentious matters, others regarded him as a religious dinosaur, an anachronism stuck in the racist swamps of a bygone age.

With his advancing years Franciszek Lewicki's ideas had become more extreme. He was a divisive force at a time when the saintly Pope, a Pole like themselves, was wearing out his shrunken body and failing heart in the attempt to foster a spirit of reconciliation. Instead of using his power to raise the standard of moral behaviour and foster brotherly love as Our Lord had instructed, the bishop was stirring up chauvinism and religious intolerance.

Although Father Krzysztof had reminded himself that hubris precedes nemesis, bowing to the will of God had failed to lighten his spirit on the journey to Nowa Kalwaria. The place was even more miserable than he had remembered. There was no doubt that the prestige of the priest increased in inverse relation to the size of the locality and Father Krzysztof was not averse to wielding power, although he preferred to think of it as benevolent influence.

His expert eye had soon sized up the parishioners. Every town and village, whatever its size, contained similar groups. There were the sycophants with calculating eyes who presented him with home-baked yeast cakes, plum *povidl* and legs of smoked ham, along with gossip about their rivals and the hope of insinuating themselves into his favour to advance their own agenda. Then there were the genuine devotees, mostly elderly women who flocked to church every Sunday and hung on his every word; the politicians eager to convert him to their cause; and the secularists who enjoyed his conversation and tolerated his status but kept away from the church.

Father Krzysztof glanced at his watch. He had made an appointment to talk to the headmistress about the curriculum that afternoon but there would still be time to drop in and see his mother. Widowed many years before, she was in poor health and the opportunity of spending time with her was the only benefit he could see of returning to Nowa Kalwaria.

Closing the door of the presbytery behind him, he paused and filled his lungs with cool draughts of autumn air. He looked across at the old church which had stood there since the sixteenth century. A turbulent time, he reflected, but which era of Polish history had been free of conflict? His mind ran through centuries of wars, partitions, annexations, insurrections and invasions by Tartars, Russians, Swedes, Austrians and Germans, who had trampled across these fields and watered them with blood and tears.

Rousing himself from his historical contemplation, he glanced at the notices pasted to the church wall, announcing forthcoming ecclesiastical events. Volunteers were sought to work on the manger and to decorate the Christmas tree, and he realised with a shock that the holy season of Christmas would soon be upon them.

As he crossed the square with his energetic gait, his long cassock swished against the cement path that bisected it. These days the square was planted with beech and maple trees, but when he was a boy it had been roughly paved with cobblestones that resounded with the wooden wheels of farmers' carts on market day. The two women in shawls who inclined their heads as he passed looked exactly like the women he remembered there forty years ago.

'*Szczęść Boże.*' He greeted the women with the traditional blessing, making a sign of the cross.

'*Daj Boże,*' they murmured in reply. One of them whispered something to her companion and they turned back to look at him. With his thick white hair brushed forward onto a narrow face with its aquiline nose, the new priest had an air of distinction.

He slackened his pace and thought he heard the wheels rumbling over the cobblestones once more and the shouts of the peasants calling out to passers-by to buy their chickens and cheeses. As a boy, he had heard that the Jews had once had shops and stalls surrounding the square, but they had all gone by the time he accompanied his mother to market. Sometimes she would mention Berish the baker, Chajcia the dressmaker and Yankel the miller — strange names that evoked exotic characters from fairy tales rather than living souls who had once inhabited his town. Her eyes would close with blissful recollection when she told him about the vanilla ice-cream that Avram used to make. 'That was the creamiest ice-cream you can imagine, heaven on your tongue, much better than the ones they make today,' she would recall. When she was in a good mood she would recite a ditty that she and the other children used to chant:

Avram młody,
kręci lody
aż mu zmarzną
ręce i nogi.

As she clapped her hands in time to the beat, he tried to visualise the strangely named Avram mixing ice-cream until his hands and feet were frozen.

Father Krzysztof turned onto the road that skirted the bare brown potato fields, striding along the centre to avoid loose stones and gravel. He stopped and looked around. Near this spot he used to swim in a pond with the other boys on hot summer days, throwing off their clothes, leaping in, splashing and shouting. Sometimes they would hide behind the hazel bushes to watch the girls. If they were lucky, they were rewarded with a flash of white buttock or a soft pink breast, enough to keep them whispering in excited voices for days.

His old friends had all married village girls and raised families, and most of them had moved to the towns years ago. Although he regretted nothing and had no wish to change his destiny, he wondered how his life would have turned out if he had not recognised and surrendered to his calling. There was no trace of the pond now and the abandoned mill at the crossroads mouldered above a muddy swamp. This stretch of road was desolate with marshy soil, straggly weeds and spindly bushes. Had his long absence confused him, or had the pond dried up and disappeared along with the summer days of his youth?

Past the stand of rowan trees, whose sour orange berries he and his playmates had used as pellets, he came to his old home and pushed open the wooden gate. A wisp of smoke from the chimney curled towards the sky. The thatched roof had been replaced with shingles, but otherwise the cottage had not changed. Inside, beneath the picture of the Virgin, his mother sat hunched in her chair in front of the tiled stove, a shawl around her thin shoulders, an eiderdown on her lap and a rosary in her roughened hands. Each time he saw her, her frailty shocked him. She seemed to be shrinking from day to day.

He made the sign of the cross above her head. '*Mamo*, how are you feeling today?'

Her sunken eyes lit up, as they always did when she saw him. 'Better now you're here, *synku*,' she whispered and broke into a paroxysm of coughing. He couldn't help smiling that at his advanced age, with his white hair, his mother still called him her little son.

'I think the Lord will take me very soon,' she said, looking into his face with the fearless candour he had always admired.

'Nonsense, *Mamo*. He needs several more years to go through all your sins.'

She chuckled. 'I only hope I die before Satan finds out!' They always joked like this. 'I'm ninety-one, God has had long enough to tally up the score! Besides, I've taken up space in the world long enough.' The smile faded. 'I'm almost ready to go,' she said.

He waited.

She fluttered her translucent hand in a weak motion. 'Sit here beside me.'

When he drew up a wooden chair, her keen eye noticed that he was sitting on the edge. 'I suppose you're rushing off somewhere this afternoon?'

While he was explaining about his meeting with the head-mistress, she sank back against her pillow. When she closed her eyes, the blue-veined lids resembled crumpled tissue paper.

Clasping her cold bony hand in his warm one, he leant towards her as she spoke in a breathless voice that was almost inaudible. '*Synku*, next time stay a little longer. There is something I've been meaning to tell you.'

The light outside was fading and the trees swayed and soughed in the wind. He sat for several minutes without speaking, listening to her laboured breathing while the branches of the rowanberry trees banged against the window pane. Then he raised her limp hand to his lips and pressed a kiss on it. '*Mamo*, next time I come, we'll talk for hours.'

Walking slowly towards the school, he wondered if some minor transgression committed long ago was weighing on her conscience. Over the years he had noticed that willpower often kept people alive long past their doctors' most optimistic predictions. Sometimes it was the desire to wait for the birth of a grandchild, or the return of a long-absent son. Even on their deathbeds, people delayed the final moment until the priest arrived so that they could meet their maker with a cleansed soul. Having to perform that service for his own mother would be a painful blessing.

Lost in his thoughts, he didn't hear the car coming towards him or see its lights until it swerved to avoid him, skidded and screeched to a halt. As he stood motionless with shock at his narrow escape, he saw the driver's alarmed expression and, beside him, a pale, anxious face pressed against the windshield. A moment later a tall woman was standing beside him, her oval face full of concern.

'Are you all right?' she asked. 'Can we give you a lift?'

Although she wasn't young, she had a youthful energy that was appealing. He wondered about her strange Polish accent and her ignorance of the correct form of address when speaking to a priest.

He shook his head. 'Thank you, but I need the exercise. Walking helps to clear the cobwebs from my muddled old head!'

As they drove off, he noticed that the Mercedes had a Warsaw number plate.

Fourteen

Nowa Kalwaria sprang up around its market square out of the commercial turmoil of the Middle Ages. Not long after it had received its town charter, a church was erected with a steeple that towered over the countryside to remind the villagers that there was a higher power to account to than the one that tempted them with material comfort. Jews who had been banished from other regions settled here, encouraged by Nowa Kalwaria's acceptance, and as soon as their numbers grew sufficiently they built their wooden synagogue.

As centuries rolled on, craftsmen tooled leather and carved wood in their huts and peasants continued to eke out a miserly existence in this somnolent backwater, tilling the soil, unaware of the industrial revolution that had exploded in western Europe. Nothing changed in Nowa Kalwaria, until the head of the noble family that owned its fields and hunted boar in its forests visited the city of Lodz. Dazed by the bustling activity caused by machines that produced fabrics with a speed and accuracy that seemed miraculous, he resolved to industrialise the village and transform the inhabitants into textile manufacturers.

Within a few years shuttles flew, looms clattered and machines whirred out of a hundred workshops as the master craftsmen of Nowa Kalwaria produced silk that became the wonder of the region. And the more the township prospered, the faster its population grew. Textile-workers as well as leather-workers, lace-makers, carpenters and goldsmiths came from miles around. In time, the textile factories of Nowa Kalwaria diversified and turned out tricot stockings and gloves. But it takes far less time to destroy than to build, and by the end of World War I Russian armies had trampled back and forth over the town, demolishing most of its houses and ruining its industries. Many of the inhabitants moved away and a sad, neglected air settled over the place which was not dispelled even after some families began to trickle back.

On her first stroll through the township Halina failed to detect any of the energy that must have fuelled Nowa Kalwaria in bygone days. In fact, its subdued, almost apologetic air reminded her of a depressed person shuffling around with downcast eyes. Spindly weeds pushed up through the paving in the village square and there were no benches where people could chat or contemplate in solitude.

Pinned onto the thickest trunks of the trees were election posters with slogans that urged people to vote for the League of Polish Families, whose slogan was *'Polska dla Polakow'* — Poland for the Poles.

It was difficult to imagine a time when this had been a bustling commercial place, surrounded by workshops where tailors had stitched suits by hand, cobblers had mended boots and ironmongers had soldered pots. In the stores, keen shoppers had examined and bargained over bolts of cloth, fine lace and leather belts. But most of the people Halina saw walked with the slow gait of those who have little joy to look back on and still less to look forward to.

On one corner, a man in a beige windcheater removed his stained cap to scratch his head and raised his hand to greet an elderly man riding the kind of bicycle that Australian workmen rode during the Depression. An elderly woman wrapped in a brown shawl was walking towards her, carrying a string bag. As she furtively glanced at Halina, a startled look appeared on her face and she crossed herself, her wrinkled lips moving as though reciting a prayer. A moment later, she was gone.

The small wooden houses around the square were built of weathered planks set horizontally under pointed roofs, like the houses that small children draw. There was something mean-spirited and secretive about these dwellings, Halina thought, as she entered a dark grocery shop where the merchandise was displayed on wooden shelves or lay in boxes on the scuffed linoleum floor.

The woman behind the counter shot her a questioning look. Halina bought a carton of raspberry juice and left, feeling the woman's eyes boring into the back of her head. Outside, two old men with purple veins on their cheeks and cauliflower noses lounged against the lamppost. They nudged each other as she approached and stared at her long after she had passed.

The church bell rang and she looked up at the only structure in town that was visible above the houses. Neatly painted behind its wrought-iron railing, the church was a handsome white building with two towers topped by baroque copper domes. Pasted onto a noticeboard outside was a poster of a woman sitting by a sickbed, with the message 'Faith works through love'. No matter where you went in the world, it was always the women who were expected to fulfil the ideal of compassion and care-giving.

The vibrations from the bell trembled in the air and Halina felt the sound waves rippling against her skin. How quaint to live in a place where the church could be seen from every part of town and its bells heard all over the surrounding countryside. Back in the days when illiterate peasants knew only what they were told in church, the priests in these communities had wielded enormous power, but she imagined that this must have changed now that people were educated and had access to mass media. Still, if the locals in the square were any indication, it didn't look as though the people in this remote rural community were very receptive to new ideas.

Although winter had not yet set in, the cold here in the north was penetrating and the wind seemed to blow unchecked from the Siberian wastes across the steppes and deserts of Central Asia. It pierced her bones and chilled her marrow, and as she pulled up the collar of her cashmere coat she regretted her decision to accept this assignment. Hopefully the exhumation wouldn't take long and she would soon be able to leave this bleak place.

It was late afternoon and there was time for a stroll before the welcome dinner at the council chambers. Around the corner from the church, she wandered down a crooked street. It was deserted. She was peering into a yard heaped with wooden crates and old rubber tyres when a fierce black dog rushed out from behind the wood shed, barking hysterically. She started as it leapt up and snapped at her through the fence, saliva dribbling from a mouth full of sharp teeth. 'Shut up, you lousy cur!' a man yelled from inside the house, and came out into the yard, brandishing a stick. The dog stopped barking and slunk back into its kennel.

In the distance, Halina saw fields and headed towards them. The lane narrowed into a dirt track and her high heels crunched over the packed earth and loose gravel. On either side of this lonely path, potato fields stretched towards the horizon. A man leant out of the window of his wooden farmhouse, looked up and down the path, spat and went back inside. She heard the burr of an engine and, shielding her eyes, spotted a farmer ploughing with an old tractor whose wheezing motor chugged over the field. A woman wrapped in a woollen shawl trudged along the path towards her, her crooked legs encased in woollen stockings. In her bony hand she held a switch that she applied to the rumps of two black and white cows that looked better fed than their owner. Halina smiled but there was no corresponding smile on the woman's face.

A few metres on, she felt a sharp pain in her foot, and saw that a stone had become lodged in the sole of her shoe. Stopping to remove it, she leant against the paling fence around a farmhouse where a pot of scarlet geraniums stood on a windowsill. As she hopped on one leg to put her shoe back on, she thought she saw someone move at the window. The white lace curtain behind the flowerpot fluttered, the shadow disappeared and there was no other sign of life inside the house.

The path ended abruptly at a low wall that enclosed what appeared to be an overgrown paddock. Curious, Halina pushed open the wooden gate. It scraped against the ground. A moment later she jumped back, startled by the flapping of black wings overhead. She had disturbed two ravens in their search for food. The hazel bushes in the field had become so intertwined that she had to push them aside to pass. As she parted the tangled bare branches and squeezed through, she stubbed her toe and looked down.

Concealed by the undergrowth, a slab of pitted stone, tilted to one side, protruded from the ground into which part of it had sunk. Jade-coloured lichens, smooth to the touch, covered one side of the rough granite surface. When she bent down for a closer look, she noticed that something had been chiselled into the stone. It was so weathered that the letters were hardly discernible but from their shape she guessed they were in Hebrew.

Pushing her way through the thorny brambles and hazel bushes, she came across other stones, more sunken than the first. She was able to make out part of a candelabra on one piece of granite, and urns and lions' heads on others — emblems she found strange. If this was a Jewish cemetery, where were all the tombstones? She looked around, but apart from the broken stone fragments saw nothing to indicate that people had been buried here.

A thick layer of wet black leaves exuded the musty smell of mildew and rotting vegetation. The light was fading and a chilly dampness rose from the ground. As Halina's heels sank into marshy patches, she shivered, wondering what lay beneath her feet.

She felt a sudden compulsion to get away, but when she turned to leave she couldn't move. She tried to pull away but invisible fingers clutched her, pinning her to the spot. Her heart pounded in terror as she mustered all her strength to extricate herself, finally stumbling forward as the grip was released. She looked back and saw that her assailant was the sharp end of a branch that had snagged her coat. Piqued that she had been spooked by imaginary ghosts, she walked briskly towards the gate.

She had almost reached it when she stopped in front of the only hazel bush that hadn't lost its foliage. Its leaves resembled flakes of sunlit amber. Suspended from the branches by invisible tendrils, the pointed leaves twirled gently in the air, and clung to the rough branches, defying fate and gravity. The heavy clouds parted for a moment and a shaft of late afternoon sunlight burnished the hazel bush until it seemed to be on fire.

Transfixed by the incandescent leaves glowing in the ruined cemetery, Halina stood there until the last rays had faded and a murky light descended over the fields.

The local council, the *Rada*, was housed in a plain rectangular building whose functional style and lack of any embellishment proclaimed its communist origin. Inside the council chambers, the mayor, Aleksander Wojciechowski, bowed and kissed her hand, surprising her with an old-world gesture that she thought would have disappeared long ago. She could imagine what her feminist friends like Claire would say about a custom that implied that women were the weaker sex, to be admired, courted and placed on a pedestal.

'*Pani Doktor*,' Mayor Wojciechowski was saying, 'on behalf of the council, I'd like to welcome you to our town and say how deeply honoured we are by your presence.'

With his thick dark hair parted on one side and a handlebar moustache, she could imagine him as a soldier in Kościuszko's army, breaking girls' hearts in his shiny leather boots and gold epaulettes as he rode a galloping steed and flourished a sabre.

'I hear that you — I mean someone told me, you were born in Poland.' It was Kazimierz Borowski, the deputy mayor, a man with a meaty complexion and a balding head beaded with perspiration. 'So I ... that is, I mean we — we hope you will understand our difficult situation here.'

Before Halina could ask what he meant, the mayor led her away and introduced the rest of the council. Polish didn't come easily to her and, to make it more difficult, they spoke it here with a slow eastern drawl. She was about to ask one of the councillors to repeat what he had said when all eyes turned to the door. In his long vestments and skull cap, Bishop Lewicki was a commanding presence and one by one they knelt and kissed his ring. When it was Halina's turn to be introduced, she inclined her head and shook the extended hand but declined to genuflect or kiss the symbol of spiritual power.

The bishop observed her with calculating eyes, his small white hands resting on his protruding belly. 'So this is our charming forensic expert from Australia!' he boomed. 'We are counting on you to come up with the right answers and put an end to this disgraceful affair once and for all.'

He turned to the deputy mayor. 'No doubt you have explained the situation for Dr Shore so that she is in full possession of all the facts?'

Flustered, Borowski flushed to the roots of his receding hair. 'I haven't — what I mean to say is, not yet, Your Excellency.'

The bishop's eyes narrowed. 'Make sure you do. We wouldn't want her to get the wrong idea from other people.' His lips were smiling but his eyes were hard as they flicked to the mayor.

Halina was relieved when Andrzej Stolarz, the leader of the Polish forensic team, arrived. Small-town politics were always a minefield and she had no intention of becoming involved in the petty squabbles and rivalries of Nowa Kalwaria. The bishop was still talking to the deputy mayor and she extricated herself from their company and turned to her colleague.

'Have you been to the site yet?' he asked. From his rapid speech and the restless way he looked around, she sensed that he felt more at ease in the field than at receptions.

Andrzej Stolarz was Poland's leading forensic archaeologist and had worked on the exhumation of the grave in Katyń, which had proved that over 20,000 Polish officers killed during World War II had been shot by Russians soldiers, and not by the Germans as the Russians had claimed.

'They all seem very worked up over this exhumation,' Halina said, indicating the group talking and gesticulating nearby.

'We're between Scylla and Charybdis here,' Andrzej whispered, his deep-set eyes roaming around the room. 'But Charybdis hasn't arrived yet. They'll be here tomorrow when we begin uncovering the site.'

Seeing her perplexed expression, he explained, 'The IPN people. Institute of National Remembrance. The ones in charge of the investigation and the exhumation, who got our team together.'

Some aspects of this investigation puzzled Halina. Wartime atrocities committed by locals against Jewish civilians had already been investigated in the Ukraine, but this was the first time she had come across such an investigation on Polish soil. What made it even more unusual was that the investigation had been initiated and organised by the Polish government. Then there was the curious timing, so long after the event. She frowned. 'What made them decide to investigate this affair now, after all this time?'

Before Andrzej could reply, the deputy mayor announced that dinner was served.

'Would you — that is, what I mean to say is, could you do me the honour of sitting between me and our worthy mayor?' he said to Halina.

The bishop had left to attend an ecclesiastical meeting in Warsaw so she assumed that the purpose of his brief appearance at the council chambers had been to declare his commitment and enlist support for his cause.

Under the Polish national emblem of the silver eagle on the red and white flag, the long table almost filled the spartan dining room. On the walls hung photographs of the Polish president and Pope John Paul II, taken during his recent visit to his homeland. The middle-aged waitress who served mushroom soup and crumbed pork chops with sauerkraut had trouble manoeuvring in the narrow space between the wall and the chairs, especially when she was called repeatedly to replenish glasses with vodka.

After they had drunk toasts to Poland and Nowa Kalwaria, the mayor rose and proposed a toast to truth, justice and reconciliation. In the instant before everyone raised their glasses, Halina noticed deputy mayor Borowski and one of his councillors exchange glances across the table.

'Everyone knows that the Germans committed the crime here, dear lady,' Borowski said. His face flushed with alcohol, he no longer stammered and his face was so uncomfortably close to hers that the sharp alcohol on his breath stung her eyes. 'We are at a loss to understand why the IPN in its wisdom has decided to waste its money on this matter. They should be investigating the crimes of the communists against the Polish population, not the death of a few communists at the hands of the Nazis.'

Halina couldn't conceal her astonishment. 'The death of a few communists?'

He took another swig of vodka and nodded. 'Everyone knows that the Germans were responsible for what happened here, but some troublemakers in America have created a sensation with their lies about this town. *Cholera psia krew.* Pardon my language, but that's all they are, bloody lies.'

Several questions sprang to her mind but she chose the least confronting one. 'Why do you think they spread these lies?' she asked.

'To make trouble for us Poles,' he said triumphantly. 'That's what the Jewish Polaphobes do all the time.'

The mayor, who had been talking to Andrzej, had also heard his deputy's comments. He turned towards Halina.

'Whatever the truth is, you and Mr Stolarz will dig it up with your spades, and then no one will be able to argue,' he said pleasantly.

His deputy flushed and, as he turned away, again she caught the meaningful look between him and his colleague on the other side of the table.

Fifteen

A policeman in a lime green vest scrutinised Halina at the checkpost set up at the entrance to the exhumation site.

'Ah, *medycyna sądowa*,' he said, waving her through as soon as his eyes slid to the words Forensic Medicine emblazoned on her royal blue overalls. The site was located at the end of the dirt path facing the abandoned cemetery but she had been so intrigued by the graveyard with its broken headstones that she had failed to notice the area nearby which was cordoned off with perimeter tape.

Even before she reached it, she heard scraping sounds as the workmen in navy blue caps, denim overalls and protective gloves pushed their spades into the ground and emptied the soil into wheelbarrows. Andrzej, in a squashed white hat, was crouched beside the test trench they had dug, examining a sample of soil in the cylindrical probe he had bored into the ground.

'This is agricultural loam weathered into the windblown loess of the last glaciation. It's not the kind of soil where you'd expect soft tissue to survive.' He was speaking rapidly to his two students, Marta and Stefan, who were nodding thoughtfully.

Andrzej rarely gave permission for students to attend the exhumations of mass graves because of their distressing nature, but he had made an exception in the case of these postgraduates.

'We are looking for changes in soil colour and texture,' he said. Ramming his hat lower over his forehead, he continued. 'It's impossible to conceal a grave, especially a mass grave. See how the darker soil and the lighter clay layers are mixed together? That happens when soil is disturbed during burial.'

Halina glanced around the site. Somewhere in this dark soil, among the skulls and skeletons, criminology intersected with history, religion, sociology and psychology. Would they be able to unravel these tightly interwoven strands of the past? Every contact leaves a trace, as Edmond Locard, the father of criminology, had stated a hundred years before. But the interpretation of those traces relied to a large extent on human powers of observation and deduction as well as on attitudes and convictions. In a case like this, where emotions ran high and so much depended on the outcome, it would be difficult to remain objective and narrow the margin between fact and hypothesis.

A big bear-like man was striding around the perimeter, head bent, intent on two metal prongs that he held in front of him. As Halina came towards him he straightened up and adjusted the small black scullcap nestling in his bushy hair. With his serene smile and mass of tight curls, he reminded her of Californian hippies of the 1970s.

'Have you met Rabbi Silverstein?' Andrzej asked her, indicating the stranger. 'He's here to supervise the exhumation.'

Marta, the personification of the blonde, blue-eyed image of a Polish girl, was staring at the prongs. 'Are we looking for water?' she whispered behind her hand.

'No, we're looking for bodies!' Rabbi Silverstein boomed in a cheerful voice. 'The divining rods respond to a change in the soil mass. If the mass changes, the rods will start to converge and then we'll know there's a grave underneath.'

Halina was shaking her head with disbelief. 'Divining rods indeed,' she muttered to herself. What mumbo-jumbo. Next they'd be consulting clairvoyants.

As the rabbi walked towards the area where Andrzej had extracted his sample, the prongs began to converge until they almost met, but after he had paced out eight long strides they began to diverge again. 'Will you look at that!' he exclaimed, his eyes shining with excitement. 'Here are the parameters of the mass grave delineated exactly where the geomagnetic device indicated. So divining rods that were used thousands of years ago are just as accurate as your modern magnetic technology!'

Just then a gust of wind blew his skull cap off and he ran to retrieve it with a speed that belied his corpulent shape, laughing as he ran. He was still laughing as he replaced the cap on his head and strode back to resume the conversation.

David Silverstein, the new rabbi of Warsaw, had recently arrived from Los Angeles and spoke Polish with a comical accent and atrocious grammar. Yet from the response of the students and the forensic team, who were all clearly enchanted with him, Halina realised that he was one of those rare people whose warm nature and charismatic personality overcame any linguistic defects. In his presence, everyone felt more alive.

A few moments later, he excused himself and became engrossed in an intense discussion with the head of the IPN delegation, Professor Witold Dobrowolski, who looked troubled.

'The professor looks like General Jaruzelski,' Halina whispered to Andrzej. 'The same narrow face, bald head and dark glasses.'

Andrzej chuckled. 'Luckily for us, he hasn't introduced martial law yet!'

As she pulled on her rubber gloves and picked up the screen to sift through the soil heaped up in the wheelbarrows, he murmured, 'I've heard that the rabbi has a problem with some aspect of the exhumation. There's a rumour that he would prefer for it not to go ahead.'

She spun around. 'What do you mean?'

He shrugged. 'Some Jewish thing. I don't understand it.'

'So what's going to happen?'

'Nothing. Dobrowolski will explain to him that the IPN needs the exhumation because they are conducting an investigation, and if anyone is to be charged with murder they'll need concrete evidence that a crime has been committed. That means bodies. Or remains. Anyway, there have been so many rumours and so much pressure from some sections of the government for an exhumation, it absolutely has to proceed. The right-wingers are desperate to prove once and for all that it was the Germans who murdered the 1500 Jews of Nowa Kalwaria, and not their Polish neighbours, as a historian in the United States has alleged. An election is coming up and the Minister of Justice needs the right-wingers' support to get back in. He's convinced that the investigation will show that the Nazis did it, which will make him very popular with his constituents. What's more, Poland has applied for membership of the European Union, and the President wants to prove to the west that we are not anti-semitic. He is determined to show that we are doing all we can to investigate Polish crimes against the Jews. You know, Caesar's wife must be above reproach and that sort of thing. So with all that going on, I can't see that they'll be influenced by any religious reservations.'

Looking across at the rabbi still engaged in an intense discussion with Professor Dobrowolski, Halina raised her eyebrows. 'I think that underneath that jovial exterior the rabbi is a man of steel. He won't give up easily.'

Halina gathered the forensic team around her. 'According to magnetic imaging — and divining rods' (there was good-natured laughter at her allusion to the rabbi's method) 'the mass grave is over there, to the right, but we're going to start here, where the barn used to be. From what one of the witnesses has said, the bodies were burnt in the barn and later buried in the mass grave, so I don't expect to find very much here, but we must make sure that nothing is overlooked. We will map and record the position of everything we find, number every item and identify and label every fragment of bone. Our aim will be to establish how many people were buried here, and their age and sex. We'll also try to determine whether the victims were burnt on the spot or burnt elsewhere and later deposited here, so we'll be observing every detail that might help us reconstruct what happened.'

As soon as the labourers had removed the top layer of soil, the sifting began. Almost immediately tiny bone fragments started to appear.

'The first thing I'd expect to see in a grave of bodies burnt at high temperatures over fifty years ago is a fusion of minerals in the bones,' Andrzej explained to the students. 'As you know, the body is self-combustible because, as the fat melts, you basically cook yourself.'

They were hanging on every word, revolted yet fascinated by his graphic description.

Holding up a larger piece of bone, he continued, 'You'll notice variations in colour. For instance, this bone is not charred, because it is part of the pelvis.' He looked at Marta.

She spoke slowly, studying the bone. 'Mmm, the pelvis is covered in a lot of flesh, so it isn't as exposed to fire?'

Andrzej nodded and picked up a white fragment. 'This was part of a radius close to the wrist, which was exposed to flames. The organic material in the bone would have become carbonised during the heating process, and the carbon would have burnt down until only the minerals remained, so it became bluish-white, what we call "calcined". Calcined bone is the most durable.'

He held up another piece of bone which displayed several colours. 'This is part of the femur, and shows the gradation from yellowish to black and white, which has become calcined. The rate of decay depends on the position in the grave. Close to the top, we'll find only skeletal remains, but at the bottom, it's possible for some soft tissue to be preserved, perhaps even hair. So we could see various states of preservation within one mass grave.'

He turned towards Halina. 'Of course the most durable part of the body is tooth enamel, but I'll leave it to my colleague from Australia to discuss that with you when she's ready.'

Although only those involved in the exhumation were permitted to enter the cordoned area, a curious crowd had gathered to watch the work from a distance. Most of the onlookers stared in silence but occasionally someone shouted to one of the villagers employed in the digging.

'*Ej tam*, Bolek, aren't you afraid the Jews will come out of their grave and point the finger at your old man?'

The man being addressed hunched over his shovel and continued digging as if he hadn't heard.

'They'll be pointing at quite a few people, if it comes to that,' an old woman in a woollen cap retorted. 'Once you dig them up we'll never get rid of the curse.'

Puzzled, Halina looked at the female archaeologist and raised her eyebrows.

'The old people around here are very superstitious,' Beata Wrobel said. 'They believe the Jews put a curse on the town. If a baby is born with a defect, or someone gets sick or dies, they say it's because the village is haunted and blame it on the curse.' A strand of hair escaped from her tightly twisted bun; she tucked it behind her ear and continued sifting.

The fragments of white bone stood out against the dark soil like crystals of salt on a black cloth. 'These bones are white because of the high temperature of the fire,' Andrzej was saying to the students. 'Calcination only takes place when bodies are burnt at temperatures that exceed 800 degrees.'

There was a sudden lull in the conversation. The scraping of trowels and the thudding of soil into barrows ceased, and even the village dogs stopped barking. In the silence Andrzej's words struck everyone, even the forensic specialists who were experienced in detaching themselves from the horrors of the crime scene, as the significance of what had happened here became uncomfortably real. On this spot, people had been incinerated alive in a conflagration of such an intensity that their bones had turned white.

'*Jesus Maria*,' Marta whispered.

As Halina continued sifting the soil, her mind wandered back to the broken tombstones in the cemetery. Although the graves had been desecrated, at least the dead had been buried with dignity, according to the rituals of their faith, not tossed like rubbish into a roughly dug pit.

Beata and Andrzej were arguing about the number of people who had been burnt in the barn. No one was certain exactly how many Jews had lived in the town in 1941.

'According to the last census, taken before the war, there were 1500, and that was the number recorded on the plaque,' Andrzej pointed out, and quoted from it: '*To the memory of 1500 Jews of Nowa Kalwaria who were killed by the Germans in July 1941.*'

Beata, however, insisted that this number was a vast exaggeration. 'You'll see, we won't find more than about 200, perhaps 300 at the most in there,' she argued.

Halina was surprised by Beata's vehemence. The dispute would be settled by the exhumation, but whether there had been 200 or 1500 didn't alter the hideous nature of their death. She closed her eyes as terrifying images flashed across her mind. The thick black smoke, the orange flames clawing at the roof, the roar of the fire. The panic. The carbon monoxide they breathed in would reduce the amount of haemoglobin in their arteries, making them feel confused, weak and dizzy. As the saturation increased, their muscles would have become uncoordinated and they'd be staggering around. When they tried to shout or scream their speech would have been slurred. Some of them probably vomited. In a short time they would have been unconscious. They were the lucky ones — unlike those who had remained conscious and died in agony.

She seemed to have stepped into a Brueghel canvas with its grotesque depiction of hell, contorted bodies and agonised faces. Acrid fumes mingled with burning flesh and the nauseating smell of kerosene. That smell was so real that Halina's stomach contracted into a tight fist while the blood drained from her head. She felt the ground shifting under her feet.

She stood very still and closed her eyes until the disturbing sensation faded away. To give herself time to recover, she walked slowly to the other side of the pit and stood apart from the others, deep in thought. A small distance away, a tractor rumbled across a potato field, as though in defiance. Until several months ago, when the government bought this land at a highly inflated price, the owner had ploughed this very spot, disregarding the fact that human blood and bones had fertilised the soil.

What would Edmond Locard have advised in this situation? Halina ran through the principles formulated by the father of forensic science as a student of religion might run through the catechism. Ask what questions you want answered, so you can clarify your thoughts and concentrate your mind, he had said. She would try to establish the age and sex of as many victims as possible and assess their number, but their identity would never be known. No gravestone would ever bear their names. And after so many years had passed, they could receive no real justice.

Inside the Quonset hut that had been erected nearby, bone fragments were spread out in trays, sorted according to size, placed on paper and photographed beside a ruler to indicate their size, before being bagged and labelled.

Halina was at her work table, looking through the bone pieces in search of teeth, when she heard a commotion outside. The team had gathered around Beata who was holding something; from their expressions, it seemed to be an important discovery. Halina rose from the table just as Beata came striding towards the hut with a cartridge case in her gloved hand.

'Now we're getting somewhere,' she said in a ringing voice. 'Poles weren't allowed to own firearms during the German occupation, so this will prove that the killers were German, not Polish.'

Andrzej regarded her for a moment before speaking. 'I don't think you can categorically say that.'

'Before we make any assumptions,' Halina said, 'we'll get the cartridge case checked by a ballistics expert and find out what type of weapon fired it.'

Beata's mouth was set in a straight line. 'It will be a German bullet. Poles didn't have guns,' she repeated, glaring at Andrzej.

Sixteen

On Łomza's main street, a notice pinned to a doorway between the police station and the post office stated that Detective-Inspector (retired) Mieczyslaw Dominik, member of the Association of Firearm and Toolmark Examiners, would be back at 2 p.m.

Halina looked at her watch and sighed. Two hours would be a long time in this town. In the course of her work, she had travelled all over the world and visited many countries, yet she felt more alien in Poland than anywhere else. Even among the descendants of the ancient Incas and Mayas in Peru and Guatemala, she had sensed a more powerful connection than she felt in her native land. Here it felt as though her skin had been peeled away and now encased a stranger's body.

Although Andrzej's student, Stefan, had volunteered to take the cartridge shell to the ballistics expert, Halina had insisted on going herself. She needed a break from the claustrophobic atmosphere of Nowa Kalwaria and welcomed the opportunity to breathe the air of another town for a few hours. Łomza was a quiet country town built around a central square but, in contrast to Nowa Kalwaria, the air seemed brighter and the people walked with a more purposeful step. Women with shopping bags and small children clinging to their hands stopped to chat on street corners, and the shops offered a wide variety of merchandise. Peering into a window displaying women's fashions, however, Halina figured that this was one place where her passion for clothes would not lead to credit-card debt.

Turning up the collar of the raincoat she had bought at the Galeries Lafayette two years before, she sighed for the boulevards of Paris. She was daydreaming about chic pavement cafés and French lovers strolling arm in arm beside the Seine as she passed a sign pointing to the archive office. Half a block further on, she stopped and retraced her steps. Esther Kennedy had mentioned Łomza. The plight of that demented old woman living out her last days in the retirement home shrieking the name of her lost niece had touched Halina. Perhaps she would find some documents here pertaining to the child. If nothing else, it would pass the time.

The archive office was located in a portable hut at the end of a passageway choked with cartons and boxes. From the musty smell of the rooms, and the tattered condition of the tomes stacked on shelves from floor to ceiling, Halina wondered how long these records would last before they disintegrated.

'You see conditions we work in?' The young archivist shrugged her shoulders, spraying Halina's black coat with angora fibres from her fluffy pink sweater. 'Can you believe that we live in a computer age?'

They both laughed at the absurdity of it. Now that the ice was broken, Halina asked for the birth records for 1939, the year Esther Kennedy had mentioned in her letters.

'Catholic records?' the clerk asked.

Halina shook her head, surprised by the question.

'Jewish records for this region we have, but not many,' the clerk explained. 'I will show.' She climbed up a ladder, ran her hand along the volumes on the top shelf and pulled out three. '1897 to 1898, 1923 to 1924, and 1938 to August 1939. After that we don't have nothing, because the Germans destroyed the Jewish communities together with their records.'

Halina needed both hands to open the thick leatherbound tome. Its spine was so worn that the gold lettering had faded and the pages were beginning to fray. There were no entries under Kleinman. Of course! Being her sister's child, Mireleh would have had her father's surname, but what that was Halina had no idea. She ran her eye down the handwritten entries looking at the unfamiliar names: the Moiszes, Szura Bailas, Itzaks and Sruleks. Some families had eight, nine, even ten children. The list of names represented so much hope, so much love. She wondered how many of them had ended up in the barn that fateful summer's day.

As she closed the volume with a sigh, she became aware of someone watching her. A man was sitting at a small table nearby, an open ledger in front of him. 'Any luck?' he asked.

Halina shook her head. 'I didn't have much to go on.'

He leant back in his chair. His grey-flecked hair was brushed back from his forehead and fell softly around his face, touching his collar, like an artist. He was a slightly built man with a square-hinged jaw, and as he regarded her with hooded eyes she imagined him in a creased trenchcoat with a fedora pulled down over his face, leaning against a lamppost, puffing on a Gauloise. His expression invited her to continue the conversation and she sank into the chair facing him, relieved to discuss her futile search.

'All I know is that she was called Mireleh,' she concluded, and added, 'I've never heard that name before.'

'It's the diminutive of Miriam,' he said. His eyes were the colour of toffee, and when he turned towards the window amber lights danced in them. 'Why don't you go through that volume and look for babies with that name? It's a long shot but you never can tell.'

Then he gave her a shrewd glance. 'But surely you didn't come to Łomza just to check on a child you don't even know. What brings you to our little town?'

'Business,' she said.

The corners of his eyes crinkled with amusement at her laconic reply. 'I knew who you were as soon as you walked in here. We don't see many women who look like illustrations from fashion magazines and speak Polish with a peculiar accent. Everyone knows who you are and why you're here. You're the biggest sensation since the Pope's last visit!'

With a broad smile he stretched out his hand and shook hers with a firm grip. 'I'm Roman Zamorski. I teach history at the high school in Nowa Kalwaria.'

It seemed that Miriam wasn't a popular name in Nowa Kalwaria in those days, so it didn't take long to skim down the columns where newborn babies' names were entered in perfectly formed copperplate script. Halina was running her index finger down the register, her eyes glazed with anticipated failure, when the first entry for September leapt off the page. On 2 September, Miriam Chaja was born to Malka Lieberman. The mother's maiden name was Kleinman, the same as that of Esther Kennedy.

'I've found her!' Halina called out and turned the volume around to show Roman who was already by her side.

Although Esther Kennedy would not be capable of reading or understanding the document, Halina felt it was her duty to obtain a photocopy, but the archivist shook her head.

'I'm very sorry but we cannot allow people to photocopy these books.'

Roman leant over the counter. '*Proszę pani*, this is a very special case,' he said. 'This lady has come all the way from Australia to search for this document. We can't let her go home empty-handed and disappointed thinking that Poles are unhelpful, can we? Poland's reputation is in your hands!' He spoke in a genial tone and concluded with a dramatic flourish that made the archivist burst out laughing.

A few moments later Halina was holding the photocopy as Roman steered her into the small *kawiarnia* next door. Over coffee and cheesecake Halina asked, 'How did you know that Mireleh was the diminutive of Miriam?'

'I'm researching Jewish life in Nowa Kalwaria before the war,' he said. 'The Jews have lived here for hundreds of years, side by side with the Catholics. They suffered through the bad times and contributed to the good times, and are part of our history just as we were part of theirs.' His voice grew more impassioned as he spoke. 'And now they are ghosts. Gone without a trace. My pupils have never met a Jew. When I tell them about Jewish culture, they look at me as if I am talking about ancient Assyrians. Some of them talk about Jews as if they are horned devils. I've been learning Hebrew so I can decipher the inscriptions on the gravestones.'

'But there are hardly any stones left,' she said. 'What happened to them?'

'That's a very sad story. They're scattered all over this area. After the Germans destroyed the cemetery, they used some of the gravestones for paving roads, and the townspeople carted away the rest.'

'What for?'

He shrugged. 'To build houses or pave yards. It's shocking.'

'I'm not easily shocked,' Halina said. She liked the way he addressed her: not in the formal third person, but '*ty*' which, like the French 'tu', created instant intimacy.

He studied her for a moment before speaking. 'No, I suppose not, in your profession. You know, there's a huge battle looming over your investigation. As far as some people are concerned, the honour of Poland is at stake and if you don't come up with the answers they want, things could get nasty.'

She was still thinking about his mission. 'Why are you so interested in the gravestones?' she asked.

Roman cleared his throat. 'The way I see it, cemeteries are the whetstones of community values. The way people treat them says as much about their morals as the way they treat the living. If churches and synagogues are destroyed, they can be rebuilt. If holy books are burnt, they can be rewritten. But once cemeteries are desecrated, they can't be put together again and the dead souls will find no peace until some restitution has been made.'

Now it was Halina's turn to contemplate her companion. 'You're very different from most of the people here. How come you're working in Nowa Kalwaria? Don't you find it suffocating?'

He took a drag of the cigarette and exhaled a column of smoke towards the grimy ceiling. 'Listen, Halina, I could tell you that I want to change the attitude of the young people, or that I'm determined to get to the truth, and maybe you'd be impressed with my idealism, but it's not as simple as that. We can always come up with reasons to justify what we do, but in the end, some things can't be explained. Reason is all right up to a point, but after that ...' He shrugged. 'My parents were born in Nowa Kalwaria but after the war they moved to Bialystok and never came back. But when a job came up here, I just had to take it.'

'Maybe the ghosts in the cemetery were calling you,' Halina said.

'That's another long story,' he said.

She found the olive-tinged pallor of his smooth angular face as intriguing as his conversation. She guessed that he was in his late forties, perhaps a little older. Married, probably. They always were. She was keen to hear his story but when she glanced at her watch it was after two. She drained the coffee and rose.

Roman held out his card. 'If you ever need anything, or want to talk, call me at the school.' The hooded eyes lingered on her face. 'Or at home. Any time.'

She was already at the door when she turned around. 'Are you coming to the dinner at Borowski's place tonight by any chance?'

He gave a short mirthless laugh. 'I'd be the last person the deputy mayor would invite.'

Detective-Inspector (retired) Mieczyslaw Dominik had cropped grey hair, an unsmiling face and an erect posture that made Halina wonder whether a metal pole had been inserted into his spine. They were very lucky to find a ballistics expert in such a small town. Professor Dobrowolski had said they would have to send the cartridge case to Warsaw police headquarters for identification, but while scrolling through a list of Polish experts on his laptop, he had exclaimed, 'Look at that! Mieczyslaw Dominik lives in Łomza!' The man who had been in charge of Warsaw's forensic ballistics section for twelve years had recently retired and returned to his home town.

Halina began explaining about the cartridge case but he cut her short. 'Witold Dobrowolski already called me,' he barked. 'Let me see it.'

He shook the case several times until the remaining grains of soil clinging to it fell onto his workbench. Then he immersed it in water and dried it with a small air compressor. Speaking in his staccato manner, he said, 'This is a 7.9 by 57 mm calibre fired cartridge case. Discharged by a Mauser Kar 98 K repeating rifle.'

So Beata was right. It was a German bullet. Halina was about to thank him and leave when he strode over to a large glass-fronted case displaying a variety of rifles and pistols, unlocked it and thrust a rifle into her surprised hand.

'This is it,' he said. 'Standard German infantry issue. Derived from the Gewehr-98 they designed back in 1898. Had a very strong action. Fired five rounds. The Americans copied it with their Springfield rifle.'

While he proceeded to demonstrate how its five-round charge was inserted, the bolt closed, the fired cartridge case extracted and then ejected, Halina's attention wandered to the walnut butt stock with its engraved eagle holding a swastika.

'Weapons have always been part of life,' Mieczyslaw Dominik said. 'Man had to hunt and protect his family. The earliest implements ever found were weapons.'

'I suppose it's not guns that trouble me as much as their potential for destruction,' Halina said, handing the rifle back to him with a haste that indicated her lack of appreciation for firearms.

He gave a sardonic laugh. 'So are you going to ban matches? And kerosene?'

He jammed a magnifying glass into his right eye socket and squinted at the base of the cartridge case. 'Aha!' he said in his dry voice. 'The headstamp tells the whole story.'

He held it out to her. She could make out some figures and letters stamped on the metal but had no idea what they meant.

'German small-arms ammunition always stamped the manufacturer's mark, the type of metal used, the delivery number and the year of manufacture.' He reached for a handbook on German headstamp codes. 'Aha!' he said again and closed the book. 'Now we know everything.'

She waited.

'See the initials "eba"? That was the German military code for the Metallwarenfabrik Scharfenberg & Teubert at Breitungen-Werra. That's where your ammunition was manufactured. We also know that it was the thirty-fourth lot manufactured that year, and that it was made of steel.'

Now that Halina knew it was a German bullet, none of this was relevant, but politeness required that she listened.

He was still looking at the head stamp. 'Here's an interesting bit of information for you. The year of manufacture was 1944.'

She snapped to attention. '1944? Are you sure?'

'Look for yourself.'

Through the magnifying glass she saw the number 44 clearly stamped on the base.

'So it couldn't have been fired in 1941!' she exclaimed.

He gave her a withering look. 'Full marks for deduction. But if you're not convinced, here's another piece of evidence. See this small "s" with the cross beside it? That stands for steel. Until 1942, the Germans were manufacturing brass ammunition, but from 1942 on they used steel because they'd run out of brass.'

Halina's mind raced as she hurried along the street. So that bullet couldn't have been fired from a German rifle in 1941 after all. Beata wouldn't like that — and she wouldn't be the only one. But if it hadn't been fired that July day in 1941, what was it doing in the ground where the barn had stood? Someone had obviously planted the shell there and, judging by its location near the surface, they had done it recently. Halina wondered who had been responsible for this clumsy attempt to fake evidence in the hope that it would clear the Polish villagers of the crime.

Seventeen

Glancing at her watch under the table, Halina found to her dismay that only seven minutes had passed since the last time she looked. She had often complained that conversations at Sydney dinner parties revolved mainly around the price of real estate, the state of the stock market, gossip about politicians and discussions about restaurants, but even those topics now seemed riveting compared with Nowa Kalwaria's council issues. Her host, the deputy mayor, had placed her between himself and one of the councillors, while the mayor, whom she found far more congenial, was seated at the far end of the table.

'So, *Pani Doktor*, how is — I mean to say, is our investigation going well?' Kazimierz Borowski asked, his red face mottled from the Żywiec beer he was drinking. His stomach was bulging beneath a tight pin-striped suit that he had probably worn on special occasions for the past twenty years.

While she was struggling to think of a noncommittal reply, he raised his arm in a deprecating gesture. 'No, don't tell me, you don't need to, it's all right, I know you can't tell secrets out of school!'

Tilting his head back, he drained another glass of beer, then replaced the glass on the table with an assertive thump. He opened his mouth to say something when her neighbour on the left, a burly man with a thick red neck, saw his chance and jumped in.

'You have your work to do, *Pani Doktor*, that we understand perfectly well,' Councillor Kruk said. 'But you're an intelligent woman, so can you explain the purpose of this investigation?' He continued without waiting for her reply. 'I don't mind telling you that I was totally opposed, *totally opposed* to it. Most of us here,' — he waved his arm around the table to indicate the other councillors, but when he came to the mayor he stopped and stared as though he'd seen a snake — 'most of us voted against digging up the area around the barn. This regrettable event happened so long ago, *bój sie Boga* — heaven preserve us!' He brought his hands together with a resounding clap to emphasise his point. 'It was half a century ago! Half a century! People want to get on with their lives, isn't that right? Everyone has suffered enough, Poles just as much as Jews. In any case, we are all Poles, dear lady, so why distinguish between the two?

'But unfortunately that's the agenda of the American Zionists. You saw what happened at the Auschwitz site. They always want to claim a monopoly on suffering. What's the point of dwelling on all these unfortunate things that were forced on us, *forced* on us, by a barbaric regime? The best thing that could happen is for the site to be covered up and a memorial erected, if they insist on it — as they always do.' He smiled conspiratorially, obviously expecting her to agree. 'After all, everyone knows the Germans did it. Jews and Poles lived side by side for centuries here, dear lady, without any problems.'

Halina noticed that at the other end of the table the mayor was listening intently. 'It isn't as obvious to some of us as it is to you, *Panie* Kruk,' he said. 'We would all like to get out from the shadow of the barn but we can only do that when the truth finally comes out.'

Councillor Kruk's face matched the colour of the beetroot *barszcz* that the deputy mayor's wife was now serving in large cups, sprinkled with dill and accompanied by croquettes filled with minced chicken.

'What are you suggesting?' he barked. 'Are you implying that Poles had anything to do with it? We're all fed up with your slanderous insinuations! And to think that you're the mayor of this town! *Wstyd i hańba!* You're a bloody disgrace. You've been brainwashed by the Jews. Aren't you forgetting that we were victims of the Russians and the Germans during the war?' Quivering with fury, Kruk clenched his fists, stood up and looked as though he would rush at the mayor when Borowski whispered into his ear and pulled his sleeve to make him sit down.

'Victims can be perpetrators too,' the mayor said quietly and turned to speak to the council treasurer who was nodding agreement.

Embarrassed by this altercation in front of the guest of honour, the host turned to Halina and suggested showing her around the house before the main course was served. Although the argument had enlivened the evening, now that it was over, it was an effort to keep her eyes open and Halina was glad of the opportunity to move around.

'My office,' he beamed, pointing to a small room with a desk. Near the doorway, on a shelf, two books caught her eye: *Poland Betrayed* and *The Jewish Conspiracy.* Taking her elbow, Borowski steered her towards the back of the house, explaining proudly that he had paved the yard 'in the Italian style', instead of leaving it like most others in the area where chickens scrabbled around in the dirt. Hearing voices, the German Shepherd poked his long snout out of his kennel and growled. 'Shut up, *Złoto*,' his master said, throwing him a biscuit. The dog caught it mid-air and flopped down to devour it with loud crunching noises.

The night was cold and crisp and Halina draped her black pashmina shawl tightly around her shoulders. When she breathed in, the frosty air chilled her lungs. The crystalline scent of snow hung in the air. She stopped in front of every rose bush, examining each bare thorny stem in turn to delay returning to the overheated dining room and the tedious conversation. When her host excused himself to check on the other guests, she lingered outside and gazed at the immense starlit sky while loneliness gnawed at her bones.

The longing for a cigarette was too strong to resist. As she struck a match, about to light up, she noticed something on the stone beneath her feet. Curious, she lit another match and bent over for a closer look. The marks resembled the inscriptions she had seen in the cemetery. Looking around, she saw similar marks on the other stones, but before she had time to look for others, her host was hurrying towards her. He shepherded her inside as his wife placed a bowl of *bigos* stew on the table, with a platter of crisply fried potato *placki* and pickled cucumbers.

That night Halina couldn't sleep. The hotel room was stuffy and, no matter how hard she tugged at the window, it wouldn't open. The eiderdown made her perspire but when she pulled it out through the diamond-shaped opening of the duvet cover, she shivered with cold. Reverberating through her mind were the mayor's words. *Victims can be perpetrators too.*

Did he know more than his colleagues or was he the only one willing to speak out? She recalled Roman's warning and decided to tell him about the stone slabs. Perhaps he would be able to decipher the inscriptions.

Early next morning, she called his home.

'That doesn't surprise me,' he said when she told him what she had seen.

'Some of those inscriptions were quite long,' she said. 'I thought you'd be interested.'

'That's extremely thoughtful of you.'

Her face flamed like a schoolgirl caught out scheming to contact the object of her infatuation.

'One of the teachers said that the deputy mayor was going to Łomza tonight to visit the bishop,' he was saying. 'When it's dark I'll get into the yard and have a look around.'

She didn't hesitate. 'I'll meet you outside his place at eight.'

'How good are you at scaling walls and running from security guards?' he asked.

'Probably better than you,' she retorted. 'I used to be a good runner.'

As she hung up, she smiled for the first time since arriving in Nowa Kalwaria.

Walking past the presbytery on her way to the exhumation site Halina came face to face with the priest.

'You're the kind samaritan who offered to give me a lift two days ago when I almost collided with your car,' he said. 'I know you're busy with this investigation, but any time you feel like a chat or a glass of tea, come to the presbytery.' He waved his arm in the direction of the small house behind the picket fence a few metres away from the church. 'My *gosposia* makes delicious *pączki*.'

At the mention of doughnuts Halina could already taste the yeasty dough sprinkled with sugar. 'With rose marmalade?'

'Of course,' he replied. 'Lots of it.'

'Unfortunately I won't be able to get there until four o'clock!' she said.

You'd think the circus had just come to town, she thought as she approached the exhumation site and took in the procession of forensic specialists walking to and from the Quonset hut, the onlookers hovering around the perimeter, craning their necks this way and that so as not to miss anything; and now reporters from all over Poland, as well as some from Germany and France, were pushing one another in their anxiety not to miss anything. Everyone was firing questions. The most persistent were the photographers, desperate for a shot of anything connected with the exhumation.

Professor Dobrowolski hurried towards her. 'We can't have this three-ring circus,' he said, squinting into the light as he wiped specks of dirt off his dark glasses. 'The reporters are getting in the way and disturbing the archaeologists with their endless questions, and as for the photographers leaping up all over the place and blinding everyone with their flashbulbs, it's just too much. It's disrespectful to the site and disruptive for the experts. I'm going to ban all the journalists until we call a press conference.'

'Get ready for the riot,' Halina commented.

'How did you go with the ballistics expert in Łomza?' he asked.

He listened gravely as she repeated what she had been told, and sighed. 'I thought as much.'

Lowering her voice, she asked, 'Do you have any idea who might have planted it?'

'I have several ideas,' he said dryly, 'but no proof. But we know that the extreme right will go to any lengths to prove that the Poles weren't responsible.'

He was cool and dispassionate, yet he was a Pole investigating a massacre that could besmirch his nation's reputation.

'Is this hard for you?' she asked.

He pursed his thin lips. 'My job as prosecutor is to find out what happened here. I was in charge of the Katyń investigation.' He inclined his head towards Andrzej. 'We worked on it together. You know the story. Over 20,000 Polish officers were found in a mass grave, supposedly killed by the Germans. But we never believed that, and didn't let it rest until we got to the truth. So how can we justify investigating one mass murder committed on our soil but resile from another? Do these people deserve justice less than the Polish officers did? Naturally I'd be happier if it turns out that the Germans committed this crime, but the truth has to come out no matter what it is.'

Halina was reflecting on the prosecutor's words as she sat down beside Andrzej, who was concentrating on sifting the soil. The faint but unmistakeable smell of smoke emanated from the ground. 'It's incredible, after all this time!' said Halina, wrinkling her nose.

'The ground eventually yields its secrets to those who are alert enough to recognise them,' Andrzej said, but stopped talking when his trowel clinked against something. He gently moved the soil away with his hands and held up a black object, round and flat, that fitted in the palm of his hand. 'A man's pocket watch!' he exclaimed. 'And there's something inscribed on the back.'

Using a tiny brush, he removed particles of soil clinging to the watch and placed it on a tray in the Quonset hut. But when he looked through the magnifying glass, he shook his head. 'It's not a name, it's a date: 1924. The hands stopped at 4.15.'

Finding a personal item once again momentarily dispelled the professional detachment that created a distance between the historical event and their emotions. With the discovery of the watch, fragments of bone that had been numbered, coded and labelled with anatomical names were now connected with human beings, people whose everyday life had in so many ways resembled their own. The find evoked a sense of kinship with the dead and aroused lively speculation.

'Perhaps it was a coming-of-age gift,' Marta ventured, wide-eyed with excitement.

'Or he could have inherited it from his father,' Stefan suggested.

Beata looked irritated. 'A man's watch,' she said. 'That's consistent with what we've always been told — that the Germans rounded up male communists that day.'

Andrzej was inspecting a small piece of leather he had come across in his sieve. 'Looks like part of a heel,' he said. After examining it with a magnifying glass, he detected signs that the leather was tooled. 'It's too fancy for a man's shoe, most probably it came from a woman's,' he said.

Beata shook her head. 'You can't assume that!' she retorted.

Stefan gave a shout. 'There's something down here!' Pushing aside the soil carefully with gloved hands, he revealed the rounded surface of a solid object wedged firmly in the earth.

Andrzej bent over to examine it. 'That looks like cement,' he said. 'Push away all the soil and take it out very carefully so that it doesn't break up as you lift it.'

It was a chunk of cement of no identifiable shape, smooth except for one surface. They examined the puzzle from all sides, wondering what it could be.

'It must have snapped off something larger,' Andrzej mused. 'Let's keep working, the answer is bound to turn up.'

A moment later there was another cry. 'Here's another piece, much bigger!'

With Andrzej supervising to ensure that it was extracted without being damaged, it took three of them to lever it out gently and place it carefully on the other side of the trench. They stared at it in astonishment. One cheek was missing, and most of the forehead, but the prominent chin was there with its characteristic pointed beard. They were looking at the head of a massive statue of Lenin.

Professor Dobrowolski spoke unusually fast, unable to suppress his excitement. 'This must have been part of the statue of Lenin that the communists erected in the small square near the Łomza road,' he said. 'We have an account from an eyewitness who testified in 1951 that ten years earlier the Jewish men had been rounded up and forced to carry the statue through the town. The locals jeered and tormented them all the way. They made them shout that they loved Lenin and that the Soviet occupation was their fault. If anyone fell over, they beat and kicked them mercilessly. And here's proof that the incident did take place.'

Halina studied the head. Even though much of it was missing, it was too heavy for one person to lift it. 'How could they carry the whole statue? It must have weighed several tonnes.'

'They were ordered to smash it first so they could carry it in pieces,' the professor explained.

They were trying to visualise this scene when Beata's penetrating voice sliced through their thoughts.

'It all adds up. First the German cartridge case and now the Lenin statue. The Germans punished the male Jewish Bolsheviks by making them carry the statue of Lenin and then they killed them.'

Halina surveyed her with an irritation she could no longer conceal. Alone among the entire forensic team, Beata insisted on imposing her preconceived notions on everything they extracted from the soil.

'As a matter of fact, it doesn't add up at all,' Halina retorted.

Beata frowned. 'How come? We've got the evidence.'

'We've got a broken statue, a man's watch and the cartridge case of a bullet dated 1944, so it certainly wasn't fired by Germans or anyone else in 1941.'

Halina turned her back on Beata, annoyed with herself for losing her objectivity and snapping at a colleague. She was considering an apology when Andrzej whistled under his breath. 'Halina, come and look at this,' he said.

On his gloved hand lay a gold bracelet. Even in its blackened state the fine Florentine work was noticeable. The clasp had melted.

'How hot must it be for gold to melt?' Halina said, unable to tear her eyes away from the bracelet that had once adorned the wrist of a woman who had probably enjoyed wearing jewellery as much as she herself did.

Her contriteness evaporated. Holding the bracelet up, she shot Beata a triumphant look. 'Do you suppose Jewish Bolshevik males wore delicate gold bracelets?'

Eighteen

Halina hurried back to the hotel, her cold hands thrust so deep into the pockets of her coat that her nails caught on the silk lining. As she approached the presbytery, she remembered accepting the priest's invitation for afternoon tea and her heart sank. A religious discussion was the last thing she felt like at the end of a draining day. Not being a believer, she would either have to argue with him or accept what he said in hypocritical silence. For a moment she toyed with the hope that perhaps he hadn't taken her jocular reply seriously and didn't expect her to come, but knew she couldn't go back on her word.

The woman who opened the door had an apron tied around her solid waist and wore frayed felt slippers. Her short grey hair was fixed with two bobby pins at the sides to stop it falling into her eyes.

'I'll let Reverend Father know you're here.'

She spoke with a slight lisp caused by a gap where her right lateral incisor and canine had been. Dental care in Nowa Kalwaria was either non-existent or beyond the reach of most people, Halina decided, recalling the missing teeth and badly fitting dentures she had noticed since her arrival.

Tapping on a door that was slightly ajar, the housekeeper poked her head inside. '*Proszę księdza*, there's a lady here to see you.'

The priest was sitting in an old-fashioned carved armchair in front of the fire, writing.

'Ah, my good samaritan,' he said, and smiled. He noticed that she hesitated. 'Just call me Father Krzysztof,' he added.

'Christopher, that's an apt name for a priest,' Halina said.

Turning his head towards the door he called, '*Gosposiu*, could you bring us some tea with those delicious *pączki* of yours?' His eyes brimmed with amusement. 'And an extra dish of rose marmalade!'

The wood fire crackled in the hearth and spat embers, making Halina's face glow. As she sipped the strong black tea and bit into the plump sugar-crusted doughnut whose fragrant jam oozed into her mouth, her bones thawed and softened along with her mood.

'These are as good as the ones my mother used to make,' she said, reaching for another.

He nodded. 'Polish home cooking is hard to beat,' he said. 'You should try *gosposia's pierogi*.'

'Does she fill them with potatoes and cheese, or cabbage and mushrooms?' Halina asked.

They were discussing the relative merits of various fillings when she burst out laughing. 'I was worried we were going to have a heavy discussion about religion and here we are talking about food!'

He laughed too. 'After all, man does not live by bread alone. *Pierogi* and *pączki* are an important part of life, isn't that so?' He leant forward. 'Tell me, did your mother pickle cucumbers and marinate *prawdziwki*?'

'She made wonderful dill pickles but Polish wood mushrooms don't grow in Australia,' Halina said.

He wanted to know about their life in Sydney, surprising her with his knowledge of Australian politics, economy and geography. 'I don't get much chance to travel overseas but I read a lot,' he said. 'Wasn't it an Australian author who wrote *The Devil's Advocate*? And another one who wrote *The Thorn Birds*?'

'You read *The Thorn Birds*?' She was incredulous.

'Well, one of the main characters was a priest!' he protested, amusement in his slate-coloured eyes. 'What did you think, that priests only read ecclesiastical bulletins?'

Then he looked at her intently. 'Tell me something about yourself.'

After she had given a sketchy account of her professional career, he said, 'I'd like to get to know you. Has life fulfilled your hopes?'

Halina was taken aback by the directness of the question. 'Professionally, yes. But if you're asking me whether I've fulfilled life's hopes, whether I've become the person I had hoped to be, I'd have to say probably not. Somewhere along the way I started shifting the goal posts.'

He nodded. 'As we all do, in spite of our best intentions. But our merciful Lord understands.'

'Do you think God understands the people who committed the crime here?' she asked.

'Only God can understand the darkness that lurks inside the heart of man.'

'No wonder, since man made God in his own image,' she blurted out.

She felt she'd gone too far but Father Krzysztof was considering her words.

'That's also true,' he said. 'Our limited imagination finds it difficult to go beyond the physical world.' He gave her a searching glance. 'I'm sure that underneath all that cynicism you have a good soul.'

She stared into the fire, conscious of her shortcomings. Did she really have a good soul? She tried to think of something unselfish she had ever done.

'I jumped into the sea a few months ago and pulled out a child who got swept off the rocks,' she said.

He was looking at her with interest. 'You must be a good swimmer, like so many Australians.'

'No, actually I'm a bit frightened of the water.'

'So you are very brave.'

She shook her head. 'I can't take any credit for what I did.'

'Why not?'

She shrugged. 'It wasn't a conscious choice. I didn't stop to weigh up the risks or decide to overcome my fear. If I'd thought about it, I probably wouldn't have done it. It was sheer impulse, that's all. I just couldn't sit there and do nothing.'

'Perhaps that's what being unselfish really means,' he mused. 'What separates the good people from the others is being unable to do nothing when someone is trouble.'

They sat in companionable silence, looking into the fire, when he said softly, more to himself than to her, '*Każde z serc ludzkich ma swych dziejów księgę.*' His beautifully modulated voice rose and fell with the lilting rhythm of the poem. 'Every human heart keeps a record of its own deeds.'

She looked at him questioningly.

'Juliusz Słowacki wrote that. He's one of our great Polish poets. Do you know his work?'

She shook her head and he began to recite the poem:

'Man and his land are inseparable, because land is the basis of life and reflects human deeds, its joys as well as its sorrows.

Quiet and sad is this land, soaked in blood and tears.'

When he came to the last line, he looked into her eyes.

'To discover the limits of noble feelings, look into your own heart.'

She watched his patrician face, flushed in the glow of the firelight that accentuated the whiteness of his hair and the inky depths of his eyes. Would he have looked equally distinguished if, instead of the black soutane, he had worn a suit? And would she have found it as easy to speak so candidly without the reassurance that his spiritual status and sexual abstinence conferred? For the first time she sensed the tantalising attraction of the cassock with its combination of intellect, empathy, humour and sexual detachment, and understood why a priest might pose a challenge that some women found hard to resist.

'And what about you?' she asked, emboldened now. 'How has life measured up to your hopes?'

He looked away as he spoke. 'Life never ceases to surprise me.'

'Is that another way of saying that the Lord moves in mysterious ways?'

He gave a short laugh. 'That's certainly true!'

Halina left the presbytery with a plate of doughnuts, a volume of Słowacki's poems, and the certainty that she would return.

The Mickiewicz Inn was the only hotel in Nowa Kalwaria that offered a reasonable standard of comfort, although Halina suspected that it would have been lucky to earn two stars in any international guidebook. Established at the turn of the twentieth century by an enterprising textile manufacturer at a time when the industry still prospered, it had fallen into disrepair as Nowa Kalwaria slid into industrial oblivion. These days, the owner struggled to keep it open, and the arrival of the forensic team had been the most exciting event in the hotel's recent history.

The hotel's one constant source of revenue was the modest restaurant where some of the villagers occasionally dined. The pallid light cast by its weak bulbs was further dimmed by the tasselled khaki lampshades that must have formed part of the original décor. Halina had to hold the menu directly under a wall lamp to read it. The others had not yet come down for dinner but she had decided to eat early to avoid their curious looks and questions when she excused herself to go out. The young waitress set the cutlery and glasses in front of her and hovered with a friendly smile, glad to have something to do to justify her continued employment, but after the doughnuts she had eaten that afternoon Halina didn't feel hungry.

Picking at a platter of cold cuts, she scanned the local newspaper. Among reports of the usual council brawls and accusations about misused and misappropriated funds, an article headed 'Foreign expert in Nowa Kalwaria' caught her eye.

In the belief that our Polish scientists are not equal
to the task of unearthing the remains of a few Jewish
Bolsheviks killed by the Gemans over fifty years
ago, our respected politicians in Warsaw, no doubt
encouraged by certain groups in the United States, have
appointed a foreign expert to collaborate with the farce
taking place in our town.

Insinuations and sarcasm marked every sentence. The journalist, who used the byline 'Patriot', had misspelled Halina's surname and omitted to mention that she was born in Poland.

Before leaving the table, Halina wrapped several chunks of the smoked *kiełbasa* sausage in a serviette and, glancing around to make sure the waitress wasn't looking, slipped them into her pocket.

In her room, the wind rattled the window and the bare branches of an elm tree banged against the pane. It was almost time. Although the quest for the stolen gravestones had captured her imagination, and the prospect of embarking on an adventure with Roman was appealing, the risks made her heart pound. She would be mortified if someone caught her snooping around the deputy mayor's house. 'Patriot' would have a field day.

But as she pulled on the thick fleece sweater, Gore-Tex weatherproof jacket and boots she hadn't worn since trekking in the Himalayas several years before, Halina suppressed a giggle, wondering whether this was a suitable outfit for breaking into someone's yard.

Creeping past the reception counter, she closed the hotel door quietly behind her and fastened the hood of the jacket under her chin to keep out the wind. The night was dark and heavy clouds obscured the stars. Hardly any lights shone in the windows of the houses she passed and the street lamps cast long shadows on the pavement. There was no one about and, although she tried to tread softly, her footsteps resounded in her ears.

She hurried along the street, astonished that such a short distance could take so long to cover. The most direct route to the deputy mayor's house was by the diagonal path that bisected the square but the lights didn't reach the centre. Reluctant to retrace her steps and take the long way round, she quickened her pace to get away from the creaking trees and their moving shadows which resembled grotesque figures. A twig snapped underfoot and she jumped, convinced that someone was standing behind the mottled trunk of the giant beech, watching her. Finally she was in the light again. Only a few more metres and she would be there.

She kept her head down as she hurried along and almost collided with Roman as he stepped out from the shadows towards her. He put out his arms to catch her, and as she brushed against his cheek she caught the fresh citrus smell of his aftershave.

'I've never seen anyone move so fast,' he whispered. 'You must have had the devil at your heels!'

They looked up and down the street to make sure no one had seen them, then crept to the front of the house, but when Roman ran his hand along the edge of the gate to find the latch, he felt a padlock.

He surveyed her dubiously. 'How good are you at scaling walls?'

'Pretty good. I got first-class honours from the Cat Burglars' college.' Halina was giggling like a schoolgirl.

'What about you?'

Without replying, he jumped up, got hold of the top of the wall and hoisted himself over, eager to display his athleticism. A moment later she heard a muffled thud as he landed on the other side. It was followed immediately by furious barking as Borowski's German Shepherd tried to break free from its chain.

'Shit,' Roman muttered. 'I forgot about the dog.'

'I didn't,' Halina whispered, taking a piece of sausage from her pocket. 'Here, *Złoto*!' she called softly and hurled it over the wall. While the dog was devouring the meat, she hoisted herself up and jumped down into the yard, then threw him the other piece.

Now that the dog was quiet, they tiptoed to the back of the house. Roman shone his flashlight around the paving. Halina pointed. 'Here's one!'

He knelt on the ground to inspect the carved inscription. 'This is the best one I've ever seen,' he whispered, his voice hoarse with excitement. He waved his flashlight to outline the shape. 'See that? Two hands. That means it came from a woman's gravestone.'

A little further on, he stopped again. 'That's part of a candelabra.' He pulled a camera out of his backpack and crawled on the ground, photographing the inscriptions. 'I'll have the photos enlarged to make the letters easier to decipher,' he said.

They were about to climb back over the wall when they heard loud voices on the other side.

'I'm telling you, I heard something just before. And I saw a light flashing,' a young male voice was saying.

A drunken laugh greeted his statement. 'You can't even stand up straight. It was stars you saw, not lights.'

His companion gave a loud belch. 'I'm not moving till I find out what's going on.'

Halina placed her finger on her lips and pointed to the other side of the house. They were creeping down the side passage when Roman tripped on a spade which clattered onto the cement. Hearts thumping, they flattened themselves against the wall.

'See? What did I fucking tell you?' the young one shouted. 'We'd better go in and look around. Borowski told us to keep an eye on his place.' He lowered his voice. 'People reckon he's got Jewish gold stashed away in there. If we catch a burglar, we'll be in his good books.'

'*Ej, tam*, who gives a shit,' the older man drawled. 'Let's get out of here. The bloody dog probably knocked something over.'

'You don't know your head from your arse, you fuckwit,' his companion jeered. 'The dog's chained up. I'll catch the burglars on my own. Just don't ask me to share the reward with you.'

They heard the sound of liquid being gulped, then several more belches. 'Gimme that!' one shouted. A moment later they heard glass shattering.

The voices drew nearer. 'You wait here with the bat while I go round to the other side,' the older man said.

Halina looked at Roman. 'We've got ten seconds to get over the back wall before they spot us,' she whispered.

They made it over the wall and ran. At the corner, Roman gave her hand a quick squeeze and they parted.

Halina's scalp prickled as her footsteps crunched on the path through the darkest part of the square. Something rustled behind her and she saw a long shadow gaining on her. This time she knew that someone was following her.

'I know you're there,' she shouted. 'Why don't you have the guts to show yourself?'

If she made enough noise she might frighten him off. She tried to remember some holds and throws she had learnt at karate long ago. The elbow was a powerful weapon. 'If he attacks from behind, I'll jab my elbow into his throat, spin around and knee him in the groin. Or perhaps ...' She was mentally rehearsing the moves when something struck her and she sank to the ground. The footsteps receded.

Too dizzy to stand up, she sat holding her head until the cold air revived her. As she struggled to her feet, she saw that the weapon was a rock wrapped in paper torn out of an exercise book. She picked it up and moved into the light. Scrawled on the paper in large, badly formed letters was a warning. *Kurva żydowska! Don't meddle in our affairs or watch out!*

'Jewish cunt, am I?' she yelled into the darkness. 'You'd better watch out, you little shit, because I'm going to get you!'

Nineteen

A white parachute was floating in the sky. They looked up from their trowels and sifting screens to stare at this surreal vision.

'Look, he's got something in his hand!' Stefan pointed. As the parachutist descended, they saw one flash of light, then another. 'That's a flashbulb going off! It's a photographer!' he exclaimed.

A few moments later, the parachutist landed in the potato field beside the exhumation site, extricated himself from his harness and sprinted across the field towards a waiting car.

'That's what I'd call *chutzpah*,' Rabbi Silverstein chuckled. 'Are you familiar with that word in Australia?'

The parachutist hadn't yet closed the door when the driver gunned the motor and the car sped off, wheels skidding on the gravel. 'That's chutzpah all right,' Halina said. 'But anyone that determined deserves to get his shot.'

Somewhere in the village a dog started barking and soon others joined in, creating an ear-splitting cacophony. The church bells clanged, resounding across the town.

'In years to come, when I think about this place, I'll think of silent people, hysterical dogs and ringing bells,' Halina said.

'I paid the priest a courtesy visit yesterday,' the rabbi said. 'What a delightful guy. So broad-minded. And what an intellect! I'm going to give him a book I think he'll find interesting.'

On the other side of the trench, Marta was painstakingly removing grains of soil from something with a bamboo skewer. With several long strides, Rabbi Silverstein was beside her. He nodded as he recognised a familiar object.

'That's a *shochet's* knife,' he said. Answering her questioning look, he explained, 'The *shochet* was the community's ritual slaughterer, and he would have used that to kill chickens. *Shochets* still use these sharp narrow-bladed knives to cause the animals as little pain as possible. So we know that at least some of the people killed here were Jews and that one of them was their *shochet*.'

They resumed sifting. Now that several objects had been recovered from the site of the barn, everyone was more sharply focused on the work. 'I'm amazed that these coins are still here,' Andrzej mused, looking at two five-zloty silver coins that had melted and coalesced into one lump. 'It's a wonder the locals didn't loot the valuables.'

Halina recalled the villagers' comments and Beata's explanation. 'Perhaps they thought the place was haunted,' she said.

As the digging, clinking, scraping, scooping and sifting continued, the number of items laid out and bagged in the Quonset hut piled up. By the time they had dug sixty centimetres down, they had found everyday objects that were touching in their ordinariness. A tailor's spool, belt buckles, a wedding band, buttons, safety pins and coins.

Halina was puzzled. 'A slaughterer's knife and part of a sewing machine. Why would people have brought these things to the barn?' She scanned the faces of her colleagues but no one could provide an answer.

The students were chattering about their Christmas plans while Beata was using a bamboo skewer and small paint brush to remove the soil from a small metal article lying on top of several fine white bones.

'These are hand bones,' she told the students. 'In cases of incineration, bones are usually fragmentary, as we've already observed. They shrink during the fire and shrinkage can vary from 1 to 25 per cent depending on bone density and the temperature and duration of the fire. There's no shrinkage until the temperature reaches 700 degrees C, maximum shrinkage between 700 and 900 degrees, but no further shrinkage at higher temperatures.

'Extensive shrinkage is accompanied by changes in colour, first to black or grey, then white. If the fragments are white, then we estimate that shrinkage was as much as 25 per cent. So looking at these white bones, you can assess the temperature of the fire.'

Stefan let out a low whistle under his breath.

Marta looked thoughtful. 'What about the length of time that the bodies have been down here? How can we determine when they were buried?'

'Forensic entomologists can sometimes work that out by examining the type of insects found in the soil of a mass grave,' Beata replied.

Halina looked up. 'A student once asked me whether a forensic entomologist was someone who investigated the death of insects!'

They all laughed, relieved to lighten the atmosphere. But the laughter soon petered out when Beata pointed to the hand bones she had found.

'Let's look at the patterns here, because they can tell us quite a lot. If you cremate dried bones, you get very different patterns from those that are cremated with flesh on them. Burning dry bones causes cracking and produces spidery patterns but no warping or twisting. But if you have a good look here, you'll see definite warping. So looking at these bones, we can say with confidence that they were burnt with the flesh on them.'

'*Jesus Maria*,' Marta whispered.

Beata was studying the metal object she had found lying on top of the bones. Its shape was familiar and unmistakeable. 'Probably a house key.' A hush fell over the group. 'The owner had obviously expected to return to his home,' Beata said. Her hair had come loose again and she pushed it behind her ears and cleared her throat.

Halina glanced at her in surprise. Displays of emotion were rare at exhumation sites. Like surgeons, who allowed themselves to focus only on the strip of flesh exposed beneath the sheet, forensic specialists were too intent on their work to be distressed by what they found. But occasionally unexpected connections broke through their defences and transformed bones into human beings. First the pocket watch, bracelet and wedding ring, and now the key. They were looking at the remains of people who had locked up their homes in the hope that they would soon return, unaware of the terrible fate that awaited them.

Marta blinked a few times and turned away. Stefan blew his nose loudly and muttered something about having a cold. It seemed to Halina that the smell of smoke that clung to the soil had suddenly become more pronounced.

She turned to Beata. 'You're assuming they were a man's bones, but they could have belonged to a woman.'

Beata shook her head. 'Everything we've found so far relates to men. Even the knife and the pin that Rabbi Silverstein said came from a prayer shawl. That could have been a young man's hand.'

'But what about the bracelet?' Halina persisted. 'Men in those days might have worn wedding rings but they didn't wear bracelets.'

'We don't know for sure that it was a wedding ring,' Beata said. 'And the bracelet could have been in a man's pocket, a gift for his wife or fiancée. Or he was a jeweller and someone could have given it to him to repair.'

Letting out an exasperated groan, Halina gritted her teeth and returned to her work. What would it take for this woman to let go of her agenda? Beata was ready to turn intellectual somersaults to avoid facing the possibility that her countrymen had been responsible.

But although Halina was irritated by Beata's selective perception, she could understand it. No one wanted to believe that their own countrymen had participated in an orgy of blood-lust against innocent people. She too had been incredulous when some historians and sociologists had accused past Australian governments of attempted genocide for tearing Aboriginal children away from their parents and their heritage. Arguments raged over the motives of the enforcers, the number of the victims and the historical context. Even if it were true that some children had been removed, most Australians maintained that they had not constituted an entire generation, and that the intentions had been benevolent, within the belief system of the time. Only hindsight condemned them.

Halina herself had found it difficult to accept the possibility that the government had used its power to oppress a helpless group in the community and destroy their culture, and that white Australians had colluded by their silence and apathy. Perhaps we identify so strongly with our nations that we cannot confront their crimes without feeling personally attacked, she thought. Surely mature people should be able to confront the good and evil in a person, as well as in a country. She was mulling over this vexing question when she noticed several white specks in the soil. Teeth.

A shadow fell across the ground and Halina looked up to see Marta standing beside her. 'Mmm, excuse me, but what can the teeth tell us?'

'Tooth enamel is the most durable part of the body,' Halina explained as they walkd towards the Quonset hut. 'The crowns of teeth, the external white part that sits around the interior dentine, often survive fires even when bones crumble, because they become calcined and resistant to the decay processes in the soil. Teeth are unique,' she went on, 'they're the fingerprints of the mouth, but to identify people, we usually need ante-mortem and post-mortem records. In this situation, the most valuable thing we can determine is age, especially in the case of young people. Dental tissue grows at the rate of four micrometres per day and that's shown by striations on the tooth. Like the age of a tree trunk, really. So we can tell the age of young people to within twenty days. If we have the entire jaw, we can assess age by taking X-rays of the teeth and dental eruptions into the mouth, but that's not an option here. Past the age of twenty-five, the biting surfaces wear down, gums recede, pulp chambers become smaller, roots are resorbed and the tips of roots become translucent, so in adults we estimate age by decades rather than years.'

Spreading the teeth on a tray on her table, she held one up. 'This is an upper right third molar. Second molars don't usually erupt until twelve to fourteen, so we can safely assume that this person was over fifteen.'

Stefan had followed them into the hut. 'What about DNA? Could that be used here?'

Halina smiled. Students the world over were fascinated by the developments in microbiology. She nodded. 'DNA has been extracted from the pulp chamber of the tooth after hundreds of years. The most useful form of DNA is mitochondrial DNA which is passed without any changes from mothers to children, generation after generation. That's how they identified the remains of Tsar Nicolas, by comparing his mtDNA with that of the Duke of Edinburgh who was related through the Tsar's mother. But there are problems with DNA technology in general, and with mtDNA in particular, where mass disasters are concerned. For one thing, you need blood relatives for comparison, and for another, it's expensive and time-consuming to check the DNA of every single victim against the DNA of all the relatives. That's assuming we have relatives we can test. But we don't have the ancestors or descendants of the people who perished here, so it's not relevant in this case.'

She picked up another tooth. 'This one is a left central incisor. Judging by its size it could have belonged to a man, but I couldn't say for sure.' She squinted as she examined it from all sides and felt the cutting surface. 'Teeth change throughout a person's life. See, there's a narrow cleft here that was probably caused by some repetitive activity. For instance, a tailor or seamstress could have developed grooves like this after years of cutting thread with their teeth. Pipe smokers sometimes wear a ridge in their central incisors. So do clarinet players.' Her mind leapt to her clarinet-playing neighbour in Paddington. She wondered whether Andrew had a cleft in his central incisors and whether he was looking after Puccini properly.

'Mmm, can we tell from the teeth whether these people died in the fire or before?' Marta asked.

Halina nodded. 'That's a very good question. If the teeth were not in the victim's head when the fire began, they would have shattered from the heat. That's because when the enamel is heated suddenly, the tiny particles of moisture it absorbs turn to steam and cause the teeth to shatter. But when they're inside the head, the temperature would increase gradually. That's why these teeth are still intact.'

She continued to study the teeth spread out on the tray until she came to something that made her stiffen.

'Stay here until I get back and don't let anyone touch these,' she told the students as she ran out of the hut.

Professor Dobrowolski was sitting on a canvas chair in his dark glasses, typing up his report on a laptop when she rushed up to him.

'*Panie Prokurator*,' she panted. 'Could you come with me? There's something you should see.'

He sprang to his feet and followed her. Inside the Quonset hut, she pointed to three white specks. 'These are milk teeth,' she said. 'They belonged to children between two and four years old.' They both stared at three tiny tooth crowns whose eruption would have been greeted with cries of delight by admiring parents and grandparents.

Halina was looking at the prosecutor. 'You know what this means,' she said.

He gave a long sigh. 'I would have given anything for this not to have been found.'

'So would many other people,' she said, thinking of Beata and some of the councillors she had met. She remembered the planted bullet shell, 'Patriot's' article in the newspaper and the assault on her the previous night. She rubbed the egg-sized bump on the back of her head as she turned her attention back to the teeth. 'We need to keep these in a safe place,' she said.

News of her find spread quickly around the site and when she emerged from the Quonset hut, everyone crowded around to ask questions, but Beata stood apart, a look of distaste on her face. 'So you finally found what you were looking for!' she snapped and strode away before Halina could reply.

Andrzej watched her retreating figure as he took off his soft hat and wiped his forehead. 'It won't be a popular find, but it's our biggest breakthrough,' he said. 'It destroys the male Bolshevik theory for good. Unless those babies were also Bolshevik males.'

He pointed to the still unopened area of the mass grave. 'That's where we'll come to the most significant finds.'

From the corner of her eye, Halina saw Professor Dobrowolski engaged in an intense discussion with Rabbi Silverstein. The prosecutor had his mobile against his ear, pacing up and down as he spoke. He replaced the phone in his pocket and returned to the rabbi. A moment later he strode towards Andrzej and Halina.

'I've just been talking to the Minister of Justice. I'm afraid we can't proceed until a decision has been made.'

Halina frowned. '*Panie Prokurator*, I don't understand. A decision about what? Are we to stop at this stage of our work, now that we're starting to find significant remains?

How long will this take? Are we talking about hours or days or weeks?'

From the vein pulsating at his left temple and the taut hinge of his jaw, she could tell that the professor was struggling to control his emotions. 'I can't tell how long it will take. It's not up to me. The rabbi is opposed to the exhumation of the mass grave on religious grounds. It seems he had no problem with exhuming the barn area, but when it comes to the mass grave, where the people were buried, he says that disturbing their remains is against Jewish law.' He shrugged wearily. 'Now the Minister will have to decide whether to alienate the Jews or antagonise the Poles.'

Twenty

Warsaw looked greyer than before, and even the reconstructed baroque square was lifeless without the Sunday artists painting at their easels and the horse-drawn *doroszki* clip-clopping on the cobblestones. Although Halina felt no affection for this city, anything was better than stagnating in the village waiting for a decision to be reached, and the prospect of having dinner with Roman, who was attending a history conference here, had been an added incentive to travel to the capital. Now that she was here, she decided to use the opportunity to visit the national archives to obtain a copy of her birth certificate.

A basket of scarlet pelargoniums hanging over the entrance of a restaurant in the square provided the only splash of colour in this wintry scene. Inside, the elderly maître d', in a bottle green waistcoat, ushered her downstairs into the vaulted dining room and fussed around her in an obsequious manner that made her uncomfortable. Forty minutes later he placed a bowl of tepid mushroom soup in front of her. Pushing it aside, she left some money on the table and hailed a cab.

The taxi driver watched her through the rear-vision mirror as she gave him an address.

'I suppose you left Poland as a child,' he commented. 'Your parents were smart. This country's always in the shit. If it's not the fucking communists, pardon my French, it's the no-hopers from the stockyards who think you can run a country like a wharf union. And this idea of us joining the European market.' He tapped his head. '*Proszę pani*, I ask you! You know how we'll end up? Screwed as usual. And on top of that, we've got a so-called liberal president trying to make out that Poles are murderers! Have you heard about the Nowa Kalwaria affair?'

His voice rose to such an excited pitch that he jerked the wheel and the car swerved across the path of an oncoming truck whose driver leant out of his cabin, yelling obscenities. Oblivious of the near-accident and the insults, the cab driver continued his harangue.

'Sure, we have to find out the truth, but there's truth and truth, isn't there? We're no angels, that's a fact, but when someone tries to tell me that our countrymen are murderers of women and children, that's where I draw the line. If there's one fact no one can argue with, it's that we Poles always behave with honour. We're being persecuted by our elected representatives! Now there's democracy for you!'

There was no getting away from Nowa Kalwaria and the national outrage at being victimised, by the government, by the Jews, by the entire world. As the driver continued his tirade Halina wondered how he would react if she said that victims could be perpetrators too. She decided against it. He jerked the car to a halt in front of the large three-storey building flanked by a row of identical government office blocks.

At the counter of the National Archives office, she filled in the application form for her birth certificate. Halina

Szczecińska, born in Warsaw, 10 March 1939, to Zofia and Józef Szczeciński. Feeling alienated in her birthplace, she sought the solace of having her entry into the world officially confirmed.

'*Proszę poczekać*,' the clerk said and disappeared inside. Halina sat down on the wooden bench and calculated what time it was in Sydney. Her fingers hovered around her mobile. Stifling the urge to call Rhys, she decided to call Andrew instead and check on Puccini. At the thought of home, a feeling of desolation swept over her. It was the clear, unequivocal light of Sydney that she missed, the innocent sky and the wide sweep of the sea, the openness and infinite space. Ever since arriving in Poland she had felt hemmed in and isolated, disconnected from everything and everyone, as though she had landed on another planet.

The clerk returned empty-handed. 'I've checked the information you gave me, but we don't have a record of anyone of that name who was born that day. Are you quite sure of the details?' he asked.

Halina pulled a face. 'Of course I'm sure. That's my date of birth. Could you check again?'

'There's no point,' the clerk said. 'Our system is very accurate. I've already checked twice, and asked my colleague to check as well.'

'Could some of the records be missing?'

'Our records after September 1939 are incomplete, but there's no problem with earlier dates.'

Halina's mind roiled with questions. What could this mean? Was it possible she hadn't been born in Warsaw as her mother had said? Perhaps she was born in a village nearby; people from small towns often claimed to come from large cities. But she dismissed that possibility. Her mother was too down-to-earth for that type of pretence. Still, it was baffling, and there was no one she could ask about her birthplace. At least while she was there, she would obtain her mother's marriage certificate. That way she would probably discover something about her father.

Half an hour later, the clerk was shaking his head again. 'I'm sorry to tell you that unfortunately we don't have any record of the marriage of Zofia and Józef Szczeciński in 1937,' he said with a sympathetic look. 'I even checked 1936 and 1938 as well, just in case. I really don't know what to suggest. Would you like to see the director?'

Halina shook her head. Her face was so rigid that if she moved a muscle she felt it would split apart.

She walked slowly out of the archive office, feeling her way along the pavement as though a chasm had opened beneath her feet and she was afraid of falling into it. Human beings were all a mystery to each other, but to become a mystery to herself in middle age was very disturbing. She fought a paralysing sense of panic. Perhaps her mother had never married. Having a child out of wedlock in Poland so long ago would have been a disgrace that she would never have revealed. That could explain her reticence to talk about the past.

Halina had trouble filling her lungs with enough air and found it an effort to keep her legs moving. With her mother dead, and no living relatives, she had come to a dead end. She was a huge question mark with no answers.

Too churned up to wander around the city, she returned to her hotel on Aleje Jerozolimskie. The elderly doorman, in tarnished epaulettes and a rakish hussar's cap over one eye, swung open the door to the Belle Epoque foyer with its fringed lamps, etched glass windows and raspberry velvet banquettes. In the coffee shop, businessmen from Germany, Sweden and the United States puffed on cigarettes or cigars while they spoke in insistent voices to local entrepreneurs, offering deals to take advantage of Poland's new capitalism. Repelled by the droning voices and the smoke, Halina retreated to the small piano bar on the other side of the lobby.

A young woman with a straight back and a sheet of glossy brown hair fanned out on her bare shoulders was playing a Chopin medley. The barman shook his head, grinned and raised his eyebrows in mock amazement when Halina asked for a Metaxa; she settled for a *wódka wyborowa* instead. He watched with an approving smile as she threw her head back and drained the glass. Almost immediately her spine softened. Vodka was the next best thing to a massage, she decided, swaying in time to the music and dancing her fingers on the polished timber bar. As soon as the mazurka was finished, she applauded so enthusiastically that the pianist turned around and inclined her head in acknowledgement.

'You have request?' she asked.

Halina didn't hesitate. 'The Nocturne in E. Do you know it?'

The pianist looked pleased. 'Is very beautiful. I will play.'

'Another vodka?' the barman asked, and she nodded. As the exquisite notes flew from the pianist's long fingers, Halina closed her eyes. Chopin's melodies seemed to have been wrenched out of his aching heart. They expressed the essence of the Polish soul with all its poetry, heroism and turmoil. As she listened, she felt something stirring. Never had she felt so intensely Polish.

The music stopped, the pianist bowed and left the bar. Halina looked at her watch, slid off the stool and walked unsteadily towards the lifts, her blood dancing in time with Chopin's music.

Upstairs in her silent room, she yearned to hear an Australian voice. She dialled Claire's number, but heard a recorded message and remembered that she had gone to Bangkok for a meeting with police about Thai girls who were lured to Australia and sold to brothels. Toula was also out, probably at her mother's. When she tried Andrew's home, she heard the opening bars of Woody Herman playing 'Golden Wedding' and a recorded message.

'If you're listening to this, Puccini, I miss you,' she said and added, 'Please call me.'

She filled the bath, and slowly trickled the hot water over her neck and shoulders as she sat submerged in a mountain of foam. Hot water trickling on the skin was a sensual pleasure that the Turkish pashas had understood when they installed vaulted marble *hamams* in their palaces. Raising one leg out of the water at a time, she looked approvingly at her long narrow feet with their neatly stepped toes. When she stood up to rinse off the bubbles, she noticed that her stomach was more rounded than usual, and when she lifted her arms, she was disgusted to see loose skin hanging down. No wonder, with all those doughnuts and no exercise. In the mirror, her oval face with its eager expression and overlapping front teeth looked back at her. A few grey hairs were showing and she needed a haircut.

But half an hour later, glowing and made-up, dressed in an Escada silk shirt and long skirt, she sprayed herself with perfume and smiled at her reflection.

The lobby swarmed with hotel guests talking to friends and business partners, and she had to push her way past several groups before she noticed Roman leaning against a column reading a newspaper, the collar of his beige trenchcoat turned up. He looked up as she approached, and when he smiled at her, the light from the chandelier caught the amber flecks in his eyes.

He took her hand and kissed it, then leant forward and kissed her on each cheek. As she started to move away, he kissed her right cheek again.

'That's the traditional Polish way,' he said. 'One kiss on the hand and three on the cheeks.'

'I had no idea you were so old-fashioned.'

'You're in a good mood this evening. Warsaw must agree with you,' he said, and looked at her again. 'You didn't look as elegant as this last time we met.'

She hooked her arm through his as they walked towards the taxi and laughed. 'I'm not planning to scale any walls tonight.'

He squeezed her shoulder and she felt her flesh yield under the warm pressure of his hand.

'You look wonderful, Halinka.'

Halinka. She repeated it in her head. No one had ever called her by that diminutive before. As she returned his gaze, her toes curled inside her boots. Loneliness was a powerful aphrodisiac and she tingled with anticipation, sensing new possibilities.

There were no tourists or pretentious waiters in the restaurant he had chosen, no stag heads or suits of armour on the walls, just small candle-lit tables covered with red and white gingham cloths and a hospitable owner who bustled around bringing crusty rolls and liver pâté while they looked through the menu. Although the food was excellent, Halina concentrated so hard on what Roman was saying that she hardly noticed what she was eating, while his eyes never left her face.

His wife had left him five years before, he told her, taking their only son to her home town, Łodz. 'She was an interior designer with social aspirations, and being married to a teacher in Nowa Kalwaria didn't suit her.' He shrugged and looked away but she saw the hurt expression in his eyes. 'First she didn't like Nowa Kalwaria and then she didn't like me. Especially after she met someone else.'

He looked at Halina again. 'And you, have you been lucky in love?'

She shook her head. 'I often wonder how couples ever manage to stay together. It must be a triumph of determination over human nature!'

'That calls for a toast.' He signalled to the waitress. 'What will you have?'

'I believe in sticking to your poison,' she said. 'Vodka.'

Over coffee, they talked about the photographs of the gravestones he had taken at the deputy mayor's house. 'I can't decipher all the inscriptions,' he said. 'I'll ask the rabbi to help me.'

'The rabbi is the reason I'm in Warsaw.'

'In that case, I'm very grateful to him,' Roman said with a smile. She felt the blood rushing to her cheeks as she met his gaze. 'I've been wondering what to do with those gravestones,' he was saying. 'I can't leave them scattered all over town to be trampled on. It's such an appalling example for our young people.'

'Why are you so involved?' she asked.

It took him a long time to reply. 'When I was about

seven, I overheard my father talking to his drinking mates. It was late and they'd all had too much to drink. He was telling them about the day he had brought the wardrobe home. "When I opened the door, a dead Jew fell out," he said. They were holding their sides and hooting with laughter. You'd think it was the best joke in the world. I could see that wardrobe from my bed. It was big and dark, and every time my parents opened it I held my breath, waiting for a dead Jew to fall out. I forgot all about it for years but when this investigation started, it came back to me. To this day I can't get that image or the sound of their laughter out of my mind.' Roman's face was white and strained. 'Trying to find out about the life of the Jews who lived in Nowa Kalwaria is my way of dealing with it.'

She reached across the table and placed her hand over his. 'You're not responsible for what happened. It wasn't your fault.'

He shook his head. 'Blame is irrelevant. It's just another way of avoiding responsibility. It's about morality, about how you feel and what you're willing to do about it, not whether you were physically present. Just because I didn't personally pick up a club and kill people doesn't mean I shouldn't feel ashamed that some of my countrymen did.'

Halina played with a piece of rye bread, watching the caraway seeds scatter over the plate. 'Can one good deed cancel out a hundred evil ones?' she asked slowly.

'I don't know,' he said. 'But denying a crime is a double evil because it perpetuates the lies. The whole town is under this dark cloud. You must have sensed it. People feel cursed by what took place there, however much they pretend it never happened. When young people move away, they're ashamed to admit they come from Nowa Kalwaria. The only way to exorcise evil is to confront it and acknowledge its existence.'

Halina sighed. The erotic fantasies her overheated mind had concocted were being squashed by the weight of their conversation. There could be no romantic conclusion to an evening spent discussing mass murder and its expiation. The effect of the vodka had worn off, leaving her feeling tired and flat.

'Shall we go?' she suggested.

As the taxi pulled up outside the hotel, Roman drew her towards him. '*Wiesz, strasznie chciałbym sie z tobą kochać.*'

For an instant her heart stopped beating. So that was how you said it in Polish. She had never heard it before, and translated it to herself, feeling more excited by these words than she had ever felt by their English equivalent. 'I'm dying to make love to you,' sounded pallid by comparison. It lacked the intimacy and urgency of the Polish phrase. Or perhaps it was the way he looked at her when he said it.

In her room, he undid the row of small covered buttons on her blouse one by one, looking straight into her eyes. She trembled, and he wrapped his arms tightly around her. 'Are you cold?' he murmured. 'Shall we have a hot shower to warm you up?'

As he soaped her body with slow, long strokes, she closed her eyes. The first time was always tentative and tense and she wondered whether she wanted to go through with this. Sex with some men resembled a workout in the gym, a display of sexual athleticism that was as exhausting as it was impersonal. Others were too timid and their continual need for instructions and reassurance turned lovemaking into a tedious multi-choice questionnaire. She longed for Rhys whose impatient fingers would have torn the buttons off her blouse, scattering them on the floor, who would have pushed her onto the bed without waiting for a shower.

'*Kochanie*,' Roman murmured as they lay on her bed. '*Moja kochana Halinka.*'

She looked at him. More caressing and intimate than the English word 'darling', the Polish endearment dislodged Rhys from her mind. So did the other words of love that Roman taught her that night. The ear was an underrated erogenous zone, and his words aroused her more than stimulating her G-spot would have done. She found it unexpectedly thrilling to be made love to in her mother tongue, as though some atavistic memory had been stirred. Patient and assertive, Roman read every sign of her pleasure correctly, and like a pianist whose strong yet sensitive fingers tease out new nuances of rhythm and melody from oft-played concertos, he delighted her with his interpretation. It wasn't an electric charge as much as an infusion of rose petals, and her skin leapt towards him with an urgency she had thought she would never feel again.

Later, as they lay with their arms entwined, he whispered in her ear, 'Would you like me to stay?'

In reply, she clamped her arms around him. 'Try leaving!' and they both laughed.

In the morning, she woke up smiling, and looked at Roman lying asleep beside her. Waking up beside a new lover was sometimes disillusioning, but she felt neither awkwardness nor regret. Turning on her side, she studied him. He was slightly built but well proportioned, and his taut body was covered with skin that felt finely textured under her caressing fingers. She was tracing the angular line of his jaw with the tip of her finger when he leapt forward and playfully bit her hand. She shrieked, then fell on top of him, pummelling his smooth chest.

'Are you hungry?' he asked.

Her eyes slid down his body. 'Mmm,' she said. 'Very.'

He kissed her chin. 'What would you like for breakfast?'

'What are you offering?' she asked.

'Anything you like, *kochanie*. From corn flakes to caviar.'

She pulled him towards her. 'You first. Then caviar and corn flakes.'

At the worst possible moment, the phone rang. 'Oh, no,' she muttered. 'Hold that thought!' she whispered to Roman as she reached across him for the receiver, expecting to hear Professor Dobrowolski's voice. In her haste, she pulled the telephone off the bedside table. Puffing and cursing, she picked it up but it slipped out of her hands and crashed onto the floor again.

The voice at the other end was unmistakeably Australian. 'Bloody hell, Halina, what's that racket? What are you doing?'

It was Andrew returning her call. Her hesitation was so incriminating and transparent that he burst out laughing. 'Oh, shit, I'm sorry! What's the time over there?'

'I have no idea what the time is,' she laughed. She squinted towards the window but the drapes were still closed. 'I think it's morning.'

'You left a message,' he reminded her.

'I was wondering how you and Puccini were getting on.'

'We're fine. He has great taste. Loves Woody Herman. I swear his paws tap out the rhythm when I play "Golden Wedding"!'

'He's probably pawing the ground in impatience,' she teased. 'Listen, can I call you back?'

'Don't you want to say a few words to Puccini? I can put him on, he's right here, waiting to talk to you.'

'Not now,' she laughed. 'Just give him a cuddle for me.' She was still laughing when she replaced the receiver.

Roman hadn't taken his eyes off her during the conversation. 'Your eyes are sparkling, Halina. It was someone you care about, yes? The special man in your life?'

She laughed. 'You're the special man in my life. That was just a neighbour.' But she couldn't stop smiling. There was a perverse pleasure in having a call from one man when you were in bed with another, even if the caller was just the man next-door.

The coffee was cold by the time the waiter arrived with their tray, but the pleasure of having Roman pour it for her made up for its defects. Although it was winter, the fruit plate was an impressionist still life of vivid summer fruit. He watched her as she picked out the strawberries and, taking the fork out of her hand, put the berries into her mouth one by one, looking into her eyes and running his finger around her lips until every nerve in her body tingled.

'What time did you say you have to be at the conference?'

He smiled. 'Not for another ten minutes.'

She pushed the plate away. 'I'm not as hungry as I thought,' she murmured.

'Or much hungrier,' he teased as they fell onto the bed.

With Rhys, sex had had an element of domination, a hint of brutality and forbidden pleasure that created conflicting emotions. But making love with Roman was as fresh and invigorating as a swim in a mountain pool. For the first time in her life, she experienced the delight of sharing an intimate encounter with an equal, surrendering yet keeping her self intact.

She watched him, wondering how to phrase her question. 'Have you been involved with anyone since your marriage broke up?'

'I've never met anyone like you,' he said, stroking her face. 'I've been waiting for you all my life.'

'Roman by name and romantic by nature,' she quipped, but the look on his face made her stop. 'You really are a romantic,' she said slowly.

'Aren't you?'

'I used to be,' she replied.

Cupping her face in his lean, strong hands he looked into her eyes. 'Halina, we are all made from warped timber. Love is the only thing that brings out the beauty of our grain.'

After Roman had left, the room was still and silent again. Halina stood on the balcony, an eiderdown draped around her shoulders, watching cars streak along the boulevard. It was raining and the tyres sprayed passers-by with water. Her euphoria receded. She would soon be back in Sydney and this interlude would be nothing but a delightful memory.

She felt restless. A brisk walk would have been a relief but it was too early and too cold to go out. The only channel that broadcast in English was CNN with its endless repeats and recaps of the news and the same talking heads discussing events they had already covered from every conceivable angle. A corner of newspaper poked under the door and she picked up the Warsaw daily, *Gazeta Wyborcza*, turning the pages in a desultory way. An article on the feature page caught her attention. She read it through twice, noted the journalist's name and keyed it into her electronic notepad.

Halina turned on her CD player and inserted the *Winterreise* disc. Listening to the poignant songs about the wayfarer travelling through a bleak winter landscape in search of love, her eyes filled with tears. It seemed that people spent their lives searching for love or turning their backs on it. She would leave Poland before spring, before this relationship with Roman had the chance to bloom. Schubert's music, perfectly balanced between delicacy and strength, captured the elation and desolation that were part of the human condition. The warped timber. She smiled, recalling Roman's phrase.

The music ended and she sat staring into space. The visit to the archive office, temporarily displaced by vodka and lovemaking, flooded back into her mind, throwing her off balance. She felt like a child abandoned by her parents in a dark, impenetrable forest. Nothing was as she had believed, perhaps not even her name. Her keystone had been removed, leaving her trembling on the verge of collapse.

'I'm not me,' she said aloud. Suddenly tears welled up in her eyes, but whether they were tears of sadness or laughter at the irony of life, she couldn't tell. All she knew was that she was a forensic dentist with crooked front teeth who devoted her life to finding out the identity of strangers, yet had no idea who she was herself.

Twenty-One

Checking the address she had jotted down, Halina ran up the wide flight of stairs that led to the sprawling apartment block then looked around, wondering whether to turn right or left. Like so many post-war Warsaw buildings, it was shoddily built and had aged before its time. The grimy walls, crumbling plaster and splintered window frames had encouraged larrikins to scribble scatological and political graffiti all over the façade.

Following a path to the back of the building, where three tousled boys were kicking a ball in the cement yard, Halina came to a security door and pressed the buzzer to apartment 61. The door clicked open and she stepped into a doorless iron cage that sighed and creaked until it jolted to a stop on the fifth floor. An arrow scrawled on the peeling beige wall pointed upstairs to the attic apartment that the lift didn't reach.

The woman who opened the door pushed a few strands of hair away from her tired face. Waving a diffident hand in the direction of the sitting room, she said in a voice that seemed to emerge from the bottom of a well, 'You can see why I wasn't thrilled when you suggested coming to see me.'

It looked as though the removalists had dumped the contents of an entire household in one room. One glance was enough to discover Jolanta Morawska's taste in books, clothes and music. Wobbly piles of CDs featuring Billie Holiday, Miles Davis and Louis Armstrong sat on top of boxes alongside old hardcover editions of Solzhenitsyn and Günter Grasse, and thick sweaters and tracksuits were heaped over chairs and cartons. Pushing folders of papers to the other end of the table, Jolanta motioned Halina to sit down on the only vacant chair in the room.

'It was very good of you to let me come when you've just moved.'

Jolanta looked at her for a moment before speaking. 'Actually I've been living here for a few months,' she said in her gravelly voice, 'but I still can't convince myself that this is home.'

Accepting an offer of tea with lemon, Halina followed her to the kitchenette which resembled a garage sale after scores of visitors had picked over the goods. Dishes, plates and saucepans were stacked on top of the small stove, and brooms, basins and buckets stood against the wall. Dropping ash into the cement sink, Jolanta picked up the electric jug from the worn lino floor, plugged it into the only powerpoint behind the narrow laminex bench top, and took two mugs from a shelf covered with brown paper. Opening a cupboard whose veneer was lifting off in the right-hand corner, she took out a piece of poppyseed cake and some biscuits from a packet labelled *Keksy*.

Throwing a pile of sweaters onto the living room floor, Jolanta flung herself into a chair with a loud sigh. 'This place was all I could find at short notice,' she said, biting into a biscuit.

'It's probably the same all over the world,' Halina said. 'A good flat, like a good man, is hard to find.'

Jolanta didn't smile. 'You said you wanted to talk about my article about Nowa Kalwaria in the paper yesterday.'

She was staring out of the window and Halina followed her gaze. Although it was only mid-afternoon, it was dark and only the spire of the Palace of Science and Culture showed above the soupy layer of the city's polluted air.

'That was the third of a series of articles I wrote about Nowa Kalwaria, but as soon as the first one appeared, the worms crawled out of the woodwork,' Jolanta was saying. 'The messages they left on my phone would make your blood freeze. *You fucking cunt. You Jewish whore. One night I'll be waiting for you and you'll wish you'd never been born ...*'

Puffing on her cigarette, she added, 'You're working in Nowa Kalwaria, so you must know what I'm talking about. Extreme right-wing groups flourish out there. Poland for the Poles, meaning Catholics only, thank you very much. They inhabit some sort of medieval fantasy land where Catholics are the heroes and Jews are the devils.'

'Are you Jewish?'

Jolanta stared at her in surprise. 'It's obvious you don't live in Poland or you'd never ask such a thing. It's like asking someone if they have genital warts.' She shook her head. 'No, I'm not Jewish, but most people assume I must be. They can't imagine that a Catholic would think like me.'

Tamping out the cigarette with angry jabs, she told Halina about the vitriolic letters that arrived at the newspaper, all anonymous, written by people consumed by hate. But more distressing than the unsigned hate mail was the reaction of her former neighbours, people she had regarded as friends. The guy next door, who used to drop in for coffee and a cigarette, and sometimes treated her to a beer, looked at her as though she'd poisoned his dog, while the woman who had once confided in her now turned her head away. Some of the tenants had even circulated a petition to have her evicted.

The shadows under Jolanta's eyes grew darker. 'That's why I moved in here. I had to get away from that poisonous atmosphere before I had a breakdown. I could cope with the venom of strangers but not with friends and neighbours turning on me like that.'

'How did you come to hear about Nowa Kalwaria?' Halina asked.

Jolanta crumbled her slice of cake, picking up the scattered poppy seeds with a moistened index finger. 'I was doing some research at the Jewish Historical Institute when I came across the memoir of a man who had survived the fire in the barn. I'd heard vague references to Nowa Kalwaria over the years but his story was so incredible that I could feel the hairs standing up on the back of my neck while I read it. I hoped that he was exaggerating but deep down I knew I'd come across a black page in Poland's history, and I had to follow it up.'

'I don't understand it,' Halina said slowly. 'How can ordinary people turn into cold-blooded murderers?'

'My dear Halina, it's always the ordinary people. That's what's so frightening. If only they were psychopathic monsters, it wouldn't be so shocking.' She sat forward. 'If you only had one week to investigate this issue, you'd come up with an answer, but if you studied it for a lifetime, you'd never get to the truth.'

She lit another cigarette and released a column of smoke towards the discoloured ceiling. 'I'll tell you something interesting. I was in Kosovo at the height of the Bosnian War, and in Sarajevo when snipers were shooting at people in the street as if they were targets at a rifle gallery, but I felt more scared when I was walking around Nowa Kalwaria.'

'Because people were afraid you'd find out who the real killers were?' Halina asked.

'They were more afraid that I'd find out who the rescuers were. Over fifty years after the event, some people are still too frightened to admit that their parents sheltered a Jewish couple for a night or saved a Jewish child, for fear of ostracism or reprisals. Imagine that!'

Jolanta reached down to a pile of books on the floor and pulled one out. Flicking through the pages until she came to a map of Poland, she pointed to a cluster of townships and jabbed her nail on the ones highlighted in yellow. 'Nowa Kalwaria was not unique, you know,' she said. 'Similar pogroms, though on a smaller scale, took place in about thirty other villages in the Podlasie region.

'All the villagers know what happened and whose father or grandfather did what,' the journalist continued. 'But when outsiders descended on them, they closed ranks, denied everything and blamed the Germans. The trouble is, they can't prove the Germans did it. The older people know the truth, and I think for some of them it would be a relief to get it off their chests, but they're too scared to speak out. I hope that's something your investigation will clear up. How is it going?'

Halina didn't want to be drawn on the progress of the investigation. She knew only too well that journalists couldn't be trusted and, besides, there was already enough controversy over the exhumation without adding to it.

She changed the subject. 'Why hasn't there been an investigation before?'

'They did investigate it after the war, but it was a joke,' Jolanta said. 'The communists who had just grabbed power were constructing a myth of national solidarity, so no one was interested in digging up divisive stories about communal violence.'

She gave a mirthless laugh. 'If you believe the witnesses and the accused, Nowa Kalwaria was a model of race relations. What's more, it must have had the best-tended fields and the biggest number of invalids in the country, because, according to their depositions, most of them were either ill in bed or out cutting grass with their scythes that day. And the ones who had described the hideous events during their first hearing later rescinded their testimony on the grounds that they had been coerced under torture to betray their neighbours. It was obvious they were too scared to testify against them.'

'So how come the villagers talked to you?'

Jolanta's voice sounded thin and dry. 'Because I pretended to agree with them. I'm not proud of it, but I decided to say whatever it took to get the truth out of them. But afterwards I felt I'd fallen into a cesspit and couldn't get the smell of shit out of my nose. It was my own moral stench I could smell. I don't know if I'll ever write anything again.'

Halina's mobile phone rang and she reached for it with an eagerness that made Jolanta smile. But instead of Roman, she heard Professor Dobrowolski's quiet, measured voice. 'I thought I should put you in the picture,' he said. 'Nothing has been resolved yet so we won't be resuming work for at least another day.'

Halina replaced the mobile on the table. 'Where did you say you read the memoir that got you interested in Nowa Kalwaria?'

Jolanta gave her a penetrating look. 'Halina, take my advice. Think of Nowa Kalwaria as a minefield. Just do your work and get out. Don't get involved.'

When Halina didn't reply, she added, 'Listen to me, I know what I'm talking about. No one who gets involved in this affair emerges unscathed.'

Outside, the cold bit into Halina's face, making her eyes smart, but instead of taking a taxi she wound the pashmina around her neck and headed towards the hotel on foot. Jolanta's melancholy mood and the disturbing story she had told had depressed Halina and she needed fresh air and exercise. The street was almost deserted, but here and there someone hurried along the windswept pavement hunched against the cold. There was no softness in the faces of people here; decades of misery had etched tense lines upon them. It was spring in Australia, but more than the cheerful blue skies, Halina missed the ready smiles of Australians. As she walked past long, featureless city blocks, her chin nestled in her shawl, Jolanta's warning echoed in her mind.

A gust of wind whipped a torn sheet of newspaper along the pavement and blew it against a lamppost where posters advertised a rock concert and a furniture exhibition. As Halina looked down at the paper, she saw part of Jolanta's article. She raised her chin defiantly. Whatever happens, Nowa Kalwaria is not going to destroy me, she said to herself.

Twenty-Two

The sky was the colour of tombstones that Sunday morning and hung low like a ceiling about to fall. Or so it seemed to Father Krzysztof as he strode towards the church on his way to conduct Mass, his hands thrust deep into the pockets of his cassock. Turning into the square, he saw a crowd gathered around the banner of the Polish Patriotic Party and stopped to hear their representative.

'Don't let them fool you!' the man bawled, the veins on his temples straining with the effort to be heard. 'The European Union is nothing but a communist plot to hoodwink the Polish nation! Make your voice heard before it's too late! Only one party will look after your interests and protect you. Vote for us!'

On a rickety table beside him among the pamphlets were a few copies of *Poland Betrayed* and *The Jewish World Conspiracy*. Standing beside the table was Każimierż Borowski's thin-faced son, Edek, who had an eagle tattooed at the base of his shaven skull.

The priest walked on, shaking his head. The nationalist groups were very active in this village, just as the pre-war *Endecja* had been. 'Extremists always pose as patriots,' he muttered as he quickened his step. The older he got, the more he talked to himself, probably not a healthy sign. In the 1930s, *Endecja* had organised a boycott of Jewish businesses, and local thugs had stood guard outside Jewish shops, clubs in hand, to make sure no one went in. They smashed the windows and terrorised the Jews. And, to its shame, the Church had supported *Endecja*'s policies.

He knew this from reading ecclesiastical newspapers from the 1930s which his predecessor had left at the bottom of a drawer in the presbytery. The papers had made his blood boil. It seemed that the majority of priests in the area had eagerly embraced political extremism with its lies and prejudices. One had even instructed his parishioners not to buy bread from the Jews, warning them that they mixed dirt into the flour and spat into it.

Father Krzysztof sighed. When the middle ground collapses, everyone scrambles for the edges. Between the wars, the world had been polarised between Communism and Fascism and, faced with extinction at the hands of the Bolsheviks, the Church had supported the Fascists, but he was distressed to see the extent of the clergy's anti-Jewish attitude. He didn't doubt that their views had paved the ground for the bloodbath that followed. If the priests of Poland had used their pulpits to warn parishioners that denouncing Jews meant collaborating with the Germans, if more clergy had set an example of brotherly love by giving shelter to Jews, then the tragedy of both groups might have been averted. They were too bigoted to see that what took place was not only a genocidal tragedy for the Jews but also a moral catastrophe for Polish Catholicism.

But why dwell on the past? There were enough disturbing things going on today. You only had to listen to the broadcasts on Radio Maryja. He couldn't understand why the station was allowed to spew its anti-semitic venom over the airwaves under the auspices of the Catholic Church. Freedom of speech was all very well, but that shouldn't mean freedom to malign other religions. Why did the Church allow some of the priests who ran the radio station to stir up religious hatred? 'Why am I surprised?' he muttered under his breath. Their legacy lived on in the pronouncements of some of the country's leading clerics. His own bishop expressed those views from time to time, in revisionist leaflets that he distributed around the diocese. In one of them he had even claimed that the head of the SS was a Jew. Someone had once said that anti-semitism was a virus for which there was no known cure, and shaking his head sadly Father Krzysztof wondered if perhaps this were true.

Noticing the priest's lips moving as he walked along the street, his eyes cast down, his parishioners assumed that he must be praying, but Father Krzysztof kept his eyes down to conceal his anger.

Last night, he had watched a program about Pope Pius XI and the Vatican Papers. It had been interrupted by an advertisement about the forthcoming referendum which would decide whether Poland would join the European Union. An actor made up to resemble a bearded Jew in a long black coat — a stereotype that would have gladdened Goebbels' heart — was rubbing his hands together as he pointed to a block of flats. Speaking ungrammatical Polish with a Yiddish accent, he said: 'Before the war, one third of the buildings in this country belonged to us. At the moment, Polish law prevents us from recovering our assets, but just wait! The minute Poland joins the European Union, all that will change. That's why we're voting for the European

Union.' This speech was followed by an exhortation to follow the Nationalist Party's advice and vote no.

Trembling with anger, Father Krzysztof had called the television channel. 'How can you allow such scurrilous material on your program?' he asked.

'Every political group has the right to have their say about the referendum but the station doesn't take responsibility for their statements,' the producer replied.

There it was, the scourge of the modern world: rights without responsibilities. He saw it now with such dazzling clarity that he stopped walking. They were all links in the deadly chain. The cardinals and bishops, the rank and file of the clergy, the politicians, and the general population who were encouraged to blame the Jews for all their problems.

As he pulled on his white surplice and green brocade vestments, Father Krzysztof examined his own attitude towards Jews. He couldn't say that he had any special affection or affinity with them. It had taken most of his life to overcome the antipathy that had been inculcated into him as a boy, hearing them described in the village as Christ-killers, exploiters, usurers, capitalists, communists and traitors. People complained that they kept to themselves but were happy enough to use Catholic girls as servants or wet nurses. They resented the fact that the Jews engaged with the outside world in a material sense but disengaged from it in an emotional and spiritual way.

As he grew older, however, some contradictions began to bother him. The Jews couldn't have been communists as well as capitalists. And if they were all communists, as many people said, how come the Russians had deported so many of them to Siberia? Whatever the truth of the matter, his sense of justice was offended by what he heard, and it was this that led him to arrive at conclusions that placed him at odds with some of his superiors. Father Krzysztof had welcomed the conciliatory pronouncements of Pope John Paul II and hoped that with his guidance, tolerance and justice would replace prejudice.

As usual on Sunday morning, the church was full. That was one advantage of a country parish: attendance was high; not like the cities where increasingly younger and better-educated people fell away, disillusioned by the hypocrisy and growing irrelevance of the Church, and the predatory sexual behaviour of some priests.

Father Krzysztof looked around the congregation and smiled. They smiled back, the women in their best dresses, the children spruced up with well-scrubbed hands and faces, hair slicked down or tightly plaited, and the men clean-shaven, in their Sunday jackets. Even the youths wore neat jeans and fresh shirts that looked as though they had been graced by an iron. There was still respect here for the Church and what it stood for. If only the Church could use that respect in the cause of tolerance.

Standing in front of the altar that was covered in the dazzling white linen cloth lovingly embroidered by the ladies' guild, with the large carved crucifix behind him, Father Krzysztof held up the chalice and the wafer and his dramatic words rang out: 'This is my body and this is my blood.' He loved the rituals of his faith, with their majesty and poetry, but he wondered how many of his parishioners realised that these were metaphors, along with Christ's miracles and the virgin birth. One by one they came forward, eyes lowered, waiting to receive the body of Christ in the form of a wafer that would dissolve on their tongue.

Just as the villagers in 1941 had received the body of Christ on Sunday and butchered their neighbours on Monday.

He almost recoiled with shock, and had to look down for a moment to regain his composure. Where had that thought come from? Had it been incubating ever since the woman had knelt before him in the confessional several days earlier? He could still hear her troubled voice as she pressed her mouth against the screen and whispered the secret that had burdened her conscience for many years.

'I've never talked about this to anyone, Father,' she began. 'It happened back in 1941, not long after the Bolsheviks left. When my Pawel came home that day, there was blood all over the cart. Puddles of it on the bottom and some splashed on the sides. I'll never forget that smell. It was thick and cloying and made me feel sick.'

Her voice was so low that he had to tell her to speak up.

'There was blood on his shirt and trousers as well, and his forehead was spotted with it.' She faltered again. 'Reverend Father, I knew whose blood that was. I saw Pawel and some of our neighbours bashing Mendel the baker and some of the other Jews. They pushed them into our cart and rode off in the direction of the woods.

'Next day, I watched some of our men round up more of those Jews and drag them towards the barn. A young Jewess I knew grabbed my arm and begged me to take her baby but I pushed her away. *Proszę księdza*, I don't know what got into me. I'm really a good person but ...' She tailed off, shaking her head. 'I don't know how to explain it. I'm ashamed to say it, but it was exciting. We were all standing together for once, our men were in charge, and those Jews were getting what they deserved. Somehow it didn't feel wrong. After the war, some magistrates came and asked everyone what had happened to the Jews. I lied to them. I said that Pawel was sick in bed all week and I didn't know anything about it. May the Holy Mother of God forgive me but I had another baby to feed by then, and I was scared of Pawel and that long knife he kept for slaughtering the pigs.'

Inside the confessional, Father Krzysztof had sighed. At times like these he was relieved that he was merely a priest entrusted with guiding and comforting people, and not a psychiatrist obliged to unravel the knots in their psyche.

A few days later, another woman had slipped into the church to confess, and she too alluded to incidents that had continued to suppurate in her memory despite her efforts to forget what she had witnessed that day. As she spoke, she painted hideous scenes that reminded him of the images of tortured souls the nuns used to show them at school to frighten them from committing sins. The nuns had warned of the inferno awaiting evildoers after death, but in 1941 this village must have been hell for the living.

Father Krzysztof's attention returned to the late-comers in the congregation, who were slipping out of their seats and walking solemnly towards the altar to take Holy Communion. The choir began to sing and as the angelic descant of a Gregorian chant rose to the vaulted ceiling, Father Krzysztof felt moved by the purity of the voices. All people believed they were intrinsically good. He had never come across an evildoer, robber or murderer who didn't believe in his own quintessential goodness. We all start life with dreams and aspirations for the future, he thought, all believing in our ability to become the kind of people God could love, but faced with temptations along life's tortuous journey, we all detour occasionally into some murky alley. Pity swept over him for all those lost hopes, for the destruction of the ideal self so often besmirched by sin. Now he felt only compassion for his parishioners who simply needed clearer directions to help them find the right path again so they could become the people they wished to be. He was so elated that he could feel the blood coursing through his arteries. He knew now what he had to do and he would do it this very morning. It no longer mattered how the bishop would react. He would take responsibility for himself and account for his actions to a higher power than his ecclesiastical superior.

The sonorous notes of the organ died away and all eyes were on Father Krzysztof as he climbed the five wooden steps to the carved pulpit, ready to give his sermon.

'Dearly beloved,' he began. 'We are all travellers on a journey that leads to the same end, but the road has many paths that sometimes confuse us and lead us away from our true destination. Like a river that rushes towards the sea, so do our souls rush to embrace our Maker, but sometimes we lose our way and wander deep into forbidden forests, far from the light. Our village has been stumbling in the dark for too long, but today we have reached the crossroads. Today we can decide whether to take the path that leads us towards the radiant mercy of Our Lord, or to remain for ever lost in the twisted undergrowth that is the domain of darker forces.'

The villagers stopped shifting on the hard wooden pews and fiddling with their hymn books. Even the children were still. Like a skilled actor, the priest dropped his voice. 'Several decades ago, before many of you were born, one half of the residents of this village died. An epidemic killed them, but although it happened long ago, the same bacteria are still infecting the good people of this blessed land.'

Some of the congregation were frowning, struggling to recall such a calamity and nudging their curious children to be quiet, while others waited expectantly. He spoke slowly and with great emphasis. 'This epidemic was caused by humans, not by microbes. I'm referring to a plague of religious hatred, prejudice and bigotry. In 1941, in this village, and others in this area, Catholics forgot the commandment that says thou shalt not kill, they forgot Jesus's instruction to love our neighbours as ourselves, they ignored the call of their conscience and turned against their fellow citizens — men, women and small children, just like your own little sons and daughters sitting beside you right now. Their crime was that they were Jews.'

A ripple passed through the congregation like wind whipping through a cornfield, as heads turned, uncertain how to react to a topic that had never been raised in church before. Some squirmed in their seats and looked down, while others hardened their faces. Even some of his most adoring parishioners now looked cold and angry. But whatever their reaction, the priest's intense gaze and compelling voice transfixed them as though they were listening to a prophet.

At the back of the church where the deputy mayor's son, Edek Borowski, sat with some of his friends, a prayer book dropped noisily to the floor, quickly followed by another. Fixing the disruptive youths with a stern look, Father Krzysztof paused, then continued speaking.

'This morning in the square I heard bigoted views that bring disgrace on those who spread them and shame to those who listen. These racists are fooling you with their lies, they are feeding you dangerous myths. That the only true Poles are Catholics. That Jews are to blame for Poland's problems. And that nothing that happened here during the war was our fault, because the Germans were in charge.'

His voice grew louder. 'Well, the time for delusion is over. It is time to face facts. The fact is that Jesus Christ our Saviour was a Jew. He was born on straw in a barn, not very different from the barns around here.' At the mention of this provocative word, an electric current passed through the congregation. He saw it in their widened eyes and the tense stiffness of their bodies. 'His mother, Mary, the blessed virgin, who we regard as the Holy Queen of Poland, was a Jewish girl. Her husband, Joseph, was a Jew. The disciples and apostles were all Jews,' he continued. 'God chose the Jews to be His people, and persecuting them is blasphemy against God.'

They were staring at him as though he had lost his mind, enthralled by his heresy like children watching a tightrope walker, breathlessly waiting for him to perform even more death-defying acts but secretly hoping that he would fall.

'The fact is that we Catholics are no more heroic and no more loved by God than any other religious group. The fact is that we have to take responsibility for what happened, no matter who was in charge. Only the criminally insane or the politically fanatical would attempt to justify the murder of innocent people. We insisted that the Russians had to stop their deceit about the murder of the Polish officers at Katyń. We insisted that they acknowledge their responsibility. And now it's our turn to acknowledge our national responsibility for the murder of Jews in our village. No nation likes to admit its mistakes, we would all like to think that Poles are noble and heroic, but if we want to claim credit for our heroic deeds we also have to own up to our shameful deeds. Although the investigation is not over, this much we know: many eager Polish hands were stained with the blood of their Jewish neighbours. As long as we do not acknowledge this crime, and ask for forgiveness, we will continue to live in the shadow of this barn, and the spirits of the people murdered there will continue to haunt this place.'

A loud clatter at the back of the church made every head turn. 'You are a disgrace to the Catholic Church and to all decent Poles!' It was Edek Borowski, his adam's apple jumping with emotion. The youth next to him made a low hissing sound. In spite of the general consternation at the priest's words, no one dared to contradict him or to misbehave in God's house, and many worshippers turned around and hushed the boys with stern voices.

Pointing to Edek with a dramatic gesture, Father Krzysztof's voice rang out, 'Sit down this instant and hold your tongue. You will be silent in the house of God or get out.'

He turned his attention back to the congregation. 'To those of you who consider yourselves Polish patriots, I want to say this: those who were responsible for the murder of their fellow Poles of the Jewish faith during the war were traitors, because they collaborated with our enemy and did their dirty work.'

Stunned by the priest's words, the villagers cast sidelong glances at each other, but he still hadn't finished.

'Our own beloved Karol Wojtyła has spoken time and time again about the need to improve relations between Catholics and Jews, whom he calls our older brothers in faith, chosen by God to fulfil His mission. Most of you have the Pope's picture in your homes. You were hysterical with joy when he came to Poland, tears streamed down your cheeks when he addressed us, but when our Holy Father speaks to you, many of you become deaf. Where were you when he acknowledged the responsibility of the Catholic Church for persecution of the Jews and apologised on behalf of the church for two thousand years of anti-semitism?'

A shocked intake of breath followed his words. The worshippers stared at each other in consternation. If Father Krzysztof had announced that the Virgin Mary was a woman of easy virtue they could not have been more appalled. The local media had not reported the Pope's apology, and few of the villagers read the national dailies like *Rzeczpospolita* and *Gazeta Wyborcza* which had been reporting and discussing the Pope's initiatives and the reaction of the Church and intellectuals for the past few years.

'I am well aware that much of the anti-Jewish sentiment before the war was tacitly encouraged and, in many instances, actively fostered by our Church. I can see that some of you are thinking that what happened here sixty years ago, before you were born, or outside your knowledge, or at the instigation of a brutal invader, has nothing to do with you. So think about this. You weren't present at the crucifixion of Our Lord either, but you assume you know who was responsible, and you continue to vilify their descendants. You weren't present at the resurrection of Our Lord, but you are willing to claim redemption as a result. Think about that while you're telling yourselves that what happened on these very streets during the war has nothing to do with you. Expressing regret does not mean admitting guilt. It is merely a human act of compassion. Many of you feel that the spirits of those dead Jews haunt this village and that the place is cursed. Well, let me tell you this: it is your guilty conscience that haunts you, and it will not let you or your descendants rest until you have acknowledged the truth and felt genuine sorrow.'

Transported by emotion, Father Krzysztof was amazed at the impassioned words that poured from his heart. 'Although I urge and encourage you to do this, each and every one of you must reach his or her own decision. What I can do, however, is take responsibility for myself. Humbly, from the depth of my heart, O Lord, I apologise to you, and to the Jewish people of this area, for the suffering inflicted on them in 1941. I apologise for the lack of spiritual guidance on the part of the local diocese to control the base instincts of the perpetrators who took part in the killing or encouraged the murderers by their silent compliance.'

As though emerging from a trance, he stood in the pulpit hardly aware of what he had said, while his parishioners stared at him in silence, their emotions stirred by his eloquence while their minds resisted his words.

Alea iacta est, he thought. The die is cast. No doubt he would hear from the bishop. Possibly he would be removed from the parish. But he felt strangely buoyant as he descended from the pulpit, as though he had just fulfilled a holy mission.

Most Sundays, a group of parishioners would crowd around the church door to share some news or congratulate him on his sermon, but today only two people were waiting for him.

The maths teacher, a middle-aged woman in a shiny black suit, spoke first. 'It's high time people heard some home truths, Father Krzysztof,' she said in her forthright way. 'Don't be dismayed by the reaction. Quite a few people agree with you but they've been too cowardly to admit it. Maybe now they will.'

Councillor Kruk cleared his throat with a dry cough. 'I have to hand it to you, Reverend Father, you're a very brave man,' he said. 'If you don't mind me saying so, you got a bit carried away this morning, but you've given me something to think about.' And he strode away before Father Krzysztof could reply.

On his way back to the presbytery, Father Krzysztof passed Edek Borowski and his gang huddled together in the square like a group of conspirators. As he saw Edek glance in his direction, he wondered what they were plotting.

Twenty-Three

The windows rattled whenever buses and trucks roared past, but inside the reading room of the Jewish Historical Institute in Warsaw the only sound was the crackle of pages being turned. Opposite Halina, a young man with a white face held his head in his hands as he read the thick volumes stacked up in front of him, and an elderly woman in a thick woollen coat buttoned to the neck jotted notes in an exercise book. Every so often the young man uttered a loud sigh, pushed back his chair, scraping it noisily on the wooden floorboards, and stared at the ceiling for several minutes before resuming his research. Now and again the librarian, a plump young woman in a black kaftan, brought in piles of books and periodicals requested by the researchers, then resumed her seat at the square table by the window.

Engrossed in the document she was reading, Halina hardly noticed the people around her. It was written in such a nervous, unsteady hand that it often required several attempts to decipher the words, but as soon as she turned each page, her hand slid to the bottom and lifted the corner in anticipation. She couldn't wait to find out what happened next, yet dreaded what the following page would reveal.

The memoir was dated 1985 but had apparently arrived at the Institute nine years later, and was signed with the writer's initials, not his full name. A note appended by the curator explained that the Institute had received an affidavit with the writer's full name, but had agreed not to publish it at his request.

> *By the time you read this I will have gone to another world. I hope that when I am reunited with my beloved family at last, I will find the peace I never found in my lifetime. I have asked my dear wife not to mail this memoir until after my death because I know that the murderers, may their names be cursed for ever, have never stopped trying to hunt me down, and would come after me this very day if they knew I was alive. I know that my wife will keep her promise although I have never told her my story.*
>
> *It has taken most of my life to find the strength to write down what happened in 1941 when my village became the devil's playground. To this day I can't think about it without trembling. I'm a simple man and never went past elementary school so words don't come easily to me. Even so, it is my sacred duty to record the terrible events of 10 July 1941, because I am the only one left who can tell the world what really happened. Until the truth is told, the dead will never rest in peace and neither will I.*

Reading this message from beyond the grave, Halina shivered as though a ghost had tapped her shoulder. In her mind she could see the writer's spectral face hovering overhead, a compelling presence in the silent room. She heard the intensity of his voice and felt his long, cold fingers on the nape of her neck.

Before I get to the events of 1941, I want to say a little about myself, to give you an idea of the shtetl where I grew up, in a world that has vanished for ever. I was the eldest of eight children. My father was a hawker. I can see him now, a big man with a deep laugh and a bushy beard that curled on his chest. He rode around the countryside in his horse-drawn cart, his shirtsleeves rolled up, a song always on his lips. He sold ribbons, buttons and lengths of material to village women during the week, but every Friday afternoon he came home to celebrate the holy Shabbas with the family.

When I was eleven, I was sitting beside him when the horse bolted and the cart overturned. Was it an accident? Did village boys throw a stone to make the horse bolt? Only G-d knows. We never found out because when Tateh fell off, he struck his head on a rock. I can still see him, his face as white as Yankel's flour, with the blood running zigzag from his temple like crooked stitching. He was never the same again. My poor mother had to bring up all of us children on her own. She never stopped worrying how she was going to feed and clothe us. I don't think Mama had a single happy day from then until the end of her life. In winter, when our window panes froze, we couldn't afford wood for heating and had to stay in bed all day to keep warm. The small children couldn't go to school because they didn't have shoes. I was strong even as a boy and worked for the miller, carrying sacks of flour all day to earn a few zlotys to buy bread and milk.

*But no matter how bad things were, Mama always
managed to put something special on the table to
celebrate Shabbas. The Jews of Nowa Kalwaria were
very devout. Our rabbi used to boast that our wooden
synagogue was the most beautiful in the whole Podlasie
district, and we believed him. Why would he lie? The
men prayed twice a day, the boys studied the holy words
of Torah at* cheder, *and the women kept kosher homes.
They would rather go hungry than allow any prohibited
food to touch their lips. That's how it was in Nowa
Kalwaria before the catastrophe.*

Halina re-read that paragraph, fascinated by the lifestyle
that the writer evoked and the contrast between the
vibrant Jewish community with its rich spiritual life and
the dejected atmosphere that hung over Nowa Kalwaria
today. She supposed the writer had omitted the middle
letter of the word 'God' to avoid using God's name in vain,
and made a mental note to ask Rabbi Silverstein about it.

*With all the praying and the poverty, and all the
responsibility on my young shoulders, you might think
I had a miserable life but you'd be wrong! I was a lively
boy, fearless, and strong as an ox. And cheerful. Why
worry? The rabbi once said that worrying was an
insult to G-d, because it meant we didn't trust the way
He organised the world. And that made sense to me.
Whenever I had a bit of time to myself, I would ride
our horse. When I galloped over the fields and heard
the blood rushing through my veins, I imagined I was
a knight riding to rescue the princess, like the legends
we read at school. My mother wanted to sell the horse*

because we needed the money, but I talked her out of it. It was a good thing she listened to me because, thanks to that horse, I rescued someone far more important than any princess.

This is what happened. You probably know that in 1918 World War I finished, but General Haller's soldiers were still on the loose. To the Poles they were heroes, but to us Jews they were vicious anti-semites like the ones who have made our life a misery throughout history. To amuse themselves, those soldiers tore off the beards of Jewish men together with the skin. They tossed Jewish women and children out of moving trains. That's how they celebrated Poland's new independence.

One day the soldiers had a drunken brawl and one of them got killed but they accused the Jews of murder. They said they would hang the rabbi together with fifty other Jews in reprisal.

Everyone was in a panic. How could we stop them? The police wouldn't help us against the soldiers. The situation looked hopeless until someone remembered that years ago, when the Russians attacked our village and captured the archbishop of Łomza, it was our rabbi who interceded with them and saved him. So the rabbi wrote to the archbishop, pleading with him to stop the murder. But who was going to deliver the letter? Łomza was over twenty kilometres away, and Haller's hooligans were prowling all over the countryside like hungry wolves, looking for Jews.

That's when I came forward. I knew all the side roads, and could rider faster than anyone else. 'I'll take the letter to the archbishop and be back before you blink three times,' I said. My mother wrung her hands. 'It's too dangerous. You're just a boy,' she said. I can still see her white face. 'Don't worry, Mama,' I said. 'G-d won't let anything happen to me.'

I don't know how to put it into words, but I knew that G-d wanted me to do this. It never occurred to me that I wouldn't get through. I jumped on the horse, dug my heels into his flanks and galloped towards Łomza through fields and side roads. I didn't notice if it was hot or cold, if I was thirsty or tired, I just kept spurring him on. I sat so close to his head that when his mane flew up the hairs brushed against my lips. Twice I flattened myself against him and jumped over barriers they had placed across the road at checkpoints, as if I was flying. One soldier raised his rifle to fire at me but we moved faster than the bullet.

Just outside Łomza, with the archbishop's palace in sight, a dog rushed out of a farmhouse near a checkpoint. The horse shied and reared up. Before I could get him to move, one soldier grabbed the reins and two others pulled me onto the ground. I rolled around in the dirt and kicked them but it was no use. 'You want to go to Łomza? We'll help you get there real fast,' one of them grinned.

They started tying my hands together in front of me and I knew they were going to attach me to the horse's tail and slap his rump to make him gallop, dragging me along the cobbled road. I once saw a man they did that to. All that was left of him was his legs. My mother used to say that a drowning man will clutch at a razor blade and I suppose that's what I did that morning. I still don't know how I did it, but somehow I sprang from their clutches, leapt onto the horse from the back and galloped like the wind until I got to the archbishop's house.

I was filthy and shaking all over, and I thought the archbishop would take me for a beggar and throw me out, but as soon as I mentioned our rabbi, he read the letter, nodded several times and said he'd send word at once to stop the execution. G-d watched over me and I got home without a scratch. Everyone treated me like a hero, and some of the hostages wanted to give me money, but, poor as we were, I refused. Mama had taught me that you never accept money for performing a mitzvah. The only thing I accepted was the rabbi's blessing. 'May the Lord bless you and keep you, may He shine His light onto you, so that neither thunder, lightning, fire or water will ever hurt you,' he said. That blessing later saved my life.

A shiver of excitement slithered down Halina's back. His story was like a biblical parable. If she had come across it in a novel, she wouldn't have believed it, but it was impossible to doubt the sincerity of the writer. Besides, no one other than Isaac Bashevis Singer would have been capable of inventing such a tale.

And now that I've told you a little about myself, I come to the part that I have tried to push away from my mind all my life. But the more you try and push something away, the more it weighs you down, and with every passing year it grows heavier, like a stone around my neck. Maybe after I have written it down, I will finally enjoy the heavenly peace of a dreamless sleep. For I have witnessed things that no one should ever see, and come face to face with the darkness that dwells inside men's hearts.

It started with the fire in Stary Most, about two weeks after the Germans arrived in our village. We saw the red sky in the distance and saw thick smoke blowing towards us. Soon Nowa Kalwaria filled with Jews who had fled from Stary Most. They told stories that made our hair stand up on the back of our necks, things no civilised person could believe. The next day, wagons started rumbling into the square from nearby villages. They were full of peasants even though it wasn't market day. Just looking at them you could see how excited they were, as if they were on their way to a football match. But this was not innocent excitement, because their eyes were hard as the clubs and scythes in their hands. They were looking for blood.

Here I'd like to make an observation. Some people can see a runaway train rushing towards them yet they don't move from the railway line, as though their brain can't connect with their eyes. Perhaps they become mesmerised by destiny. And that's how it was in our village. Most people could not believe that we were in terrible danger. 'Why would our neighbours hurt us?' my mother said. 'We've lived side by side all our lives, and our parents before us.'

But I remembered the cruelty of Haller's soldiers, and the way none of the goyim *protected us against them, and I believed it. The Russians had just retreated, the Germans were arriving, and there was no one in charge in our village, only a self-appointed council who welcomed the Nazis with bread and flowers. They didn't answer to anyone.*

Anyway they knew the Germans would approve of what they planned to do. When power is in the hands of people with hate in their hearts and weapons in their hands, the law of the jungle takes over. I ran to warn my brothers and sisters to take their children and hide in a safe place until this was over, but they looked at me as if I was crazy. 'Leave our homes? Where should we go? If we're not safe in our own village, how can we be safe among strangers?'

As it turned out they were right, because no hiding place was safe once the frenzy of blood-lust was aroused. We lived through three days of terror, when people who had lived beside us for generations turned into wild beasts, getting drunk on our blood, because they knew no one would punish them. They could do with us as they pleased. The morally weak were getting their revenge on the morally strong. That's when we realised how profoundly they hated us. For being more frugal, more sober, for keeping apart. For being 'Christ-killers' as their priests had been drumming into them for two thousand years. We were everything and everyone they hated: Satan's children, capitalists and communists. An avalanche of bile and spite spilled over us. They became the hunters and we their prey. Even if some good-hearted neighbour let a Jew hide in his barn, another neighbour would report him. The corn had grown very tall that summer, but if we hid in the cornfield, village children would call out 'Żydek! Żydek!' and at the sound of the word Jew, the thugs would come running, scythes and axes in hand. A cordon of villagers stood guard at the exits of the village, to make sure none of us escaped. They were going to finish us off for good.

I could write a book about those terrible days. The screams still ring in my ears, and scenes no normal

person could imagine still haunt my dreams. But this
was just the prelude to the pogrom. I have to save my
strength to tell the story of the last hours of the Jews of
Nowa Kalwaria.

After warning my family to hide, I ran to a
neighbour's farm. The farmer let me stay in a dugout
in his field, but his son told someone I was hiding there.
When you are hunted, your senses become very sharp,
like an animal's. I sensed the ground vibrating with
footsteps and started running through the cornfield.
I would have made it to the other side but they had me
surrounded and their dark shadows fell across the yellow
corn. I was looking into Bogdan's face. He always had
a sly grin and never looked you in the eye but for once
he was looking straight at me. As he raised his stick,
something glinted in the sun. Fragments of razor blades.
I lunged at him, but he struck my head.

Everything spun around and I fell. When I tried to
stand up, his companion Franek bashed me with the butt
of a Russian rifle and I fell down again. I thought he'd
finish me off when I heard Bogdan say, 'Don't waste
your bullet. Bułka said we were to take them all to
Zielinski's barn, like we did with the two we found at
Piotr's place.' He gave his braying laugh. 'It'll be much
more fun watching them roast.'

They pushed me ahead of them, prodding me in the
ribs when I staggered, and bashing me with the rifle
butt when I fell. Every breath felt like a spear being
twisted inside my body. I knew that some of my ribs
were broken, but whenever I slowed down and clutched
my chest, Franek bashed me again with the rifle butt
and Bogdan gave that idiotic laugh of his. 'Don't worry,'

he almost spat the words out. 'Soon all your troubles will be over.' But above the pain, my mind was clear. I knew I mustn't panic. My only hope was to stay as hard and cold as steel.

When we came to the dirt path that led to a barn near the Jewish cemetery, I could see a long column of Jews. Men, women and even small children, being driven along the road by villagers armed with clubs and whips. A little boy in a blue cap suddenly ran away from the group and disappeared into the cornfield, but the swaying of the corn gave him away. The ironmonger's son, Tadek, and one of his pals rushed after him, clubs raised. The child's screams made the skin crawl down my spine but the silence that followed was worse.

A few moments later, the two criminals emerged, smiling happily. When I looked over at the field, I saw the boy's blood-stained cap lying in the corn. Everything happened fast, yet at the same time it was in slow motion, and I watched as if in a dream, my body and feelings frozen solid. All this time, our people were being tortured by villagers they had known all their lives, while some of the women were tearing the clothes off the Jewish women and children. 'You won't be needing these any more,' one of them said. Others were standing by the side of the road, craning to see what was happening and jeering. 'Now you'll see who's boss, you filthy Jews, you've sucked our blood long enough, now we'll see how high and mighty you are!'

Just ahead of me, a young Jewish woman I knew was cradling her baby. She clutched a bystander's arm and begged her to take her child. 'He's only a week old,' she pleaded. 'He hasn't hurt anyone. At least let him live.'

But the woman she spoke to yanked her arm away, her face cold and pinched. We could expect no pity from them now that they had tasted blood and were drunk with power and greed.

My poor father, who could hardly walk, was being pushed ahead of me and when Bogdan looked away for a moment, I moved closer to him, but where the rest of my family was I had no idea. I only hoped they'd managed to hide in time. Some of the villagers had encircled the barn to make sure no one got away. I wasn't surprised to see those three bandits, the Lewicki brothers, that drunken layabout Grochowicz, Bogdan's father Stach, or some of the self-styled militia who crawled up the arse of our Nazi-loving mayor, if you'll pardon the expression. What shocked me most was seeing that among that crowd people I'd always considered decent folk, who had so quickly lost every human feeling.

My father and I were among the last to be pushed into the barn. Tadek Zamorski stood guard, axe in hand, ready to split the head of anyone who tried to escape. He used to be in my class, we used to kick a ball around together after school and I often did his maths homework for him. After we left school, he shod my horse in his smithy and I sold his wife silk for her wedding dress. But now he looked at me with eyes that could have sliced through granite. That's when I knew we couldn't expect mercy from any of them. It was as if they'd all got infected with the same poison and had turned into mad dogs. Just before they slammed the wooden door shut and hasped it, I caught sight of the postmistress's son, Wacek, coming towards the barn with a big can of kerosene.

Halina read that paragraph several times. Just because the surname was the same didn't mean they were related. In these villages, where people had lived for hundreds of years, the same names often recurred. She made a rapid calculation. The age tallied, but that probably didn't mean anything. Just the same, she wondered if Roman knew anything about this Tadek Zamorski and her eyes kept straying back to that name.

We were pushed inside, jammed against each other, men, women and children. I never would have believed that you could fit so many people into a barn. It looked as though the whole Jewish community was in there. 'Help us!' people were shouting and banging on the walls. They stood on each other's shoulders, trying to climb out. When someone lifted a small boy up through the thatched roof, one of the fellows guarding us threw the poor child back in, head first.

They had propped a ladder against one wall. Someone climbed up, flung liquid over the roof, ran down and dragged the ladder away. The sharp smell of kerosene filled my nose and throat. There was laughter outside and a moment later I heard crackling above me. The thatch was on fire and I saw orange flames licking the roof and running down the walls. People panicked and the smell of fear was even stronger than the smell of kerosene or smoke. Children whimpered, parents clutched their babies and sobbed or screamed, while others yelled, 'Let us out! Save us! Don't let us die!' But we knew that no one would help. As if to mock us even more, the church bells rang out, and it was bitter to know that even the village priest had done nothing to stop the pogrom. Suddenly a fanfare blared out: one of the murderers was playing a trumpet or clarinet. I could hear them laughing. They were having a wonderful time outside, like children at the circus when the clown pokes his head around the curtain.

Fiery embers flew around us and fragments of burning thatch started falling. The roof was collapsing but there was nowhere to go and no way of dodging the flames. We were jammed too tightly together. All we could do was hold the people closest to us and pray. Thick black smoke, as deadly as the fire itself, descended over us and the coughing was even louder than the moaning and crying. As I write this, I know it's impossible for anyone who wasn't there that accursed day to have any idea what it was like to be locked in that barn and to know that we would die in agony. In the twentieth century, we were about to be killed like the medieval martyrs we had read about. No words could possibly describe it.

Some of the people near me were already unconscious. They were the lucky ones, drifting out of life through lack of air. I could imagine the Angel of Mercy lifting their souls to heaven through the opening in the roof. I turned and saw a burning shard strike my father's head. I moved towards him to protect him but the flames were already leaping up from the back of his jacket and I beat them out with my bare hands. When I looked at his face — this is so hard for me to write, even now after all these years — I covered my mouth with my hand so he wouldn't hear me scream. His left eye was sliding down his cheek. A moment later he was dead.

The flames were jumping from one person to another. Parents tried to shield their children with their own bodies, but there was no place that the flames couldn't reach. Those screams of agony, that heart-racing panic, the smell of singed hair and scorched flesh, never will I get them out of my mind. There was no air to breathe and every fibre of my body was squeezed dry of fluid. I would have given anything for one drop of water on my tongue. We were in hell, but this wasn't Judgment Day, it was the day that civilisation died.

I looked across at our rabbi, a saintly man with a long white beard that grew in two triangles below his chin. He was chanting the Vidui, the prayer we recite on Yom Kippur or before death to confess our sins, beg forgiveness for our transgressions and cleanse our souls. Soon the barn, like the synagogue on the Day of Atonement, filled with the sound of humble voices begging G-d's forgiveness, while flames leapt around us, licking our hair and our clothes. That prayer was followed by the Shema which affirms the existence of a single G-d whose glory must be extolled. Hear O Israel, the Lord our G-d, the Lord is One. You had to hear a barn full of people condemned to a hideous death affirm their belief in the mercy and loving kindness of G-d to understand the power of the Jewish faith.

And that's when a strange thought flashed through my mind. In this desperate moment, about to be burnt alive, we were freer than the men who put us there. Because we hadn't abandoned our faith or compromised our principles; we still clung to the values of our fathers that bound us to each other and to our covenant with the Creator. Those hyenas outside had abandoned all the moral precepts that elevate man above beasts. They had descended into barbarism and that was the real hell.

I looked across at the rabbi and thought of my horseback adventure. This time I wouldn't be able to rescue him. Our captors were making sure there would be no survivors, no one who would be able to confront them with their crime. And suddenly, don't ask me how or why, I knew I was going to get out of there. At that moment the door blew open. Maybe a scientist could explain that the heat created a draught, or the expanding gases pushed the door, or perhaps it was the rabbi's blessing long ago, but who can say what methods the Almighty uses to help us?

In that instant, I squeezed through the space in the door and saw that Tadek was holding the axe, ready to split my skull open. Without thinking, I jumped forward, grabbed his arm and threw him off balance. Just then I saw a small child looking up at me. She must have slipped out the same moment I did. Tadek was getting to his feet and reaching for his axe with a murderous look on his face, so I picked her up and ran.

I ran faster than my legs knew how to run and didn't stop until I reached a barley field where I threw myself down on the ground. When I looked up, a young woman was standing there. Without uttering a word, she beckoned to the little girl and held out her hand. When I saw she was safe, I ran until I got to Zenek Woźniak's barn. He was a decent man and hid me for four days, even though he was already hiding my cousin.

'*Proszę pani*, can I get you a glass of water?' The librarian was looking into Halina's face with concern. Halina looked up and stared. She hardly knew where she was, dazed by the apocalyptic scene she saw before her eyes. She nodded gratefully and returned to the account.

The writer's suffering didn't end there. Not long afterwards, the Germans deported him to the ghetto in Bialystok and for the next four years he experienced the cold-blooded German machinery of death at Auschwitz. Unable to take any more of his harrowing story, Halina skimmed the next section until she came to the last page.

My whole family was murdered in the fire in Nowa Kalwaria, not only my father but also my sisters and brothers. I state categorically that the people who carried out this massacre were Poles, not Germans. The Nazis have a lot to answer for, no one knows that better than I do, but this is one crime they did not commit. This was an act of genocide, carried out before Hitler hit on the Final Solution. I saw a few Germans wandering around the town the previous day, but on 10 July 1941, I did not see a single German near the barn. I believe that they approved of the pogrom and allowed it to take place, but they didn't force anyone to bash, humiliate, torture or burn the Jews of Nowa Kalwaria. Those who committed these terrible crimes did so with eager hearts, of their own free will.

I know that they hunted me from that moment, not only in the villages but even in the concentration camps, because I am the only living witness of their crime. That's why I didn't want them to find out that I was still alive or where I was living. As soon as I could leave Poland I migrated to the other end of the world, to put two continents and several oceans between us, but I know they have never stopped hunting for me.

*May the Almighty continue to bless me and my
family, and may we all live to see the coming of the
Messiah who will bring Peace to Israel and to the
entire world.*

It was signed J.E., Australia.

So the survivor had migrated to Australia and, despite
all the horrors he had experienced, he had not lost his faith
in God. Halina hoped that he found the peace he craved.

That evening, alone in the Warsaw hotel, grotesque images,
more harrowing than any documentary footage she had
ever seen, flashed across her mind. Mingled with these
disturbing scenes was a sense of personal confusion and
anger as she struggled to comprehend the significance of
the missing documents. All her life her mother had deceived
her, lied to her. How would she ever discover the truth?

'With your silences and your secrets, you kept from me
facts I had a right to know. What were you trying to cover
up? An illegitimate pregnancy? Some village scandal? Did
you think I'd care?'

Had her mother ever stopped to think how her daughter
might feel one day, not knowing where she was born or who
her father was? Or was that the plan, to have the last word
from beyond the grave?

Later that night as she and Roman lay in bed together, she
tried to push aside her anguish, knowing that this would be
their last night together for some time. The claustrophobic
atmosphere of Nowa Kalwaria would preclude nightly
rendezvous. Halina couldn't risk damaging her professional
reputation and becoming the subject of local gossip by
sleeping with the village teacher. Like a prisoner on death

row she was determined to capture every sensation. The silken nightdress brushing against her warm thighs, the tenderness of his hand on her cheek, the shiver that rippled down her back when he whispered 'Halinka' in a voice hoarse with desire. But in the midst of her sensual delight, a perverse thought wormed into her mind and the pleasure evaporated into the cool air.

'You told me your father left Nowa Kalwaria when you were very small,' she said. 'Do you know why?'

Roman shrugged. 'People often leave villages to look for better opportunities,' he said. 'There's not much going on in Nowa Kalwaria today, so you can imagine what it was like straight after the war.'

'Did he ever talk about the war years?'

His angular face tilted to one side in surprise. 'Apart from the incident with the wardrobe I told you about? No. Why are you so interested in my father all of a sudden?' He was still stroking her but his movements felt less loving than before.

'Just curious,' she said. 'I don't even know your parents' names.' She said it casually.

'Well, for the record, Detective-Inspector Halina, my mother's name was Jadwiga, and my father was Tadeusz. Everyone called him Tadek.'

She had to look away.

Long after he had fallen asleep, Halina stared at the ceiling, her mind a kaleidoscope of dark thoughts and hideous images. Drained, she finally fell asleep. In her dream she was standing on a narrow verandah with lozenge-shaped tiles and she recognised the semi-detached cottage in Newtown where she and her mother had lived after moving to Sydney. Her mother handed her an urn made of porcelain so fine that it was almost transparent, with golden handles and sprigs of flowers with delicate petals edged in gold. 'This is priceless,' Zosia was saying in a stern voice as she placed it on a pedestal. 'Take good care of it. One day it will be yours.' Halina thought she would burst with pride at being entrusted with such a work of art. But a moment later, while running out of the house, she tripped on the pedestal and sent the urn crashing to the floor. Her hands shook as she reached for a tube of glue, but no matter how she arranged the shattered fragments, they didn't fit.

Her heart was drumming against her throat and her palms were moist with sweat when she woke up. She knew that the heirloom was smashed beyond repair and a terrible retribution awaited her.

Twenty-Four

The fire was crackling cheerfully in the hearth when Halina put her head around the door and Father Krzysztof rose from his armchair, stretching out his arms to greet her. With a contented smile, she flung herself down in the chair facing him with the ease of a daughter coming home for a visit. She found it curious that a presbytery should feel like home and that she should feel so comfortable in the company of a priest.

'You must have smelled the *naleśniki*!' he teased.

'I did.' She laughed. 'I could smell them in Warsaw!'

He studied her for a moment. 'And how was Warsaw?'

She heaved an involuntary sigh. 'Interesting. Confronting. Distressing.'

'Would you like to talk about it?' he asked gently.

There was a tap on the door, and the housekeeper pushed it open with her slippered foot while she backed into the room holding a tray.

'Ah, here's *gosposia* with our afternoon tea,' he said and slid a pancake filled with sweetened cream cheese onto her plate.

After a sip of scalding black tea, Halina wanted to say that the earth had lurched off its axis under her feet and she no longer knew who she was, but the turmoil and confusion were too fresh to discuss. Her only happy moments in Warsaw had been spent with Roman, but she had no intention of telling Father Krzysztof about that.

'Is there something on your mind?' Father Krzysztof was observing her with his penetrating gaze.

'If you found out something terrible about someone's father, would you tell them?'

He chuckled. 'My dear child, what a question to ask a priest! I spend my life finding out terrible things about people that I'm forbidden to reveal to anyone.'

She smiled. 'I almost forgot it!'

'Think of it this way,' he went on. 'Who would benefit by the disclosure? You or the other person?'

She bit into the pancake and caught the cheese oozing out of it with her tongue while she considered his question. 'It's not that clear cut. I don't really know who would benefit.'

'I think you do,' he said gently. 'In a contest between truth and love, love usually wins.'

She glanced at him in surprise. How did he know that love was involved?

'Truth for truth's sake can be destructive,' he said.

'But is it right to wash your hands of it?'

'You don't have to be Pontius Pilate, but you don't need to throw the truth in someone's face either. You can know the truth and keep it to yourself until the right moment comes.'

'How will I know that moment?'

'You'll know.'

'But won't this knowledge become a barrier?'

He picked up the iron poker and stoked the fire until a spray of embers flew towards the chimney. 'That depends on the depth of feeling,' he said.

Reaching for another pancake, she said, 'I feel so comfortable with you. It's as though I've known you all my life.'

He looked deep into her eyes. 'That's because I accept you exactly as you are, as Our Lord does. What you see in me is the reflection of your own goodness.'

Tears filled her eyes and, vexed at this unexpected show of emotion, she asked, 'What's been happening here?'

Now it was his turn to sigh. 'The Lord took my dear mother three days ago.'

She reached forward and touched his arm, surprised at her boldness. 'I'm so sorry,' she said, and added, 'I didn't realise you came from Nowa Kalwaria.'

'Things have a way of turning out for the best, if we trust the Lord. When the bishop appointed me to this parish, I was unhappy, but as it happened, it enabled me to comfort her in her last months.'

'Were you with her when she died?'

He shook his head. 'I saw her a few days before —' He stopped mid-sentence and looked out of the window. He hadn't returned in time to hear what his mother had wanted to tell him.

Halina sensed that the conversation was over and wondered what lay beneath the pained look on his face. The death of a mother always left children with regrets but she had imagined it would be different for a priest.

'While you were away, I aroused the enmity of the local nationalists,' he said.

'Don't tell me you've been telling them truths they didn't want to hear?'

He wagged his finger at her playfully. 'Touché! But I knew for whose benefit I did it!'

While he was describing the episode in church the previous Sunday, she was seized by an overwhelming urge to tell him all about herself. For the first time in her life she wanted to tear off the mask of professional confidence that concealed her personal uncertainty. She wanted to stand before him as she really was, stripped of the superficial image she had built up layer by layer to conceal her true nature even from herself. She longed to unburden herself of all the pretence, pain and sadness, lust and ambition, of the anger and resentment she felt towards her mother who had deceived her, and the confusion she felt about herself, certain that he would listen, understand and not judge. She wanted to tell him that somewhere along life's journey she had ceased being the person she had always wanted to be. Never had she felt such absolute trust in another human being. Irrational though it was, she felt that if he rested his hand on her head, she would feel absolved and never leave his side.

The moment passed and, anxious to dispel her maudlin thoughts, she asked for another glass of tea.

Father Krzysztof was studying her, his chin resting on his intertwined fingers. 'I wonder why we stifle our noblest instincts and feel too inhibited to reveal our real selves,' he mused. He had read her thoughts again.

As she rose to leave, he took both her hands in his, looked into her eyes with his steady gaze and made the sign of the cross over her head. 'Take good care of yourself, Halina. May Our Lord Jesus bless you and your work, and may His mercy always shine on you.'

His words resonated in her mind as her heels clicked along the cold, empty street towards the hotel. She had to speak to Rabbi Silverstein while there was still time.

The rabbi was in the foyer of the hotel, his mobile phone clamped to his ear and a perturbed expression on his usually jovial face.

'My daughter is angry with me,' he sighed, raking his curly hair. 'It's her birthday and I'd promised to be back in L.A. but as you know, we're holding our press conference this afternoon and I have to be here. My wife isn't impressed either.'

Halina felt for him, a conscientious man trying to juggle a demanding job with personal commitments.

'I'd like to speak to you before you make a decision about the exhumation,' she said.

'I've made a decision,' he replied.

She took a deep breath to calm herself. 'I'd like to discuss this with you. If you don't mind.'

'Sure, fire away,' he said in his Californian accent. 'So what's on your mind?'

'First, could you explain to me why you are against continuing the exhumation?'

'Okay. Well, to fill you in, from the very beginning some of the impetus behind this exhumation was politically motivated. Sure, there was a genuine quest for truth and justice, but there were other considerations as well. Some members of government wanted to use it to prove that Poland wasn't anti-semitic, while others wanted to lay to rest the ghost of Polish responsibility for the pogrom. They thought that exhuming the grave would prove beyond any doubt that the Germans had done it.'

'But that's not our concern,' Halina burst in. 'Surely that's not why you've decided not to continue.'

Rabbi Silverstein gave a short dry cough that heralded disagreement. 'My reasons are spiritual, not political. According to Jewish law, once a body is buried in the ground it must not be disturbed. The only exception is when moving it is for the benefit of the deceased.'

Halina frowned. 'Under what circumstances would that happen?'

'If the body was going to be buried in Israel. Or if the cemetery was beside a river and the water table was rising and threatened to flood the graves. But even then, that's on the assumption that you could move the entire body, and that's obviously not the case in Nowa Kalwaria where the bodies were burnt and broken up.'

'But how much of a body is left after a few years in the ground, even when it is buried whole?' she broke in.

He coughed again. 'In those cases, the body is wrapped in a shroud and placed inside a coffin.'

'So you can pretend it was whole.'

He surveyed her for a moment. 'I understand your point of view,' he said. 'But I have a duty to Jews here and all over the world to uphold Jewish law.'

'What about your duty to the dead?' she asked. 'Don't they deserve to have the truth about their death revealed?'

He spread his hands in a gesture of mild exasperation. 'But your team has already found bones and artifacts that revealed the way they died.'

'Yes,' she persisted, 'but people are disputing the facts and the numbers. If we exhumed the mass grave, we could prove exactly how many were murdered here, how many adults and how many children. Don't you think we at least owe them that?'

'Listen, no matter how many bones you dig up, you'll

never convince some people. Your team has already shown that the victims were burnt to death. Do you think that's going to convince everyone? Will the lunatic right ever believe that the exhumation is genuine or that Catholic Poles did this? Tell me, how many bones do we need to dig up to prove that people were murdered here? And does it matter if there were 300, 1000 or 1500? Once the basic fact has been established, that there are charred remains of men, women and children in this mass grave, any further digging is merely a forensic exercise. All the locals know what really happened, and the others just don't want to know.'

'We're here to discover the truth, regardless of what people choose to believe,' she countered.

'Well, that's where the forensic and the spiritual differ,' he said. 'I cannot allow the desecration of Jewish bodies to satisfy forensic science.'

'I'm not speaking as a forensic scientist,' she said, struggling to keep her voice under control. 'I've just been to the Jewish Historical Institute where I read the testimony of a man who survived the fire.'

His thick eyebrows shot up in surprise. 'Someone got away from that barn?'

She swallowed. 'I'd like to tell you his story.'

He listened in silence while she recounted it, with all the details that had been seared into her memory. With an impassioned voice she said, 'Rabbi, these people were martyrs. Their death has meaning and must be publicly acknowledged. If their bones are just covered up, the arguments will never cease. Once doubt is cast over one aspect of a historical incident, the doubters focus on that and shake the credibility of the whole story. A whole community was burnt to death here. Don't you think we owe it to them to discover as much as we can, and try and account for each one?'

Rabbi Silverstein was nodding slowly. 'Let me think about this,' he said. 'Perhaps I'll find a compromise.'

The reporters were already milling around waiting for the rabbi to arrive. As soon as they caught sight of his portly figure striding towards the exhumation site, they surged forward, tape recorders, microphones and cameras poised. Standing to one side with the forensic team, Halina noticed that not only were the major Polish newspapers, television and radio stations represented, but international media as well.

Beata pointed to the German television team and whispered to Andrzej, 'Wouldn't they love to report that the Poles did it? Then they could say that the Germans weren't the only perpetrators.'

He regarded her for a moment without speaking. 'But they weren't, were they,' he said quietly.

'You've all come to the wrong place — Michael Jackson isn't coming here today!' the rabbi joked with the journalists, immediately dispelling the tension as laughter broke out.

'Rabbi, can you tell us when the exhumation will resume?' asked a young reporter, a beat ahead of the others who were shouting across each other.

'Hey, boys, gimme a break!' the rabbi laughed and waited for the hubbub to subside. 'This exhumation is a delicate and difficult matter, because we're trying to abide by Jewish law and tradition but at the same time we also want to abide by Polish legal requirements and, beyond that, by the demands of humanity. The Jewish law that forbids disturbing the dead has evolved over thousands of years. It's not in my power to alter that. I'm only an agent of that law.'

The quality of listening changed as the reporters realised that something momentous was about to be said.

'The issue for me is not that Germans or Poles committed this crime. For me, the fundamental issue is that neighbours did it. I know that some people, who consider themselves Polish patriots, maintain that the victims were all men and that they were all Bolsheviks. That is a lie, and in repeating that lie they are damaging the name of Poland around the world and violating the integrity of this nation.'

Three brindle cows meandered along the path, driven by an old woman bundled up in a thick grey shawl. A moment later a flock of jays flew overhead, cawing so raucously that the rabbi had to stop talking. A sudden gust of wind blew off his skullcap and, replacing it on his bushy hair, he continued. 'I would like to say at this point how much I appreciate the sensitivity of the Polish government in this matter and the professionalism and dedication of the forensic team.' His gaze rested for a second on Halina's face. 'The exhumation is part of a criminal investigation and the evidence that it produces may assist in future prosecutions. But more than that, it is the duty the living owe to the dead to discover the truth. It has been my challenge, and my responsibility, to reconcile these requirements.'

The reporters moved forward, holding their microphones and recorders closer, not to lose a syllable. The rabbi blinked as flashbulbs exploded in anticipation of his next statement.

'After a great deal of soul-searching and consulting with my ecclesiastical colleagues in Israel and New York,

I've reached a decision. We believe that in this unique situation, the exhumation may be permitted to continue. But as soon as it is concluded, all the remains must be replaced in the grave.'

As the reporters and photographers scrambled to their waiting cars, Halina closed her eyes and breathed out in relief.

Twenty-Five

The woman pushed open the church door and looked around as she tied a black chiffon scarf over her grey hair. She dipped her fingers into the font of holy water, genuflected and made the sign of the cross. Taking a note from her purse she dropped it into the alms box, lit two candles, and knelt at the back of the church, resting her pointed chin on her hands as her lips moved in silent prayer. She remained there with her head bowed until she saw the priest's black cassock near the altar.

The church was as cold as a cemetery vault. Father Krzysztof rubbed his hands together to restore the circulation, and wondered about the woman whose footsteps echoed on the stone floor as she approached. She didn't look familiar. Sometimes women came from other villages to confess their sins and be absolved by a priest who didn't know them, but he had never seen this one before. As she asked him to hear her confession, a shaft of winter sunlight slanted down from the stained-glass window and lit up her face. The sweetness of her expression reminded him of Fra Angelico's painting of the Annunciation which he had seen once on the wall of a church in Florence. The solemnity of the Archangel's face as he announced the Holy Virgin's destiny had moved him deeply, and looking at the woman in front of him, he was struck by the resemblance.

She knelt in the confessional. 'Forgive me, Father, for I have sinned.'

When she spoke, he could detect lilting traces of the distinctive local speech that marked the inhabitants of the Podlasie region. So she did come from these parts after all.

'We are all sinners, my child,' he responded. 'When was your last confession?'

She hesitated. 'A long time ago, Father.'

'What sins have you committed?'

Her voice trembled. 'I didn't keep a promise to the dead.' She blew her nose.

'The spirits of the dead understand our earthly dilemmas,' he said softly. 'Can you still keep that promise?'

She blew her nose again with a loud finality and sighed. 'Yes, Father, but it's probably too late. So many years have passed.'

'It's never too late to keep a sacred promise. God is not a timekeeper. A thousand years is a blink of an eye in His sight, but the good intentions of a pure heart like yours light up the darkness of this world for all eternity. Say five Hail Marys and keep that promise as soon as you can.'

She didn't move. 'I have another problem,' she said.

'A problem or a sin?' He was glad she couldn't see him smiling.

'A dilemma, Father.'

'It's cold and uncomfortable here, my child. No good for my rheumatic old bones. Come and talk to me at the presbytery in an hour. We'll have a glass of tea in front of the fire and I'll see if I can help with your dilemma.'

He watched her as she walked away with her straight back and quick, firm steps. You could tell a person's character by their gait as much as by their gaze, and from his long years of observing people, the priest knew that this woman had strong principles and a good heart.

The woman walked out of the church and, without hesitating, turned onto the unpaved road that led towards the potato fields. She was surprised to see that some of the farmers still covered their roofs with thatching, just as in the old days. After passing several farmhouses, she came to a large area cordoned off with police tape. Inside the enclosure, people were digging, sifting soil, and carrying various objects towards a makeshift hut. Some of them wore overalls with the word Forensic or *Medicyna Sądowa* in large letters across the back.

Even from where she was standing, she could hear the clinking of trowels and the buzz of conversation. A man in a soft white hat was holding up something he'd picked out of the soil. He walked over to a tall slim woman with reddish hair, who nodded, took it from him and headed towards the field hut. Caught up in their excitement, the stranger wondered what they were looking at when she remembered that this was where Zielinski's barn had once stood. She trembled so violently that she had to lean against the fence to stop her knees from buckling.

Although she had her back to the farmhouse, she sensed that someone was watching her, but when she turned around the only sign of life was the flutter of a curtain. Further on, she came to a farmhouse that seemed to be sinking crookedly into the loam. Stach's house. Some of the shingles were broken and the yard was cluttered with crates, boxes and rusty farm implements. It was deserted. Stach must have died long ago, and Bogdan had probably moved away. Even after all this time, the tendons on her neck jumped and her throat closed up at the thought of them. Her legs wobbled and she slowed down, wondering whether she had the courage to keep going. This path evoked such painful memories that each breath struggled against the tightening inside her chest. Perhaps it won't be there any more, she thought, and felt ashamed of her cowardice.

But the apple tree was still there. So was the farmhouse, forlorn and neglected now with its overgrown garden, because she hadn't been able to go on living there or to sell it. She forced herself to look at the tree. Its branches were bare and, despite all the years that had passed, it had not grown. It was gnarled and stunted, and she sensed with a farmer's instinct that its spring blossoms were sparse and its summer fruit were as bitter as her memories.

The ground seemed to loosen under her feet and she felt herself being sucked down. With a shudder she pushed herself on, and didn't stop walking until she came to the Catholic cemetery. Unlike the rest of the village, it had changed so much that she didn't recognise the paths or the names on the tombstones, and couldn't find the ones she was searching for. With growing panic she wandered among the graves, reading the inscriptions behind the wilting floral wreaths and framed photographs of the deceased until she looked down at two slabs side by side, marked simply Anielcia Marczewska and Piotr Marczewski. She sat on the stony ground for a long time in silent contemplation, and brushed the pile of withered leaves and fragments of rock away from the gravestones. Finally she traced her father's name with her finger.

'I've come back, *Tata*,' Kasia whispered. 'I've come back to keep my promise.'

Slowly she retraced her steps to the square.

In the warmth of the presbytery, encouraged by the priest's kind face, she spoke in a quiet voice, considering each word.

'*Proszę księdza*,' she began. 'I don't know where to start.'

'Take your time, my child,' he urged.

She took a deep breath. 'It happened in 1941,' she said. 'The Russians had just retreated, and the Germans had just arrived.'

As she spoke, she was twelve years old again, her skinny little plaits tied on top of her head with a ribbon, sitting beside her father on the cart on their way home from the market, watching the cavalcade of German cars and motorcycles with their riders who smelled sharply of eau de cologne.

Like a newsreel documentary unrolling on a movie screen, Father Krzysztof saw the events she described so vividly. She was looking past him as she spoke, her eyes fixed on an internal landscape, and he listened gravely to the torrent of words that spilled out as though she was possessed and powerless to stop until the story was told. He heard the knocking on the farmhouse door, saw the exhausted Jewish couple collapsing on the doorstep, and sensed the anguish of the secret birth in the barn. But when she came to the terrible moment when the father had to smother his newborn son, Father Krzysztof closed his eyes as though to shut out the unbearable scene.

'What a tragedy,' he sighed. 'What terrible times. To be forced to kill your own child.'

Kasia sat forward and there was a strange expression on her face. 'But that's just it, Reverend Father. The baby didn't die.'

She had stood in the doorway, watching as her father walked out of the barn, head bowed, a small wooden box in his big hands. When he came to the old apple tree, he placed the box gently on the ground and picked up a spade, sighing each time his rubber boot pushed it deeper into the soil. She tried not to think of the tiny body inside the box, no bigger than a doll. Did Jewish babies go to Limbo if they died before being christened? From time to time her father stole a glance at the box and brushed away the leaves that fluttered onto it, and as he leant on the spade and wiped his face, she sensed his distress.

She wished he would hurry. What if someone came and saw what he was doing? Suddenly she heard a faint mewing sound. A moment later she heard it again. It sounded like a baby. Her father stiffened and looked around, and their glances met. Was conscience playing tricks on them? The sound stopped and Piotr dug faster now. He was about to give the spade one last push when he stopped in mid-air. There it was again. He put his ear against the box. There was no mistaking it this time. A baby's cry. Piotr flung down the spade and with trembling fingers opened the box.

Kasia crept forward. '*Rany boskie!* Christ's blessed wounds,' she whispered. The baby's mouth was open, his face was red and scrunched up, and he was crying.

Piotr sank on his haunches, trembling all over. It was a miracle.

'We could take him to the nuns, they might look after him,' Kasia suggested.

Piotr looked glum. 'They'd know it was a Jewish baby and would want to know where I found it. If only it was a girl, it would be easier, but they say that Jewish boys are made differently.'

Kasia examined the baby. He looked exactly the same as the boys she had seen swimming in the creek.

Piotr stared in disbelief. 'It's a miracle,' he whispered. 'The Lord wants this baby to live.'

Late at night, when the younger children were asleep, he wheeled his rusty old bicycle out of the shed. Kasia sat on the handlebars, holding the box. They took the path through the woods, away from the houses, and Kasia gripped the box and tried to steady herself whenever the bicycle bumped over a tree root. It was a dark night and a sliver of a moon spotlit the birch trunks which gleamed with a ghostly light. An owl hooted, and Kasia screamed and almost fell off as she looked up into its unblinking yellow eyes. A few moments later her father stopped outside the thatched hut of a childless couple they knew. Slipping off the handlebars as quietly as she could, Kasia placed the box on the doorstep. Village girls were always getting into trouble and they would think that one of them had abandoned her unwanted child.

The following day Piotr and Kasia were on tenterhooks, wondering what had happened to the child, but didn't dare to make any enquiries. Kasia took bread, water and potatoes to the bunker in the swill bucket but couldn't look at the Jewish couple's grief-stricken faces. They hardly touched their food, and turned away from each other, not speaking. Yossel seemed to have shrunk, and he stared into space. Malka's dull eyes followed Piotr with an accusing gaze. Kasia longed to tell them that their baby was alive, but her father said they'd better make sure the couple had kept the child before saying anything.

It didn't take long before the villagers started gossiping about the baby that had miraculously appeared on the doorstep of the childless woman who told everyone that the Holy Virgin had answered their prayers and brought her a little angel from heaven. As soon as he heard that the baby was safe, Piotr rushed home, whistling all the way, impatient to tell Malka and Yossel the good news.

But when he entered his yard, the smile froze on his lips. Kasia was standing there, gripping the bucket with white knuckles as Stach and Bogdan loomed over her.

'Just swill for the pigs,' she said, tilting her pointed chin defiantly.

Turning to Piotr, Stach sneered, 'Well, *panie gospodarzu*, let's see what the Marczewski pigs eat these days.' He yanked the bucket out of Kasia's grasp, spilling its contents on the dirt. 'Just look at that. Bread, milk and potatoes. What lucky pigs,' he said, and turned towards the barn.

Kasia broke into a cold sweat as her father shouted, 'You piece of shit! You German-loving scum! Get off my land!' He moved to pick up the scythe but Stach was running his finger along the edge of the axe. Not taking his eyes off Piotr's face, with the other hand he reached out and pulled Kasia towards him, hooking his arm around her throat.

'Or what?' he smirked. 'What will you do? Call the police?'

At this Bogdan gave a shrill laugh. 'We're the police now!'

Stach pushed Piotr in the chest with the axe handle, still holding Kasia against him, while Bogdan jabbed the pitchfork into the hay spread over the barn floor, tossing it aside to see what lay underneath. Watching Piotr's tense face, Stach gave an insidious smile. 'We've seen Kasia hanging around here with her bucket, haven't we, Bogdan?'

Kasia's eyes widened with fear. So that was the sound she'd heard behind the lilac bushes.

'Let her go,' Piotr said through clenched teeth. 'This has nothing to do with her. Bogdan should find something better to do than sneak around spying on his neighbours.'

Stach scratched his prominent chin with the axe handle. 'As it happens, we do have something better to do today, don't we, Bogdan?' Turning to Piotr he said, 'We're going to clean up our town today, and we're starting with your visitors.'

Bogdan had stopped poking around with the pitchfork. 'Now what have we got here?' he shouted. Pushing aside the hay, he whooped as he saw the trapdoor. Piotr closed his eyes, his lips moving in prayer.

Kasia held her breath as Bogdan threw down the pitchfork and, like a dog that has scented truffles, panted with anticipation as he raised the door. 'Look what we have here!' he shouted. 'Well, the game is over!' Leering, he leant down and shouted, 'You'd better come out quick before I come down and break your necks!'

Piotr rushed at Bogdan. 'Leave them alone, you bastard!'

Stach studied him for a moment, as if trying to figure something out. He looked around the barn until his eyes fell on Bogdan's razor-studded stick. He smiled and said something in a low voice to his son.

'I don't think you understand, *Panie* Piotru,' he said. 'We're only carrying out orders. And I wouldn't make any nasty remarks if I was you. And as for this one here,' he indicated Kasia, 'what if we tell the Commandant that she's been feeding Jews?'

It was too late for caution. 'Tell him what you like,' Kasia said. 'I'll tell him you and your son go around terrorising decent people.'

Piotr gave her a warning glance but Stach merely shrugged. 'You'll keep.'

Malka was still screaming as Bogdan picked up his razor-studded stick and waved it in front of her. 'Shut the fuck up or I'll cut both of you into tiny pieces,' he yelled.

As they dragged Malka and Yossel away, Piotr looked into Kasia's eyes and spoke with a forceful intensity she had never heard in his voice before. 'Watch carefully. Notice everything. Never forget,' he told her. 'One day you will need to remember this.'

Kasia turned her gaze back to Father Krzysztof with a start, as though she had forgotten his presence.

'We couldn't save Malka and Yossel,' she said in a dull voice. 'We didn't even have time to tell them that their baby was still alive.' A loud sigh escaped from her mouth. 'That's why *Tata* made me promise that one day I had to tell what I knew about the baby.'

Father Krzysztof spoke slowly. 'How come your father didn't do it himself?'

But tears were streaming down Kasia's face and it took her several minutes to compose herself.

She closed her eyes. This was the part she had tried to shut out of her mind all these years.

'Later that day Stach and Bogdan came back for my father,' she began in a tremulous voice.

It was as raw and vivid as the day it happened, but at the same time it was also unreal. Stach's horrible smile as he turned to her father and sneered, 'Now we'll deal with you. We have to teach Jew-lovers a lesson.'

She had watched helplessly, but when Bogdan threw a rope over the thickest branch of the apple tree, she had grabbed the rake and run towards him, screaming at them to leave her father alone. Just then Marysia had run out of the house and Bogdan picked her up. 'Get inside and shut up or I'll cut her throat,' he said.

Kasia swallowed and her voice broke. 'I never took my eyes off *Tata* and he never took his eyes off me. The rope was cutting into his neck and he could hardly talk. The last thing he said was "Tell them". All I could do was nod. Then Stach kicked the stool out from under him and his eyes bulged and his legs swung in the air and all I could hear was someone screaming and screaming and it was me ...'

She was trembling so violently that the priest rang the little bell and asked the housekeeper to bring more tea.

Cupping the glass with hands that shook, Kasia continued. 'Before they went off, Stach said he'd be watching me and if I ever told anyone what had happened, I'd find my sisters at the bottom of the well. I was too scared to stay around so the following day I packed all our things in bundles, loaded up the cart and we went to live with my aunt in Bialystok. I never wanted to see this place again. All my life I've tried to forget what happened here. I've never told anyone what I've just told you. Not even my children.' Her voice dropped to a whisper. 'Only I couldn't forget. The more I wanted to forget, the more I thought about it.'

'My poor child,' Father Krzysztof said. 'What a heavy load you've had to carry. But what made you decide to come here now?'

'As soon as I heard about the investigation I knew I had to come back and put things right. Only I don't know how. People have been living in ignorance all these years, so what right do I have to come here and tell them that things are not the way they thought? My parents always said that we must tell the truth, but is truth the most important thing?'

For the second time that week, the philosophy of truth was being debated in his sitting room.

He looked at his hands. 'If you were to "put things right" as you say, how would you do it?' he asked gently, evading her question.

She bit her lip. 'I'd have to find the people who brought the baby up and tell them who the real mother was. But I'm afraid that will come as a terrible shock to them after all this time.'

'Do you remember who they were?' he asked.

She nodded. 'It was *Pani* Agata.'

Father Krzysztof's mouth felt as though he had swallowed a cup of sand. 'The carter's wife?'

Kasia nodded again.

He gripped the table with white knuckles as the room started spinning around him. His voice was muffled as though his tongue was swollen. 'The Lord gathered *Pani* Agata up last week.'

'So I've come too late!' Kasia cried out. 'Now I can't keep my promise.'

He didn't reply.

Suddenly Kasia looked up. 'Reverend Father, do you happen to know what happened to the child?'

He seemed not to have heard. She repeated the question, and waited again. When he finally replied, his voice was so faint and weary that she felt alarmed.

'Leave it with me, my child.'

As she turned to leave, he added, 'The good Lord knows that you've kept your promise.'

Father Krzysztof sat in the darkening room without stirring. Although he occasionally looked out of the window, he saw nothing. The temperature had dropped sharply and snow would soon fall but he wasn't aware of the cold, only of the tumult raging inside his head. Every fibre in his body was screaming that this wasn't possible, there must be some mistake. He could not be a Jew. The Lord would not have played such a cruel trick on him.

How was it possible that he hadn't realised he was different? Glancing into the mirror, he saw the close-cropped white hair, the oval face and the aquiline nose. Digging into his youth, he searched for signs of awareness, and recalled times when he had noticed that he resembled neither parent, that his features seemed to have been moulded by a different sculptor. But his mother had always allayed his doubts by saying that the good Lord made us all unique because we all had a special purpose to fulfil. His was to dedicate himself to the service of God.

He recalled the stories that his mother — he would never be able to think of the kind, simple woman who had brought him up as anything else — never tired of telling about his infancy. She had repeated them so often that he knew them word for word.

'You were blessed. You radiated goodness and everyone loved you,' she used to say, her face shining with pride.

'When poor old Stefcia was paralysed after she fell off the ladder, you just touched her hand and the very next day she got up and walked. Everyone said you had miraculous powers. People came from villages all around with presents, hoping for a blessing. You were a little angel and goodness shone from your face. You were clever too, and people whispered that you'd go far, maybe even to Rome. That's why your father and I knew you were destined for the priesthood.'

Contemplation was replaced by anger. His life had been a mockery. His real father had tried to kill him, and when he failed to die, he'd been abandoned on a stranger's doorstep like a bundle of unwanted rags. And his adoptive parents had lied to him all his life, pretended he was theirs. Wild thoughts spun around his head, raging, accusing, blaming, until he felt wrung out.

How could the parish priest of Nowa Kalwaria be a Jew? Ever since he'd read Pope John XXIII's Vatican II encyclical, he had known that the Jews could not be blamed for the death of Christ. In any case, they were all Jews in those days, apart from the heathen Romans. And if God had ordained that his only begotten son should die, then it was blasphemous to blame the agents of his will. Jews and Catholics shared the same God and the same Holy Bible, the Old Testament. But having a tolerant attitude towards a religious minority did nothing to diminish the shock of discovering that he himself belonged to the race that was despised by so many of his countrymen.

Time after time his housekeeper tapped on the door to ask whether he wanted dinner, a glass of tea or more wood for the fire, but each time he waved her away with a distracted gesture. Nothing about his life made sense any more, and the volcanic anger that threatened to erupt terrified him with its fury. Occasionally the rage subsided and for a while he was able to stand back from his pain. He reasoned with himself, turning the horrifying facts over in his mind in an attempt to find some other interpretation. It was impossible to imagine the despair of a father forced to suffocate his own child, or the grief of a mother who gave birth only to have her baby snatched away for ever.

Perhaps this was the secret that his mother had wanted to tell him. But recalling Kasia's story, he realised that his adoptive mother hadn't known whose child he was. Kasia's family alone had known the truth. He thought about his birth mother, a phantom called Malka, who had borne a son on a pile of hay scattered in a stranger's barn, surrounded by people who wanted her dead. The stories he had recently heard in the confessional shocked him with a new force. His parents must have been among those unfortunate souls who had been tortured by the villagers during their calvary on that summer's day in 1941.

He covered his face with his hands. A Jesuit priest who was a Jew! The turmoil was unbearable. He was too churned up to think clearly. What should he do? Perhaps no one need ever discover his secret. But he knew that he could never live with deceit. Should he resign from the priesthood? His whole life lay in ashes around him. He dropped to his knees and buried his face in his hands.

'O Lord, with your infinite wisdom and mercy show me the way for I am lost. If this is part of your divine plan, give me the strength to bear it so that in time I may learn to turn my tragedy into your triumph.'

Twenty-Six

Twenty-two young faces, their expressions ranging from grudging interest to sullen boredom, turned towards Halina when she entered the classroom. She shook hands demurely with Roman, surprised that even this fleeting touch sent ripples through her body. As she looked down to avoid giving herself away, she felt no older and certainly no wiser than the girl with the untidy fringe who was staring at her from the front row. Tearing her gaze away from Halina's high-heeled boots, the girl swivelled around to whisper something to her friend, who craned forward for a better view. One of the boys flicked a paper dart across the room while the others regarded Halina with an insolent stare.

'No one in Nowa Kalwaria has ever met an Australian,' Roman had said the previous night. 'Most of these kids have never even been to Bialystok, let alone Warsaw. It would be good for them to meet someone from another country. Besides, *kochanie*,' he was nuzzling her cheek, 'I'd like you to come and see where I teach. And here's the *pièce de résistance*: you'll be able to see the Wojciechowski Auditorium before they change its name.' He gave a wry smile.

Halina knew that an acrimonious dispute was being waged between the school board and the councillors over naming the auditorium after the mayor. Ever since he had announced that he was in favour of the President's plan to hold a ceremony of repentance in Nowa Kalwaria, many members of the *Rada* were campaigning to have him removed from office.

Roman's invitation had aroused her curiosity. It was tempting to have a legitimate excuse to spend time with him and to expand the students' horizons at the same time. But now that she was face to face with these resentful teenagers, she regretted her decision. In his eagerness to include her in his daily life, Roman had clearly overestimated their interest in Australia.

Her eyes wandered around the classroom and stopped at a striking poster. A bird splashed in exotic colours was flying towards the sky, closely pursued by a flock of black ravens with pointed beaks and predatory eyes. On the ground were dozens of other ravens. Some looked excited, others showed no emotion, while the majority looked away, as though determined not to see the drama taking place overhead. She glanced around the room and wondered whether the students had understood the poster's underlying message.

'Dr Shore lives in Australia. You remember we talked about Australia yesterday,' Roman began. At the back of the room, an overgrown youth stood up, raised his hands in front of him and hopped around while another made a clicking sound. They had obviously seen reruns of 'Skippy' on television. 'I'm sure she won't mind answering your questions,' Roman continued, ignoring the interruption.

Halina caught his eye and they both looked away, avoiding each other's glances in a way that a perceptive observer would have interpreted correctly.

As no one volunteered any questions, Halina said, 'People usually want to know whether water in Australia flows the wrong way around and whether kangaroos hop along the streets.'

A few students smiled politely, others rolled their eyes, while the rest continued to stare blankly. After a long pause, one student raised his long thin arm. 'I want to know why you've come here.' His tone, sharp as a spear, hurled a challenge. For the first time since she had entered the room, there was silence.

'The Polish government invited me to take part in the investigation,' she replied, ignoring the meaning behind his question.

'Why do we need people from other countries to meddle in our affairs?' he persisted.

'The forensic team was chosen on the basis of expertise,' she said. 'But I was actually born in Poland. A long time ago, as you can probably tell from my accent.'

A glimmer of interest greeted her remark. A plump girl with a shiny pink face was frowning. 'Do people talk about Nowa Kalwaria in Australia?'

'As a matter of fact, most Australians have never heard of it,' Halina replied. 'Why do you ask?'

The girl looked down at her hands. 'My father says everyone knows what happened here. He reckons foreigners think that the Poles were no better than Nazis.'

Suddenly they were all talking at once. 'Have you heard the latest Nowa Kalwaria joke?' the boy with the long arms called out. 'A guy leans out of a car and asks the way to Nowa Kalwaria, and the villager says, "Just keep going until you see the smoke!"'

A few of them tittered. One girl frowned and her neighbour leant over to explain it. The girl with the round face nodded. 'See, we are famous!'

'Well, my dad says it's all a load of crap,' the lanky youth shouted. 'There weren't even that many Jews living here. Anyway, lots of Poles were killed during the war so who gives a shit about the Jews?'

'It's all the mayor's fault.' Everyone turned around to look at the speaker. 'They killed Jews in Stary Most, and in Tykocin too, but no one talks about that.' Antek's loud voice shouted everyone down. 'If the mayor hadn't made all this fuss about saying sorry and wanting to have that pathetic ceremony, no one would have known anything. And Father Krzysztof is just as bad, standing there in church trying to make us feel ashamed of being Polish.'

Halina looked at him, struggling to remember something, when she was distracted by another question.

'How would you feel if every time you mentioned the name of your town, people looked at you as if you were a murderer?' The speaker was Irena, the girl with the shaggy fringe in the front row.

Halina glanced at Roman, unsure whether to continue this awkward conversation or let him steer it to a less controversial topic, but he gave an almost imperceptible nod.

'I suppose I'd be upset like you,' she replied. 'I'd feel it wasn't fair.'

The hostility in the room began to recede. 'When I go and see my auntie in Krakow I tell people I live in Bialystok,' Irena said. 'When you say you come from Nowa Kalwaria people look at you as if you're some kind of criminal.' Some of her classmates were nodding.

'Well, fuck them. Let them think what they like.' Antek almost spat the words out.

Roman held up a warning hand. 'Watch your language, Antek.'

'Anyway, whatever happened, it was only natural,' Antek spluttered. 'People shouldn't mix. Whites go with whites. Blacks go with blacks, Catholics with Catholics. That's how it should be. Poland is a white Catholic country and it should stay that way. People should stick to their own.'

Roman looked around the class. 'I don't see anyone here who's exactly the same as everyone else. I can see a lot of differences.'

One of the girls giggled. 'What about girls, Antek? We're different but I've never heard you complain about that!'

As his classmates laughed, Antek reddened and made a rude gesture in her direction.

Irena was waving her arm around to attract Roman's attention. '*Proszę pana*, it's like that poster, isn't it? All those black birds going for the coloured one, and the rest of them just watching it happen.'

Roman caught Halina's eye and gave her a quick conspiratorial smile. She watched as he moved around the room with boyish lightness, his long grey-speckled hair brushed back from his forehead.

A girl with tiny features in a broad face broke in. 'I'd be looking on. I wouldn't want to chase it away but I'd want to see what was going on.'

Someone let out a belly laugh. 'Oh, yeah, Ewa, that's typical. Sit on the sidelines and watch everyone else fight it out!'

'You're too chicken to protect your own territory, but you'd be happy for the others to do it for you.'

Ewa was shaking her head. 'Trying to help would be a waste of time, anyway. One person can't make a difference.'

Most of the students nodded.

Antek was bristling with disdain. 'I can't stand people who go on with that crap about everyone being equal and how we have to love each other. I'd be up there with the strong ones, getting rid of the foreigner. And then I'd come and deal with you lot!' He looked around the classroom, defying them to argue.

Halina looked at him again when the buzzer signalling the end of the lesson cut across her thoughts.

'That was an interesting lesson,' Halina said later. 'I wonder if they were aware of the parallels.'

'They might see them when they've had time to let it sink in,' Roman replied. 'You saw how emotional this topic is. Not that it's surprising. Quite a few of them have the same names as the perpetrators. Antek's grandfather owned the barn. It's a terrible heritage.'

She nodded absently and wondered how Roman would react if he knew about his own father.

The exhumation site buzzed with activity again. Rabbi Silverstein was in deep discussion with another rabbi whose flowing white beard reminded Halina of a biblical prophet, but from the yellow stain on his moustache, it seemed that this prophet was addicted to nicotine. Nearby, Professor Dobrowolski was sitting on his canvas folding chair, recording the day's proceedings on his laptop. Having concluded the exhumation at the site of the barn, the forensic experts were turning their attention to the mass grave and were discussing the position of the bodies as indicated by the reading from Andrzej's theodolite.

Halina was about to pick up her textbook to check the age of a tooth when she noticed a folded piece of paper lying on the floor. A crudely drawn coloured bird was plummeting to the ground with blood gushing from the Star of David on its chest. Underneath, scrawled in big badly formed capitals were the words 'Poland for the Poles!' So the message had got through, though not in the way Roman had hoped. She re-read the note and, with a thoughtful expression, tucked it into her wallet.

Large flakes of snow had started falling and she stood in the doorway of the hut shivering. She glanced at her watch. It was ten past three and the light was fading. Throwing on her coat, she locked the hut and headed towards the square, licking off the flakes that dissolved on her lips. Before she realised it, her feet had led her to the presbytery door. Father Krzysztof would put the day's events into perspective. As she rang the bell with cold-stiffened fingers, she pictured them sitting in front of the fire, talking over a glass of tea and the housekeeper's delicious cakes.

She had to ring twice before she heard footsteps coming down the hall. The door opened slightly but this time there was no mouth-watering aroma of vanilla, yeast or sweetened cream cheese. The housekeeper didn't invite her inside but kept her on the doorstep like she was a hawker offering unwanted goods.

'I'm sorry, *Pani Doktor*, but Reverend Father isn't feeling well today.'

'What's wrong?' Halina asked.

The housekeeper merely repeated her statement.

'Perhaps a visit will cheer him up.'

The housekeeper shook her head. 'Reverend Father doesn't want to see anyone.'

It must be serious. 'Has the doctor been?' Halina didn't have much faith in the local doctor who looked as though he hadn't yet caught up with penicillin. 'I could drive to Łomza and fetch a doctor from there,' she suggested.

The housekeeper remained silent. What was the matter with the woman?

'Could you at least tell him I'm here?' Who knew what fantasies filled the head of an elderly unmarried woman who took care of a charismatic priest? Perhaps she was jealous of his friendship with Halina and was attempting to discourage her visits.

With an exasperated sigh that seemed to confirm Halina's suspicions, the housekeeper left her standing in the corridor while she tiptoed towards the last door on the right. Halina strained to hear Father Krzysztof say in an exhausted voice, 'Please thank Dr Shore for her concern and tell her it's nothing serious. With the Lord's help I'll feel better in a day or so.'

A moment later the housekeeper reappeared. Halina was about to ask more questions but one look at her set face convinced her not to bother. Whether the woman liked it or not, she intended to come back the following day.

As soon as she returned to her hotel room, a dog started howling and, as usual, others joined in the daily canine cacophony. She reached across to draw the curtain, whose original crimson colour, still visible along the edges, had faded to a sickly puce. It had stopped snowing and the light coating of flakes on the ground had turned into dispiriting brown slush. Back in Sydney, the startling summer light would be pouring over the city, the currawongs would be gargling in the fiddlewood trees, and everyone would be rejoicing in the blissful warmth and blue skies.

Sudden longing for Rhys overwhelmed her. Was he pressing hot kisses on another woman's body and seducing her with his velvet voice? Visualising him with another lover pinched her heart. So the thought of Rhys still had the power to arouse lust and pain. Perhaps love never died but continued to lurk in the veins unseen and undetected, an emotional infection that the system could never eliminate.

Andrew would be sitting beside the pond in the park, the sun shining on his ponytail while he played 'Night and Day'. Puccini would be rubbing against the door in anticipation of his chicken dinner, and Claire and Toula would be sipping cappuccinos and watching the waves breaking on the beach. And she was sloshing around in this miserable village in the freezing cold, examining dental remains and reading poison pen letters.

Halina pulled out her suitcase from behind the door and started rifling through the zippered compartments. She plunged her hand into each one in turn, throwing receipts, tickets and brochures onto the floor. Where had she placed that note? Surely she hadn't thrown it out by mistake. There it was, to her immense relief, in the outside pocket: the warning note that her attacker had wrapped around the rock he'd aimed so accurately at her head the night she and Roman had broken into Councillor Borowski's yard.

She laid the note on the table, spread beside it the drawing she had found in her hut, and looked from one to the other several times. 'Just as I thought,' she muttered.

Twenty-Seven

After pacing out the perimeter of the mass grave, Andrzej showed the labourers where to cut the trench and remove the topsoil. Ramming his soft white hat on his head he picked up a handful of soil and watched it trickle slowly through his fingers.

Following his gaze, Marta looked puzzled. 'Mmm, the georadar indicated the site of the mass grave but why didn't it show up the remains under the barn as well?'

'Because the ashes from the fire blurred the image,' Andrzej explained.

Stefan was looking from where the barn had stood to the site of the mass grave several metres to the right. 'How did the bodies get from there to here?'

Before Andrzej could reply, a commotion interrupted the conversation. Two high-school students had sneaked into the cordoned-off area and were arguing with the security guard. Poking her head out of the hut, Halina recognised Irena and her plump friend, Janka.

'*Proszę pana, niech wejdą*. It's all right, let them in,' she called. 'I've given them permission to come.'

With a shrug he waved them through.

'You look different,' Irena said, surveying Halina's overalls and wellington boots.

'No high-heeled boots this time!' Halina laughed.

The girls looked around in awkward silence.

'Would you like me to show you what I do?' Halina asked.

She led them into the hut. 'Be careful, it's very cramped in here,' she warned as Janka bumped into the portable dental X-ray machine. Pointing to the developing tank Halina explained how the X-rays of the roots and crowns enabled her to assess the age of children and teenagers.

'Why do you want to know that?' Irena asked.

'It's very important, because some people say that only men were killed,' Halina said. 'So by examining the teeth I can either confirm they're right or prove them wrong. If some of the teeth belonged to children, then we can tell how old they were and how many of them there were. So aging the teeth helps us build up a picture of what really happened.'

'What else can you tell from teeth?' Janka asked.

They listened attentively as she ran through a few famous cases. 'Dental records and dental X-rays helped us identify the remains of Hitler and Eva Braun about fifty years after their bodies had been burnt beyond visual recognition,' she said. Encouraged by their interest, she went on to explain the technology that enabled them to extract and compare mtDNA.

'No school today?' she asked. Then she remembered. Roman was taking his class on an optional excursion. 'Didn't you want to go to the museum in Łomza?'

The girls exchanged conspiratorial glances. 'We said we had colds because we wanted to come here instead,' Irena said, and added, 'My dad would give me a belting if he knew where I was. He thinks you should all be sent packing.' She gave a high-pitched giggle. 'He reckons you're all a bunch of troublemakers and should go back where you came from.'

'Why is he so upset about this?'

Janka nudged her friend to keep quiet but Irena said, 'It's because of my *dziadek*.' She chewed her lip and looked down.

'What does your grandfather have to do with it?' Halina asked.

Irena was picking at her thumbnail as she struggled with the temptation to reveal the secret and the need to conceal it. Janka was still signalling with her eyes but Irena blurted out, 'Everyone in Nowa Kalwaria knows anyway so I may as well tell you.' She lowered her voice. 'My *dziadek* was here when it happened.'

Halina looked at her in surprise. 'During the war?'

Irena nodded. 'He was only a kid then. About fifteen, I think. He saw everything.' She emphasised the last word in expressive capitals.

'Does he ever talk about it?'

'He used to. When my mum was growing up he did. It used to make her sick. She thought he was making it all up to scare her so she'd behave. But he hasn't talked about it for years.'

'Does your *dziadek* still live here?'

Irena pointed towards the fields. 'He's awfully old now but he still ploughs and looks after the cows. He went a bit funny after *babcia* died.'

'I'd like to meet him,' Halina said. 'It might help me understand what happened. Do you think he'd talk to me?'

Irena looked doubtful. 'I don't know,' she said. 'There was a reporter here from Warsaw about a year ago. She was poking her nose into everything, pretending to be everyone's best friend, but my dad didn't trust her and when she wanted to talk to *dziadek* Dad told her to push off. If he found out I'd been talking to you, he'd kill me.'

A crowd had gathered around Andrzej. Beneath the layer of sandy topsoil, charred bones appeared among the ashes. 'Look at this bone,' said Andrzej, holding up a femur for the students. 'What do you see?'

Marta examined the calcined bone. 'A bone burnt at temperatures between 700 and 900 degrees.' She looked troubled. 'Could any of these people still have been alive when they were thrown into the mass grave?'

Andrzej nodded. 'It's possible.'

Halina closed her eyes. She saw people whose hearts were still beating being hurled into this pit along with the dead. Had the black soil felt heavy on their chests as it pushed out their last breath? How long did the soil heave with the bodies pulsating underneath?

Her thoughts turned to Irena's grandfather. Back in the hut, she made a call on her mobile. Jolanta was either out or wasn't answering her phone. There was no message She recalled the journalist's gravelly voice reiterating her warning. *Nowa Kalwaria is a minefield. Do your work and get out.*

But it was too late. She was involved. With Roman, with the exhumation, and with these charred remains.

'Do you know Irena's family?' she asked Roman that evening. They were sitting on high stools in the hotel bar, facing a faded photograph of a stream running through a pine forest. At the other end of the maplewood counter stood bottles of Żywiec and Heineken beer, sickly-sweet Russian champagne and overpriced French Bordeaux.

'Wine will be cheaper when we join the European Union,' the barman said, pushing a saucer of salted pretzels towards them. They chose Żywiec and sat down at the far table. Roman took some papers from his briefcase to create the impression that this was a professional meeting, but the barman, studiously polishing glasses, glanced in their direction several times and smiled to himself. They didn't fool him.

Roman was squeezing her knee under the table. 'Looks like we couldn't keep away from each other for very long,' he whispered. He was struggling to keep a straight face. 'So we're meeting to discuss Irena's family, are we? I've only ever met her mother. A sensible, hard-working woman. Why do you ask?'

She shrugged. 'Just curious.'

He raised his eyebrows. 'It wouldn't have anything to do with the fact that Irena came to the site today, would it?'

'News travels fast around here. I didn't know if I should tell you in case she got into trouble.'

'She told me herself,' he said. 'You've probably noticed that discretion isn't her strong point. Tell me, what's this sudden interest in her family?'

'I'd like to talk to her grandfather if I can find out who he is.'

Roman looked thoughtful. 'That shouldn't be too hard.'

The cold, as insidious as a traitor's smile, sucked every bit of warmth from her body. No matter how many layers of clothing she wore, or how many glasses of scalding tea she drank, the heat failed to reach her hands or feet. Her fingers were stiff as she glued together and X-rayed pieces of jaw that they had recovered throughout the afternoon from the ashy soil, along with charred femur and humerus bones. Plunging her arms into the sleeves attached to the developing tank, she looked through the plastic cover and made notes about the teeth.

As she worked, she puzzled over her emotional involvement, so different from her usually dispassionate approach. Although her working life had been marked by horrific cases, this time she found it difficult to distance herself emotionally. Perhaps it was the scale of the atrocity, or her connection with Poland, or the nightmare she'd had in Sydney, but whenever she closed her eyes she imagined the tiny children whose milk teeth she was examining. Children whose future had been hacked off by a savage mob. She could see the children, terrified and bewildered as the flames leapt all around them, feeling the searing heat and the suffocating smoke, hearing the screams and moans and clinging to their frantic parents. How had the parents soothed their children in those final moments before they were all burnt to death? Did they hold them close and promise to meet in heaven? She thought of J.E. and his miraculous escape, and of his old schoolfriend Tadek Zamorski who guarded the door with an axe to make sure no one got away.

She longed to talk it over with Father Krzysztof. The strange attraction she felt for this priest was unlike any feeling she had ever had. Not sexual yet not purely platonic, it was an intriguing mixture of admiration and affection, devoid of the tension and uncertainty that accompanied her relationships with other men.

How did a man with Father Krzysztof's intellect and integrity reconcile faith in God with his knowledge of the evil in the world and the darkness within the human soul? She found it difficult to believe that in the era of space travel, gene therapy and cloned embryos, people still prayed to some benevolent figure with a white beard who supposedly resided above the clouds and directed events on earth like some kind of moral traffic warden, keeping a log of everyone's good and bad deeds.

How would the priest explain this pogrom? In a secret recess of her sceptical mind lurked the forlorn hope that his faith would give her the reassurance and spiritual comfort she craved. Because if the world was the result of chance and chaos, and human beings, given the slightest opportunity, descended into atavistic savagery, then progress was a myth, and literature, music, philosophy and science were gaudy tinsel covering up a stinking pile of filth.

'Father Krzysztof is still unwell and not up to seeing anyone,' the housekeeper said, planting herself across the doorway.

This time Halina refused to be fobbed off. Edging forward, she said in a firm tone, 'It's you I'd like to talk to, if you can spare a moment.'

Inside the sitting room, where no fire had been lit, she faced the old woman. 'I know you're devoted to Father Krzysztof, but I'm worried about him too. Perhaps he should be in hospital. Please tell me what's going on.'

The housekeeper hesitated. 'You see, *Pani Doktor*, it's like this,' she began. 'I'm not an educated woman like you, but I don't think a doctor will help. Reverend Father is suffering from a nervous problem.'

'A nervous problem?' Halina repeated. 'Father Krzysztof isn't a nervous person. What do you mean?'

The woman shuffled in her slippers and sniffed into a large handkerchief. 'Well, you see, that's just it, I can't express myself like I should. My mother wanted me to stay at school, but my father wanted me to start working ...' She tailed off, uncertain how to extricate herself from this morass of words.

Halina took a deep breath and tried to infuse a conciliatory tone into her voice. 'I didn't mean to hurt your feelings. You're an intelligent woman and no one could take better care of Father Krzysztof than you. Can you give me some idea of the problem?'

Mollified, the housekeeper sniffed again. 'Well, he's not in pain or anything like that. But he has this look in his eyes. I don't know how to describe it. If it was someone else, I'd say he looked angry, but that can't be right. And he doesn't want to eat anything, which is unusual because Reverend Father usually has such a good appetite. He won't even touch the chicken broth I made him. He just paces up and down his room, up and down, or else he stares out of the window. Yesterday, to cheer him up, I said, "Doesn't the snow make everything look lovely?" but he gave me this strange look and I could tell he had no idea it was snowing.'

Now that she'd started talking, there was no stopping her. 'It's upsetting to see him brood like that. His poor dear mother died not long ago, a fine soul she was too. I suppose he's grieving for her. It's not fair is it? When we need comfort, we come to him, but who can he go to?'

In his cold, high-ceilinged room, Father Krzysztof watched snowflakes fluttering past the window. They landed on the bare branches and formed white pillows on the boughs. Some fell against the panes, melted and formed crystals of ice that made feathery patterns on the glass.

He had sat by the window like this as a boy, watching as his warm breath misted the pane for a second and dissolved the snowflakes that slid down. He recalled a winter of fierce blizzards many years ago, when snow reached halfway up his parents' door, and a solid mountain of it had piled up on the roads which became impassable on foot or by cart. Snow threatened to engulf the village. It seemed as though no one would be able to leave home to go to the marketplace, to school or to church until the snow thawed. He had sat by the window for hours, watching it mount higher and higher, until he figured out a solution.

'We can't climb over the snow, but why don't we make a tunnel through it?' he asked his father. The men set out with their spades and scooped out a hollow inside the snow big enough for people to walk through. It was hailed as another example of the boy's exceptional powers.

If only the problem he was grappling with now had such a simple solution. For the past week, anger and confusion had destroyed his equilibrium and made him question his vocation. The reply he had received from the Vatican had been swift but enigmatic. *Your suffering is a sign of God's love*, His Holiness had written. Did the Holy Father mean that God had sent this trial to test him, just as he had tested his only son? Did he mean that Father Krzysztof had been selected to endure this anguish? Or was he referring to the redemption implicit in suffering?

Father Krzysztof's mind wandered back to the snowstorm of his childhood. It was shortly afterwards that he had announced his decision to become a priest. What had prompted that decision? Had it been merely his enchantment with church ritual and the Latin liturgy, or a desire to fulfil his parents' dreams? Or had it also stemmed from an awareness that he was different, from an unconscious desire to find security in a vocation beyond doubt?

And now his choice had turned him into a human paradox. A fraud. A Catholic priest who was a Jew. How could he face his congregation? It was unthinkable to announce the truth and impossible to continue living a lie. Yet the Holy Father's letter had implied that he should continue, regardless of the distress and confusion he felt. He rested his chin on his hands. There was a divine purpose behind everything that happened in life, of that he had no doubt. Perhaps that's what the Holy Father had in mind: that he should accept the suffering just as Our Lord had done, because this cross had been placed on his shoulders for a reason.

Two days later, he felt a spark of energy returning. Perhaps he was destined to become a living parable and to transform his anguish and suffering into a message for others. Instead of rejecting his Jewish roots he could embrace them. Jesus of Nazareth, that beloved Jew, had also had a Jewish mother. It was He who had rescued him from the fate that had awaited him in 1941, and delivered him to this crossroads in his life. He bowed his head as he became aware of the two rivers of faith that flowed within his soul. 'Help me to become your bridge, O Lord,' he prayed, 'so that through me, people might come to understand that we are all interconnected, that Jews and Christians are two stems with a single root.'

The Holy Father had said recently that genuine cooperation between Christians and Jews would require courage and imagination. Father Krzysztof almost smiled. Our Lord had certainly chosen an ingenious instrument for reconciliation. But did he have the strength to confront this challenge? He realised now that, far from being punished, he had been singled out and blessed to become the personification of that vision. His own life would show that reconciliation and redemption were accessible to everyone.

The long black night of the soul was over.

The housekeeper knocked on his door to announce that Halina had arrived. For the first time since the crisis began, he could envisage talking to her, but needed more time to compose himself.

The front door closed and he heard Halina's heels clicking towards the gate.

'*Gosposiu!*' he called. 'You look tired. I'm feeling stronger now. Why don't you take a few days off?'

The housekeeper gave him a grateful look from the doorway. 'My sister in Krakow hasn't been well. If you can spare me, I'd like to go and see her.'

Alone again, Father Krzysztof pondered on his heritage. Perhaps he should begin to study Judaism. Rabbi Silverstein would advise him what to read. His mind kept returning to his parents, Malka and Yossel. Only a few days ago, he had been secure in the knowledge of who he was and where he belonged, but now he knew little more than a newborn child. He had been too stunned to question Kasia, and now it was too late. She had returned home without leaving her married name or address. He longed for the peace of mind he had lost for ever. With a deep sigh, he reminded himself to accept God's will with good grace and a humble heart.

There must still be people in Nowa Kalwaria who remembered Berish the Jewish baker and his family. He made a mental checklist of the parishioners who could help him. Again he felt a jab of regret. His mother, Agata, would have been able to tell him whatever he wanted to know. She would have known the baker and his daughter, Malka. Like so many of the villagers, his mother had probably bought Berish's bread. He had heard that Jewish bakers were renowned for the plaited loaves they baked on Fridays and wondered now how those *challahs* tasted.

How would his mother have reacted if she had discovered she had brought up a Jewish child? Perhaps she had had her suspicions but, knowing her compassionate soul, he felt certain that she would have felt pity for the parents forced to give up their child in such terrible circumstances, regardless of their religion.

When he was a small boy, his mother had taken him to a fair. One of the sideshows was a maze of distorting mirrors. Whether you stood in front of it or turned sideways, the image reflected back a grotesquely elongated or swollen figure. At first it had made him laugh, but after a while he cried and tugged his mother's arm to take him away because he was frightened that he'd remain a freak. That was how he felt now, but this time the distorted image was permanent.

Twenty-Eight

The old man hobbled around the yard on bowed legs, making clucking noises as he tossed scraps from an iron bucket. 'Come on, my little pets,' he called out to the chickens. 'Come here, my little beauties.'

Looking up, he saw a tall slim woman standing by the gate. '*Dzień dobry*,' he greeted her in the sing-song drawl of the locals.

'*Proszę wejść*. Come inside, don't stand there holding up the fence. Quick, shut the gate so the chickens don't run out.' His accent together with his ungrammatical Polish made her strain to catch his words.

Everything in his body seemed to have collapsed in on itself. His lips had sunk inwards around his toothless mouth, his small eyes had almost disappeared within the folds of his lids, and his thin shoulders jutted over a concave chest. She introduced herself, extending her hand, but he hung back. '*Ej tam*, you don't want to shake my hand, look how filthy it is!' he said. It was a peasant's hand, roughened and callused from farm work, with yellowed nails hardened and rimmed with dirt.

'You'd better come in out of the cold,' he said, holding open the door to his small wooden house. With its weathered shingle roof, horizontally laid rough-hewn planks and sagging window frames, the house looked as though he had nailed it together himself. The skinny dog chained beside the wood pile gave a threatening growl as Halina passed, and his owner picked up a stick with a threatening gesture and yelled, 'Shut your gob, or I'll give you something to growl about!'

Stepping over muddy boots, he weaved between dirt-encrusted buckets, rakes and wheelbarrows lying in front of the doorstep, and unhasped the wooden crossbar that fastened the door, mumbling about the mess. One space served as kitchen and bedroom, where a crocheted cover with fraying threads was thrown untidily over the bed. Above it hung a large crucifix and a picture of the Virgin Mary. Clearly visible under the bed was a chipped enamel chamber pot which he kicked out of sight as he passed.

'The shit-house is outside but I don't go out these cold nights. That's what happens when you get old,' he said with a wheezy cackle. 'You end up doing things just like your parents and grandparents did, that you swore you'd never do.'

He pointed to the wooden chair beside the bed. 'Sit down, sit down. It's not often I have visitors. It was different when Urszula was alive.' Tears gathered at the corners of his eyes and left a trail on his hollow cheeks.

'You're sitting on half your arse, as if you're about to run,' he observed. 'I won't bite. Sit back. That's it. Now, what did you come about?'

It hadn't taken Roman long to find out where Irena's grandfather lived, but now that Halina was face to face with Wacek Podobas she felt awkward. He was watching her with eyes narrowed to slits. 'You must want something because it isn't often that smart young ladies visit old Wacek.'

It was a long time since anyone had described her as a young lady and she smiled, wondering how to bring the conversation around to the past. She felt like a stage actress whose script had been changed just as the curtain went up.

'I wanted to meet you,' she began.

'Meet me?' he cackled. 'What for? All I know is raising chickens and pigs, and growing beets and potatoes. Urszula knew lots of things. She read books sometimes but I only finished second class.' He squinted at her again. '*Ale co gadać*, you didn't come to talk about farm things, did you, eh?'

She shook her head. 'I was hoping you'd remember what it was like here during the war.'

'Aha! I thought so!' he exclaimed, spraying saliva into the air between them. He rubbed his hands with glee at having divined her motive.

'You don't mind talking about it?'

He shrugged his bony shoulders. 'A long time ago they shut me up. A group of them came, like those posses you see in the cowboy films. "Shut your mouth, Wacek, or we'll shut it for you," they said. Those buggers weren't kidding so I shut up. Not a word.

'Let's see, there was the so-called mayor, Bułka. You didn't argue with him. Then there was Krolik, his deputy. He was sly, that one. When the Ruskis was here, he worked for them, but as soon as the Krauts arrived, he started licking their arses.'

Halina frowned. Why would a communist be collaborating with the Nazis?

But Wacek was shaking his head. 'He couldn't wait to show them what a good Nazi he was, see, or they'd have shot him for working with the Bolsheviks. He was scared of some of the villagers too. Because of him, a lot of people ended up in Siberia. So he toadied up to the Germans!'

It made sense to her. An opportunist who had collaborated with the Russians would go to any lengths to prove his loyalty to the Nazis to save his skin. The whole place must have been a nest of traitors and collaborators, who switched sides depending on the way the political wind blew and whose boots were trampling over their fields.

'The other one that came over with them that day was Zielinski,' Wacek was saying. 'He had a grudge against the mayor but kept it to himself until after the war, and then he dobbed him in. Zielinski was the guy whose barn got burnt down. He was sorry after.'

'Sorry because all those people died?' she broke in.

'*Zaraz, zaraz.*' He held up his callused hand. 'You city folk are always in a hurry. He was sorry because they cheated him.' He chuckled. 'See, he'd just built it so he didn't want it burnt down, but in the end he said they could use it to burn the *Żydeks* provided they compensated him for it. They agreed, but later on he was spitting chips because they didn't give him as much as they'd promised.'

Halina's voice was icy. 'So he didn't mind donating his barn to burn all those people, as long as they replaced its full value,' she said slowly.

'*Ano tak,*' he nodded. 'That's right. Well, it was a big barn, see, built on a stone foundation, not one of the cheap jobs they used to nail together out of a few planks.'

She took a deep breath. 'How did you get involved in all this?'

'Look, I was just a snotty-nosed kid at the time, about fourteen or so. I wasn't good at nothing.' He lapsed into silence and there was a faraway look in his sunken eyes.

It wasn't a time he liked to think about. At school he could never remember the multiplication table, and no matter how hard he tried he always wrote the letters of the alphabet back to front. He could still hear the swishing sound of the birch switch as the teacher brought it down on the backs of his bare legs until they were crisscrossed with welts and he cried till the snot ran down his chin. Then his schoolmates would make fun of him as usual. It was a relief to leave school after second class even if he never did learn to read or write. At home, his father belted him with the buckle end of his strap and called him a hopeless idiot. 'If someone put a scythe in your hand you wouldn't know which end to use,' he always said.

Wacek had been hanging around the square as usual that afternoon when that big-shot Bułka told him to go and get the kerosene. This was his chance to show those buggers that he could do something right. He ran all the way to the garage on the Łomza road and hauled the jerry can to Zielinski's barn. It was so heavy that the handle dug into his palm and he had to keep changing hands.

He roused himself from his reverie. 'You know it's a funny thing, but I can remember that day better than last week. That can was fuckin' heavy and the sweat was pouring off me.'

'So what happened when you brought the kerosene to the barn?' Halina prompted.

'*Zaraz, zaraz!*' Again he cautioned her to slow down and continued reminiscing at his own pace. 'You'd think they would've been pleased, but they made fun of me just like they always did. "You took your time, Wacek! Did you come through Warsaw or did you stop for a nap in the cornfield on the way?" Anyway, someone got a ladder, put it against the barn and told me to climb up and chuck the kerosene all over the roof.'

'Did you know what it was for?' She moistened her dry lips with the tip of her tongue.

'Of course I knew. Everybody knew. All the shops in town were closed that day, you could have fired a machine gun in the square and not hit a soul.'

'I heard that it was just a few ringleaders that were involved,' she said deliberately.

'*Proszę pani!*' His voice hovered between ridicule and disbelief. 'Whoever told you that? Just about everyone was there that afternoon. The women were standing around, watching and gossiping, their tongues working overtime as usual. And the kids were running around. It was like watching the circus setting up. And when the fire started, everyone was staring at it, you'd think their shoes were nailed to the ground. See, in its own way, the fire was beautiful — bright orange outside and white in the centre, and it jumped and curled around all the time and made these patterns —'

'Did you know what was going on inside the barn?'

He shrugged. 'There was a lot of crying and banging and screaming. Some weird gabbling too.'

He paused for a moment, as though trying to recall those sounds. 'Marćin Lewicki said they were chanting magic spells, but his fat wife laughed and said, "Much good it'll do them!"'

Wacek's small eyes suddenly lit up. 'I'll tell you what else I remember! When the roof was going up in flames and the fire was running down the sides too, Bolek picked up his trumpet or bugle or whatever it was, and played as loud as he could.'

She stared at him. 'Why?'

'To drown out all the noise. But we could still hear them screaming in spite of him blowing so hard his face was like a boiled beetroot.'

She swallowed. There was something surreal about this conversation. She might have been talking to a fifteenth-century Spanish peasant happily describing how the infidels had been burnt at the stake during the Inquisition, or to a Parisian *citoyenne* calmly knitting while the tumbrils rolled towards the guillotine and the bloodthirsty mob cheered. If what Wacek said was true, then everyone in Nowa Kalwaria knew what was going on that day, and there weren't many families untainted by the pogrom.

Hardly able to control her anger, she asked, 'Didn't you care that all those people were going to be burnt alive?'

'*Proszę pani*,' he protested. 'I just did what they told me to. There weren't any Poles inside there, you know, just *Żydeks*. Everyone knew they were going to cop it that day.'

'Why? What had they done?'

He shook his head at her ignorance. '*Ej tam*, I had nothing against them personally. The *Żydeks* in my class let me copy their homework and after school I kicked a ball around the fields with them. They were lucky, their parents used to buy them toys. When the harvest was bad, some of them gave my dad credit. But they weren't like us. They kept to themselves, they wouldn't eat or drink with us. And they weren't patriots. When the Bolsheviks came, the *Żydeks* sang and danced. *Tata* said they'd pay for it one day. He used to say there were too many of them, that they'd take over the country if we didn't do something about it.'

Halina made an effort to sound calm. 'What about that deputy of Bułka's, the one you said collaborated with the Bolsheviks and sent people to Siberia. Did they burn him in the barn too?'

He gaped at her. 'They just burnt the Jewish Bolsheviks, that's all.' He looked longingly out of the grimy window at the chickens scrabbling in the dirt.

'What about the women? There were women in there too, weren't there?'

He nodded slowly.

'And children?'

He shifted in his chair. 'When the roof was on fire, a little boy tried to run away. It was Itzek the tailor's son. He was about two. Stach grabbed hold of him and said, "This little bugger's not getting away. Quick," he said to me, "grab hold of him and throw him back in."'

Halina's mouth could hardly form the words. 'Did you?'

Wacek nodded. It was no use trying to explain that he couldn't refuse. Fear pushed you to do strange things that made no sense afterwards. What was it he'd been so frightened of? He saw the gleam of their axes and some of them even had rifles they'd nicked from the Ruskis. He had seen them bashing up the Jews. By the time they'd finished with them, you could hardly recognise anyone. And what they'd done to the girls that day, he didn't want to think about. But it was exciting too, being on the side of the folk with the power to do whatever they wanted. He wanted to be part of it, to show that he was one of them, that he could be trusted to do things, so they'd stop making fun of him. So he had picked the child up by his legs. He could still see his red face and hear him bawling, the tears all mixed up with the soot. The kid was driving him crazy with all the screaming, and there was Stach and Bogdan and all the others looking at him, watching to see what he'd do. Waiting for him to stuff up again so they could give him a kick up his arse.

Wacek's voice faded to a whisper. 'I told myself that this way, at least the kid would be with his people. What was the point if he lived and his parents didn't? He'd be all alone, wouldn't he?'

'Weren't you afraid of being punished for what you did?'

'*Gdzie, co,*' he scoffed. 'Who from? Bułka was in cahoots with the Germans. They weren't going to complain about a few dead *Żydeks*!'

As if coming out of a trance, he shook himself and looked down at his hands. 'I haven't talked about that day for over fifty years. I'm not a bad person, you know. I've always left a few coins on the collection plate in church. And I've been punished for what I did. My daughter was born a cripple, my son's a useless drunkard, and now my wife died and I'm all alone.' Tears of self-pity welled in his eyes.

Halina tried to say something but couldn't find the words. It was Wacek's matter-of-factness that stunned her, his lack of feeling for the neighbours he had known all his life. He'd felt no pity, not even for the child he'd thrown into the fire, and later had justified it to himself as a good deed. Perhaps when you dug down to the core of evil, all you found was a void, an emotional numbness more terrifying than any malevolence. Was the demarcation line between decent people and bloodthirsty brutes so faint that it was possible to step over it without even feeling a twinge of conscience?

She forced herself to continue. 'What happened after the fire?'

He didn't seem aware of her revulsion. '*Ano tak*. Oh, yes. The next day the Germans were back in town. See, they came in just before the fire and then most of them drove away — they left Bułka and his gang to deal with the *Żydeks* in any way they wanted, but the day after the fire they came back.'

He could see them now, all spruced up like wedding guests, spotless and gleaming. You could see your face in their boots. The uniforms were so stiff they crackled. You had to admire soldiers that looked like that.

'Well, it didn't take them long to find out what had been going on. This terrible smell was all over town.'

It was a greasy smell, thick and sweetish, like nothing he had ever smelled before, that clung to his nostrils and never really left him. It hung over the town for months like a curse, and they couldn't help breathing it in. When the Commandant, a big fat guy with a smooth pink face, came to see what was left of the barn, he pulled a terrible face and took a big white handkerchief out of his pocket to cover his nose. 'This time you people have gone too far,' he told Bułka in disgust and ordered him to have the bodies buried immediately or there'd be an epidemic or some such thing. That was when Bułka had grabbed hold of him and some other fellows, and ordered them to dig a pit beside the barn and throw all the bodies into it.

From the way his tongue flickered in and out of his toothless gums, Halina could see that Wacek was having trouble going on. With a quavering voice he said, 'When I looked at what was left inside that barn, I bent over and kept vomiting until bilious yellow stuff came out my mouth.

See, the fire had sort of melted the bodies together and instead of having one head and two arms, there were these black shapes all joined together. They didn't look human. One of the boys screamed "Devils!" and threw down his spade and ran away. I wanted to run too, but they'd only say I was good for nothing. So I stayed.'

He lapsed into silence and she waited for him to resume his story.

'I worked for hours there, knee-deep in those bodies. After a while, I stopped vomiting. I just kept dumping all the bones into the pit. On and on it went, there was no end to it. And that smell! A lot of them I couldn't budge because they were all stuck together.'

'So what did you do?' she whispered.

He looked at her and shrugged. 'I had to chop them apart with an axe.'

She stared at him. She would have liked to see a two-headed monster with one eye in the middle of his forehead, blowing smoke through his nostrils. Instead, she saw an ordinary old man who had felt stupid all his life, who loved his chickens and missed his wife.

Wacek's voice was still in her ears as she walked slowly towards the exhumation site. The silence was the first thing she noticed; silence that had a gritty texture and trembled in the cold air and alerted her to something unusual. The entire team, as well as the two rabbis, were standing on the edge of the grave, looking down. For once, no one was laughing or chatting. Andrzej saw her approaching and nodded in her direction without saying a word. Closer now, she saw that Marta's hand was pressed against her mouth and her eyes were wide with horror. The others had sombre expressions. Now and again someone let out a deep sigh. They might have been mourners at the funeral of a close relative, she thought, and quickened her pace.

A lower section of the grave had just been exposed after the topsoil and loose bones had been removed, and it seemed they were looking straight into hell. The skeletons that lay in the grave were conglomerates of blackened bones twisted and fused together like abstract sculptures created by an artist with a surreal vision of the inferno. A closer look revealed crushed skulls, long rib bones and some mandibles with teeth still attached.

Halina walked away, head down, her hands thrust deep into her pockets. In her mind she saw an image of the village simpleton hacking at charred bodies with his axe.

Twenty-Nine

The housekeeper put her head around the door for the fifth time that morning and Father Krzysztof looked up reluctantly from his book. On the flyleaf of *Commentaries on the Torah*, Rabbi Silverstein had inscribed, 'From one man of God to another', and Father Krzysztof had been struck by the timing of the gift. A sign from God, he was certain of that.

His hands trembled as he read, daunted by the magnitude of the chasm he was attempting to bridge. Was he capable of confronting the intellectual and theological challenges that threatened to transform every aspect of his life? Beguiled by the wisdom and insight of the Jewish thinkers he encountered in these pages, he jotted down ideas that he found illuminating. He wrote more rapidly than usual, excited by the theology he was discovering. The truths they contained were universal, pertaining as much to Catholics as to Jews, and indeed to all people, irrespective of colour or creed.

Not content with elucidating the past, the author related historical events to contemporary life. The heroism of the Maccabees and the mass suicide at Masada had a resonance that echoed to the present day. These were true heroes who had chosen death in the spirit of the Catholic saints and martyrs. As he read on, he felt the hairs on his arms prickling as these commentaries enabled him to look at past events with new understanding. It seemed that the Jews had always lived in interesting times. But it was more than a new interpretation of history that excited him. It was the realisation of a shared heritage. After all, this history, this theology, these people and their values flowed into the river of humanity on whose tide every being swam to this day. 'My people,' he whispered to himself.

From the church he could hear singing, and recognised the ethereal melody of Mozart's *Ave Verum*. The retired music teacher had found her niche in conducting the choir, and although some of the singers complained that she treated them like schoolchildren, her insistence on punctual and frequent rehearsals had produced singing that made him shiver with joy. If only the peace and harmony of that music could be reflected in his parishioners' lives. Elections to the *Rada* were approaching, and the atmosphere in the township was growing tense as candidates vilified each other. Above the baritones and altos, a soprano's pure voice soared to the sky. This must be how the host of angels sang in heaven.

Heaven was one of the issues discussed in the commentaries. Father Krzysztof felt he had embarked on a journey of discovery — perhaps the most significant one of his entire life, because it contained guidelines that pointed to ways of achieving peace and serenity not only for himself but for all mankind. The light of the Torah illuminated the dark corners of life and reached out to his soul, to help him enter a world that had hitherto been closed to him. As he read on, the world began to emerge from chaos and became a place where it was possible to reconcile all things, if, as the Torah and Our Saviour both instructed, we truly loved our neighbours.

He was meditating on the beauty of this concept, its simplicity and complexity, when the housekeeper's face appeared at the door once again. From the way she was hovering it was clear that she had not gathered the courage to say what was on her mind.

'What is it, *gosposiu*? Come out with it.'

She shuffled in and stood leaning against the door but her injured tone refused to admit to any subterfuge. 'I only wanted to know what Reverend Father fancied for dinner.'

'And before that you wanted to know what I wanted for lunch, and before that whether I wanted the room dusted or needed my galoshes,' he teased her. 'Come now. What's all this about?'

She reddened at being caught out. There was no point trying to keep anything from him. 'Well, I was wondering, wasn't that Kasia Marczewska I saw here a few days ago?'

He put his book aside. 'Do you know her?'

Liberated from her self-imposed reticence, the housekeeper moved closer. 'Poor Anielcia, her mother, died young. And her father, Piotr, was a decent type. Didn't spend his money in the tavern or beat his wife like so many of them did. But he came to a tragic end.' She shook her head several times and clucked her tongue. 'They were terrible times, Reverend Father. Kasia left with her sisters soon afterwards and I haven't seen her since, but I would have known that little pointed chin anywhere. There was a lot of bad feeling about Piotr. Many people called him a traitor, and said good riddance to the traitor's daughter.'

'Did you think he was a traitor?' Father Krzysztof asked.

She shifted from one foot to the other and examined her chapped hands. 'It was so long ago, Reverend Father, it's hard to remember exactly.'

As so often in conversations with his housekeeper, he had the impression that she held back more information than she offered. He gave her a shrewd look. 'Go on with you! You've got a memory like an elephant!'

'Well, I suppose I did think that at the time. Everybody did. And if they thought differently, they kept it to themselves.'

Her discomfort was visible. He leant forward and said in a conspiratorial tone, 'Why don't you bring some tea and two glasses and we'll talk about the old days.'

She was soon back with tea and poppyseed cake, fussing around with plates and forks. It wasn't often that she was invited to have tea with the priest.

'You know that fairy tale about the evil spell that was cast on everyone?' She spoke slowly, struggling to articulate her thoughts. 'Well, that's what it was like here during the war. It was as if someone had put a spell on the people that made them do terrible things.'

'Are you saying they weren't responsible for what they did?'

She breathed out heavily. 'I can't explain it, Reverend Father. All I know is that they had to be possessed by Lucifer himself to do those things. It was like the plague that spread from one to another. And once it started, there was no stopping it.'

He smiled inwardly. No one ever remembered that Lucifer, the bringer of light, had once been God's favourite angel.

'They say Kasia was there while they hanged her father,' the housekeeper mused as she slid another wedge of cake onto his plate. 'Poor girl. Makes you wonder if anyone can get over something like that.'

He was looking at her intently. 'Did you know everyone in the village?'

She took a mouthful of tea, turning it over and over in her mouth as though she was chewing it, but refused to touch the cake. That was carrying familiarity too far. 'I knew most people.'

He would have to ask the question more directly than he would have wished. 'Do you know why they hanged him?'

She rolled more tea around her mouth. 'It was because of a Jewish couple,' she said carefully, glancing at him out of the corner of her eye. She wiped her lips on the back of her hand to avoid staining the damask napkin and fell silent.

Perhaps an oblique approach would be more successful. 'You must have been an eligible young lady at the time. How come some handsome fellow didn't come along and sweep you off your feet?'

In spite of her age she blushed and gave him a look that was almost girlish. 'I had my admirers, Reverend Father,' she said coyly. 'You mightn't believe it from the way I shuffle along on my poor old legs these days, but I could outdance anyone then. You should have seen me kick my heels up when the band struck up a polka.' A melancholy look glazed her eyes. 'But the ones that wanted me, I didn't want. And the one I wanted left me for another girl. That Bogdan was after me, but he was a violent drunk like his father. His sister was the only decent person in the family.'

'You seem to know everything that went on in the village,' he said slowly.

She looked pleased. 'I didn't miss much. Your mother was a good woman,' she added, stealing a quick look at him over her teacup.

'Then you know that I was a foundling.'

She raised her eyes to meet his and from her expression he could tell that she knew everything.

They were sitting in reflective silence when the doorbell rang. A moment later, Halina was in the room.

'You look very serious today,' Father Krzysztof commented while his housekeeper scurried away with her glass, as though removing incriminating evidence.

'I've been looking into the jaws of hell,' Halina said, rubbing her hands in front of the fire. 'I have to know what you think about evil. What makes people capable of inhuman cruelty?' He was about to speak but she interrupted. 'And please don't tell me about original sin!'

He chuckled. 'As long as you don't quote Rousseau and tell me that man was born perfect but was corrupted by his environment!' They both laughed.

'For the past two thousand years, philosophers and theologians have torn their hair out trying to find the answer and you want it distilled into one sentence!'

She waited.

'Have you ever been in a car when the brakes failed?' he asked.

She shook her head, baffled by this sudden change of subject.

'As long as the brakes work, you can predict where the car will go, because you're in control. But if the brakes fail, you're at the mercy of external conditions. Perhaps it will skid into a wall, slam into another car or plunge into a river. Nothing you can do will affect the outcome. In

1941 in Nowa Kalwaria, the moral brakes failed, and when the car finally came to a halt it lay at the bottom of a foul swamp.'

The priest walked over to the heavy dark sideboard and took a coin from a drawer, placed it on the table and then flipped it back and forth, before sinking back into his winged armchair. 'All I can tell you in one sentence is that good is as much of a mystery as evil, but both are as inextricably connected as the two sides of that coin.'

Halina stared moodily into the fire. Atheists often searched for answers among believers but it had been childish to imagine that he would produce an illuminating explanation. Perhaps he was right. The heart of man was as unfathomable as the meaning of life.

'When I was in the seminary, our supervisor once posed a conundrum,' Father Krzysztof said. 'Is God capable of creating a lock that is too complex for God to unpick?'

She nodded. That was probably as close as she was likely to get to the mystery of human behaviour. 'I had hoped that you'd shed some light on this, because I can't make any sense of the things that happened here during the war.'

He considered her words like an alchemist carefully weighing out gold dust on his scales. Everyone searched for reasons, but there were only circumstances that, like volatile gases, occasionally combined to produce violent reactions. And once the explosions began, there was no stopping them.

'It isn't possible to be slightly inhuman any more than it is possible to be slightly pregnant,' he mused. 'There are no degrees of inhumanity.' He cast her a sympathetic glance. 'Perhaps that's your challenge as a scientist: to accept that some things make no sense and can be neither explained nor understood.'

'That's like asking you to accept that there's no God.'

'Perhaps we're talking about two sides of the same philosophical coin.'

He walked over to his bookshelf and took out a thin volume of poems. 'Do you know the work of a Sufi poet called Rumi?' She shook her head. It sounded like something Claire would read. He scanned several pages until he found what he was looking for. 'Rumi wrote a wonderful line, just for you. He said, "The eye goes blind when it only wants to see why."'

He handed her the book to read for herself.

'So it looks as though I'll soon be needing glasses,' she said, and smiled.

'Moving from the sacred to the secular, how is the romance progressing?'

Halina looked at him in surprise. She had always assumed that, having married the Church and embraced celibacy, priests were out of touch with the sensuality that spiced the lives of others, but Father Krzysztof's eyes twinkled expectantly as he waited for her to reply.

She could think of no simple answer to his question. Roman was a gift that, at her age, she had never expected to receive. After breaking off with Rhys, she had thought that sexual love was destined to become an aching memory, like the endless summers of childhood. But the memoir she had read in Warsaw, and old Wacek's story, had affected her relationship with Roman. Although she knew that these events had nothing to do with him, they had cast a menacing shadow, creating a distance which seemed to be widening.

It had been a mistake to start this affair. If they had continued as friends, she wouldn't be in turmoil now. Affection aroused no expectations that were doomed to disappointment, it created no demands that curdled a relationship. Love was the Cagliostro of relationships: conjuring visions, passing off base desires as solid gold and tricking the mind into false emotions. Sexual love was the most illusory and transient of all, but no kind of love could be trusted. Even her mother, who had supposedly loved her, had deceived her and deprived her of her identity. She looked at Father Krzysztof, his close-cropped white hair backlit by the fire. Perhaps there was something to be said for a celibate existence, life lived in the temperate zone.

The priest sat very still, watching the conflicting emotions flit across her face, his slim white hand with its spatulate fingers resting on the small table between them. In a sudden surge of tenderness, she reached out to place her hand over his, but, embarrassed by the impulse, swiftly withdrew it.

'Sometimes putting feelings into words is like brushing the bloom off a butterfly's wings,' he said.

She assumed he was referring to her silence. But later, in the solitude of her room, she was no longer certain.

Thirty

Like lava bubbling unseen beneath the ground, resentments and recriminations gathered force and began to erupt. At night, brawls in the taverns became more violent as tongues and fists lashed out at those with dissenting views. Council elections were approaching and the main topic of conversation was who should be elected to the *Rada*, and, more importantly, who should be voted out.

Inside the municipal chambers, accusations and insults grew more vicious as the campaign against the mayor gathered momentum. Its most powerful weapon was the local newspaper where anonymous articles relentlessly besmirched his good name. A front-page article attributed to 'a staff writer' that morning accused the treasurer, one of the mayor's supporters, of diverting funds allocated for the upgrading of the Łomza road and questioned her honesty. On the next page, an article quoted 'a reliable source in Chicago' who insinuated that the mayor was in the pay of American Jews who were paying him a fortune in return for his support. 'It seems that the Mayor of Nowa Kalwaria has gone to the Jews,' the writer alleged.

Mayor Aleksander Wojciechowski strode into the conference room with a grim look, brandishing the paper.

'Don't think I don't know the cowards who hide behind this disgusting slander.'

He looked straight at his deputy who stared at the wall behind him, not blinking his protuberant, lashless eyes, while Councillor Kruk squirmed in his chair. In church, only a few days before, he had been carried away by Father Krzysztof's eloquence, but the fervour had cooled and now he vacillated between throwing in his lot with the mayor and risking political oblivion, and playing it safe by supporting the deputy. Apart from Kruk, two other members of the council were calculating whether to risk the enmity of the deputy by expressing support for the mayor. The rest, however, regarded the mayor with faces that might have been hewn from granite.

'I'm not even going to bother denying the nonsense about these millions I'm supposed to be getting from America, but if anyone has evidence to support the rumour about our treasurer, they'd better produce it immediately or ...'

He was shouted down by fists thumping a drumroll on the table and cries of 'Traitor! Traitor! Resign! Resign!'

In the uproar that broke out, a high-pitched voice rose to an indignant squeal. 'Don't you realise you're paving the way for an invasion of Jews from all over the world? They'll rush over here claiming compensation. You'll bankrupt the town! It'll be your fault when they throw us out of our homes!'

'Throw you out of your homes!' the mayor repeated. He wheeled around to face the speaker, whose bald head seemed polished to a high gloss. 'What a short memory you have, Councillor! Have you forgotten whose home your father couldn't wait to move into? I'll remind you. It was Berish the baker's home, after his family were all killed. So don't bother putting on this righteous tone about your home!'

The councillor's face flushed and swelled. 'Turncoat!' he hissed.

Some shifted in their chairs or examined their hands. One man shouted, 'Apostate!'

The mayor gave him a contemptuous look. 'The traitors in this room are those who cling to malignant lies. I'd also prefer to believe that Poles were innocent of killing the Jews in this town. Believe me, I'd also be happy to blame the Germans. But what kind of world are we leaving to our children if we hide behind lies?' Ignoring the hostile murmur in the room he continued. 'Whether you like it or not, I've been elected mayor of this town and I intend to carry out my duties in an honourable manner. The murdered Jews were Polish citizens just as much as we are, and deserve the respect that's long overdue. I support the President's decision to apologise on behalf of the nation. And if I'm voted out, so be it. I'd rather lose the election than lose my soul.'

With that he flung down the newspaper and strode out of the room.

As he walked towards the square, the mayor felt anger simmering in his veins. Three generations of his family had tilled the soil of this township, and while growing up he had always felt secure that his roots reached deep into this land. He had never been able to understand why people gave up lives in their ancestral communities for an anonymous existence in the big cities. But ever since the investigation had begun, he had been troubled. Snippets of memory began to haunt him. He remembered walking home with his parents one long summer evening when he had been no more than eight or nine. When they came to the house three doors away from theirs, his mother had shuddered and he heard her say to his father, 'I can never go past there without seeing poor Salcia lying at the bottom of the well.'

'Who's Salcia? Why is she at the bottom of the well?' he had asked, looking from one parent to the other.

Above his head, the adults had exchanged meaningful looks. 'I told you not to talk about it in front of the boy!' his father had warned. For years afterwards he avoided walking past that house at night, imagining the ghost of the dead woman rising from the well and clutching at him with bony fingers to pull him into its murky depths.

Another time, while playing chasings near where Zielinski's barn had stood, one of his friends had said, 'I dare you to go there at night! All the *Żydeks* they burnt there come out and pull Catholic children into their grave.' He guessed that the dead woman in the well was somehow connected to the ghosts who haunted Zielinski's barn and, from then on, he avoided going near there as well.

Until the investigation began, like most of the others, he had blamed the Jews for Poland's problems. But the more he found out about the vanished people who had shared this town for centuries, the more obvious it seemed to him that the stories he had been told couldn't be true, and that the truth about the fire in the barn had to be exposed and acknowledged, no matter how unpalatable it was.

Father Krzysztof's recent sermons had strengthened his resolve, despite his growing social isolation and the prospect of the destruction of his political career. Always a popular, genial man, he now had implacable enemies for the first time in his life. He could have made things easier for himself and his family by compromising his convictions, but rejoiced that, when tested, he had found the strength to stand by his principles. He was fortunate that his wife, Anka, supported him even though she herself had recently become the target of threats and abuse.

'Watch out or we'll throw a match into your house!' one lout had yelled.

'Look, she's got Jews in there!' Zielinski's daughter had jeered when Rabbi Silverstein came for tea.

'That's right, I've got thousands of Jews in here, and tomorrow I'm hanging a Star of David around my neck!' Anka had yelled back.

Aleksander Wojciechowski smiled. His wife was a feisty woman. Just as well, because he suspected that she would need all her courage in the weeks to come.

Undeterred by the antagonistic glances that followed him wherever he went, the mayor continued to attend the exhumation every day. It was his duty as the elected representative of the town to be present, but it wasn't merely obligation that directed his footsteps to the site of the barn every afternoon. Rabbi Silverstein was the first Jew he had ever met, and he was surprised how much he enjoyed talking to this amiable man with his ready laugh. He admired the rabbi's lack of rancour towards the townspeople and admired his generosity of spirit. It was a rare man who was able to pray for the souls of the murderers as well as for their victims. Moreover, the forensic work intrigued him. As he passed Halina's hut now, he looked inside.

She was studying part of a mandible with three teeth attached. Beside her on the folding table lay another piece of bone and an open textbook. As she reached for the tube of superglue to secure the teeth, she saw him at the entrance and beckoned him inside, wondering how long he'd been standing there, waiting for her to look up so as not to disturb her work. She admired his humility, so rare in a politician.

'This jaw belonged to a teenager of around fourteen or fifteen.' She pointed to the X-ray inside the developing tank.

He was tall enough to see over her shoulder. 'How can you tell?'

'From the development of the third molars.'

His eyes were fixed on the teeth as she marked them on the dental chart, recorded them, and placed the jaw in a brown paper bag.

'I feel ashamed.' He spoke with such intensity that she laid her pen aside and waited.

'Not just for the past. For the present as well.'

'But there are some good people here too. Like the history teacher.' She liked bringing Roman into the conversation.

He nodded. 'Unfortunately, his influence is limited.'

'I've heard about the death threats against you,' she said. 'Are you worried? Do you think they're serious?'

'The police have given me a permit to carry a pistol but as you can see ...' He ran his hands down his body to show there was no firearm secreted inside his coat. 'We all have to die one day, and I don't intend to spend my life looking over my shoulder. What worries me much more is that they'll poison the air with all their lies and denial, so that our children and grandchildren won't be able to breathe in this place.'

While Halina took a radiograph of the piece of bone and placed it in the developing tank, he glanced outside.

Beata was taking small bones out of the sifting screen while Andrzej and his students were looking at a twisted torso in the soil.

The mayor turned towards Halina, a half-smile playing around his lips. 'And they thought they'd kill off all the Jews once and for all!'

His words echoed in her mind after he left. There didn't seem to be an issue in this town that didn't revolve around the Jews, whose presence in death seemed far more powerful than it had ever been in life. Sometimes it required a great effort of will not to believe in a God who meted out punishment with such exquisite irony.

A shadow fell across the floor of the hut and when she looked up Roman was already standing beside her, pressing a kiss on each cheek. He laughed when she broke away after the second kiss.

'Halinka, you never remember, this is Polish way! Right cheek, left cheek and then right one again.' He demonstrated the whole ritual from the beginning again and added a personal variation — a long kiss on the nape of her neck. She pulled away in case someone saw them.

'What are you doing here?'

'My class will come soon. We go to clean up the Jewish cemetery. Last time I was there, I saw beer bottles, squashed cigarette packets, condoms and all kinds of rubbish.'

'How did you persuade them to come?'

'It was Irena's idea.'

She shook her head, marvelling that Wacek's granddaughter had initiated this project.

Roman was watching her, his head tilted to one side, eyes narrowed like an artist with paintbrush in hand, considering the best angle to pose his model.

'You've seen Nowa Kalwaria at its worst,' he said. 'You should stay and see the spring.' He described the meadows sprinkled with snowdrops, crocus and forget-me-nots, birch trees covered with delicate spear-shaped leaves that shimmered in the light, the wistful scent of lilac, and the call of the cuckoo in the woods.

'You should be writing poetry,' she said lightly and turned away to suppress a sigh.

The students straggled past a few at a time, the girls giggling self-consciously among themselves, the boys swaggering as they feigned indifference or made wisecracks. Someone in a bright blue quilted jacket was waving to her.

'*Dzień dobry, Pani Doktor*,' Irena called out. Assuming a proprietory air, she turned to the girl beside her. 'Dr Shore can tell how old people were just from their teeth.' She was standing in front of Halina now. 'Can you show her?'

Halina pointed to a speck she had placed in a small plastic bag. 'That tooth belonged to a child about five years old,' she said.

One of the girls looked shocked. 'My little brother is five,' she said, unable to take her eyes off the tooth.

The last group of boys slouched towards them.

'Better watch out or the ghosts will get you!' one of them bellowed. It was Antek, dragging his feet at the back. As he passed Halina, he fixed her with an insolent stare and whispered something to one of his pals who gave a belly laugh.

'Hello, Antek,' Halina said in a loud, clear voice. 'Did you come looking for more rocks? You're bound to find some in the cemetery. Are you planning to throw them at anyone in the square tonight? Oh, and if you're going to leave any more anonymous notes, I'd do something about that handwriting if I were you. Those crooked letters will give you away every time!'

Roman looked perplexed. 'What's this about?'

Halina smiled sweetly. 'Antek sent me a love letter in the square a week ago, but I don't think he'll be writing any more.'

Flushing dark red, the youth muttered something under his breath and slunk away.

Thirty-One

The howling wind shook the branches of the willow trees that bent and swished against the ground. Walking head down across the square, Halina didn't see the elderly woman with the basket until they collided. Picking up the bread, cheese and tomatoes that rolled on the ground, Halina looked into the face of the woman she had seen crossing herself near this spot on her first day in Nowa Kalwaria. She was about to speak to her but, with a startled look, the woman hurried away.

Father Krzysztof had a visitor when Halina arrived at the presbytery, and she followed the housekeeper into the cavernous kitchen. Ever since the priest's illness, the housekeeper's attitude towards her had become more friendly, and while she bustled around peeling potatoes and shredding cabbage with swift movements of her large knife, Halina leant against the warm tiles of the big stove and chewed a slice of carrot.

'Things are hotting up in town,' the housekeeper said. As she levered up the lid of a large wooden barrel, the kitchen filled with the sour smell of pickled cabbage which she ladled into the saucepan of pork, sausage and beef simmering on the stove. 'It'll be a miracle if the mayor gets re-elected.

Pity, he's a good man. I heard his wife had a run-in with Zielinski's daughter,' she chuckled. 'Anka Wojciechowska gives as good as she gets. They won't scare her!'

Like many sharp-witted old women with no family of their own, the housekeeper thrived on other people's news. She knew the skeletons most of the villagers tried to keep in their closets and, when the occasion required, could retrieve the information faster than any computer. She remembered whose violent husband had met with a suspicious accident, whose unmarried daughter was sent away to have her child in another town, and whose wife had an affair with the philandering chemist. She only had to see a student loitering in the square for his family tree to scroll through her mind. Knowing everyone's secrets gave her a sense of power.

'That schoolteacher now, *Pan* Zamorski.' While she talked she peeled apples in one continuous motion so that long pale green spirals fell into the worn enamel sink. At the mention of Roman's name, Halina's heart jumped. 'He made a bad choice with that wife of his. I knew the minute I met her that it wouldn't last, but I thought he'd have found someone else by now. There's no shortage of women looking for a decent man.'

Did Halina imagine it, or had the housekeeper given her a sly look out of the corner of her eye? She changed the subject. Perhaps the housekeeper knew something about the nervous little woman she had collided with in the square.

'Oh, the convert!' the housekeeper exclaimed. 'She was a *Żydoweczka*,' she added, using the diminutive form of the word for Jewess. 'She converted when she married Zenek Wozniak. She took on the name Cecilia and went to church

354

more often than any born Christian. Her mother-in-law turned her into the most devout Catholic in town!'

Zenek Wozniak. That name was familiar. Then Halina remembered. He was the man who had hidden J.E. after his escape from the barn.

'When did she convert?' she asked.

The housekeeper threw the last handful of apple slices over the cake batter in the baking tin and slid it into the oven. Wiping her flushed face with the corner of her apron, she made a rapid calculation. 'Let me see. It must have been around 1945.'

'That's over fifty years ago! And you still call her the convert?'

The housekeeper shrugged. 'Everybody's always called her that.'

So there was one Jewish woman left in Nowa Kalwaria. Intrigued by the woman's timid demeanour and the fervent way she had crossed herself, Halina was about to ask another question when she heard a door open and voices sounded in the hall. A moment later Father Krzysztof put his head around the kitchen door and invited her into his sitting room.

Although he was pale, he looked more cheerful these days, as though the demons he had been wrestling with had finally been defeated. Or perhaps he had surrendered. But what it was that he had defeated or surrendered to, she had no idea.

Referring to the visitor who had just left, he said with a quiet smile, 'I'm not very popular with my bishop.'

Not that he was surprised. A priest using the pulpit of a Catholic church to say *Kaddish* for Jews was novel to say the least, especially when they had been killed by the relatives of some of the parishioners. The bishop regarded his behaviour as a dangerous provocation, and his view on this vexing subject was reinforced by the indignant letters he had received from some of the people in the diocese, and by the editorials in the local paper.

'Rabbi Silverstein, who has come here to supervise the exhumation, has prayed for the souls of the murderers as well as for their victims,' Father Krzysztof had told the worshippers, a commanding presence with his white hair and green brocade vestments. Although he noticed some empty chairs, he was gratified that the numbers hadn't dwindled significantly. He knew that among the congregants he had a small core of supporters as well as some timorous souls who secretly agreed with him, but he was also well aware that the majority were antagonistic to his views. Perhaps it was his entertainment value that kept them coming. They wanted to see what outrageous things he would say next. It gave them something to discuss all week, an outlet for their discontent with life in general. He smiled to himself. Controversy was one way of keeping the church full and the congregation attentive.

'I believe that, as true Christians, we too should pray for the souls of those who were killed in our town. And what could be more fitting than saying *Kaddish*, which, like our own prayers, extols the glory of the Almighty,' he had begun.

To their amazement, he had proceeded to recite the traditional Jewish prayer for the dead, which did not mention death but praised God's infinite mercy and compassion, and thanked Him for bestowing the gift of life. Spellbound by the strange cadences of ancient Aramaic, they had listened, but left the church feeling confused and manipulated.

'Do you think they're ready for your revolutionary ideas?' Halina asked after Father Krzysztof had given her an account of his latest sermon. She admired his crusading courage but her conversation with the mayor had made her aware of the dangerous passions this issue had aroused.

'They will never be ready unless they're pushed out of their narrow bigoted existence,' the priest said. 'Think of me as the broom that reaches into the dark corners and sweeps out cobwebs that have accumulated for years.'

His simile did not allay her concern. 'Make sure the broom doesn't snap under the weight of all those cobwebs,' she warned.

The housekeeper put her head around the door. 'Proszę księdza, I've made a big pot of krupnik soup with lots of barley, the way you like it, and there's a saucepan full of bigos and a platter of potato pierogi. Oh, and there's an apple szarlotka in the baking tin.' She looked worried. 'I hope that will last for two days.'

'Gosposiu, knowing the quantities you make, it will last me for two weeks,' he laughed. 'Relax and enjoy yourself at your sister's. You deserve a break.'

A few minutes later they heard the front door close softly behind her.

'She treats me like a helpless child,' he said. 'I'm surprised she didn't remind me to light the fire, heat the soup and keep breathing.'

'I'll check up on you every day to make sure you do,' Halina laughed.

The mood in the hotel dining room that evening was unusually sombre. Even Andrzej, who could usually be relied on to amuse them with a joke or an anecdote, remained silent, and no one seemed able to muster any light-hearted conversation. Every exhumation had its occasional low days, when the gruesome nature of the work and the human tragedy it represented made lightness impossible. The low-wattage globe in the dining room cast a gloomy light and the food seemed heavier than usual. The waitress's false brightness and the clatter of plates and glasses only accentuated their low spirits. Halina checked her watch several times under the table, impatient to make an excuse and slip away to meet Roman.

The urge to see each other had proved too powerful to resist. Most evenings he came to the hotel and waited until no one was about before running up to her room two stairs at a time. The instant she heard three soft taps on the door, she opened it a fraction, and as soon as he slipped inside they would throw themselves on the bed and shake with stifled laughter like teenagers who have managed to evade vigilant parents. Occasionally they had dinner at his place. His culinary repertoire was limited to thick potato soup that often stuck to the bottom of the saucepan, and to overcooked omelettes into which he threw pieces of smoky *kiełbasa* and whatever vegetables happened to be languishing in the fridge.

'It's a good thing you show more imagination in other areas of your life,' she told him the second time he had produced his burnt soup. She had enjoyed going to his neat little house on the other side of the square, but ever since her conversation with the mayor, she caught herself wondering whose house it had been and whether there had once been a well in the yard.

Restless in her hotel room, waiting for him to arrive, she turned on the small television set and switched channels until she found CNN. The reception was poor and it required determination and patience to watch the blurred image. Suicide bombings in Israel, kidnappings in the Philippines, atrocities in Liberia, child killers in the Congo and famine in Ethiopia. Nothing ever changed. She switched back to the Polish program. The local channel was interviewing candidates and voters about the forthcoming elections and the likely outcome of the referendum.

'The question is, will Poles vote for the past or for the future?' the finance minister was saying in a quiet, precise voice while his opponent waved his arms about and shouted that the government was selling out to foreign interests.

Every rustle she heard in the corridor made her glance at the door but there was no sign of Roman. He had never been as late as this. The sensual pleasure of lying in a foaming bath and changing into her eau-de-nil silk nightdress in anticipation of his visit had already evaporated along with the perfume she had sprayed over her warm body. The room was overheated and her eyes were beginning to close. He was never late. Anxious, she called to find out what had delayed him, but the answering machine replied with its standard message and his mobile was switched off.

Thirty-Two

Two cigarette ends glowed in the dark. Leaning against the beech tree, two shadowy figures spoke in excited whispers, occasionally glancing in the direction of the presbytery.

'Are you quite sure there's no one home?' Janusz asked for the third time.

'Get a hold of yourself, I've already fucking told you, the place is empty. The old woman's gone to her sister's, she won't be back for two days, and I've made sure the priest is out,' Edek hissed back.

He couldn't help grinning at his own cunning. Muffling his mouth with a scarf, he had called the presbytery. If the old witch had answered the phone, she would have suspected something and might even have recognised his voice, so he'd waited until she had left. It was a pity that the only person who knew about his scheme was Janusz, who was a bit of a wimp, but he could hardly brag about it in public. Still, it made him feel good to know he'd covered every possibility and anticipated all the problems, just like Dirty Harry and those other guys in the action movies he watched over and over again on video. He didn't tell Janusz how nervous he had been when Father Krzysztof answered the phone or that he'd almost lost his voice.

'*Proszę księdza*,' he had whispered in a tone that feigned urgency and distress. 'My old woman has collapsed on the floor in a fit or something. She's dying.'

'Have you called the doctor?' the priest asked.

'*Ano tak, proszę księdza, naturalnie*, but he can't do anything for her. Could you come as soon as possible, give her the last rites? She won't last long.' He managed a sound resembling a strangled sob and gave the name of an old couple who lived on the other side of town, almost choking with suppressed laughter as he replaced the receiver. By the time the priest would have got there, discovered that he'd been given the wrong address and got back home again, they'd have plenty of time to get away.

This priest sure had it coming to him. Crawling to the rabbi, trying to make the villagers feel guilty. Apologising. He was turning them into a laughing stock. The party's leaflets explained how the Jews had insinuated themselves into Poland so that they could take it over. They would have succeeded too, if the Nazis hadn't stopped them. Jews weren't real Poles. You only had to look at those disgusting pictures of the men in their long black coats and black hats to know they were a sinister lot, always taking advantage of the Christians. Anyway, his father said that the story about the fire in the barn was a lie, a conspiracy to malign the Poles when everyone knew the Germans did it. But that was typical of the Jews, to try and put the blame on the Poles so that they could demand millions in compensation. Everyone knew they were money-hungry and ran the banks in the whole world. They were the ones behind the plan to make Poland join the European Union, to ruin their nation. And their gullible President had been sucked in.

It wasn't as though they hadn't tried to put Father Krzysztof straight, but their attempts to enlighten him had been useless. That apology of his was the last straw. Let the Jews apologise for what the Bolsheviks had done. But instead of being reprimanded or removed, he continued ranting his provocative crap Sunday after Sunday. Well, if the bishop, the Church officials and the pathetic mayor didn't have the guts to take action to protect the village, he'd teach the priest a lesson himself. For once his father would be proud of him. Who knows, maybe one day he'd even go into politics and look out for Polish interests.

Janusz's whining voice broke into his daydreams. 'How can you be sure he'll stay out long enough?'

Grabbing his companion by the collar, Edek hissed, '*Odpierdol sie.* Get a grip on yourself, or piss off before you shit your pants.' In a menacing tone he added, 'You'd better not do anything to make me regret I let you in on this.'

Janusz fell into a resentful silence. He tossed his cigarette stub to the ground and pulverised it with his sneaker. Planning this had been exciting but the reality made him nervous. If not for the fear of appearing cowardly, he would have happily abandoned this escapade.

They had never been friends, but Edek exerted the fascination that ruthless personalities often have on their weaker acquaintances. While repelled by his vicious nature, Janusz admired his confidence and envied his power. Especially with girls. The more indifferent Edek was, or the more roughly he treated them, the more they hung around him, while he himself never had any luck. Only last week he had bought a chocolate bar for that flirty blonde with the long legs, but she had laughed in his face, turned on her heel and walked off. When Edek had casually mentioned this adventure, Janusz had been flattered to be asked and jumped at the chance of showing that he wasn't afraid of anything. Girls liked heroes, so perhaps some of Edek's aura would rub off on him and make the blonde sorry she'd rebuffed him. It was only now that he asked himself why, out of all the guys Edek knew, he had been chosen as an accomplice.

Edek was checking the time. 'Now,' he said.

Janusz quivered with anticipation. It was like his favourite scene in *Where Eagles Dare*, when all the commandoes synchronised their watches before the raid.

They crept through the square, flattening themselves against each tree in turn until they were in the street, but Janusz couldn't help looking over his shoulder.

'Look straight ahead, for fuck's sake,' Edek hissed. 'Son of a bitch, you'll attract attention if you keep turning round like that.'

When they came to the presbytery, Janusz stiffened. A lamp was shining through a side window, casting a small pool of light on the dark grass outside. 'See, there's someone inside,' he whispered.

'He's just left the light on. Keep down and stay near the fence while I check things out.'

Janusz stared at the window, mesmerised as a rabbit caught in headlights, his breath coming in uneven gasps. What if the old woman had returned? Suppose the priest hadn't gone out after all?

Edek gave him a scornful look. 'You're a fucking moron. Of course he's gone out. What priest wouldn't go to give a parishioner their last rites?'

Janusz's teeth chattered but he didn't say any more. It was too late now. He tried not to think about his father and what he would do if he ever found out, but consoled himself that he never would. He sighed. Only another few minutes and this would be over and he could go home and forget about it.

Edek was back. 'I've found a way to get in,' he whispered. 'There's a door round the side that leads into the kitchen. I think we can jemmy it open.'

Janusz's dinner was rising into his throat. He swallowed hard to push down the sour taste. 'We haven't got anything we can use,' he said, brightening up at the prospect of having to abandon their plan.

But Edek was grinning. 'There's a crowbar behind the bushes. I hid it there this afternoon.'

'When we get inside —' Janusz began.

'Belt up. I'll force the door open and hand you the crowbar so you can put it back.'

The old alloy lock had rusted into the door and it took much longer to prise open than Edek had expected. At one point he dropped the crowbar with a loud clunk that reverberated along the silent street and made Janusz jump.

Janusz was shaking all over with fear. 'How do you expect to do anything with those gloves on? Why are you wearing them, anyway?' he grumbled. 'Quick, let's get out of here before someone comes. The whole town must have heard that.'

'Go on, run home to Mummy, you cowardly little prick,' Edek snapped. 'I'm going to see this through. I don't give up as soon as things get tough.'

The lock finally gave and the door creaked open. 'Quick! Get inside!' Edek whispered, and turned the handle gently to close the door behind them.

Edek's flashlight swooped around the kitchen. There were dirty plates in the sink and saucepans on the stove. He turned and waved his arm, motioning for Janusz to follow him inside. Heart hammering under his parka, Janusz forced his legs to move forward. 'Where do we start?' he asked, but Edek placed a warning finger against his lips and shook his head.

Guided by the beam of the torch, they crept into the hallway, and caught their breath when the grandfather clock started to chime. They flattened themselves against the wall until it had chimed ten times, then tiptoed into a room on the other side of the corridor and almost fell against the armchair in front of the dying fire. Shining the torch around the room, Edek picked up a book from the small table.

'This is what I think about *Commentaries on the Torah*,' he said and, flinging it to the floor, stamped on it. With a violent motion, he swept framed photographs and a glass vase off the mantelpiece and sent them crashing to the ground. Emboldened by Edek's action, Janusz swiped his arm along the bookshelf and smiled as the books tumbled all over the parquet floor. This was fun. He took a box from his pocket and was about to strike a match when the room was flooded with light.

'What do you think you're doing?'

They spun around. Standing in the doorway was Father Krzysztof, a grim expression on his face.

'Next time you play your childish pranks and make stupid calls impersonating someone, make sure the people are in town,' the priest said in a cutting tone. 'How dare you come and vandalise my house, you despicable hooligans?' He strode towards Edek, glaring. 'I know you. You're the deputy's son.'

Edek made a sudden run for it and, pushing past the priest, darted down the hall and bolted out of the house.

Janusz was about to follow but Father Krzysztof blocked his way. 'Not so fast!' he said, grabbing his shoulder with a strong grip.

That was when Janusz remembered that he still had the crowbar in his hand. Before he had time to think or decide on a plan of action, his arm, independent of his body and his brain, raised the crowbar and struck the priest on the side of the head.

He raised his arm again when he saw that the whites of Father Krzysztof's eyes had turned crimson. Those terrifying eyes fixed Janusz with a gaze that bored through the flesh to the marrow in his bones. It dissolved his will to escape and nailed his feet to the floor.

Janusz watched as the priest raised his hands to his head, tottered forward, stood perfectly still, then crumpled to the ground. He didn't take his eyes off Janusz until the back of his head struck the corner of the fireplace and he fell on top of Edek's flashlight. The priest lay motionless, arms and legs outstretched, a circle of light shining eerily around his head. With that image imprinted on his mind, Janusz ran sobbing into the street.

Halina stood at the window, drumming her fingers on the sill as she gazed up and down at the empty windswept street. If he wasn't able to come, why hadn't he let her know?

Only two more weeks at most and this assignment would be over. It would be good to be home again. The petals would have fallen off the jacaranda trees and the creamy scent of jasmine would no longer linger in the air, but she would still see the sun-drenched golden robinia when she sat on her balcony and stroked Puccini's silky fur. She could already imagine herself describing this trip to Toula and Claire, and to her clarinet-playing neighbour as well. She tried not to think about saying goodbye to Roman and Father Krzysztof. Premature sadness would darken the time that was left.

There was a tap on the door, louder and more urgent than Roman's discreet signal, but it was Roman standing there, swaying on his feet. The blood had drained from his face and there were dark hollows around his eyes. Her hand was already covering her mouth when he sank onto the chair. He didn't need to tell her that something terrible had happened.

Thirty-Three

Halina sat with her head in her hands, rigid with shock. She wanted to scream that it wasn't possible, that such things couldn't happen, but apart from the involuntary moans that escaped from her numb lips, no words came out. The depth of her grief took Roman by surprise. He sat beside her stroking her head like a relative comforting the bereaved.

'It can't be true,' she said finally, shaking her head as though in a trance. 'It isn't possible. There's some mistake.'

'Halinka, I went in there, I found him,' Roman said as he held her closer. 'I was on my way to see you, but when I walked past the presbytery I sensed there was something wrong ...'

She pulled away. 'You can't know for sure. You can't.' She was speaking rapidly and pulling at his coat sleeve. 'He could have just collapsed. It happens. Sometimes it's hard to feel a pulse ...'

Halina sprang up, grabbed her coat and rushed out. She was still pushing her arms through the sleeves and fastening the buttons as she ran along the street, oblivious of the needles of sleet biting into her bare legs. Roman had to be mistaken. The figure he had seen lying on the floor was only unconscious. 'Let him be alive, let him be alive.' She repeated this mantra over and over as she ran through the square, the blood roaring in her ears.

Time stopped and distance ceased to exist as she strained every muscle, her face distorted with the effort. This was the way she had won races at school and university, her mind focused only on the destination as her spikes flew over the 200-metre track, hardly touching the ground.

She had just reached the presbytery when a police car pulled up and a uniformed officer jumped out, ramming his cap on his head as he strode up the path. Ignoring him, she ran down the side passage.

'Keep out! Stay back!' he yelled.

'It's all right, I'm a forensic scientist,' she called.

Sergeant Rosiak did not take kindly to assertive women and the lines in his face deepened with disapproval. 'I don't care if you're Lech Walesa. You're not going in there.'

As luck would have it, his colleague had been taken ill, and until the detectives arrived from Łomza, he would have to control the situation on his own. He moved towards her to block her way.

'You're not keeping me out,' the woman said in a strangled voice.

'If you don't get out of here I'll arrest you and have you locked up!' he bellowed, but she pushed past him and ran inside the house.

All the forensic training Halina had received, the basic principles about not compromising a crime scene or touching anything without gloves, evaporated. Only one thing mattered.

Dropping to her knees beside the cassocked figure on the ground, she alternately placed her mouth over his and thumped his chest in an attempt to breathe life into him, but his lips were as cold as granite and no air moved inside his lungs. The side of his skull had caved in, and the blood oozing down from the wound accentuated the waxy pallor of his face. A pool of blood, sticky and dark, spread on the floor beneath him. The torch was still switched on and she stared at the halo shining around his head. A moment later she rushed out of the room and stood in the garden, shivering as she repeated to herself, 'It can't be true. He can't be dead.'

The sergeant was standing over her, hands on hips, a condescending expression on his face. Women acted tough but couldn't cope with dead bodies. 'If you come inside the house again I'll arrest you,' he shouted.

Two car doors slammed. Thank God, the plainclothes guys from Łomza had arrived. He couldn't preserve the scene, run around to make sure there was no one else on the premises, and deal with this hysterical woman by himself.

Detective Myśliwski kept his hands in his pockets and his thoughts to himself. His eyes darted all around the room, taking everything in. 'Did I see that woman coming out of here?' he asked in his slow laconic way. 'I hope we've preserved a virginal crime scene here.'

These village cops were a hopeless lot. He surveyed the ill-fitting uniform, the cap slapped crookedly on the sergeant's head and the bumbling manner, and only hoped he hadn't smeared his paws all over the place and contaminated the evidence. The only cases he'd probably ever dealt with were petty theft, drunken fights and domestic brawls.

'Has anyone pronounced this man dead? Where's the ambulance? Have you called for the forensic pathologist and the crime scene examiner?' From the sergeant's expression he could see he hadn't. Normally they wouldn't bother calling forensic experts or conduct expensive tests for ordinary people, but when a priest met a violent death, you had to think laterally, something that would never occur to this buffoon.

Reading the detective's expression, Sergeant Rosiak scowled.

The gravel crunched on the outside path as the younger detective walked up to Roman who was comforting Halina outside. 'Were you the one who called the police? What were you doing here?'

Roman had been walking towards Halina's hotel when he saw a youth in a hooded parka rushing from the presbytery as though pursued by the proverbial devil with a pitchfork. Roman's curiosity was aroused. What was the fellow doing there at night and why was he running away? It was possible that he had been visiting Father Krzysztof, but recalling the distraught look on the youth's face, Roman felt uneasy. He rang the presbytery bell several times, but when there was no answer, he started looking around. Unable to see anything through the front windows, he hurried down the side passage. The door was open and the lock plate was smashed in. With a sense of foreboding, he went inside and saw the priest's motionless figure spreadeagled on the floor.

He was giving the detective a description of the youth he'd seen running down the side passage when he recalled something else. 'Just before that, I saw another young fellow running across the square. He came from the direction of the presbytery too.'

'Ah, so there were two of them, not just one as you said before?' The young detective's voice was heavy with sarcasm. He looked up from his notebook and fixed his narrow eyes on Roman. 'Is that all, or was there a whole relay team?'

His senior colleague stepped in. 'Why don't you look around the house for clues,' he suggested. These university-educated officers were too abrasive, too smart for their own good.

A moment later, his colleague's voice rose with excitement. 'Here's the murder weapon!' he exclaimed, pointing to the crowbar that had rolled behind the curtain.

'We don't know what it is yet,' Detective Myśliwski growled, unwilling to concede premature credit. 'So far it's just a crowbar. Until the crime scene examiner arrives, we won't even know if we're dealing with murder.'

The young detective was stubborn. 'There's a body with a wound to the head, a bloodstained crowbar that was used to break in, and two youths seen running away from the house. I'd say that points to murder.'

The older man gave him a scathing look. It was all theory nowadays and no common sense. 'What do they teach you guys at the academy? You're a bubbling fountain of assumptions. We don't know if he died from a blow from the crowbar or from tripping over and hitting his head on the fireplace. And as for you,' he glared at Halina, 'I don't know what you think you're doing here but this is a crime scene not a paddock. We can't have people roaming all over the place like a herd of cows.'

'If it's a crime scene, where's the crime scene examiner?' she snapped.

Without bothering to explain that the examiner had an hour's drive to reach Nowa Kalwaria, the detective's eyes slid over her body, taking in her bare legs and the flimsy garment showing under her coat. It resembled a nightdress, but was nothing like the flannelette tent his wife wore to bed. He asked himself why this educated woman with the expensive cashmere coat would have worn such a nightdress in winter, and why this schoolteacher would have rushed over to see her immediately after discovering the priest's body at the vicarage. He smiled to himself as he drew his own conclusions.

They could make the police courses as high-powered and academic as they liked, but there was no substitute for years of observing human nature to figure out what made people tick. It made no difference whether they were rich or poor, professors or plumbers; it all boiled down to some passion that coursed beneath the deceptively smooth surface of their lives. Of course, you never knew until you were tested what your own obsession might lead you to do. That was another thing you learnt on the job. He knew only too well the fine line that divided the law-abiding citizen from the law-breaker. You were offered a glass of vodka here and a jar of caviar there, and before you knew it you were accepting gifts that could be misconstrued as bribes. You went to bust a brothel and ended up spending the night with a girl who did things that made you so crazy that you risked everything you had built up in your life and became a sex junkie. You had to get your nose out of the books and smell the raw sewage of life to understand it, and that's what his colleague, so quick to make judgments, knew nothing about, and probably never would.

A hush fell over the village. Shaken by the death of Father Krzysztof, people spoke in whispers. The violent death of an ordinary individual was a private matter that aroused curiosity and conjecture, but the murder of a priest, even one whose ideas were unpopular, was a public event, an offence against the Almighty that reflected badly on the whole village. Some of the older villagers took the priest's death as proof that the village was cursed. Such a sacrilegious deed could only occur in a place that God wanted to punish. Others whispered about the vengeance of the Jews; but whatever their theories, most people were affected by this demonstration of the destructive power of hate. Even among Father Krzysztof's most vociferous opponents, some looked back on his sermons with the belated admiration of children who realise that their strict parents had their welfare at heart. Guiltily, they remembered his kindness and compassion in times of trouble. 'He stood up for what he believed in,' they said. 'He tried to make us better Christians.'

At the presbytery, the housekeeper's eyes were so swollen that she could hardly see. '*Oyey*,' she kept sighing. '*Oyey*. If only I hadn't gone away this would never have happened and Reverend Father would still be alive. I can still hear his voice saying *"Gosposiu*, how about some of those delicious *naleśniki* of yours for afternoon tea?" I can't believe he'll never come through that door again or call me.' She covered her blotchy face with hands knobbly with arthritis and sobbed noisily, working her sodden handkerchief like a rosary in a vain search for a dry corner.

Sitting beside her, Halina sighed. The presbytery evoked conflicting emotions. Although she felt Father Krzysztof's absence most keenly here, she felt closest to him in the room where they had sat and talked among his books, where the air seemed to be imbued with his spirit.

The housekeeper blew her nose again. 'If I could get my hands on those murderers! Killing a saint like that. Death's too good for them. They should fry in everlasting hellfire.' Tears as big as peas fell down her cheeks and splashed onto her hand-knitted grey sweater, producing a collar of dampness around the neck. '*Pani Doktor*, I pray to *Matka Boska* every night, but tell me, how could the Holy Virgin have allowed this to happen?'

Halina was about to say, 'Ask Father Krzysztof.'

The funeral procession wound through the town towards the Catholic cemetery. At the head of it came the bishop in his ceremonial purple and gold regalia. Behind him walked the altar boys in white surplices, the older ones with solemn expressions assumed for the occasion, the younger ones jabbing their neighbours' ribs and pulling faces at each other. Church officials followed, holding aloft holy pictures and statues of Jesus and Mary. Rabbi Silverstein walked beside Halina, who could hardly keep up with his long strides. She kept her eyes on the ground, trying to control her rage and grief. Behind them came Roman and the other teachers, followed by their pupils carrying floral wreaths.

At the back was a long line of parishioners, come to pay their last respects to a man they honoured more in death than they had in his lifetime. Nowa Kalwaria came to a standstill. Schools, shops and businesses closed and work on the exhumation stopped for the duration of the funeral. As the cortege passed, people crossed themselves, while the superstitious ones among them clasped a button for good luck.

At the graveside, as the bishop intoned a Latin prayer for the repose of Father Krzysztof's immortal soul, Halina felt anger choking her. 'Love, hope and charity but the greatest of these is love.' The bishop was quoting St Paul's letter to the Corinthians, unaware that his own voice was as empty and meaningless as a tinkling cymbal. If, instead of mouthing platitudes and stirring up the extremists, the bishop had lived up to his noble sentiments and supported Father Krzysztof's struggle to recalibrate the township's moral compass, the priest might still be alive today. 'I can't listen to this hypocrisy,' she whispered to Rabbi Silverstein and edged away from the crowd.

The frosty air pierced her lungs like a bamboo spike. As she walked towards the square, snow began to fall. Fine as iced powder, it fluttered and settled softly on the silk scarf over her head and speckled her black coat. She brushed away the melting snowflakes from her face and licked her lips, surprised to taste salt. For the first time since Father Krzysztof's death, Halina was weeping.

That night she dreamt about the broken urn again. Studying its vivid colours and swirling patterns, she was confident that she would be able to match the fragments, but no matter how many configurations she tried, not one of the pieces fitted, not even the handles. Unable to control her fury she hurled them onto the floor where they smashed into even smaller fragments. She woke up with an ache in her heart knowing she would never be able to make the urn whole again.

Thirty-Four

The voice at the other end of the phone sounded wary. 'Why do you want to speak to my mother?'

'I'd like to talk to her about the old days,' Halina said lightly.

'Is it Polish–Jewish matters you want to discuss?'

Taken aback by her bluntness, Halina was figuring out how to reply when Ola Pałka snapped, 'I can't allow you to talk to her. She's being treated for nerves and I don't want her upset.'

'I won't upset your mother,' Halina protested. 'I just wanted to have a chat.'

'Well, I'm afraid that's not possible.' With that, Ola banged down the receiver.

The housekeeper was sorting her belongings into forlorn little piles when Halina dropped in to the presbytery. After a lifetime of service, everything she owned fitted into one small brown suitcase.

'I'm going to Krakow next week, to live with my sister,' the old woman sighed as she padded to the kitchen to make tea, glad of the opportunity to interrupt her melancholy thoughts about the future. 'So you talked to the convert's daughter, did you?' Her eyes gleamed with mischief. 'Her children would tie her up and gag her if they could. The son is a councillor. A big shot, or so he thinks. He's worried he won't be re-elected if his mother starts talking to reporters and digging up dirt about the past. His waste disposal business has flourished ever since he got elected to the council so he doesn't want to get voted out. And the daughter is active in the Polish Legion of Families and doesn't want to be reminded about her mother's origins.'

Perhaps that was why the little woman had scurried away without speaking when Halina collided with her in the square several days before.

'Why does she allow her children to run her life?'

The housekeeper surveyed Halina for a moment. You couldn't expect outsiders to understand; even a smart woman like *Pani Doktor* had no idea what life was like in a small place like this. 'Ever since the convert's husband died, her health hasn't been good and her daughter insisted she move in with her. That one's got a tongue on her like a barber's razor. I get the feeling she was just waiting for her father to die so she could control her mother.'

Halina looked thoughtful. 'Isn't she ever home on her own? The daughter must go out sometimes.'

'Even if you get her on her own, she won't talk to you. She's scared of her daughter and doesn't want to do anything to ruin her son's career.' With a knowing smile she added, 'He's not a bad fellow but he's under his sister's thumb.'

When Halina was about to leave, the housekeeper said, 'Father Krzysztof didn't have any family so I suppose all this' — she waved her arm in the air — 'will be taken over by the church.' Placing her knobbly hand on Halina's arm she said, 'You were attached to him and I know he was very fond of you, so if there's anything of his you'd like to have, take it.'

A knot formed in Halina's throat. She was about to refuse when her eye fell on the book lying on the small table beside the empty armchair. The jacket was torn now and the cover had come away from the spine, but she remembered that he had been reading it before his death and been excited by its ideas. 'Just this,' she said and slid *Commentaries on the Torah* into her bag. She was about to leave, but walked back to the bookcase and scanned the titles. Father Krzysztof's voice was in her head as she pulled out a slim volume. Turning to the housekeeper, she wanted to say something but her throat locked. With a quick nod she hurried out of the presbytery, clutching Rumi's poems in her hand.

The death of Father Krzysztof overshadowed the election campaign. Although Mayor Wojciechowski hoped that this tragic event would convince the voters that reconciliation was the only antidote to the toxins of prejudice and hate, he refrained from making political capital out of the priest's death.

His restraint, however, was not shared by the opposition who pointed to the tragedy as the inevitable outcome of the mayor's obsequious attitude. They blamed him for dividing the community and creating rancour and resentment. You only had to look at most countries in Europe to see the chaos that followed when foreign ethnic groups were introduced to formerly homogeneous nations, they insisted. 'We have to fight these do-gooders because they're the ones who want to foist the European Union onto us,' the deputy mayor told his supporters at a reception in his home which was attended by the bishop. 'If that unfortunate 'state of affairs ever comes to pass, you can say goodbye to Catholic Poland,' he said to thunderous applause, whistles and cheers.

'Do you think you'll get back in?' Halina asked the mayor at the exhumation site later that morning.

'I hope so. Not so much for myself as for the town, because a vote for me would be a vote for tolerance.'

The anonymous calls to his home continued unabated. Most were made in slurred drunken voices but his wife, Anka, had recognised the caller who had rung that morning.

'One of these days your house will go up in smoke so you can go and join your Jews,' the woman had hissed. It was Zielinski's daughter, a fervent supporter of the deputy mayor.

'Well, you're the right person for the job,' Anka had retorted. 'Setting fire to people runs in your family.'

The mayor had suggested that his wife leave town, at least during the campaign, but Anka had refused. 'As if I'm going to run away from that witch and the other halfwits in this place,' she had retorted.

Halina looked up from the fragments of jawbone she was gluing together. 'What will you do if you lose the election?'

'I'll carry on until my successor takes over,' the mayor said. 'But I'm going to stay in Nowa Kalwaria. This has always been my home. Besides, you can't influence events from a distance.'

At the thought of spending a lifetime in this haunted village, Halina shuddered. Ever since Father Krzysztof's death, she had felt more alienated than ever, and increasingly distanced from Roman. He had become tarnished by association with everything that distressed her about Nowa Kalwaria.

He had noticed her coolness and was bewildered by it. 'Halinka, what's wrong? Are you upset about something?' he had asked when she had refused to meet him at the hotel the previous evening. Too drained to discuss feelings she couldn't explain, she had insisted once again that she was too tired.

She tried to push this unresolved situation out of her mind as she walked along the dirt road towards Cecilia Wozniakowa's house in the afternoon. As she neared the neat cottage with its steeply pitched shingled roof and white-painted window frames, she recognised it. This was where she had seen a shadow moving behind the curtain when she had walked towards the Jewish cemetery on her first day in Nowa Kalwaria. It had probably been Cecilia Wozniakowa, like a wistful prisoner gazing at the outside world.

Past a small vegetable patch with spindly tomato plants tied to stakes and cucumbers growing between rows of radishes and beets, she came to the front door. Knocking softly, she braced herself in case the daughter opened it. A corner of the curtain moved and she sensed rather than saw someone peering at her from behind the cotton lace. A moment later the door opened just wide enough to allow a lean tabby to bolt outside. Standing in the doorway was the shrunken woman with iron-grey hair with whom Halina had collided in the square. She looked even more frightened than before.

'What do you want?' she whispered. 'Why did you come here?'

Like many old women in this area, she wore thick woollen stockings, a printed scarf tied under her chin, and several layers of clothes showing beneath a long knitted jacket.

'I just want to talk to you,' Halina began.

The woman glanced around like a hunted fox expecting the snapping dogs to rush at her any moment. 'What about?'

Halina took a deep breath. 'I heard that your husband saved one of the Jewish villagers after the fire in 1941. Is that true?'

The little woman's mouth was moving as though pulled in all directions by invisible strings, and her hands fluttered around her apron. 'I don't have time,' she said. 'I've got too much to do. Sorry.' She was already closing the door.

'Please don't be afraid. I only want to know about the man your husband saved,' Halina said softly.

Moisture gathered in the corners of Cecilia Wozniakowa's eyes. 'My husband was a good man,' she said, in such a low voice that Halina had to step forward to catch her words. 'An angel, that's what he was.'

She was looking at Halina, trying to read her face like a pack of tarot cards, to divine whether she could be trusted. She looked around again. 'I can't talk here,' she whispered. 'Meet me at the far end of the Jewish cemetery tomorrow at two. And don't tell anyone.' She quickly closed the door.

When Halina's mobile rang after dinner, she didn't need to look at the display to know who was calling.

'Halinka, how are you today?'

'You mean, do I feel like seeing you tonight?' The words shot out faster and sharper than she had intended.

'I mean, how are you today.'

'I'm fine. Really.' An uncomfortable silence followed. She opened her mouth to tell him about the convert but remembered her promise.

'I think we should talk, don't you?' His voice was unusually stiff. 'If you're not too tired I'd like to come over.'

His lips felt cool as he kissed her. Sitting down in the chair and not on the bed as he usually did, he said, 'Something has changed between us, Halinka, and I'd like to know why. Have I done something to upset you?' He was looking into her face with the searching expression she used to find so alluring but this time she felt like a plank of wood.

'I don't know,' she said. 'It isn't anything you've said or done. It's me.'

'Are you depressed because of Father Krzysztof?' His voice was tender.

She shrugged. 'I don't know if it's that.'

Roman put his arm around her and drew her close to him but for once her skin did not leap towards his hand. She pulled away. 'I don't feel like making love,' she said.

'Why are you misunderstanding everything tonight? I wanted to hold you, that was all.' He rose. 'I can see there's no point trying to talk to you when you're in this mood. If you want to see me you know how to get in touch.'

She watched him go without speaking, although one word from her and his warm arms would embrace her and thaw the ice in her heart. But she couldn't bring herself to say anything, just as she hadn't been able to listen to Rhys's professions of love after the newspaper article. Although she wasn't angry with Roman, she didn't want him to hold her and couldn't explain why. Suddenly she felt very tired.

Relationships were confusing and deceptive. At first they enchanted but inevitably they disappointed. With work, the boundaries were clear and she was always in control. She wondered whether she had rushed into this relationship too soon, and for the wrong reasons, but deep down she knew it wasn't true. Her feelings had something to do with a body that fell out of a wardrobe, a can of kerosene, a priest whose loss made her eyes ache, and a shattered urn.

Thirty-Five

Andrzej was looking moodily at his mud-caked boots. 'Frost,' he said. 'I told them November was too late to get started, but politics is politics.' Seeing the questioning look on Marta's face, he added, 'Once the soil freezes, we won't have a hope of getting the remains out.'

Beata nodded. 'Wasting a week while the rabbi was making up his mind didn't help.' She glanced meaningfully at Halina. 'Of course, some people didn't mind the delay.'

Halina closed her eyes in irritation. Beata had seen her with Roman at the bar and had immediately guessed their relationship. Women were always sensitive to the body language of sexual intimacy that revealed itself in the way lovers leant towards each other and in their secret smiles. Was Beata jealous or was she still angry over their dispute about the cartridge case? Halina was about to snipe back but controlled herself. It was this tiresome proximity. There was no privacy on this site. At every other international exhumation she had worked on, members of the team had been accommodated in apartments spread around the town so that at five o'clock they could close their door and not see their colleagues again until the following day. But here it was impossible to get away from each other. Even when she dined early to avoid their company at meals, the knowledge that they were likely to appear at any moment made it difficult to relax. And now, in addition to the usual tensions and conflicts, they had the pressure of encroaching winter.

Now that the remains from the top layer of the mass grave had been exhumed, they were digging further down. Having detected some unevenness in the soil, Stefan laid down his trowel and began removing the soil from around the protrusion with his gloved hands. They all crowded around to look at the cranium that had been crushed almost as flat as a cardboard box. Andrzej pointed out the coronal suture that joined the back and front of the skull, and the malar and temporal bones that were clearly visible.

Scattered around the ridges of neck vertebrae and rib bones of the upper torso were fragments of charred wood and bone, and a calcined finger bone. Andrzej turned his attention back to the cranium. 'We'll have to be extremely careful lifting it out or the crushed pieces will fall apart as soon as we move it,' he said. While he discussed his strategy for extracting the remains, Marta was gently brushing particles of soil away from a small mandible with four teeth attached.

It was a child's jawbone. Studying it, Halina was struck by the fact that, like so many other bones they had removed from the mass grave, it showed the classic brown staining of unburnt bone, as well as charring. The finger bone they had just removed, however, and most of the bones they'd recovered from the barn had the bluish-grey patina of unglazed pottery with transverse cracking, indicating that all the organic matter had been burnt away, leaving only the mineral elements.

She leant back in her canvas chair and went over the sequence of events that day in July 1941, to find a possible explanation for the discrepancy. Exhuming a mass grave containing bodies burnt to death half a century ago was rare, and there was little documentation to help them to interpret what they found. From the memoir of J.E. and the account given by old Wacek, everyone had been pushed into the barn which was then set alight. Some fainted from lack of oxygen or were asphyxiated by smoke inhalation. The rest were consumed by flames ferocious enough to melt gold. The following day, Wacek and his companion had dug this pit and hurled the bodies into it.

'That's it! I've figured it out!' she cried when Andrzej came into the hut with Marta and Stefan. 'The bodies were buried in reverse stratigraphy.'

He waited for her to explain it to the students.

'Picture the scene,' she said. 'When the grave-diggers arrived, the barn was a pile of dead bodies. The ones at the bottom probably died first, they probably fainted or were asphyxiated before the fire engulfed the barn. So their bodies were shielded from the flames by the ones who were incinerated and fell on top of them. The grave-diggers would have thrown the bodies that were on the top into the mass grave first, and they're at the bottom now. The remains we're uncovering now came from the bottom of the barn.'

'So if your hypothesis is right,' Stefan said slowly, 'we should find more calcined bone as we go further down.'

Halina nodded. 'It would explain why these bones weren't affected by fire to the same extent as the ones in the barn.' She pointed to the anterior section of the mandible which had a russet colour. 'This part hasn't been affected by fire at all — it's just discoloured from being in the ground so long. But the rest of it is charred. That's interesting: one bone that's been subjected to two conditions.'

She studied the jawbone for several minutes before taking an X-ray. Through the red cover of the developing tank she saw that the permanent first molar hadn't erupted yet. It was the jaw of a child under six years old. This tiny jawbone touched her in a way the other bones had not. A scenario unfolded in her mind. Someone in the barn had tried to shield their child with their own body, and that sacrifice had protected part of the child's face from the flames.

With a start, Halina realised it was time to meet Cecilia Wozniakowa. She hurried along the dirt path leading to the cemetery, knowing that the woman would be too nervous to stand around and wait. Moisture had swollen the wooden gate and it scraped against the ground as she pushed it open. The first time she had stood here, the last golden leaves of autumn had still clung to the branches, but not a single leaf remained now on the thorny brambles and intertwined hazel bushes that stood stark and black against a watery sky.

As she made her way through the cemetery, she noticed that it looked less desolate than before. The area around the gravestones had been cleared. The weeds had been pulled out, the overhanging twigs trimmed back and each stone was encircled by wooden poles joined by a cordon, like an exhibit in a museum. Roman's work, she was certain of that. What a fool she had been to allow the emotions evoked by the exhumation to affect their relationship. For a moment she considered calling him, but paused and put the mobile away. She was behaving like a capricious schoolgirl.

While her emotions were swinging like a compass at the North Pole it was better to keep her distance.

The gate creaked, twigs snapped and she saw a stooped figure wrapped in a shawl slipping in between the bushes.

'I can't stay long,' Cecilia Wozniakowa whispered, her eyes darting in all directions. She spoke ungrammatically, in the sing-song drawl of the local peasants, and wore a man's old suit jacket over her bulky skirt. Her eyes came to rest on Halina, studying her face. 'My age must be playing tricks on me, but I feel as if I know you,' she said.

They sat down on a fallen tree trunk.

'My grandparents were buried in this cemetery, but their tombstones are gone,' Cecilia sighed. 'We had a mill over the stream on the Łomza road. It was in the family for generations. Everyone came to my father to have their grain ground.'

Her lips trembled at the memory of the day so long ago when her father had stood beside the foaming stream, watching the big millwheel turning, his muscular arms folded across his loose shirt. 'Watch and learn, my girl, because one day all this will be yours,' he had boomed. Everything about him had been big — his stature, his hands that could lift a man off the ground, his long dark beard and his voice that always had a laugh in it. But the men who had joked with him all their lives, whose corn he had ground for years, had clubbed him mercilessly to death that summer's day in 1941. And none of it had become hers. First the murderers had moved into their home, and later the communists took over the mill. Even after the communist regime had been overthrown, she didn't dare claim her inheritance.

'How did you survive?' Halina asked.

Cecilia sighed. It was a long time since she had spoken about her family, a subject that was taboo in her daughter's home. But although pulling the scab off her memory was painful, it was also unexpectedly liberating, like shouting a secret to the stars on a remote hilltop. She hardly knew how to begin telling it.

'When they started bashing us Jews up, *Tateh*' — the Yiddish word for father, unspoken for decades, slipped out of her lips before she could stop it — '*Tateh* told me that if I ever needed somewhere to hide I should go to Zenek Wozniak's farm. He used to live with his mother on the edge of town.'

From Cecilia's faraway expression, Halina could tell that she had stepped back into that July day in 1941. 'Everyone went crazy, that's the only way I can explain it,' she whispered. 'When we looked at our neighbours we didn't recognise them. It was as if they'd drunk an evil potion and turned into vampires that only our blood could satisfy. They didn't just want to get rid of us, they wanted to make us suffer as much as possible. And the more our blood flowed, the more excited they got. There seemed no limit to their cruelty.' She looked at Halina and shook her head. 'I could spend the rest of the day describing atrocities you wouldn't believe. By the time they'd finished their sport, the living envied the dead.'

Her face was white and she gripped Halina's wrist. 'You know the house on the corner of the square, where Borowski lives? My best friend, Dvorcia, lived there. She was the rabbi's daughter, a gentle soul who never hurt anyone. Two bandits burst in there. They tore the baby from her arms and smashed his little head against the tiled stove. When his brains spattered over one of the murderers, he ordered her to go and wash his shirt. Poor Dvorcia just stood there, she couldn't move. They dragged her outside. One of them picked up a saw from his workshop. They threw her on the ground near the bridge.'

Cecilia's nails were digging into Halina's wrist and her voice was hoarse and urgent. 'I was hiding in the field among the corn, as close to them as that.' She pointed to a tree two metres away. 'I saw everything. Everything. Her screams were enough to make a stone weep. I still hear those screams every night.' She was whispering. 'They sawed her head off, as if she was an animal. They made jokes about it. One of them said it was like cutting a pig to make neck chops. Suddenly a bright red fountain spurted up. It went all over everything, everywhere. I never knew a body had so much blood in it. I felt something wet on my forehead, and when I touched it, my finger was red. Dvorcia's blood had spattered over my face!'

Cecilia was looking at her hands as though expecting to find blood still on them. She spoke as if in a trance, her eyes staring into the distance. 'I must have fainted. When I came to, I could hear them laughing. At first I thought maybe I'd had a nightmare and none of it had been real. Then I looked and saw what they were doing. I had to clamp my hands over my mouth to stop myself from screaming. They were throwing her head to each other like a football. Her beautiful blue eyes were wide open.'

Halina's throat closed up. 'Oh my God,' she whispered. 'Oh my God.' She was trembling. 'Was that just outside town on the Łomza road?'

But before Cecilia nodded, she already knew. That was where she'd seen the vision of a pool of blood the day she had arrived in Nowa Kalwaria.

'That's when I ran to Zenek's place,' Cecilia was saying.

Her father had judged Zenek Wozniak correctly. He was young, with a strong back and broad shoulders, and a steady honest gaze which had rested with respectful admiration on the miller's black-haired daughter whenever he came to have his corn ground.

'He was a good man,' she told Halina. 'He hid me in a bunker in his field, knowing he was risking his life. They would have killed him if they found me. That afternoon I smelled smoke. Later, Kuba Einhorn rushed into the farm house, bleeding and covered in soot, looking for a place to hide. Zenek didn't hesitate, he hid him too. He said, "They can't kill me twice."' Her eyes shone with tears.

'Kuba was a distant relative of mine,' she continued. 'He was the star of the soccer team, strong and fearless as a lion. I don't know how he managed to get out of that barn. Anyway, that evening when Zenek brought bread and milk to the bunker, he had a plan worked out. "Marry me and become a Catholic," he said. "The priest will baptise you and that way you'll survive."'

'He was a simple, uneducated farm lad but he had an honest face and a good heart. I wanted to live. So I took the name Cecilia and went to church every Sunday.'

The change of name and lifestyle made it easier to push the past away, to pretend that the loved ones she had lost had been part of someone else's life. In her determination to be accepted, Cecilia had to appear more pious than the other village women. Her mother-in-law tested her every week to make sure she knew the catechism and all the prayers, but that didn't stop the villagers whispering behind her back, because, converted or not, she was the only Jew left in Nowa Kalwaria. Her presence was an unspoken accusation that dampened their joy in their newly acquired houses, dresses, eiderdowns and tablecloths.

'After the war ended and the madness was over, Zenek became unusually quiet. He wasn't a talkative man but from the troubled expression on his face and his frequent sighs, I knew something was worrying him. One evening he came out with it. "I've loved you ever since the first time I saw you at your father's mill, but I know you only married me to save your life. So now that the war's over, it wouldn't be right to hold you to it. I know you wanted to be a teacher. You'd be wasting yourself here on the farm. If you want to leave me and go back to your own people, I'll understand."'

Tears glittered in her eyes. 'That's how noble he was. But how could I do that to him after he'd risked his life to save me? Besides, where could I go? My whole family had been killed. And if I was going to remain here, I knew I'd have to go on living as a Catholic for the rest of my life.'

Halina looked pityingly at the woman before her and recalled the first time she had seen her, startled as a fawn, crossing herself in the square. Ever since the age of eighteen, Cecilia had been compelled to live a lie. Not only had she been forced to abandon her faith, but she was doomed to live among those who had murdered her family and the rest of her community. Although she had finished high school and was well-spoken, she had deliberately acquired their way of speaking so she wouldn't stand out. She even dressed like the peasant women. But the most painful aspect of this masquerade was that she had lost not only her entire family and way of life, but her heritage as well, because she was unable to pass on her traditions or share her memories with her own children.

Cecilia opened her mouth to say something, but pressed her lips together and remained silent. Some things could never be spoken. She remembered the last time she had spoken to the God of her forefathers. On the day she discovered that out of her entire family she alone had survived, she had walked deep into the pine forest and turned her face up to the heavens. 'We prayed to you so devotedly,' she had begun, quietly and deliberately. 'We extolled your compassion and mercy. So where were you when we were hunted like animals, roasted alive, raped and tortured? You showed your mercy to the murderers. After all their atrocities, they got to take our homes, our mills, our shops and everything we had ever owned. Even the candlesticks that we lit every Sabbath in your honour. No one was more devout than Dvorcia.' Her voice had become shrill. 'Where were you the day they smashed her baby against the stove? How come you looked away when they sawed her head off? Why did you let them kill *Tateh* and Mama? Is this your idea of taking care of your chosen people?'

Emboldened by her tirade and astonished that a bolt of lightning hadn't struck her down, she had shaken her fist at the sky. 'No wonder you hide up there, out of reach. You know that if you made yourself visible, you'd have to face us and answer for all your false promises, for the pogroms and persecution you've permitted for thousands of years.' Quivering with rage, she had shouted, 'You hypocrite! I'd like to spit in your face!' Then she had sunk onto the pine needles, sobbing at her own blasphemy.

'I have to go now,' Cecilia said, and there was a note of panic in her voice. 'My daughter will be home soon.'

Halina was dazed by Cecilia's story and her transformation. 'Please stay a little longer. There's so much I'd like to know about your life before the war.'

Cecilia shook her head. 'Not now. Maybe another time.'

Before Halina could reply, she was already hurrying towards the gate.

Thirty-Six

Although it was barely four o'clock, the street was already enveloped in wintry gloom. One by one, lights were switched on in the shops and homes around the square as Halina walked back to the hotel, glad that another day spent examining jaws and teeth was over. She looked up to see Cecilia coming towards her, but for once the old woman didn't avert her gaze or scurry away.

'Tomorrow morning, same place,' she murmured, hardly moving her lips as she passed.

Inside the hotel, Halina made straight for the bar. Aching with cold, she tossed down a glass of *wódka wyborowa* and flinched as the spirit burnt her throat. Another lonely evening stretched ahead. She looked moodily at her glass. Only a month ago she had felt confident and in control of her life, but now she was confused and uncertain. The more she tried to figure out why her mother had lied, the angrier and more frustrated she became. There had to be an explanation, and her scientist's mind rankled at the possibility that she might never discover what it was, that the question mark that hung over her life might never be answered.

As the ice in her veins began to dissolve, she considered ordering another vodka but held back. She wanted solace, not oblivion. As the alcohol released the springs coiled tight inside her body, she reached for her mobile.

Before Roman had time to take off his coat, she flung her arms around him, pressing her warm cheeks against his cold face.

'I know I've been elusive lately,' she began but he was kissing the words off her lips as he pushed her gently towards the bed.

He was trying to pull everything off at once, her sweater, shirt and slacks, but under each layer of clothing, his hands met with more impediments.

'Wait, wait,' she protested, laughing at his impatience.

'I've been waiting for days,' he said, struggling with a silk spencer. 'You should supply a map for this obstacle course!'

They fell onto the bed together, wriggling and tugging. It wasn't an alluring striptease, but instead of feeling awkward she laughed at their jumble of limbs and clothes.

'I read somewhere that it isn't possible to make love and laugh at the same time,' she gasped as he tried to free her legs from pantyhose that, instead of coming off, continued to stretch.

'Are they made of elastic?' he asked. 'Is it some kind of catapult?' When the pantyhose finally lay on the floor, he pretended to wipe his brow. 'I'm exhausted now,' he said. 'Do you always wear all your clothes at once?'

'Only when I want to stretch out the foreplay.' They were both laughing now.

Later, nestled against his smooth chest, she let out a long, contented sigh. 'I guess we've just dispelled a myth.'

He was lying on his side, his arm around her, humming. '*Halinka, Halinka, Halinka maja.*' She was delighted at the way he changed the words of the Russian folk song 'Kalinka'. He stopped humming. 'Halinka, why did you keep away? What was wrong?'

She had hoped he wouldn't raise this subject. 'I was overwhelmed. By everything.'

'It would have been better to talk about it, no? And if tomorrow you are overwhelmed again?'

She kissed his left eye, then his right, and covered his lips with hers. 'You think too much,' she whispered.

'No, *kochanie*, I feel too much. You're the one that thinks too much.'

Stung, she wanted to defend herself but couldn't think of anything to say. Vodka and sex must have dulled her brain. Perhaps he was right. She jumped out of bed and started dressing. 'I'm starving. Let's go downstairs and eat.'

He pulled her against him. 'By the time you've put all that back on, it will be time for breakfast.'

Cecilia was waiting for her at the cemetery the next morning. 'I've brought something to show you,' she said in an animated voice.

Unfastening a large black handbag, she took out an envelope. Inside, wrapped in several layers of yellowed tissue paper, was a sepia photograph with worn edges. Holding it in both hands, she said, 'This is the only photograph I have of my family. It was taken at my sister's wedding in 1937.'

Several generations were arranged in a formal pose around the bride and groom. At the back, the patriarch of the family — a man with a grey beard that rested on his chest — sat unsmiling beside a formidable matron in a black wig, a pearl choker around her plump neck. In the front, boys and girls in sailor collars and long white socks sat cross-legged on the floor. The middle rows were occupied by dark-eyed women with hair combed flat around their faces, and men in suits with large lapels and wide ties.

'Those are my grandparents at the back.' In front of them, a giant of a man with a black beard sat next to a small woman with marcelled hair and a set mouth. '*Tateh* and Mama,' Cecilia said proudly. She craned over Halina's shoulder. 'They made a handsome couple. And that was me.'

Now that she had lost her hunted look, Halina could see a faint resemblance to the young girl in a long-waisted floral dress standing shyly beside the bride.

'And here is Kuba Einhorn, the man who escaped from the barn.' Transported into the past by the exquisite pain of nostalgia, Cecilia had dropped her acquired local drawl and spoke with an educated accent.

Halina studied the faces, captured at a time when the trajectory of their lives seemed to stretch ahead of them in a predictable cycle, where joyous milestones marked the passing of the years. They were looking confidently into the camera, unable to imagine the destiny that was already rushing towards them. Her gaze moved to a stocky man whose flashing eyes exuded energy and confidence.

'Kuba,' she repeated. 'What kind of name is that?'

'It's short for Jakub. He was the town hero.' Even now, after all these years, the admiration in Cecilia's voice was unmistakeable. Halina wondered whether Jakub Einhorn had reciprocated her feelings. Jakub was the man who had escaped from the barn, Cecilia had said.

Halina caught her breath. Could he have been J.E., whose memoir she had read at the Jewish Historical Institute in Warsaw?

'Do you know what became of this Kuba?'

The shawl slipped off Cecilia's head, revealing wavy iron-grey hair that looked as though someone had picked up a pair of scissors, bunched her hair together and cut it straight across. 'After he left the bunker he was caught by the Germans. They deported him to a concentration camp but I heard he survived.'

Halina was shaking her head with wonder. Jakub Einhorn had survived the super-efficient machinery of death in the camps but his family hadn't survived the tribal blood-lust of their neighbours.

'Anyway, he never came back to Nowa Kalwaria and I never saw him again.' Cecilia tried to swallow a sigh. 'Someone said he went overseas but I don't know if that's true.'

Halina stared at the photograph again. Something about the man's intense expression looked familiar.

She looked at Cecilia. 'How could you bear living among these people after what they did?'

Cecilia fell silent. 'My husband was a wonderfully kind man,' she said finally. 'And my mother-in-law was a decent woman. At first she was unhappy that he married me, but eventually she accepted it. She was good to me.'

It was impossible to explain to this sophisticated Australian scientist what life had been like in Nowa Kalwaria for the rest of the war, that you weren't safe even after you converted, because to the Nazis a Jew was always a Jew. Yet no one in the village had pointed the finger at her.

'Can two good people make up for the brutality of the rest?' Halina mused.

After a pause, Cecilia said, 'After they got all that poison out of their system, most of them became normal again, no better and no worse than anyone else.'

Halina wondered whether Cecilia truly believed that, or whether it was a conviction born of emotional necessity. She turned her attention back to the photograph.

On the left-hand side, in the middle row, a young woman's face leapt out of the picture. A hairclip with two satin rosebuds pinned onto it pushed back a mass of curls, and a mischievous smile showed slightly protruding front teeth. Halina's throat was so tight that she seemed to be speaking through broken glass.

'Who's that?'

Cecilia leant over and followed her fingertip. 'That was Malka, the baker's daughter. They were distant relatives on my father's side but I never figured out exactly how we were related. She married Yossel not long after this photo was taken. See, there he is on her right.'

Halina couldn't take her eyes off Malka. Her heart was pounding with a strange dislocated rhythm. 'Tell me about her,' she said hoarsely.

Cecilia sighed. The joy of being able to show someone her precious photograph of her parents had evaporated as the stark reality of her existence reasserted itself. Perhaps the long silence that had been imposed on her had been a blessing after all. It was better to leave the past alone, safer not to disturb the ghosts of Nowa Kalwaria but let them rest in peace. Her eyes darted around nervously, signalling that any minute now she would scurry away.

'Tell me about Malka,' Halina repeated, the words catching in her throat.

Cecilia heard the urgency in her tone. Suddenly she smelled the yeasty aroma of Berish's Sabbath *challahs* that wafted over the square every Friday, and felt faint with longing. The recollection of that smell released memories long suppressed and half-forgotten, about people who had become shadows and a way of life that had been wiped out together with the community. One by one they rose from their graves and stood before her again. Malka had a mischievous sense of humour and, although they were friends, Cecilia had sometimes been the target of her wit. She was vivacious and entertaining but could also be cutting, and intimidated most of the young men.

'She was temperamental but Yossel knew how to handle her,' Cecilia said. 'After they married, she went to live in Stary Most and I didn't see much of her after that.'

'What happened to them?' Halina's voice was low and urgent.

'After the pogrom there, they fled and came to Nowa Kalwaria. Out of the frying pan and into the fire. Literally. By then they had a little girl, and she was expecting another child. That was the last I heard of them.'

'A little girl?'

Cecilia nodded. 'I saw her once, when Malka came to visit my parents. A sweet little thing, she looked just like Malka. You know what,' she sounded animated again, 'I remember her name. Mireleh, they called her.'

'Mireleh!' The name shot out of Halina's mouth. 'Are you sure?'

'They named her after Yossel's grandmother. My mother told me that.'

Halina's mind was jumping from one improbable thought to another. Get a grip, she told herself. Stay focused. Mireleh was probably a common name in Jewish families in those days. 'Did Malka have any brothers or sisters?' she asked.

'She had an older sister. I can't remember her name but I know she and her husband were sent to Siberia when the Bolsheviks started the deportations. What a shock that was, because he was such an ardent socialist. But to the Bolsheviks everyone was an enemy. They deported communists, socialists, Jews, Catholics. It didn't make any sense.'

'Was her sister's name Esther by any chance?'

Cecilia's eyes lit up. 'That's it. Esther. How did you know?'

Halina's voice was hoarse. 'What happened to that child, Mireleh?'

'I suppose she died in that barn along with all the others, in that fire you're investigating,' Cecilia said. She was looking around again with a hunted look. 'I have to go.'

Her eyes lingered on Halina's face. She saw something familiar but what it was, she couldn't say.

'I've seen you coming out of the presbytery a few times. Since you're so interested in Malka and Mireleh, why don't you talk to the priest's housekeeper? She might know something.'

On her way home, Cecilia stopped and stood motionless in the centre of the road for a long time, lost in thought. Suddenly she knew who Halina reminded her of.

Thirty-Seven

Halina couldn't get Malka's face out of her mind. It was as though she had looked into a magic mirror and seen a younger version of herself. In her hotel room, she saw that face with its mischievous smile and cleft chin while she stared at the feathery patterns of hoar frost on the window pane and played *Winterreise*.

It always shocked her that destruction, not deliverance awaited the solitary wanderer at the end of his journey. '*A stranger I arrived and a stranger I leave,*' Dietrich Fischer-Diskau sang while the pianist provided a delicate accompaniment to the tragic words.

Halina tore off the earphones, pulled on her coat and boots and slammed the door behind her. Perhaps there was still time.

Inside the presbytery, the housekeeper was tightening the frayed webbing strap around her worn suitcase. 'Ah, *Pani Doktor,*' she beamed. 'Thank goodness you've come. I'm catching the afternoon bus to Krakow and I hoped I'd see you before I left.'

She gestured around the room. 'Just look at all this. And new ones keep coming all the time.' Wreaths and garlands tied with ribbons were propped against the walls, and floral arrangements covered the table. The sickly scent of wilting flowers hung in the air.

Ever since the priest's death, the presbytery had become a shrine. Some villagers left sheafs of flowers on the doorstep, while others knocked on the door and, with tremulous voices, asked to see the room where he had died. Some of the women crossed themselves and left with tears in their eyes, but the most surprising visitors were Reverend Father's former enemies.

That a wily old politician like Borowski should have been among them couldn't be taken as an indication of a change of heart. Ever since his son, Edek, had been questioned in connection with the violent death at the presbytery, and a charge of manslaughter hung over him and his accomplice, both of whose fingerprints had been found on the bloodstained crowbar, the deputy mayor had good reason to pray for the priest's forgiveness. But among the visitors, she had even noticed some members of the League of Polish Families who had formerly reviled the Reverend Father.

Halina nodded absently. The housekeeper was delighted that the house had become a place of pilgrimage and reconciliation but Halina knew that Father Krzysztof would have been sceptical. 'Saints are created for secular not spiritual reasons,' he had once told her.

The housekeeper was still enthusing over all the tributes that had poured in, and Halina's attempts to interrupt the garrulous old woman failed. Only after she had listed every single person who had visited the presbytery to pay their respects, and given a detailed account of everything they had said, did the housekeeper finally stop for breath.

Halina came to the point. 'You've lived here all your life, so I hope you can help me.'

The housekeeper clasped Halina's hands in her roughened ones. 'What is it you want to know, my dear?'

'I heard that there was a Jewish woman called Malka who hid in Nowa Kalwaria with her husband a few days before the barn was set on fire,' Halina began.

The housekeeper shot her a quick look. Over the years, she had wondered whether she would ever be called upon to tell the story she had kept to herself for over half a century. And now, just as she was leaving Nowa Kalwaria for ever, when it seemed as though the opportunity would never arise, someone had finally broached the subject. It was enough to convince her that Reverend Father was still watching over them all.

'Let's go into the sitting room and I'll make us a glass of tea,' she said gently. 'It's a very long story.' It seemed fitting to tell it in the room imbued with his presence.

'I was living with my parents at the time, over on the other side of town, not far from where the synagogue once stood,' she began, waving her knobbly hand in the direction of the Łomza road. Those words unlocked the door to the past. She was surprised how quickly she was transported to that summer's day in 1941, when their little town resounded with screams and yells, and men armed with clubs and razor-studded sticks roamed the streets, terrorising the Jews, even the women and children.

Her mother had covered her ears with her hands and wailed, '*Jesus Maria!* They call themselves Catholics. I couldn't bring myself to drown a kitten and they're killing babies! But the day of reckoning will come and one day God will punish them. *Vengeance is mine, saith the Lord. I will repay.*'

'And my mother was right,' the housekeeper said. 'Look at your investigation — isn't that justice from beyond the grave?'

Halina wished the old woman would stop digressing but it was impossible to hurry her. Finally she came to the day when a Jewish couple with a small girl knocked on her parents' door.

'It was the sixth of July,' she said. Halina sat forward. 'No, wait a minute, it was the fifth because it was my birthday. Or was it the seventh?' Halina shifted in her chair.

The housekeeper described Malka's wild-eyed gaze and her husband's white face. They were swaying on their feet, you could see they were about to collapse. Her mother wanted to let them in but her father's words sent shivers down her spine.

'Do you want to get us all killed? We can't hide three people. Anyway, look at her, she's pregnant, she's going to have a baby any day. Babies cry. It's impossible to conceal them.'

While their fate hung in the balance of the conversation, the little girl had peeped out from behind her mother's shawl and stared at them silently.

'I could see that my mother was torn apart,' the housekeeper continued. 'She knew my father was right, but she couldn't bear to send them away knowing what would happen to them. Finally she made up her mind. "We can't hide all three of you but I'll keep the child."'

'Do you remember her name?'

'She had a strange name. Sounded like Mira.'

Halina's heart was thumping. 'Could it have been Mireleh?'

'That was it!' the housekeeper exclaimed. 'But we called her Basia and told her she must never mention her other name. She was such a good child. Did whatever she was told, and never cried. We told her if anyone came to the door, she had to run and hide in the recess behind the stove and stay there till we told her to come out. Little as she was, she seemed to know that all our lives depended on her being as quiet as a mouse.'

'How long did Mireleh stay with you?' Halina asked.

The housekeeper's face sagged. 'She'd only been with us for a few days when Bogdan and some of his pals banged on the door. "We know you've got a Jewish kid in there," they yelled. Careful as we were, someone must have noticed a small child and reported it. I signalled to Basia to hide, but those devils went through the house as if they were looking for buried treasure. In the end they found her and dragged her out. "You bandits, you won't get away with this! God will punish you!" My mother shook her fist at them. One of them knocked her down. When I rushed to help her up, he kicked me. I'll never forget the way that child looked at me when they took her away.' She wiped the tears that trickled down her wrinkled cheeks.

Halina was thinking of the tiny milk teeth in the mass grave. 'So Mireleh perished in the barn.'

'I'll come back to her,' the housekeeper said. 'But first I want to tell you about the baby.'

Halina frowned. 'Which baby?'

'I'm going to tell you.'

Halina sighed. She was only interested to hear what had happened to Mireleh but she resigned herself to yet another of the housekeeper's digressions.

'A few days after Mireleh arrived, word got round that

someone had left a baby on *Pani* Agata's doorstep,' she began. 'Everyone said that some peasant girl had gone to the field with her boyfriend, got herself into trouble and dumped the baby. Of course my parents and I knew straightaway whose baby it was but we didn't say a word. Malka must have had her baby and we were glad that the poor little mite had a chance to survive.'

Halina was listening intently now, trying to connect the threads of this story. It reminded her of a type of puzzle where you had to locate the picture concealed among dense, swirling patterns. At first the eye perceives only chaos, but by focusing on a particular detail, the elusive picture becomes clear and, once seen, it leaps to the eye from that moment on.

'What became of that baby?' she asked.

The housekeeper was looking at her with a strange expression. '*Pani Doktor*, it was Reverend Father!'

Halina thought she must have misheard. Perhaps her attention had wandered during this long story and she had missed some vital piece of information. The housekeeper couldn't possibly be saying that Father Krzysztof had been the Jewish baby who was left on a Polish doorstep and raised as a Catholic. But the housekeeper was nodding.

'Did he know?'

'He found out only a short time before he died. It was very hard for him. He suffered like Our Lord in the Garden of Gesthemene.'

Halina was struggling to make sense of these revelations. There were too many strands to disentangle. If Mireleh was Malka's child, and Malka later gave birth to the baby that was left on Agata's doorstep ...

'Just a moment.' She spoke very slowly. 'This can't be right, but from what you are saying, it sounds as though Father Krzysztof and Mireleh were brother and sister.'

The housekeeper nodded. 'As God is my witness, that's the sacred truth.'

Halina could only shake her head. Esther had only mentioned her niece: she hadn't known about her nephew.

They sat in silence broken only by the ticking of the old clock. Time was passing and the housekeeper would soon be gone. 'You were going to tell me what happened to Mireleh,' Halina reminded her.

The old woman clapped her hands and exclaimed, *'Istny cud.* It was a miracle, that's what it was.'

It was a time of horrors and miracles, all scrambled up together in a way that made your head spin. That anyone got out of that burning barn alive was beyond belief, but there was this wide-eyed child, smudged with soot but otherwise unhurt, standing in the cornfield.

'That's where my best friend found her,' the housekeeper said, waving her hand in the direction of the fields. She saw it all as though it had happened yesterday. Her friend leaning against the door in the middle of the night, moaning softly, her arm around the silent child.

'Can I stay here just for tonight?' Her mouth was so swollen she could hardly speak.

'What happened to you?' she had cried out. Blood was trickling from the girl's left nostril, her nose was splayed across her face, and her neck and arms were covered in welts and dark bruises.

'They beat me up two days ago and came back tonight, intending to finish me off,' she gasped. 'They were looking for her.' She indicated the little girl standing beside her.

'I'm all right, don't fuss, it doesn't hurt. I'm just worried about her.'

'Who did this to you?'

Her friend shrugged. 'My father and Bogdan. They said now we've dealt with the Jews, we'll deal with the Jew-lovers. I said I'd never tell them where she was, even if they killed me. But if they do, who'll look after her?'

The housekeeper heaved a sigh that seemed to rise from the soles of her feet. 'I wanted to put my arms around her but she didn't have a patch of skin that wasn't bruised or bloodied. I cried with her until she dropped off to sleep.' She sighed again. 'The things people do to each other in wars can never be understood in normal times.'

'I wonder what made her risk her life like that.'

The old woman stared straight ahead for a long time without speaking. Then, rousing herself from her reverie, she turned towards Halina. '*Pani Doktor*, do you always know why you do things?'

Taken aback, Halina hesitated as the image of the drowning child floated into her mind, but the housekeeper didn't expect a reply.

'It's strange the things that stick in your mind,' she was saying. 'One thing she told me, I can't forget. She was shuddering so violently when she was telling me this that her teeth chattered. When she was running home barefoot, clutching the child tightly so she wouldn't be seen, she was in such a hurry that she ran right through a pool of blood.'

Halina's hands flew to her mouth. 'On the Łomza road?' she whispered.

'That's where it must have been,' the housekeeper nodded. 'How did you know?'

Halina shook her head. She couldn't account for her vision of blood on the outskirts of Nowa Kalwaria.

But the housekeeper was already going on. 'I never would have guessed she'd do a risky thing like that, and she probably wouldn't have either. "For heaven's sake, think what you're doing. You don't even like Jews," I said to her, but she just gave me that look and said, "What's that got to do with it?" I suppose it was an impulse. She saw the child and that was it.'

It was still so vivid. As she tried to bathe and dress her friend's welts and bruises, she felt helpless. She knew how vindictive Stach and Bogdan were. 'They'll come after you. Are you sure you know what you're doing?'

But her friend was unshakeable. 'I know what I'd be doing if I deserted her.'

Lost in thought, the housekeeper stared out of the window. 'In a way she needed that child as much as the child needed her,' she said slowly. 'But she never said much so it was hard to know what was going on in her head a lot of the time.' There had been something strange and secretive about her friend's violent household. There was that time she had been sent away to her grandmother's in Łomza and didn't come back all summer, but she never talked about that either.

'Even after she fled to Bialystok she didn't feel safe,' she sighed. 'She wrote to tell me she'd caught sight of Bogdan and heard he was looking for her. She moved to another part of town, but noticed someone hanging around the house, watching her and the child, and knew she'd never have any peace as long as she stayed in this country.

'Perhaps she was frightened that they'd track her down through me, because I only got one more letter after that, and she didn't give me her new address. She wrote that a United Nations' organisation was helping people to migrate to Australia and that's where she decided to go. "At least my father and Bogdan won't find me there," she wrote. I never heard from Zosia again.'

Halina's heart seemed to stop beating. 'Did you say Zosia?' she whispered.

The housekeeper nodded.

She stared at the rigid, white-faced woman in front of her. '*Pani Doktor*, what's the matter? You look as if you've seen a ghost.'

Thirty-Eight

Halina had no idea how long how she had been staring at her knees. They were blurred and slid crazily from side to side. Beyond them, an empty vodka bottle lay on the floor. She pushed it away with her foot, watching idly as it rolled backwards and forwards until it bumped against the wall. Splinters of thought were being tossed around in her head but disappeared before she had time to catch them. Occasionally an emotion floated up like flotsam tossed in wild seas after a shipwreck. There was a strange sensation in the pit of her stomach and her head was spinning. If only the rocking would stop.

A moment later, she stood up and staggered to the bathroom. Kneeling in front of the toilet bowl, she clutched her sides and vomited as though a chain had been pulled inside her throat, releasing a torrent of yellow curds.

The tiles felt cold against her bare legs as she sat on the floor, staring at the crumbling plaster on the ceiling. She leant over the bath and splashed water over her head until it formed a pool on the floor. Someone was knocking on the door, calling out 'Housekeeping!' but she shouted 'Go away!' with a ferocity that startled her. The knocking stopped. Now she could go on sitting there for ever.

Tears were rolling down her cheeks. Why was she crying? It had something to do with a photograph. Or was it a barn? The top of her skull was about to blow off and she clamped her hands over it to keep it attached. She crawled back to the bedroom and opened the minibar just as the phone shrilled. She jumped with shock but didn't pick it up. They would assume she wasn't there and hang up. But the phone kept ringing. 'Go away!' she hissed into the receiver.

A man's voice was saying, 'Halinka, what's wrong? Are you ill?'

His reasonable tone enraged her. 'Leave me alone! I don't want to see anyone!'

She threw the receiver down but the voice was still talking. She had to make it stop but her hands were made of jelly and she had to yank the cord three times before the plug came away.

It was quiet in the room once more. She sat back against the wall, eyes closed. It was soothing to feel nothing and be as mindless as a potato. This made her laugh until she remembered that there was no vodka in the minibar, and now that she'd wrecked the phone she wouldn't be able to call for room service. She would have to go downstairs to the bar, but first she would have to stand up, have a shower and get dressed. Groaning, she pulled herself up, took one step, and fell back onto the bed.

Her lids flickered apart and she struggled to focus but the light stabbed her eyes so she closed them again. Almost immediately such a rage seized her that she felt she would burst and explode all over the room. How could that woman have concealed everything from her, lied and deceived her all her life? She had removed every trace of her identity and turned her into a fictitious creation, as fake as a mannequin in a store window. If only she could tell Zosia — she would never be able to think of her as her mother again — what she thought of her duplicity and dishonesty.

'You're a selfish monster, you don't have any human feelings, how could you trick me like this? Now what am I supposed to do?' she screamed at the wall. 'You pretended to care about me but you deprived me of every single thing in my life that was real. You even deprived me of my brother!'

At the thought of Father Krzysztof, she cradled her head in her arms and sobbed. She had always believed that she was alone in the world, but to discover now, when it was too late, that the man with whom she had felt such a powerful connection had been her own flesh and blood would tear at her for the rest of her life. If only she had known. All those wasted years, and now to be left alone in the world without the brother she admired and loved. What joy it would have been to retrace the paths that had separated them, yet ultimately brought them together in such a miraculous way.

Did he ever suspect that his life had also been a lie? Would he have shared her delight at discovering that the bond that existed between them was biological? When she reflected on the inexplicable strength of that connection, she wondered whether some unconscious chamber of her heart had recognised their kinship in a way that no logic could explain.

She had grieved over him when he had died, and now she grieved again. But this time the grief was more for herself, for the loss of her last remaining flesh and blood, for the relationship that hadn't had time to blossom, like a baby stillborn with its future encoded within its cells but never realised. If they had known, he might still be alive today and she wouldn't be alone in the world. She recalled his face and scoured her memory for signs of resemblance. Was it the slate colour of his eyes? The oval face? She didn't even have a photograph of him. Overwhelmed by her loss, she rocked from side to side and moaned.

Exhausted by her emotions, she dozed for a short time and awoke with a jerk, panic-stricken but unable to move. A stone was lying across her chest, squeezing the last breath from her body. Her hands fluttered to her chest. The stone was no longer there but someone was hammering a nail loudly into her head. The hammering was at the door and someone was turning the handle.

'*Proszę pani, przepraszamy*, we're sorry to intrude, but your phone isn't working and we were worried that something was wrong.'

The duty manager, a tall young man in a grey suit, was standing in the doorway in front of a repairman holding his tool bag. The manager's expert eye took in Halina's haggard, blotchy face and dishevelled hair, the empty bottle and the phone lying in the centre of the room. He tactfully averted his gaze. 'Are you ill? Do you need a doctor?'

She struggled to sit up and pressed her hands against her forehead. 'I'm all right.' She spoke slowly in an effort to control the words that kept slipping out of her mouth before she had time to enunciate them. 'I don't need anything. I just need to rest.'

'Would you like me to reconnect the phone?' he asked.

She nodded and closed her eyes.

When she opened them again, it was dark outside. Chilled, she pulled up the eiderdown. Claire. She had to talk to Claire.

'Halina! I've just got back from Thailand. I've been thinking about you. How's it going?'

But Halina's almost inaudible voice could only repeat her name. 'Claire,' she whispered. 'Claire.'

'What's up? Halina, are you okay?'

Halina began to cry. Softly at first, and then with loud gulping sobs. In between paroxysms, she tried to apologise but the weeping continued.

'Don't try to talk. Take your time,' Claire said.

'This is insane.' Halina was laughing through her sobs. 'Crying like a baby on an international call.'

Halina made several attempts to explain but gave up.

Claire was alarmed. She had never heard Halina so distraught. 'I don't know what's going on there,' she said, 'but I hear that you're in a lot of pain. Halina, listen to me, don't do anything stupid. Get help. Whatever it is, it can be dealt with.'

'I'm not about to kill myself,' Halina said wearily. 'It's just the shock of it all. I feel angry and confused. So betrayed.'

'Don't try to deal with this on your own. You need to go and talk to someone. Do they have counsellors in Poland?'

Halina smiled through her tears.

'Listen,' Claire was saying, 'call me any time of the day or night, whenever you want to talk. Or if you just need to cry. And if you need me to come, say the word and I'll be on a plane the next day.'

Halina swallowed, too choked to speak.

She stood for a long time under the shower letting the water flow over her. She was reviewing her life with the secretive woman she had called mother. Like a prospector sieving through a mountain of soil in search of gold chips, she raked through shreds of half-remembered conversations looking for clues about her past.

Zosia's obsessive ambition for Halina and her emphasis on studying and achieving. Was that prompted, as she had always maintained, by her own lack of schooling or by a sense that Halina must fulfil the potential that was her birthright? That cold obstinate silence that greeted questions about their early life. Her mouth had become a narrow, tight line whenever Halina asked about her father or Poland. An image of Zosia stubbornly bent over her darning flashed into her mind. The rapid way her large roughened hands produced the perfect mending that was almost undistinguishable from the fabric. Looking back on it now, Halina sensed that Zosia was sewing her secrets into the tiny stitches, making them so strong that the threads would never unravel. Had she suffered from the guilty burden that she had shouldered all her life, the burden that was born from her possessiveness and her selfish love?

Her head was throbbing with choked-up anger. Malka, Yossel, Mireleh and Zosia. Pieces of a puzzle that added up to a non-existent woman called Halina.

The fire in the barn. How chillingly accurate her nightmare had been. Was it possible that her memories of that traumatic day, suppressed for a lifetime, had finally risen to the surface and revealed themselves in that dream? Had she really been inside that furnace? She went over all the facts yet again. Tears of pity welled in her eyes for that tiny girl who had ceased to exist on that day in July, who had become a person devoid of a heritage. Mireleh was a stranger. She must have felt the heat of the flames, and heard them crackle and roar while people around her screamed and prayed. Halina clutched her throat as another wave of nausea swept over her. How bewildered and terrified she must have been, separated from her parents, left with strangers, and then dragged away by men with cold hard eyes who pushed her into that inferno.

Her mind turned to her parents. Did they find her in that crowded barn? She recalled a voice whispering 'Run. Quick. While there's still time.' Did she really hear that or was it just a dream? A new rage seized her: fury at the murderers who had killed her parents. Thugs like Roman's father who had exulted in their power to kill, who thought they were supermen because they could terrorise defenceless people.

She paced around the hotel room, her heart racing. If only she could get her hands on the monsters who had dragged her parents away. Stach and Bogdan their names were. But didn't the housekeeper say that Bogdan was Zosia's brother? One had killed, the other saved. Halina sank to the floor and rested her forehead on her knees, her head pounding with the effort of putting the shredded pieces of her life together.

Zosia was a heroic village girl who had risked her life to save a child she didn't know. But Zosia was also the treacherous foster-mother who had deceived her. How could she love and hate the same person, and remain sane?

Her mind turned to the haunting memoir she had read at the Jewish Historical Institute. The writer, who had identified himself only by his initials, had escaped from the burning barn carrying a little girl. According to the housekeeper, that little girl had been Mireleh. Propping her head in her hands, Halina tried to piece the story together step by step. While they were hiding in the cornfield, a young girl had beckoned to the child and taken her to safety. She knew now that it was Zosia who had taken pity on her and saved her. From Cecilia Wozniakowa's account, she realised that the heroic J.E. must have been Jakub Einhorn.

There had been something familiar about Jakub Einhorn's brooding face in Cecilia's family photograph and suddenly she knew why. It reminded her of the photo of Richard Enfield's father amongst her mother's belongings. Halina was trembling now. J.E., like Jakub Einhorn, had migrated to Australia after the war and had changed his name. He had been too frightened to reveal it, even on a historical document, to prevent the killers of Nowa Kalwaria, who continued to haunt him for the rest of his life, from ever finding him. There was no doubt in her mind. Jakub Einhorn and Jack Enfield must have been the same man.

So this was the man who had looked down, noticed the tiny girl standing near him and, on impulse, picked her up and carried her out of that furnace. Halina felt sad that she couldn't remember him. Finally she understood the connection between Jack Enfield and Zosia, but how or where they had met after the war, or why he'd sponsored them to Australia, Halina would never know.

So many gaps, and no one to fill them in. The Enfields had been the only people Zosia had known in Australia, yet she had slammed their door and never contacted them again. What could have provoked that lifelong feud?

In another world, the telephone was ringing. Dazed, she picked up the receiver.

'*Pani Doktor*, we have message for you. We bring to your room,' the receptionist was saying.

A few moments later, she heard paper rustling and watched an envelope being slipped under the door.

'Halinka,' Roman wrote, 'I know you want to be left alone but I had to get in touch. Let me know if there is anything I can do.'

'Thanks for your message but this is something I have to deal with on my own,' she told his answering machine. 'I don't know how long it will take but I'll call you when I can.' On reflection she hurriedly added, '*Ściskam*.' A verbal hug implied the promise of future intimacy.

She was drifting off into a light sleep, Roman's note clutched in her hand, when an image of Esther Kennedy floated into her mind. How did that demented old woman fit into the tangled story of her life? Esther was Malka's sister, so she was Mireleh's aunt. Halina sat up as a new realisation struck her. There was no Mireleh. She was Mireleh. Esther was her aunt. When the Enfields had shown Zosia the letter, she must have panicked. With the threat of having Halina taken away by relatives after all she had gone through, Zosia fled to Sydney and changed their surname to ensure they would never be found.

At the thought of Esther, Halina felt despondent. Esther, who had loved her so much that she had spent years searching for her, was her only remaining relative, the only person who could have told her about her parents and grandparents. But Esther hardly knew her own name these days and what could have been a heart-warming reunion would only be a succession of blank stares punctuated by an occasional shriek calling Mireleh's name.

When she finally fell asleep, she saw the shattered urn again. Crouching on the floor, shoulders slumped, she surveyed all the pieces and knew that her mother's priceless heirloom was beyond repair. She was about to sweep the fragments into a dustpan and throw them away so that she would be released from the torment, when she paused and studied them again. Perhaps it wasn't necessary to restore the urn. With a little imagination, the smashed pieces might be fashioned into a different form, one that would not replicate the original, but would possess its own intrinsic beauty.

Thirty-Nine

Still unsteady on her feet, Halina felt that she would shatter if anyone tapped her on the shoulder. She stayed in her hotel room alone for two days, struggling to make sense of a world that had spun out of control and hurtled into another galaxy, leaving her panic-stricken and desolate. Her mind was a battleground, where hatred alternated with love, resentment with gratitude, rage with guilt. She blamed Zosia for her duplicity then castigated herself for despising a woman who had sacrificed so much to keep her alive.

The third time Claire called, Halina started talking. The words spilled out like a tidal wave but Claire listened without interrupting.

'I'm falling apart,' Halina sighed finally, too exhausted to continue. 'I don't think I'll ever be myself again.'

When she fell silent, Claire said, 'My God. What a terrible shock. I can't believe it. You're having to deal with more in one week than most people ever do in a lifetime. Tell me everything from the beginning, slowly.'

After they had talked for almost an hour, she said, 'I'll call you again tomorrow. And Halina. You're a strong woman. You won't fall apart.'

The following day Halina called Roman. 'Just hold me,' she whispered when he arrived. As he embraced her, she clung to him like a lost child safe at last in her father's strong arms. It was a relief to surrender and feel the security of dependence. They lay for a long time without moving or speaking. As though waking from a spell, she opened her eyes slowly and looked straight into his.

'It's so good to see you.'

He tightened his arms around her without speaking.

'I don't know whether I've been here for a day, a week or a year,' she said. 'What have I missed?'

'Not much,' Roman said. 'You won't be surprised to hear that the mayor lost the election.'

The depression that had begun to lift descended again. She sighed and looked away.

He stroked her cheek. 'Don't be sad, Halinka. I have good news too. My students have been helping me search for Jewish gravestones for a project we're working on.'

At the mention of the gravestones, her heart started racing. That was another issue she would have to resolve. Was she Jewish? If so, what did that mean? Who should she talk to? She sat up, chewed the skin at her thumbnail and started pacing around the room.

He watched but made no comment about the cause of her agitation. 'Halinka, come and lie down,' he said.

She shook her head. 'I can't sit still. It feels like thousands of ants are crawling under my skin.'

He took her hand and gently pulled her onto the bed, turned her over and began to rub her neck and shoulders, pressing his warm firm hands into the tightly knotted muscles. As he pummelled and kneaded, the knots gradually began to loosen and dissolve until her body felt like butter.

His tenderness released emotions she couldn't control and she exploded with harsh sobs.

'It's all right,' he soothed her. 'It's all right. Just let go. The tears are washing out all the pain and stress.'

Nestled against his chest, she splashed warm tears over his shirt. When she stopped crying, she felt still and calm for the first time in days.

Roman was looking into her face. 'Halinka, you're very thin. Can I cook dinner for you?'

By some miracle, her face still remembered how to smile. 'Don't tell me. You're going to make an omelette.'

'No, I will make vegetable soup. I've been experimenting.'

Vegetable soup sounded wonderful.

Although Halina knew it was too soon to return to the exhumation, she was impatient to get back to work. Always more comfortable with action than emotion, she was relieved to focus on something outside herself. As soon as she was at her workbench, an idea occurred to her, so obvious that she was astonished she hadn't thought of it before. For years she had been telling students of the value of extracting mitochondrial DNA from the pulp chamber of molars even decades after death. Somewhere in that mass grave lay her mother's remains, and by comparing her mtDNA with that of her mother, she would be able to identify those remains. This would be the only certainty she could have.

If the rest of the team were curious about her prolonged absence, they didn't allude to it. Someone made a sympathetic remark about the flu and Halina said nothing to dispel that impression.

'*Cześć!*' Andrzej greeted her with a wide smile. 'I've put some mandibles and maxillas on the table for you to examine.' He took off his soft white hat, scratched his head and rammed the hat back on again. 'We'll have to wind up soon because the soil is getting too iced up. We're obviously not going to be able to exhume the entire grave so I've decided to cut a trench down to the base, so we can see a cross-section and estimate the number of bodies from that.'

The sense of purpose Halina had felt was replaced by a feeling of panic as she surveyed all the plastic bags in the field hut containing hundreds of jawbones she had coded, numbered and labelled. She had handled thousands of bones. Some of them must have belonged to relatives who had leant adoringly over her cradle and marvelled at her first tooth, her first step and her first word. Perhaps some of these remains had belonged to her parents, or grandparents. She sank down in the chair and propped her chin on her hands. Unlike her friends in Australia, she had grown up without grandparents or any extended family. All that was left of them were these fragments of ash and bone.

For the first time in her life, she felt crushed by her lack of objectivity and dejected by the grisly nature of the work. Women at her stage of life often retired. Perhaps she should do the same.

As he was pushing open the door to leave, Andrzej turned around. 'While you were away we found quite a few pelvic bones.'

These were the bones that confirmed sex. She looked up with interest. 'Any women among them?'

He nodded. 'Thirty-two. And some of the mandibles that I've brought you belong to the women whose pelvic bones we found over the past few days. Most of them had borne children. Anyway, you'll probably be able to confirm their ages from the teeth.'

Her heart was beating fast. She couldn't wait to get started.

The molecular biologist took off her glasses and slipped them into the top pocket of her white coat, her eyes brimming with unspoken questions. 'I don't think we've ever been asked to perform this test, but in any case, we don't have the facilities to do it here in Łomza,' she said. 'We'd have to send the samples to Warsaw.'

She folded her short arms over her ample stomach and waited. When Halina didn't reply, she added, 'I think it's a very expensive process. Would you like me to call them and find out? Is it just one sample?'

Halina hadn't considered the cost. Surely the Institute of National Remembrance would approve the testing once they understood its significance?

That evening, Professor Dobrowolski adjusted his red polka-dot bowtie and cleaned the lenses of his dark glasses. 'My dear lady,' he said in his confidential whisper. 'Unfortunately what you ask for is impossible. Do you have any idea how much this costs? We don't have the funds. This is Poland, not the United States or Australia.'

'Isn't the aim of this exhumation to get as much information about the victims as possible?' Halina argued. She took several sips of her mineral water to gain time. Keep your voice down and stay calm, she reminded herself. 'I'm probably the only surviving descendant who could identify one of them. Perhaps even several. Surely that would be worth doing?'

The professor drained his glass of Żywiec beer and wiped the foam off his upper lip before replying. 'Believe me, I know how important this is for you, but we've so far recovered several hundred molars and we can't test them all. Each sample costs around 3000 American dollars. IPN has other investigations in the pipeline. As soon as this one is finished, we're going to investigate Ukrainian atrocities in Poland. We don't have the funds for this kind of testing.'

She turned her top lip inwards and chewed it. There must be some solution. There had to be. She couldn't give up and walk away from her only chance of identifying her mother.

'What if I paid for one sample myself?' she began.

Professor Dobrowolski stood up. 'I'll call Warsaw tomorrow. Perhaps the laboratory has special rates for government bodies. We'll see what can be done. But don't expect too much.'

The exhumation was drawing to a close. Halina watched from the field hut as Rabbi Silverstein and his white-haired colleague from Jerusalem stood by the side of the grave, supervising the final days. Soon all the bags containing the bones of the dead would be returned to the grave and prayers would be said to entrust their souls to God.

The hut suddenly darkened and she looked up to see Andrzej standing in the doorway, grunting as he scraped the mud off his boots.

'Halina, if you're not too busy, we need to do the MNI today so we can finalise the numbers,' he said, pulling up a folding chair beside her.

To avoid doubling up by counting bones that could occur twice in one body, they had agreed to count only the long bones as well as mandibles, whose right and left ends could be distinguished. The largest number of any of these that had been exhumed would represent the minimum number of victims in this mass grave.

'I've recorded 328 proximal left femur ends, 316 proximal right femur ends and 287 distal ends of the humerus. So according to my figures, we know that there were at least 328 people in the layer we've exhumed,' he said. 'How many mandibles have you got?'

Halina scanned the spreadsheet and started counting. As the dense bone of the mandible tended to split at synthesis, she had recorded not only whether the jawbone in question came from the left or right side, but also whether it belonged to its forward or rear section.

'I've got 426 left rear mandibles and 374 right forward mandibles.'

Andrzej had been jotting down her figures as she read them out. 'That gives us an MNI of 426 of the bodies we've exhumed,' he said. 'The trench we dug to get a cross-section of the grave extended another metre further down, so we can assume that the same number of people were buried in that lower layer. Extrapolating from those figures, we can estimate that the MNI in the grave as a whole was 848. That's the figure I'll give when I hand in my report for the IPN.'

Halina nodded slowly. A minimum of 848 people accounted for. But how many others had died whose bones hadn't withstood the ravages of fire, decay and time? And in which group were her parents?

The walls of the hut were closing in on her. She needed some cold air on her face.

❋

Seeing Halina emerging from the hut, Rabbi Silverstein walked towards her with a smile. 'Hey, it's great to have you back. That must have been some virus.' The eyes that rested on her face gave nothing away, but she sensed he understood that her absence had not been caused by any physical ailment.

'Rabbi, could I talk to you in private?'

'Sure you can. But call me David, right? I don't feel too comfortable with these European formalities.'

She smiled back. 'Neither do I.'

Later, in the hotel dining room, he listened attentively while she spoke. 'The answer is simple, but how you cope with it may pose a problem for you,' he said. 'According to our tradition, if your mother was Jewish, then automatically you are too. Jewish identity is based on matrilineal descent.' He chuckled. 'They figured out way back then that there may be a question about paternity but you always know who your mother is!'

'Not always,' she sighed. 'But I get the point.'

She sipped a glass of tea with a wafer-thin slice of lemon while mulling over his words.

'So that's it?' she asked. 'There's nothing I have to do?'

He spread his hands and shrugged. 'Correct. But if you decide to practise Judaism, you'll need to study and learn about religious observances, holy days, *kashrut* ...' Her raised eyebrows stopped him mid-sentence. 'Keeping kosher. Dietary laws. Like not eating pork or shellfish, and not mixing meat and dairy products at one meal. If you wanted to marry in a synagogue, have your sons bar-mitzvah'd, or be buried in a Jewish cemetery, you'd have to produce proof that your mother was Jewish.'

'What kind of proof?'

'Birth certificate, documents confirming that your mother was part of the Jewish community. That sort of thing.'

'It's just as well I'll never need to prove it then,' she said.

In the short time since he had taken over the rabbinate in Warsaw, David Silverstein had been astonished by the number of Poles who sought him out to confide their conviction that they had Jewish roots. Men and women, young and old, had come to him, determined to discover the truth, often against their parents' wishes. Even when their suspicions were not confirmed by documentation, many still asked him for guidance and religious instruction. For most of them the doubts had originated with a remark inadvertently made by a parent or grandparent, while others simply felt a strong emotional affinity for Jews and Judaism that they were unable to explain. He admired their courage. The human spirit at its best was inspiring. At its worst, it defied all understanding.

He looked at the woman in front of him and gave a short, dry cough. 'Since arriving in Poland I've heard some amazing stories, but yours is the most extraordinary one I've ever come across.'

Halina pulled a face. 'I would have preferred not to be living proof that life is stranger than fiction.'

They sat in pensive silence.

'You're a religious man,' she mused. 'How do you explain what happened here? How come your God allowed this to happen?'

He wagged a playful finger at her. 'Unfortunately God hasn't taken me into His confidence.'

The concept he understood as God was the universal yearning for love, compassion and salvation, a journey

432

that took people along different paths but, if honestly and sincerely followed, they all led to the discovery of God within themselves.

'I'll share my personal view with you,' he said. 'I don't see a division between the human and the divine any more than I believe in a schism between body and mind. I believe that being humane means being in touch with the godlike qualities present in us all. Whatever increases love and compassion in the world is divine, and whatever diminishes humanity is evil.'

Halina nodded, recalling a line from *Winterreise* which touched her profoundly each time she heard it.

'If there is no God on earth, then we ourselves are gods.'

Forty

The project Roman was engaged in occupied so much of his time that they saw each other briefly, and each time Halina found parting from him increasingly difficult. She cursed the perversity of fate that had ordained that the first man with whom she felt neither like a doormat, sex object or personal assistant, who didn't dominate or bore her, happened to be a history teacher in a remote part of Poland. At least Shakespeare's star-cross'd lovers had lived in the same town but she and Roman were destined to live out their lives on opposite sides of the world.

Time was running out. For her, for Roman, for everything. It would soon be too late and she would never know which of those remains had belonged to her mother.

'Can I speak to you for a moment?' Professor Dobrowolski was at the door of the hut. She pushed a folding chair towards him, heart beating so loudly that she was certain he could hear it.

An hour later, she was tapping her foot in the reception area of the laboratory in Łomza, waiting for the molecular biologist to rub the inside of her cheek with a cottonwool swab to collect some buccal cells to send to Warsaw.

Selecting the molars to be tested had been an agonising

process. Halina had studied every adult female jaw and scrutinised every molar, her hand hovering above each one in turn like a clairvoyant poised over an ouija board. Churned up and anxious, she had finally decided on three jaws and taken two molars from each. This was a biological lottery in which she had been given three tickets.

On the way back to Nowa Kalwaria, hardly noticing the thatched farmhouses, roadside shrines and brown fields that flashed past, she wondered how she would survive the suspense of waiting for the results. Over and over she ran through the process in her mind. First the mtDNA would have to be extracted from the tooth pulp. The technician would fill the base of a freezermill resembling a five-litre esky with liquid nitrogen. This froze the tooth and made it so brittle that it crushed easily into a fine talc-like powder. The powder was then transferred to a reaction tube where chemical buffers broke down the cell walls. When the sample was relatively fresh, it took about eighteen hours to extract the DNA. Halina figured that her long-buried samples would take at least twice as long.

Once the cell walls had been broken down, phenol chloroform was used to take out all the protein and cellular pieces. What was left would be rinsed, run through a filter system, and then spun in a centrifuge, forcing all the liquid to flow through. Sitting on top of the filter, invisible to the naked eye, would be the DNA. By the end of the entire process, there would be around sixty microlitres of mtDNA sample left in the reaction tube. The aim was to obtain ten picograms: a thousand millionth of a gram. A thousand times less than was needed in the case of nuclear DNA.

The nail-chewing part would follow, when they compared her sample with that taken from the molar. Just thinking of seeing the two sequences coalesce on the computer screen made Halina's heart bounce against her ribs. Imagine the joy of looking at the part of her mother that each of her own cells contained, of seeing the minuscule matrilineal thread that linked both of them with their own female ancestors, from time immemorial and for all eternity.

When the call came from the laboratory in Warsaw, Halina's heart pounded so much that she had trouble hearing the soft voice of the molecular biologist. 'Dr Nowak speaking,' he said. 'I'm ready to compare the samples. The process only takes about five minutes but I wondered if you'd like to be present while I do it?'

One phone call in five minutes' time and she would know. But unbearable as the suspense was, she was reluctant to end it. She had clung to this possibility of identifying her mother as to a life raft. It was preferable to prolong the uncertainty than face possible disappointment. Until the results were known, she could continue to hope. An hour later she was on the train to Warsaw.

'*Proszę, proszę*, please, come right in, do come in,' the biologist stammered. His moist hand rested in hers like a lump of boneless meat. '*Oyey.* You've come such a long way. Can I get you a glass of water? Some coffee perhaps? You must be very tired.'

In spite of her tension, she smiled at his perception of great distance.

Maciej Nowak ran his hands through the two patches of hair that edged his freckled scalp like strips of lawn either side of a garden path. Placing a chair for her in front of the monitor, he asked several times whether she was comfortable. Halina took a deep breath. If only he'd stop fussing and get on with it.

'Do you understand mtDNA and how I arrived at the sequence that I'm going to put on the screen?' he asked.

Her raised eyebrows were all the encouragement he needed.

'Mitochondria are minute sausage-shaped structures we find inside cells. But while a cell sometimes contains only one copy of the nuclear DNA, it could have hundreds or even thousands of copies of the mtDNA, which is why these tests are more successful. Mitochondria are responsible for producing the energy that cells need, and that's why we call them the powerhouses of the cells. The fertilised egg contains a mixture of the father's and mother's nuclear DNA and an exact copy of the mother's mtDNA — but none of the father's mtDNA.'

She tried to break in to say that she already knew this, but there was no stopping him. Gone was the shy, bumbling man and in his place was a focused scientist, in love with his chosen subject. 'You know, the mitochondria are really the genetic breadcrumbs of our race that are sprinkled from one generation to another, along the matrilineal line, starting with Eve. Did you know that English scientists have traced the living descendant of a skeleton that was buried 9000 years ago by matching the mtDNA in his tooth cavity to that of a villager! One day mtDNA will enable us to decode our human origins, like a kind of biological Rosetta stone!' He was beaming like a proud parent showing off the brilliance of his child.

She nodded politely without speaking, hoping to induce him to turn his attention to the samples. But he hadn't finished yet. 'Unlike nuclear DNA, which changes every generation because it combines the DNA of both parents, mitochondrial DNA never changes because it's only passed along the matrilineal line, so any maternally related people would share the same mtDNA sequence.' He glanced at her. 'Of course, that's why you're here.'

He started to explain why he had magnified certain parts of mtDNA samples and not others, but Halina's throat was closing up. In a hoarse whisper she asked for a glass of water.

'*Oy boże,* my goodness, so sorry. I've probably bored you. My wife always tells me I forget that others aren't as enthralled by molecular biology as I am.'

He almost tripped over her chair in his haste to reach the sink, where he overfilled the glass and spilled some water over his hands.

'I've amplified the variable regions in the mtDNA of the tooth to get a sequence, and now I'm going to compare it with the sequence we got from your buccal cells,' he explained, returning to his scientific persona. 'We'll place the two sequences on the screen, one under the other, to see if they correspond.'

Halina cleared her throat several times, uncrossed her legs and crossed them again. Five minutes. That's all that lay between her and certainty.

Dr Nowak was fiddling with the knob on the monitor. 'First we'll look at the tooth sequence.'

She craned forward as a graph appeared. He turned another knob and split the screen to show her mtDNA sample underneath. They might have been graphs showing the financial ups and downs of a company over two years. He traced the troughs and peaks with a pointer. 'You see, these don't correspond.'

An invisible whalebone corset was being pulled so tightly around her body that she could hardly breathe. Two chances left in this biological roulette game. Again he screened two sequences. This time the similarity was unmistakeable.

'But look at this,' he was pointing. 'Here the samples diverge. There's no such thing as similar mtDNA. Either they are identical, which proves the relationship, or they're not and they belong to total strangers.'

He turned towards her. 'It's always such a joy to get a match. One lives in hope. Well, let's have a look at the last one.'

Gripping the edge of her chair with white knuckles, Halina could hardly bear to look.

A quick glance and her last hope crumbled.

When she tried to rise she felt as though a sack of cement had been placed on her head. Her legs wobbled so much that she had to sit down again. 'Is it too late to change my mind about that cup of coffee?' she asked. If he had offered her a glass of vodka, she would have been tempted, despite her decision to stop drinking.

The coffee was weak and tepid and, after a few sips, she thanked him and left, her slow footsteps echoing along the corridor.

She stumbled onto the street, hardly aware of the people she passed or the cars that honked angrily when she stepped into the road without looking. She had almost reached the station, sighing inwardly at the prospect of returning to Nowa Kalwaria. On an impulse she made a call on her mobile and a moment later she was in a taxi speeding to an apartment on the other side of Warsaw. This time she didn't need to check the directions, and as soon as the creaky lift lurched to a halt, she ran up the last flight of stairs.

'*Cześć,* Halina!' Jolanta Morawska kissed her on both cheeks.

There were still a few boxes piled up in the living room but it no longer resembled a railway lost property office. A bowl of oranges stood on the table, a pot plant soaked up the wintry light on the windowsill, and books were neatly stacked on the shelves.

'So tell me, how are things in Nowa Kalwaria?' Jolanta tamped her cigarette into the flower pot. 'Ash is good for plants,' she said in her gravelly voice and laughed. The tension that had pulled her face so tightly on Halina's previous visit had loosened its grip and she looked younger and more relaxed. 'Wait, I'll make tea.'

She glanced at Halina and frowned. 'Maybe you need something stronger. How about brandy?'

Halina hesitated for the briefest moment before shaking her head. 'Tea is fine.'

Jolanta pushed away a pile of newspapers. 'The papers have run quite a few articles about Nowa Kalwaria and the exhumation. I hear it's about to finish. What was the final number?'

'The conservative estimate is 848,' Halina said wearily. 'Which means there were considerably more than that.'

'I suppose you'll be writing your report soon.' Jolanta expelled a long breath and her hands flew to her head in mock alarm. 'The shit will really hit the fan when that gets published! But that's what we need — a national discussion based on forensic evidence. That might make it easier for people to face the fact that we weren't all heroes.'

She didn't notice that Halina remained silent.

'I was furious about the council election,' Jolanta continued. 'Pity Wojciechowski lost. The new mayor made it sound like Poland's biggest victory since Jan Sobieski repelled the Turks!

She glanced at Halina's face and stopped talking. 'You look terrible. What's up?'

Telling her story, it sounded unreal even to herself.

'*Jesus Maria.*' Jolanta looked shaken. 'My God, Halina. I warned you not to get involved, but this ...' She trailed off, lost for words. 'So are you saying that the priest you were so close to was your brother? And to lose him just before you found out!' She was frowning with the effort of trying to grasp the twists of the story.

She put her arm around Halina's shoulders. 'To think that you're the little girl who walked out of that barn. When I read that memoir, I never imagined ... And the woman you thought was your mother was your rescuer. Unbelievable. Absolutely unbelievable.'

They sat in silence, contemplating the broken threads of Halina's life.

Jolanta lit a fresh cigarette and took a long drag. 'Do you have any idea why she did it?' she asked.

Halina shook her head. It added to the torment not to know whether she had been saved as the result of moral principles, a cold sense of duty or a sudden impulse. Did Zosia's heart melt when she saw the little girl in the field that day, or did she feel unable to live with herself if she left the child to her fate? Was she trying to make amends for the brutality of her father and brother, or for some moral lapse of her own? Perhaps she had resolved to live according to Christ's teachings. Or did she harbour a secret love of danger and feel more alive when living on the edge? None of these characteristics seemed to relate to the woman who had brought her up, who was neither religious, sentimental

441

nor thrill-seeking, but as Halina now realised, she had not known Zosia at all.

She recalled her own dash into the surf to pull out the drowning child. Five minutes before she had plunged into the ocean she would not have imagined herself capable of such a thing, nor could she give any rational explanation for what she had done. It was almost as though some force outside her conscious self had directed her actions. And yet of all the people at the beach that day, she alone had been impelled to save the child.

The housekeeper had described Zosia as an average girl, not one in whom she had ever glimpsed any intimation of saintliness or self-sacrifice. Apparently she hadn't even liked Jews. And yet she had become a lone raindrop in that desert of indifference. If only Zosia was still alive so that she could ask her; but Halina doubted whether the tight-lipped, stolid woman she had called mother would have been capable of analysing her motives.

She could visualise her shrugging impatiently in reply. 'What do you mean, why did I do it?' she heard Zosia's voice. 'I didn't have to like Jews, but I didn't want to see them killed. I saw a helpless little girl looking at me in the cornfield. Another minute and that mob would have killed you. So I took you home, that's all.'

'She didn't even like Jews,' Halina said aloud.

'She took pity on you. It was an impulse,' Jolanta mused. 'As time went on, she grew into her role.'

'But why didn't she tell me who I was when I was older?' The question tore out of her.

'And risk losing you after she had cut herself off from everyone and everything to save you? You were all she had.'

At the door, Jolanta gave a lop-sided smile. 'It's tough being human, but the alternative is a lot worse.' She gave Halina a hug. *'Trzymaj sie.* Be strong.'

Her words echoed in Halina's mind as she stared out of the train window. She didn't feel very strong. As the train rolled along the tracks towards Nowa Kalwaria, the disappointment of not finding a match for the mtDNA jabbed at her. Over 800 people had been killed in that barn. What irrational hope had made her imagine that she would be able to identify her mother's remains? Like a gambler, she had become fixated on the fantasy of winning the jackpot. If only she could have tested more teeth. But she knew that even if she had taken several hundred molars for analysis, there was still no guarantee that her mother's would have been among them.

Every few minutes the train stopped at small windswept stations where people huddled under the kiosk awning, rubbing their hands together to keep warm. Greasy paper bags and chocolate wrappings blew along the platform and onto the track. A young soldier in a khaki uniform got into her compartment and stole an occasional glance at the mini-skirted girl wedged in the corner reading a textbook on economic theory. A clatter in the corridor announced the arrival of the tea trolley pushed by a little woman with an infectious grin and a friendly word for everyone. Halina bought a polystyrene cup of hot water and a tea bag. Twice the conductress opened the door to check their tickets and slammed it behind her, leaving a blast of icy air in her wake.

Halina closed her eyes and saw a little girl inside a burning barn.

I survived that, she thought. I'll survive this too.

Forty-One

Roman's voice was low and persuasive. 'Halinka, I know this is very hard for you, but please think about it.'

She turned her face away. 'I don't think you have any idea what you're asking.'

He took her hands in his. 'Believe me, I do. And if you say no, that will be the end of it. But you have the power to make an enormous difference to these young people. Perhaps to the whole town.'

'Is this a fantasy of yours, about some miraculous transformation?'

'Of course not. But it will start them thinking. Don't forget, they've never met a single Jew, let alone one from this village.'

'I can't say the idea of being a living history exhibit appeals to me.'

Her decision to shield him from the truth suddenly evaporated. 'Should I also tell them about your father?' she blurted out.

As soon as she shot her barb, she regretted it.

His eyes darkened and the amber flecks disappeared. 'What would you like to tell them about my father?' he asked evenly.

She told him what she had discovered, unable to gauge his reaction because he was looking down. 'I'm sorry,' she said. 'I didn't mean to tell you. And certainly not like that.'

'But you did.'

A tangle of reasons spun around in her head. Resentment, anger, distress. And malice. She couldn't deny the desire to wound.

'I really am sorry,' she said. With a self-deprecating shrug she added, 'As you can see, I'm not very good at relationships.'

There was no warmth in the gaze he turned on her. 'On the contrary, you get exactly what you want out of your relationships.'

She walked to the window, her back to him, and looked down at the street. Black branches poked into a sky the colour of tears. It seemed as though spring would never come. She couldn't think of anything to say.

After an awkward silence, she felt his hands on her shoulders and turned around. His face was pale and the blood had drained from his lips. 'I already knew,' he said. 'I've known for a long time. But I was afraid if you found out, it would ruin everything between us.'

'Did you think I'd hold you responsible for your father's actions?' But although she was reluctant to admit it, she knew he was right. Ever since Wacek had mentioned Roman's father, the knowledge had chafed like a grain of sand caught between her toes.

'You might not blame me consciously, but deep down you must be angry,' he said. 'You probably feel like a traitor when you're with me.'

It was all true, even her sense of betraying her past. But now that he had articulated the feelings she had suppressed, she felt the burden lift. They couldn't allow the past to affect their relationship without conceding victory to prejudice and hatred. It was not the past itself that was eroding their relationship but their lack of openness about it. This had been the rhinoceros sitting on the table between them that they had pretended not to see.

'You're right,' she said slowly. 'I did feel that way. I tried not to, but the more I pushed those feelings away, the more they bothered me.' She looked steadily into his face. 'Roman, I don't want this to destroy us.'

His arms were around her, and he was kissing her eyelids.

The anger that had gnawed at Halina began to recede. She saw him clearly now, a man of rare integrity who had risen above the brutish violence of his father, just as Zosia had done.

Time and place had no meaning in the continuum of life. It no longer mattered whether they had spent one day together or a lifetime. The love they shared was what mattered, and it would illuminate the rest of their lives.

She leant forward and gently kissed his lips. 'Roman, *kocham cie.*'

A film of moisture brightened the amber of his eyes. It was the first time she had told him that she loved him.

Halina's face was white and strained when she walked into the classroom the following morning. She couldn't suck enough air into her lungs and, although she kept breathing in, instead of feeling calmer she became more anxious with each breath. The students seemed restless and their fidgeting and muttering unsettled her. How would she cope with their inattention or, what would be even worse, their indifference? Another deep breath, a reassuring smile from Roman, and she began.

'When I was two years old, some men threw me into a barn, locked the door and set it on fire.'

The chattering stopped and twenty-two pairs of eyes were instantly fixed on her. Encouraged by their shocked attention, she began to tell her story. She interlocked her fingers to stop them shaking, but at times her whole body trembled so much that she had to grip the side of the table to steady herself.

'The flames were leaping all around us, and the smoke was thick and suffocating, but there was no way out,' she continued.

She seemed to be in a trance now, simultaneously narrator, observer and participant, watching the scene while she felt the scorching breath of the fire and heard its swirling roar. As she spoke, her eyes rested on each of them in turn. Suddenly her hand flew to her throat and she began to cough. Roman handed her a glass of water but she waved it away. When the paroxysm subsided, she returned to the scene she saw so clearly in front of her unblinking eyes. No one moved, no one made a sound, afraid of breaking the spell of the vision she had conjured up.

'The barn was crammed with men, women and children. People were screaming, crying, praying, singing, moaning. Some banged on the walls or threw themselves against the door yelling for help, but no one could hear because outside someone was playing on a musical instrument that blared louder and louder.'

She no longer knew whether the repressed memories of the past had flooded back or whether she had pieced together the events in the barn, a collage of her nightmare and the recollections of others. Nevertheless, she trusted the truth of the scene in front of her eyes. 'All around the perimeter of the barn, men were standing guard to make sure none of us escaped.'

The faces fixed on her became even more taut as they waited anxiously to find out what happened next, yet dreaded what she would reveal. She had transported them so completely into the past that even though she stood in front of them they were not convinced that she had survived.

'I don't know how I came to be standing near the door,' she said in a low, urgent voice, 'but suddenly it blew open. That instant, a man picked me up in his arms and rushed out of the barn before the guard with the axe could stop him. But I never saw my parents again. They died in that fire.'

Her voice dropped to a hoarse whisper and the students sat forward transfixed, anxious not to lose a single word.

'He ran with me in his arms, until he couldn't run any more. We flopped down exhausted in that field over there, among the corn stalks.' She waved her arm in the direction of the Łomza road and there was a collective intake of breath as they turned in the direction she indicated, shocked that this had taken place so close to the school.

'A young village woman happened to be standing nearby and saw a bewildered little girl peeping through the corn. She beckoned to me, held out a piece of bread, and took my hand.'

Halina's voice cracked and a loud sob burst from her throat. She glanced at Roman, who swallowed hard and nodded to encourage her. She looked down for a moment to compose herself. When she raised her head, she looked at Irena's face. The girl was crying silently, big tears streaming down her cheeks. Some of the students were watching her with tear-swollen eyes, while others, including some of the boys, looked down at their hands or brushed their arms against their eyes. Overwhelmed by their empathy, Halina buried her face in her hands and wept.

Forty-Two

Walking towards the Jewish cemetery on her last day in Nowa Kalwaria, Halina wondered why Roman had asked her to come. 'It's a surprise,' was all he would say.

He was standing near the gate discussing something with his students when she arrived, and for once the cemetery's desolate air was enlivened by cheerful activity, as though a school concert were about to begin.

'We are about to enter a Jewish holy place, so all the men must cover their heads,' Roman said, placing a small round skullcap on his own head and handing others to the male students who stole sheepish glances at each other or shuffled awkwardly.

Only Antek demurred. 'I'm not putting that stupid thing on my head,' he grumbled.

Irena glared at him. 'The only stupid thing here is you.' Some of the girls giggled.

'It's a sign of respect,' Roman pointed out. 'It's your choice whether you wear it or not, but you can't stay here and take part in the ceremony without it.'

'Who gives a shit about the ceremony,' Antek muttered, but grabbed the head covering and stuck it on the back of his head.

So there was to be a ceremony. Halina looked around and saw Rabbi Silverstein approaching.

'Ah, so they're wearing the *kippahs*!' he beamed. 'That's something I never expected to see.'

Footsteps crunched on the dirt path and Halina turned to see the former mayor, Aleksander Wojciechowski, coming towards them, his head held high. He nodded to the group of bystanders crowding around the entrance, ignoring the indignant murmurs and hissed insults that rippled among several people as he passed.

'Just look at him, the arse-licker, hobnobbing with those who blacken our name. Good job we got rid of him,' one woman said in a loud voice.

'It's ridiculous having all these ceremonies,' her neighbour said. 'Our government has been brainwashed. Kowtowing to the Jews. As though Poles didn't suffer enough during the war, they're trying to make out we were killers.'

'Anyway, the Jews got what they deserved in 1941,' the first woman spat out. 'We can't let up, we have to let people know what's really going on, so we can fight the conspiracy against Poland.'

Halina turned and looked into the grim face of the woman whose father had owned the barn. Shaking with anger, she clenched her fists inside her coat pockets. A retort about paranoia rose to her lips but she swallowed it. No victory was complete and no war was ever wholly won.

Next came the headmistress and several teachers at the head of a long column of students. Walking a small distance behind them, with stiff shoulders and a fixed expression that reflected his lack of ease, was the person she least expected to see at the Jewish cemetery. Władysław Borowski, the newly elected mayor was panting, his face redder and blotchier than ever as he hurried along the path trying to catch up with the others.

The rabbi caught Halina's eye. 'Our history teacher has worked a miracle here today,' he chuckled.

As they entered the cemetery, Halina noticed that there was no trace of the Żywiec beer bottles, condoms or squashed cigarette packets she had seen on her last visit. Roman's students had done a thorough job. Past the bare hazelwood bushes and stumps of gravestones, the procession stopped in front of a large irregular shape draped in a white sheet.

Some of the locals, mostly women, stood at the back of the crowd, like a group of gate-crashers trying to blend in with the invited guests without being noticed. A solitary figure was standing apart from the villagers and Halina was surprised to see that it was Cecilia Wozniakowa. Instead of the shawl she usually draped over her shoulders like the old peasant women, this time she wore a woollen coat, but the most striking change was her posture. She held herself proudly with a straight back. The hunted, furtive look was gone and her eyes glinted with triumph.

Touched by the courage it had taken to make this public appearance, Halina walked over to her. 'It's good that you've come,' she said.

Cecilia nodded. 'It was time.'

A small distance away, Halina noticed an elderly woman in a black scarf looking at her with undisguised interest. She wondered who the stranger was, but her attention was distracted when Roman stepped in front of the gathering.

'Thank you for taking part in what I believe is a historic and significant event for Nowa Kalwaria,' he began. 'A wasted opportunity is a loss, but a wasted tragedy is a crime.

I hope that, in our small way, we have done something to prevent a double tragedy.' His gaze lingered for a moment on Halina's face before he continued. 'Gravestones belong in a graveyard, but the stones that were laid to commemorate the Jewish citizens who lived and died here for hundreds of years were torn out, defaced and scattered all over the village during World War II. Restoring the fragments to their rightful place was the respectful and honourable thing to do, and I'd like to thank my class for their hard work and commitment.' He paused while they cheered, whistled and clapped. 'But I'm not going to take up any more of your time — I'm sure you'd rather hear from a young lady who has worked very hard on this project.'

More cheers and applause rang out as Irena stepped forward to address them.

'Well, I've never made a speech before and I don't know how to do it so anyway here goes,' she said in one breath, flicking her fringe out of her eyes. 'Before I start, I want to thank someone who has made a big impact on us this year.'

Halina leant forward expectantly to see how Roman would react to this tribute. But Irena was looking straight at her.

'*Pani Doktor*, it was generous of you to share your life story with us. You had most of us in tears. Until then, what happened here seemed like ancient history, but thanks to you, we've realised that it wasn't really that long ago. When you talked to us, we saw a barn full of people just like us, and a frightened little girl who lost everyone, until a good-hearted village girl saved you.'

She stopped, looked around at her classmates and made a self-conscious grimace to cover up her emotion. Taking a deep breath, she went on. 'I know now that we don't have to feel guilty about what happened. We only need to feel sorry. You are an inspiration to us all. Mr Zamorski' — she glanced at her teacher — 'is always telling us that history is people, and you've been the best history lesson we've ever had. Thank you for telling us your story.'

The knot in Halina's throat swelled so much that her neck ached.

Roman nodded to a youth with large glasses who stepped forward and pulled off the sheet, revealing a stone wall with irregular edges. Clearing his throat several times, the boy spoke in a slow, solemn voice. 'Behind every fragment of stone there's a life story, not only of the individual, but of a whole family. These stones represent a whole world that has vanished. Our class has decided to become the caretakers of this orphaned graveyard.'

A hush fell over the gathering. Out of the corner of her eye, Halina saw Cecilia wiping her eyes.

'On behalf of our class I'd like to thank the people who made this memorial possible,' he continued. 'In particular we want to thank Councillor — sorry, I mean Mayor — Borowski who so generously donated some of the stones.'

Władysław Borowski turned from side to side smiling and bowing like a proud benefactor, giving no indication that his contribution had been made under duress. When polite requests had failed, gentle blackmail had persuaded him to dig up the stones that paved his courtyard. After all, as Roman had so pleasantly put it, he wouldn't want to be featured in national newspapers as the town mayor who paved his courtyard with stones pilfered from Jewish graves.

Startled by an unfamiliar sound, they all turned in the direction of the impassioned voice that rose in a prayer for the dead and thanked the Almighty for the gift of life. It was the second time that week that Halina had heard Rabbi Silverstein intone the haunting ancient Aramaic words, the second time they had floated over the fields of Nowa Kalwaria.

The first occasion had been several days before, at the conclusion of the exhumation. 'It is a custom at Jewish funerals for the mourners who were closest to the deceased to be first to place a spadeful of earth over the coffin,' the rabbi had said. 'If anyone here would like to perform that duty, please step forward.'

Without hesitating, Halina had taken the spade from him, scooped some soil onto it and tipped it into the grave. The loose earth pattered against the bags filled with the remains of the victims. In the silence that followed, she stood on the edge of the grave, head bowed. She thought of her brother who had been snatched away from her. Father Krzysztof — she could not think of him as anything else — would have stood by her side on this day and shared the grief and closure of this ceremony. She thought of the parents she hadn't known, whose remains were finally being interred with a fitting religious ritual, and felt a pang that she could not recite the Kaddish prayer for them herself.

The rabbi finished chanting the prayer and people began to disperse. Halina snapped to attention. She had almost forgotten she was attending the consecration of the gravestone monument. When the cemetery was still and silent at last, she studied the memorial. It was a mosaic of tombstones. One was carved with two branches of a candelabra; another with two hands. Some stones were inscribed with several lines of Hebrew script, while others were so worn that only a few letters were decipherable. The fragments were arranged around a larger stone.

Halina recognised the centrepiece as the stone she had spotted at Borowski's house. This was the one that Roman had photographed when they had broken in and they had later deciphered it together. Above the inscription, two hands were poised over a candelabra, as though raised in benediction over the Sabbath candles. There was something else carved on the other side, and with difficulty she made out part of an urn whose handles had been broken off. On a plaque underneath she read the translation: *Rivka Kleinman of blessed memory. A dear and honest woman. Died 1937.*

It was her grandmother's gravestone.

A light hand rested on her shoulder. She put her own hand over it but was too choked to speak. There were no words to thank him. She could only shake her head while tears rolled down her cheeks.

'It's all right, Halinka,' Roman said, cradling her head against his chest. 'It's all right.'

Together they bent down to read the cards that the students had written to the dead. *Although you have gone, your spirit is still here*, one message said. Another said: *Why can't people live in peace with each other? I hope that this will never happen again.* In flowery letters, Irena had written: *I feel sorry about what happened here. Your community lost everything but we are losers too. We have lost your culture and our good name.* Underneath a painting of a flock of birds of various colours, all feeding together, someone had written: *We can't change the past but we can change the future.*

A shadow fell on the ground. Halina turned to see the stranger she had noticed earlier.

'*Pani Doktor*, I hope I'm not intruding,' the woman said. 'Do you have a few minutes?'

Halina nodded, more from politeness than a desire to talk. Her eyes were on Roman who was walking towards the cemetery gate with the last of his students.

'My name is Kasia Sulikowska. I was born in Nowa Kalwaria and lived here during those terrible war years.'

Halina looked at her with new interest. Perhaps she knew Zosia. She was about to ask when Kasia blurted out, 'I would have recognised you anywhere. You look just like your mother, the same protruding front teeth, the same dimple in your chin. She had the same thick reddish hair too, but hers was long. And of course she was much younger than you back then.'

'My mother?' Halina repeated slowly.

'We hid your parents in a bunker on our farm.' Kasia's head was to one side and she was looking at her with a tender expression. 'Until those murderers dragged them away.'

Every muscle in Halina's body was stretched so tight that she gasped to allow the air to reach her lungs. She listened, suspended between the urgency to know and the pain of finding out about her parents' last days. As Kasia spoke, she relived the tragic episode of the young couple and their baby born on a pile of straw in the barn.

Kasia's eyes brimmed with unshed tears. 'I was only twelve at the time, but young as I was I could tell they cared about each other. The last I saw of them, they were being dragged along the road. Your father put his arm around your mother to hold her up. The terrible thing is, they thought their baby was dead.' She wiped her eyes. 'Just before they strung my father up on our apple tree, he told me I had to let that baby know who his real parents were, but I couldn't bring myself to come back here until a few months ago.'

The iron band around Halina's heart tightened as she grappled with this double tragedy, hers and Kasia's. Piotr had been killed because he had wanted to save her parents; Zosia had almost lost her life for trying to save hers. Was evil the manure that gave goodness a chance to flourish?

She stepped towards Kasia who held out her arms to enfold her. Connected by their loss, they were also linked by courage and compassion. They clung together for a long time, holding each other in silence because no words could express their emotions. When they drew apart, their cheeks were wet with mingled tears.

Halina looked into Kasia's soft eyes. She had so many questions to ask she hardly knew where to start. Soon Kasia would leave, and take with her the last memories of her parents. As though reading her mind, Kasia began to describe every detail she could recall, from Malka and Yossel's first desperate knock on the farmhouse door to the trauma of the secret birth in the barn.

Then she stopped and looked searchingly into Halina's face. 'Did you know about the baby?'

Halina swallowed several times but could not dislodge the hard lump in her throat. She could only nod in reply.

The gratitude she felt towards Kasia and her father overwhelmed her. She longed to do something for Kasia but nothing seemed appropriate. It felt insensitive, even insulting, to offer material help in return for a debt that could never be repaid.

But Kasia shook her head as she took Halina's hands and pressed them between her own. 'There is nothing I need,' she said gently. 'It's enough for me to know that you survived and you've had a good life. That's what your parents and my father would have wanted.'

Alone in the cemetery, Halina stroked the rough surface of her grandmother's gravestone and traced the inscription with her index finger. She felt like a medium rubbing a hand on the outside of a glass, trying to evoke the spirit of the dead. For a long time she studied the memorial. Out of these jagged, broken fragments the artist had created a work of art that was beautiful and moving. These stones spoke of a time when this community had flourished and played an important role in village life, a time when its members had been buried according to the rituals of their forefathers.

As she stood there, Kasia's last words came back to her and the turmoil began to recede. She felt as though she had received a blessing from beyond the grave. Halina looked around at the bare black winter branches that would soon burst into buds and tender green leaves and suddenly she knew how she could thank Kasia in a way that had meaning and would transcend time and place. She had read about a memorial in Jerusalem that commemorated the humanity of those who had risked their lives to shelter Jews. This memorial consisted of an avenue of trees, each one planted in memory of a courageous person. Trees were a symbol of hope, of life's eternal renewal. Piotr Marczewski's life had come to a tragic end on an apple tree, but she would see to it that a tree was planted in his honour, so that his sacrifice would be acknowledged and his story recorded for all posterity.

Her attention returned to the memorial to the vanished Jews of Nowa Kalwaria that Roman and his students had created. Had any of these stones belonged to her relatives who had died in the barn that day? It was painful not to know, but as she turned and walked slowly out of the cemetery, she realised that in a sense all the people buried there, like those in the mass grave, were part of her family.

She would have to leave it at that.

Epilogue

As the jet ripped through the black night, Halina dreamt she was back in Sydney. A white cat was strolling towards her, and as she bent down to stroke its sleek fur, it looked into her face and burst out laughing. With each peal of laughter its whole body shook and its citrus eyes crinkled at the corners. The cat's hilarity was so infectious that she joined in, and they laughed like close friends sharing a joke. It seemed natural that a cat should possess such a keen sense of humour, and she was delighted but not at all surprised.

Suddenly, the cat sprang up and bolted across the road. Panic-stricken at the thought of losing this magical creature, her heart hammered in her throat as she rushed after it, weaving between speeding cars, oblivious of her own safety until she scooped it up, clutched it in her trembling arms and buried her face in its soft fur. Now she would never let it go. Then she heard a faint clink and looked down. Attached to its collar was a disk with the name and address of its owner in Nowa Kalwaria. The cat wasn't hers and never would be.

The cabin was dark when she awoke. Halina reached into her bag and her fingers closed around the books that

461

had meant so much to her brother. She sighed, comforted by this link to the past with all its unrealised possibilities. Glancing outside, she watched the flashing lights of the engine illuminating the darkness. The surreal flicker of these silvery filaments conjured an image of celestial threads that had been spinning back and forth ever since her birth, enlacing her and Roman into their glittering web. Clasping her hands together so tightly that they ached, she sensed that destiny, which had brought them together, would find a way of linking their lives again. The lights still beamed into space, but whether these interwoven motifs were random phenomena or part of a vast design created by a maestro's guiding hand was a mystery she would never solve.

The dream left a lingering sense of sadness. To have found such a bewitching creature, only to discover that it could never be hers. Suddenly Halina recalled the cat's rollicking mirth, and laughed until tears rolled down her cheeks. In focusing on the loss, she had almost overlooked the fanciful quality of the dream. Even if she couldn't keep the cat, the memory of its joyous laugh would always remain hers.

Dreams, like people, could be analysed in a hundred different ways and no one could ever know which interpretation was right. Good was as much of a mystery as evil, and it was beyond the capacity of the human mind to comprehend either. They didn't cancel each other out but both were so intricately woven into the fabric of human nature that they were impossible to disentangle.

Halina opened the volume of Rumi's poems and turned the pages until she came to the verses she was looking for. As she read them, the poet's vision rose from the printed page, reached out and touched her heart.

An eye is meant to see things.
The soul is here for its own joy.
A head has one use: for loving a true love.
Legs: to run after.

Love is for vanishing into the sky. The mind,
For learning what men have done and tried to do.
Mysteries are not to be solved. The eye goes blind
When it only wants to see why.

A moment later she heard Zosia's voice, speaking in her thick Polish accent: 'You think too much, Halina. Not everything can be explained. Just live.' Locked inside her silence, Zosia alone had known at what price that life had been salvaged from the ashes of Nowa Kalwaria.

'Thank you,' Halina whispered. 'Thank you.'

She raised the blind and caught her breath. A slash of colour so incandescent that it hurt her eyes split the sky in half. High above the earth, flying in the starlit vastness of the heavens, she watched as light tinted the night sky and pushed away the darkness.

The sun rose gloriously on an imperfect world.

Author's Notes and
Acknowledgments

Although *Winter Journey* is a work of fiction and Nowa
Kalwaria is a fictitious place, the story is based on incidents
that took place in the Polish village of Jedwabne and, to
a lesser extent, in nearby villages during World War II.
In July 1941, the Jewish inhabitants of Jedwabne were
rounded up, locked in a barn and set on fire by their Polish
neighbours. The truth about this atrocity was covered up
for over fifty years and the Nazis were blamed, but an
investigation conducted in 2000 by Poland's Institute of
National Remembrance confirmed that the perpetrators
were not Germans but Poles.

It was Professor Jan T. Gross's groundbreaking historical
account, *Neighbours: The Destruction of the Jewish Community
in Jedwabne, Poland*, that brought the events of 1941 to my
attention and inspired this novel.

The story of J.E. is based on the heroic life of Yankel
Neumark whose memoir is included in *Yedwabne: History and
Memorial Book*. My admiration goes to Rabbi Jacob Baker,
not only for his dedication in compiling and publishing this
extraordinary book, but also for his inspiring humanity.

During the Holocaust, cases have been recorded of Jewish parents being forced to smother their babies so that their crying would not expose their hiding place and risk the death of their rescuers and companions. The remarkable case of one baby who survived in this situation is documented in the Sydney Jewish Museum.

Like Father Krzysztof Kowalczyk, my fictitious character in *Winter Journey*, Father Romuald Weksler-Waszkinel is a priest who was born a Jew, but was not told about his origin by the family who raised him as a Catholic. To this day Father Romuald continues to build bridges between the two faiths.

In Poland, I was extremely fortunate to have the assistance of several outstanding people. Jan Pieklo, who is dedicated to fighting intolerance, put me in touch with the remarkable Annamaria Orla-Bukowska whose vast knowledge, passion for improving relations between Jews and Catholics and irrepressible sense of humour are matched by her gift for friendship. I'm very grateful to Marta Kurkowska for her warmth and help, and for arranging my stay in Jedwabne. My heartfelt thanks also to Agnieszka Arnold, Rabbi Michael Schudrich, Alex Wasowicz, and Danuta and Eugeniusz Janczarski, for all their kindness and help. In Jedwabne, I'd like to thank Joasia Godlecka, Stanislaw and Jadzia Michalowski and Jagoda Smugarzewska for their hospitality. Thanks also to historians Krzysztof Persak and Andrzej Zbikowski.

In the United States, I'd like to thank Jack Goldfarb, journalist extraordinaire, for his generous spirit; Krzysztof Godlecki, a man of great integrity; and Coleman Barks, for permission to quote from *The Essential Rumi*.

I am deeply indebted to the forensic experts who have been so generous in their help. My biggest debt is to the doyen of Australian forensic dentists, Air Commodore Chris Griffiths, Assistant Surgeon General, Australian Defence Force, who gave me a crash course in forensic dentistry. In spite of all the demands on his time, he answered endless questions, explained the arcane aspects of odontology, and read the relevant sections of the manuscript. Without his input, this book could not have been written. I'm very grateful to Richard Wright who was willing to put aside his own work to help me. His help in clarifying issues connected to forensic anthropology and archaeology have been invaluable. Sarah Robinson was kind enough to elucidate the complex world of molecular biology. My thanks also to Jane Taylor, Sue Cole, Estelle Lazer and Pat Fell.

Detective-Inspector Wayne Hoffman, commander of the Ballistics Section of the New South Wales Police, devoted his valuable time to acquaint me with firearms and cartridges produced during World War II. My friend and colleague Jenny Cooke made time in her frantic schedule to read parts of the manuscript and give valuable suggestions. I'd like to thank Dasia Black-Gutman for her empathy, encouragement, and her concept of the 'Painted Bird'. My husband Michael, as always, was my first reader. I'm more grateful to him than I can say for his careful reading of the manuscript, sound suggestions, and above all, his encouragement and unfailing support.

From the moment I conceived the idea for this novel, the team at HarperCollins have shown me the support that most authors dream about. In Linda Funnell I have an enthusiastic and considerate publisher who has sought my input at every stage of production. Julia Stiles' sensitive spirit and insightful editing have enhanced the novel. I've had the benefit of Nicola O'Shea's sharp eye for detail and literary taste in copy-editing the manuscript. In-house editor Catherine Day has been a marvel of efficiency and competence. As for my agent Selwa Anthony, no author could have a more caring, diligent and feisty advocate.

P.S.

Ideas,
interviews
& features
included
in a new
section…

About the author

About the book

Read on

Meet the author

DIANE ARMSTRONG was born in Poland and arrived in Australia with her parents on the SS *Derna* in 1948.

She received a Commonwealth scholarship to the University of Sydney where she gained a Bachelor of Arts degree majoring in English and History.

Having decided to become a writer at the age of seven, Diane became a freelance journalist. She has won national and international awards for her articles, including the Pluma de Plata from the Mexican government and the George Munster Award for Independent Journalism in Australia. Over 3000 of her articles have been published in newspapers and magazines in Australia as well as in England, Hong Kong, Holland, Hungary, Poland, India and South Africa.

In 1997 she received an Emerging Writer's grant from the Literature Board of the Australia Council to write her first book *Mosaic: A Chronicle of Five Generations*, a memoir which was published in Australia in 1998. It was acclaimed by the late Joseph Heller and Nobel prizewinner Elie Wiesel, and was shortlisted for the Victorian Premier's Literary Award for NonFiction and for the National Biography Award.

When *Mosaic* was published in the United States, Barnes & Noble booksellers selected it for their 'Discover Great New Writers' series, and Amazon.com listed it among their ten best memoirs of the year.

In 1999 Diane received a Developing Writer's grant from the Literature Board of the Australia Council to assist in writing

*The Voyage of Their Life: The Story of the
SS* Derna *and its Passengers*, which was
published in 2001 and became a bestseller.

Winter Journey is her first novel.

Diane lives in Sydney with her husband,
Michael. She has two children, Justine and
Jonathan, and twin granddaughters Maya
and Sarah. ∎

Diane Armstrong

Life at a glance

BORN

1939 in Krakow, Poland

EDUCATED

BA at Sydney University

MARRIED

to Michael Armstrong, with two children, Justine and Jonathan, and twin granddaughters, Sarah and Maya

CAREER

Freelance journalist and travel writer

PREVIOUS WORKS

Over 3000 articles published worldwide.

Mosaic: A Chronicle of Five Generations (1998 Random House and 2001 St Martin's Press, New York.)

The Voyage of Their Life: The Story of The SS Derna and its Passengers (HarperCollins 2001)

AWARDS AND HONOURS:

Journalism:
- 1983 Government of Mexico's Pluma de Plata for best article written about Mexico; 1986 Gold Award, Pacific Asia Tourist Association, for best article about Asia-Pacific Region
- 1993 MBF Award (joint winner with Jennifer Cooke) for investigative article about Creutzfeld-Jakob disease

- 1997 Air New Zealand Award for Destination Journalism
- 1998 George Munster Award for Independent Journalism.

Mosaic: A Chronicle of Five Generations
- 1997 Grant from the Literature Board of the Australia Council to write *Mosaic*
- 1998 Shortlisted Victorian Premier's Literary Award for Non-Fiction
- 2000 Shortlisted National Biography Award.
- 2001 Selected for Barnes & Noble book stores' Discover Great New Writers program and chosen by Amazon.com as one of the Best Memoirs of the year

The Voyage of Their Life
- 2000 Grant from the Literature Board of the Australia Council to write *The Voyage of Their Life*
- 2002 Shortlisted for the NSW Premier's Literary Awards
- Featured on 'bestseller' lists around Australia

Winter Journey
Winter Journey will be translated and published in Poland

Discussion with
Diane Armstrong

What is your idea of happiness?
Getting together with my family makes me happy. Where writing is concerned, my happiest moments are when time seems to stand still, the creative mind takes over and the words just flow without any conscious effort.

What is your earliest memory?
Scattering rose petals in a church procession with two other little girls when I was about four or five. This was in the Polish village where my parents and I had to live as Catholics in order to survive during the Holocaust.

> ❝ I never pass a rose without smelling it, and try not to take anything or anyone for granted ❞

What do you take with you when you travel?
Far too much. People think that because I travel so much and write about travel, I must have packing down to a fine art, but I still haven't learned the art of travelling light.

What are your pet hates?
People who sue when they have an accident instead of taking responsibility for themselves. Judges who believe that drugs or alcohol are mitigating circumstances for violent behaviour.

What is the last thing that made you laugh?
My little granddaughters, Sarah and Maya, rolling around the floor like bear cubs.

Which living persons do you most admire?
Ordinary people who find the strength to face calamities bravely and without bitterness. And those who devote their lives to helping others.

What do you most value in your friends?
Caring, empathy and honesty.

What single thing would most improve the quality of your life?
Living in the present.

What is the most important lesson life has taught you?
That life is a gift. I never pass a rose without smelling it, and try not to take anything or anyone for granted.

What would be your desert island luxury?
A CD player with discs of my favourite music. They'd have to include the works of Chopin, Schubert, Beethoven and Mahler, as well as entire operas including *Tosca*, *Cavalleria Rusticana* and *La Bohème*.

What is your favourite meal to cook?
I love cooking festive birthday meals for my family, because it's wonderful to celebrate happy occasions together. The latest addition to my culinary repertoire is creating party cakes for my little granddaughters.

Which book do you wish you'd written?
There are thousands! But if I have to choose one work, it would be the plays of Shakespeare. No one has matched his wisdom, insight, wit, brilliant characterisation and magnificent poetry.

Where do you go for inspiration?
I find that inspiration comes with perspiration. When I sit at my computer and start writing, the ideas start coming.

What are you writing at the moment?
Articles based on recent trips to The Galapagos and Norway; the outline of my next novel. ∎

❝ When I sit at my computer and start writing, the ideas start coming ❞

Behind the scenes

Diane Armstrong reflects on her personal connections with Winter Journey

My father, who was a dentist, loved his profession and wanted me to follow in his footsteps. 'Dentistry is an ideal profession for women,' he would urge. 'You can work part-time, be independent and always support yourself.'

But this was one battle he was never going to win because at the age of seven I had decided to become a writer. Study dentistry? No way. What could be more boring than measuring out your life by filling molars?

Finally he conceded defeat. I enrolled in Arts, majored in history and English and became a journalist.

About two years before he died, to my surprise, my father handed me a sheaf of typed pages. His detailed memoir of life in a large orthodox Jewish household in Krakow before World War I was a sharply observed time capsule that was revealing and poignant. As I read it, I became acquainted with the unhappy little boy that my father had once been.

My first book, *Mosaic: A Chronicle of Five Generations*, was a family memoir inspired by his reminiscences and by the stories he had told me about his family. My second book, *The Voyage of Their Life*, described the voyage of the post-war migrant hellship on which my parents and I arrived to Australia.

With my new book, *Winter Journey*, however, I felt I had moved away from personal stories. Although this is a novel, it was inspired by an event that took place in a Polish village during World War II. What happened in that village in 1941 enabled me

❝ "Dentistry is an ideal profession for women," my father would urge ❞

to explore the unfathomable complexity of human nature and the behaviour of ordinary people thrust into extraordinary situations.

It wasn't until I'd finished writing that I realised the story had a personal resonance after all. Strange as it seems, I'd forgotten that the village in which my parents and I had spent three terrifying years during the Holocaust was not far from the village where the war crime of *Winter Journey* had occurred. What's more, we had been living there at about the same time as the events I was describing, and the fate that had overtaken the Jewish inhabitants of Nowa Kalwaria could easily have been mine.

My unconscious played an even stranger trick on me. Having made my heroine Halina a forensic dentist, I undertook what amounted to a crash course in forensic dentistry. During this process, I pored over tooth charts, found out how to assess age by teeth and discovered that teeth survived long after flesh and fingerprints had disappeared. I learned that the majority of victims of the Bali bombings and the tsunami had been identified by dental records. It turned out that dentistry, which I had once considered so irrelevant and dull, was a vital forensic science that often held the sole key to identity.

In those arguments with my father so long ago, I had been adamant that I wouldn't follow his profession, but by making Halina a forensic dentist, in a vicarious way I honoured his wishes and studied dentistry after all!

My father would have been pleased! ■

> ❝ The fate that had overtaken the Jewish inhabitants of Nowa Kalwaria could easily have been mine ❞

**TEN BOOKS THAT HAVE
INSPIRED ME**

····································

The Long Voyage by Jorge
Semprun. I was moved by
his insights about
retaining one's humanity
in the face of oppression.

The Fixer by Bernard
Malamud made me realise
there are times when it's
impossible to remain
neutral.

Nineteen Eighty-Four by
George Orwell. This
prophetic book was
overwhelming in its
chilling view of
totalitarianism and its
effect on human
behaviour.

An Evil Cradling by Brian
Keenan is an inspiring
account of courage and
compassion in the face of
evil.

The Outsider by Albert
Camus. The hero's heart-
wrenching epiphany, as his
life is about to end, that it
would have been so easy to
enjoy life, has made a
profound impression
on me.

Shosha by Isaac Bashevis
Singer. A beautiful love
story that touched me by
its simplicity and depth.

The inspiration

'I've always been fascinated by the behaviour
of ordinary people in extraordinary
situations, when their moral values are put to
the ultimate test,' says Diane Armstrong.
'That's a theme I've explored in all my books.
One of the questions at the heart of *Winter
Journey* is, "What makes some people capable
of slaughtering their neighbours while others
risk their lives to save total strangers?"'

But what inspired her to write this novel?
'A few years ago I read the work of an
American historian who researched the
massacre of the Jewish population of a Polish
village. As I read about that incident in
Professor Jan T Gross's book *Neighbours*, I felt
the shiver of recognition that writers sense
when a story taps them on the shoulder. I just
knew I had to write a book based on this
incident, and that it had to be a novel.'

She also found inspiration in the
Yedwabne Memorial Book, in which she read
the compelling memoir of Yankel Neumark,
on whom she has based the character J.E.

Diane's meticulous research and her
visual style of writing gives her work great
power. 'I try to remember what the great
Polish writer Joseph Conrad once said, that
good writing makes you feel, makes you hear
and, above all, makes you see,' she says. As part
of her research for *Winter Journey*, Diane
travelled to Poland, studied forensic dentistry,
visited the morgue, and was inducted into the
arcane world of mitochondrial DNA.

She also researched ballistics: 'One day I
found myself at the headquarters of the New
South Wales Police Department, having a
tutorial about German weapons and

ammunition from World War II. At one point, the Commander of the Ballistics Section, who was my mentor, thrust a rifle into my astonished hand and said, "You're writing about shells, so you need to know what the rifle that your shell was fired from feels like!" Thanks to his tuition, I was able to write about a ballistics expert in Poland with far more credibility than I would have done otherwise.'

Readers sometimes wonder whether there are any parallels between Halina Shore and Diane Armstrong. Is there is any of her in the character of Halina? 'Although Halina is a very different kind of person, some of the problems that she has to confront as an adult were ones that I faced early in life. The problem of identity, for one — I was brought up as Catholic until I was seven. This was necessary to save my life, but when I found out that I was Jewish, it required readjustment to a whole new set of realities. As we know, things that happen in childhood have a profound effect on our lives. Perhaps this is why I've always been able to see things from different points of view, but this ambivalence has been valuable for me as a writer.'

Was it important to Diane to end the novel on a positive note? 'My vision of life is realistic. I don't see perpetrators as monsters and rescuers as heroes. I believe that we all possess the potential for good and evil. In fact, I believe that good is as much of a mystery as evil. But I'm basically an optimist about human nature. So with that vision, I had to end *Winter Journey* with the hope of redemption and a better future. For Halina, for the villagers, and for Poland.' ■

Favourite *books*
(continued)

The Leopard by Giuseppe di Lampedusa. The theme of this nostalgic story set in Sicily is change and letting go of the past. It haunted me long after I'd finished reading it.

The Diary of Anaïs Nin. I was captivated by her zest for life, lack of inhibition and exquisite writing.

The Second Sex by Simone de Beauvoir was a revelation. For the first time I understood the inequality of the sexes.

Voss by Patrick White. White's powerful language created a mysterious landscape that I found compelling.

The connections

Each of my books has been marked by extraordinary coincidences, but the one that happened recently is the most amazing of them all.

John, a Polish builder I know, happened to mention that when he looked up his surname on Google the previous week, he'd found an interesting item about his family. Intrigued, I keyed in his name and started reading.

Apparently John's grandfather had hidden a Jewish couple in a recess in his barn for several years during the Holocaust, and his father, then a lad of eighteen, used to bring them food secretly every day. In case the neighbours spotted him bringing food to the barn, and became suspicious, the grandfather bought a cow. It was heartwarming to know that this family had risked their life to save Jews who were being hunted and killed by the Nazis.

But as I read on, this story started sounding very familiar. During the couple's long stay in the barn, the wife gave birth to a baby. As its crying would have given them away and threatened both families with death, the baby was left on a villager's doorstep.

I could hardly believe my eyes. This was the story that a Holocaust survivor had told me in Sydney years before. His description of their terrified and cramped existence in a recess of a barn, and the traumatic circumstances of the birth of their baby, had made such a powerful impact on me that I had based part of the plot of Winter Journey on it!

6 But as I read on, this story started sounding very familiar. 9

And now it turned out that the people who had saved him and his wife were our builder's father and grandfather!

Shortly after I'd made this astonishing discovery, I shared it with an audience at a Writers' Festival in Sydney. As soon as I'd finished speaking, a woman came forward and introduced herself. 'I froze when I heard you telling that story,' she said. 'You see, I'm married to the man who was born in that barn!' ∎

> ❛ This was the story that a Holocaust survivor had told me in Sydney years before. ❜

Have you read?

Mosaic: A Chronicle of Five Generations
(1998, Random House Australia,
ISBN 009183998X)
Starting in Krakow, Poland in 1890, and
spanning more than 100 years, five
generations and four continents, *Mosaic* is
Diane Armstrong's moving account of her
remarkable, resilient family. An
extraordinary story of a family and one
woman's journey to reclaim her heritage.

'Diane Armstrong's book is a source of
delight to the reader. Written with fervour
and talent, it will capture your attention and
retain it to the last page.' — Nobel Prize
winner Elie Wiesel

'*Mosaic* flows like a novel, which once
started, is hard to put down. It is a compelling
family history of extraordinary people played
out against some of the most frightening
events of our century. The depth of emotions
evoked is stunning. I was thrilled and deeply
moved.' — Joseph Heller, author of *Catch 22*

'A stirring and powerful tapestry into
which she has masterfully interwoven the
story of her family with the enormity of the
Holocaust, commuting fluently between the
individual and the historical, the particular
and the universal.' — *Australian Jewish News*

'It is no small achievement and it bristles
with life ... *Mosaic* is a work of many levels.
But ultimately it succeeds because most of its
characters demonstrate how the human
spirit can soar way, way above adversity.' —
Sydney Morning Herald

'A most remarkable book about one
family's experience ... a rich and compelling
history ... Just as A.B. Facey's *A Fortunate Life*

and Sally Morgan's *My Place* have become part of the national literary heritage, so too has *Mosaic* earned its place in our social dialogue as part of our cultural tapestry.' — *Daily Telegraph*

The Voyage of Their Life: The Story of the SS Derna and its Passengers
(2001, HarperCollins Australia, ISBN 0732281504)

In August 1948, 545 passengers — from displaced persons camps in Germany, death camps in Poland, labour camps in Hungary, gulags in Siberia and stony Aegean islands — boarded an overcrowded, clapped-out vessel in Marseilles to face an uncertain future in Australia and New Zealand. The epic voyage on this hellship lasted almost three months and was marked by conflict and controversy. As the conditions on board deteriorated, tension and violence simmered above and below decks. But romances and seductions also flourished, and lifelong bonds were formed.

Diane Armstrong set sail on the Derna with her parents when she was nine years old, and located over a hundred of the passengers to retell their stories. A unique portrayal of a migrant ship and its passengers.

'She is a natural sleuth … her writing is clear, incisive, yet imaginative' — *Sydney Morning Herald*

'Armstrong's triumph in this history is to avoid judgment or argument … she allows readers to enter into the mindset of the refugees, to empathise with them' — *Weekend Australian*

If you loved this, you'll like…

There, Where the Pepper Grows by Bem Le Hunte (2005, HarperCollins Australia, ISBN 0732279917)
The story of Benjamin, who fled his native Poland during the Nazi occupation, aiming to fulfil his father's long-held dream of settling in Palestine. But along the way he and his fellow survivors are stranded in Calcutta, and somehow it becomes inevitable that he will stay …

The Bone Woman: A Forensic Anthropologist's Search for Truth in the Mass Graves of Rwanda, Bosnia, Croatia and Kosovo by Clea Koff (2004, Hodder Headline, ISBN 0733616410)
Clea Koff's unflinching account of her time as a forensic anthropologist with Physicians for Human Rights in Rwanda, Bosnia, Croatia and Kosovo.

If you loved this, you'll like...

Human Traces by Sebastian Faulks (2005, Arrow, ISBN 0091794900) Jacques Rebiere and Thomas Midwinter are united by an ambition to understand how the mind works and whether madness is the price we pay for being human. As psychiatrists, their quest takes them from the squalor of the Victorian lunatic asylum to the crowded lecture halls of the renowned Professor Charcot in Paris; from the heights of the Sierra Madre in California to the plains of unexplored Africa.

The Way The Crow Flies by Ann-Marie MacDonald (2003, HarperCollins, ISBN 0007171722) For eight-year-old Madeleine McCarthy, her family's posting to a quiet air force base is at first welcome, secure as she is in the love of her beautiful mother, and unaware that her father, Jack, is caught up in his own web of secrets. But the base is host to some intriguing characters, including the unconventional Froelich family, and the odd Mr March, whose power over the children is a secret burden that they carry.

Have you read *(continued)*

'[Diane Armstrong] has turned out an absorbing and very human work, laced with drama, love, hatreds and problems with almost Marx Brothers or Monty Python humour ... A rewarding read.' — *Australian Jewish News*

'Armstrong weaves in these individual tales with great skill. They flow in and out of the narrative in rhythm with the ship's slow movement from the old world to the new' — *The Age*

'While it is a good read, *The Voyage of Their Life* is also an important historical document in that it gives humanity and dignity to the stories of dispossessed people arriving in post-war Australia.' — *Wentworth Courier*

'The characters become familiar and absorbing ... almost unbearably moving' — *Australian Book Review*

'Diane Armstrong's study of the *Derna* is an important contribution to postwar Australian history. Her careful research combined with her excellent writing skills make this book essential reading for anyone interested in the development of Australian society.' — Dr Suzanne Rutland, *Australian Historical Society Journal* ■

Find out more

ON THE WEB

www.naa.gov.au
National Archives of Australia — a searchable database of the documents held by this important organisation.

www.dianearmstrong.com
The author's website, which includes photographs by her husband, Michael Armstrong.

www.holocaust.com.au
Australian Memories of the Holocaust: as well as fascinating first-person accounts, this site includes comprehensive lists of resource materials for further reading, viewing and other study of the topic.

www.ozco.gov.au
The Australia Council is the Australian Government's arts funding and advisory body.

VISIT

Sydney Jewish Museum
The Holocaust and Australian Jewish history
148 Darlinghurst Road
Darlinghurst NSW 2010
Ph. (02) 9360 7999
www.sydneyjewishmuseum.com.au

The town of Jedwabne in Poland
For historical information see
www.dialog.org/hist/jedwabne-en
For information on travelling to Poland see the Polish National Tourist Office's website www.polandtour.org or
www.poland-tourism.pl

If you loved this, you'll like…

Mao's Last Dancer by Li Cunxin (2003, Penguin Books, ISBN 067004024X)
The true story of a young Chinese peasant boy who was chosen to be moulded into a faithful guard of Chairman Mao's great vision for China. But one day he would dance with some of the greatest ballet companies of the world. One day he would be a friend to a president and first lady, movie stars and the most influential people in America.

The Secret River by Kate Grenville (2005, Text Publishing, ISBN 1920885757)
After a childhood of poverty and petty crime in the slums of London, William Thornhill is sentenced in 1806 to be transported to New South Wales for the term of his natural life. With his wife Sal and children in tow, he arrives in a harsh land that feels at first like a death sentence. But when, as a free man, Thornhill stakes his claim on a patch of ground by the river, the battle lines between old and new inhabitants are drawn.

Joe Cinque's Consolation by Helen Garner (2005, Picador, ISBN 0330364979)

In October 1997 a clever young law student at ANU made a bizarre plan to murder her devoted boyfriend after a dinner party at their house. Helen Garner followed the trials of the student and her best friend and accomplice, and probes the gap between ethics and the law; examines the helplessness of the courts in the face of what we think of as 'evil'; and explores conscience, culpability, and the battered ideal of duty of care.

READ

The Second World War by Martin Gilbert
The Holocaust: the Jewish tragedy by Martin Gilbert
Neighbours: The destruction of the Jewish community in Jedwabne, Poland by Professor Jan T. Gross
Yedwabne: History and Memorial Book, compiled by Rabbi Jacob Baker
The Essential Rumi by Jalal al-Din Rumi

LISTEN

Symphony of Sorrowful Songs (Symphony No 3, op. 36 — 2nd Movement), composed by Henryk Gorecki

WATCH

Hotel Rwanda (2004): an inspiring and moving film about Paul Rusesabagina, who saved over 1000 Tutsis from genocide at the hands of the Hutus in Rwanda in 1994.

Shake Hands with the Devil: The Journey of Romeo Dallaire (2004): a documentary about the Canadian General who was a UN peacekeeper in Rwanda.